LIGHTNING RUNES

LIGHTNING RUNES

CITY OF SHADOWS
BOOK TWO

Harry Turtledove

SHAHID MAHMUD
PUBLISHER

www.caeziksf.com

Cover art by Dany V.

ISBN: 978-1-64710-177-0

First Edition. First Printing. March 2026.
1 2 3 4 5 6 7 8 9 10

An imprint of Arc Manor Inc.

www.CaezikSF.com

It all started with a knock on the door.

You never know what's going to happen after that. Well, I knew one thing that would happen. Sure as hell, it did, too. Old Man Mose had been sleeping on the beat-up old sofa in my office. My fuzzy red accomplice is no braver than he has to be. He disappeared under the sofa, just in case.

"It's not locked. C'mon in," I called, wondering who or what would. In this part of L.A., you never can tell.

The door opened. In walked … no, not a beautiful blond vampire, though I've had that happen. Not a cop, either. I've had that happen, too, more times than I care to remember. A man. Darker than I am, but not real dark. Somewhere just on one side of thirty or the other—close to my age. Not real big. On the thin side. Dressed sharp, the kind of clothes you'd be likelier to wear to a Central Avenue club than to visit a private eye.

"Mister Mitchell?" he said, as if he didn't want to believe the name on the other side of the door.

Well, who could blame him? I don't look like Sam Spade or Philip Marlowe. Hell, I don't even look like Humphrey Bogart. I look like, mm, a guy. I could be anybody. I could be anything.

Sometimes that comes in handy. Sometimes it makes me wonder if I'm really anything at all.

If I am anything, though, I'm Jack Mitchell. So I nodded and said, "Guilty. Have a seat. Tell me who you are and what you think I can do for you."

"Uh, thanks." He sat down. The buttsprung sofa cushions made unfortunate noises. They do that. Seeing a couple of ashtrays on my desk, he leaned forward, grabbed one, and fired up a Kool. I lit an Old Gold of my own.

After blowing a stream of smoke at the ceiling, the fellow said, "My name's Oscar Ricks. I play guitar wherever I can, you know what I mean?"

"Oh, I might," I said. Private eye's a chancy way to make a living. So is playing music. A few people get lucky. A few have more talent than they know what to do with. Most musicians scuffle to pay their bills. I waved for him to go on.

"I put songs together, too," he said. Not *I write music*. Chances were, he didn't. He'd noodle around till he had a sound he liked, then put words to it. Or maybe he'd find words first, though most guys don't.

"Okay," I said. "So?"

"I've got a tune I like a lot. I want to make a record of it. I think it can sell. I think it'd be hot like a salamander, to tell you the truth." He stopped. "Did I say something wrong?"

"Never mind." He'd caught me by surprise. I don't want to know what kind of face I made. He must have figured I was thinking of the giant salamanders that cremated Hiroshima and Nagasaki and finally made the Knights of Bushido knuckle under a few years ago. But no, it wasn't that. The little salamander that burned down my apartment building was meant to get me, too. And it would have, if only I'd been home. "Go on."

"Uh ..." Ricks didn't seem sure he wanted to. If he'd walked out, I'd be telling you a different story, that's all. After another drag on his cigarette, he decided to keep going. "Getting it made, though, getting it out there, that's the hard part."

"It always is," I agreed.

"No, not like that." He shook his head. "I can finish things. I don't give up. You've got to be stubborn if you play music. You've got to be stubborn if you want to make it and—" He brushed the first two fingers of his right had against the back of his left wrist, then waited to see if I knew what he meant.

I told you, I can be anything. He wanted to make sure I was the same kind of thing he was. An ofay wouldn't have followed him. But I did, and finished his sentence: "—if you're the color you are."

"Yeah." He relaxed. I'd passed the test. "Thing is, finishing it isn't enough if I'm making a record. Other people, engineers and wizards, they make the copies. Other people get the copies into stores and juke boxes. Other people …" He ran down again.

One more time, I knew where he was going. "Other people who're white."

"That's part of it. But they aren't just white folks. They're white hoodlums. The contracts they've got—" Oscar Ricks rolled his eyes. "Vampires wouldn't suck the blood out of you the way they do."

"You've worked the clubs, right?" I said. He nodded. I went on, "Then you've got to know those same people you're beefing about, they back most of 'em." I'd seen Mickey on Central plenty of times—a dapper little Jew who'd rub you out in a second if you got in his way. Oh, he likely wouldn't do it himself, but he had soldiers who would.

"Yeah, yeah, but it's not the same there. We're the ones who draw people in. We make money for the mob. It's a plantation, but we're house slaves, not field hands. With records, we're pickin' cotton."

"The Plantation's way the hell down Central, at the corner of 108th," I said. Ricks made a face at me. I stubbed out my Old Gold. "Never mind. I know what you're saying."

"Okay. I found me a little place even farther out than that is, out in Gardena—ass end of nowhere," Oscar said. "They're a label called Grampus Records, on Normandie near the high school. They make their own records, even—they work with a plant down there somewhere. Contract looks okay. I hear they live up to it, too. They don't stiff you like a lot of people do."

"That all sounds great. What do you need me for, though?"

"Can you, like, give 'em a once-over and see if they're really legit?"

"I can. I can't do it for nothing, though." Gardena. The name rang a bell in my head, but I couldn't remember why. One of those dinky South Bay towns that are half cows or walnut trees or something. Something different about it, though, something I couldn't think of now. I knew it'd come to me as soon as Oscar Ricks walked out of my office.

He flinched a little when I said that, but only a little. "Yeah, I know. How much you need?"

"Let me have a hundred to start with. I'll see where we go from there." I tore the top sheet off a scratchpad and slid it across the desk at him along with a pencil. "Give me your address and phone number, too."

"A hundred?" He sounded sad, but he gave me the money. He didn't live far from the office. That figured. Either he'd seen the place or he'd heard of me from somebody who'd been here before.

"Obliged," I said. And I was. A hundred bucks will feed you for a while. I approve of eating.

"When will I hear back from you?" he asked.

"I'll take the Red Car down there tomorrow, see what I can find out, if I find out anything."

"All right. I guess it's all right. I hope it is." He stood up. So did I. We shook hands. Out he went.

As soon as he was gone, Old Man Mose came forth. "What was that all about?" he asked.

"He wants me to check some things for him. He paid me. I can keep you in cat food a while longer now."

"Good!" Mose knows what's important: he is. I'm just the help. If you don't believe me, ask him yourself.

I didn't leave the office till half past ten. I keep reminding myself I slept regular hours till I went overseas. A year and then some slogging up the Italian boot took care of that. I learned to sleep anywhere at any time. Light didn't bother me. Neither did noise. As long as the fylfot boys didn't drop one in my foxhole, I wouldn't wake up.

And I stayed the same way after the Army turned me loose. In my line of work, it's a handy knack to have. It's been extra useful since I started hanging around with Dora Urban last year.

I had a fifteen-minute walk back to her place. Vampire Village lies just south of what the LAPD, in its infinite warmth and generosity, calls the Negro Belt. One of the few things the LAPD is honest about, if you ask me. But you didn't, did you?

Vampire Village by day sleeps the sleep of the undead. Between sunset and sunrise, a lot more goes on there. I stayed alert, the way you do when you walk anywhere after dark. A guy came up to me with a big smile on his face. It wasn't a friendly smile. It was one that said he saw dinner. Vampires are as self-centered as cats, often without the charm.

Instead of sinking fangs into my neck, though, he sheered off. The smile disappeared. "Oh. You're marked." He sounded disgusted, the way Old Man Mose does when I peel an orange in the office.

"Yup." I nodded. The night before, Dora'd set her lips on my forehead for a few seconds. It wasn't exactly a kiss; I thought of it as a benison, which only goes to show I've read too many old books. Whatever you want to call it, it showed other vampires I belonged to her … and Dora Urban was someone to reckon with in VV. She did it every few days to keep me safe there, because it wore off over time.

When I came to her building, I walked up the stairs and let myself into the apartment that had been hers but became ours when I got burned out of my place. How long would the apartment stay ours? Till one of us didn't want it to be ours any more, however long that turned out to be.

Being what she was, she didn't need to cook in there. I had a hot plate, and used it to warm up a can of beef stew. It was better than what the Army gave us in C-rats, which is praising with faint damn if anything ever was.

Dora came through the door while I was cleaning up. She didn't bother to open it first. By now, I'd seen that enough so it didn't unnerve me … much. Wizards have been working on duplicating the effect for live people. They've been trying for years and years, and they haven't done it yet.

"Hey, honey!" I said, and kissed her. She looked at me with her ancient eyes, as if to remind me I ought to know better than to waste her time with endearments. I kept doing it anyway, because I liked to. She didn't get as upset about it as she had right after we turned into a couple. I told myself I was wearing her down.

Even I knew how stupid that was. Suppose we stayed together as long as I lived—another forty years, maybe fifty if I was really lucky. Never mind that that wasn't likely. Suppose. At the end of that time, I'd be old and gray and go into a hole in the ground to feed worms. Dora? Dora wouldn't have aged a day. How do you age when you aren't alive to begin with?

She said, "I cannot help admiring your … enthusiasm." She always spoke very precisely. Her Hungarian accent made that more apparent, not less.

"Enthusiasm?" I kissed her again. "Whose fault is that?" I held on to her. I never wanted to let her go. That she was much stronger than I was and could shake herself free any time she pleased was something we understood but mostly didn't talk about.

"How went your day?" Dora sometimes had an old-fashioned turn of phrase, too. Was that because English wasn't her first language? Or had she learned it back in the days when people said things like that all the time? I didn't know how old she was, not to the nearest hundred years.

I told her about Oscar Ricks. "I'll get up early tomorrow, go down to Gardena and see what I can find out about Grampus Records." Early, for me, meant eight or nine o'clock these days. Dora couldn't keep my hours, so I'd moved toward keeping hers.

"Be careful," she said when I ran dry. "This Ricks person is sensible to fear these mobsters. They are dangerous. They are, or their leaders are, less stupid than most criminals. They are not less vicious."

I nodded. Most crooks are dumb as rocks. Mob bosses aren't. They're plenty smart enough to have cops in their pockets, for instance. What they pay the bulls lets them make more than they would if they didn't.

"What have you been up to?" I asked her. "Did you visit the blood bank up at County General?" She'd been on the slow side lately. I knew she was hungry. Some vampires will grab blood wherever they can. The one who'd come up to me while I was on my way to the place would have if Dora hadn't marked me. They give the rest of their kind the bad name they have with live people. Dora isn't like that. Or she hasn't been as long as I've known her, anyhow.

"No. I was visiting a secondhand bookshop, but they had nothing new I cared to read." She sounded disappointed. Time hangs heavy for the undead. A book worth reading is a treasure.

But I clucked at her as if I were her mother, which is pretty damn silly when you get down to it. "You know you need to feed."

"I thought about going up there. But then I remembered—it has been a couple of months since the last time we did. We can again, if you care to."

I thought back. She was right. She wouldn't have lied about something like that. In her way, she's scrupulous. So I said, "Sure, we can do that."

And we did. We went back to the bedroom. This time, she kissed me, murmuring, "You give me a great gift." Then, well, she fed. She is scrupulous. She didn't take any more from me than the blood bank would, or take it more often. It doesn't hurt. And I can't think of anything more intimate, and that includes twitches and moans.

"Are you better now?" I asked her when she raised her head from my neck.

She licked her lips very quickly before she said, "Ever so much so. You were right—I did have the hunger. I had it, and you drove it from me. I am in your debt. How may I repay you?"

I didn't answer. She found a way all the same. The first time she did that, I wondered if I had enough blood left to use it for what she had in mind. Turned out I did, I'm glad—I'm delighted—to say. I did this time, too.

And, after that, I rolled over and went to sleep. You'd best believe I did. I had the usual man's excuse, and I was also light on my little red cells. Yes, I know that should be little gray cells. I've red my share of stories about the Belgian with the mustache and the hairnet. You can take it from me, he wouldn't last long as a private investigator in our fair city.

Of course, I often thought I wouldn't last long here, either. I was liable to be as right about me as I was about Hercule.

When I got up the next morning, the lid on Dora's coffin was closed. She'd placed it so the sun never touched it at any season of the year. Lying there in it, she'd be undead to the world till nightfall.

I'd got a little fridge when I knew I'd be staying there a while. I could make coffee on my hot plate and put real cream in it, then scramble a couple of eggs in a small pan afterwards. I don't cook anything fancy, but I learned in the service that whatever you can fix fresh for yourself is bound to taste better than what's in those lousy cans.

After I policed up, I went downstairs and out. Rivke the Shabbas-goy Jew was at the corner keeping an eye on things, the way they do in VV. I nodded to her. "Good morning!"

"Good morning! How are you?" She smiled at me. She was very pretty when she did that, but she didn't do it much. She'd come out of one of the fylfot boys' camps more dead than alive, which put her ahead of most people who went into them. She wore their emblem and a number branded on her arm. She'd take them to the grave with her, to remind her of what she'd been through.

"Your English gets better every time I talk with you," I said.

"Not yet good," she said, which was true. But I hadn't been lying, either.

I went on down to the Red Line stop. On the way, I passed a couple more Jews who kept watch in VV during the daytime. We smiled and nodded or waved back and forth. By now, they knew I was an acceptable human. Considering which vampire's person I was, I might even have been a little more than that. Not royalty, but nobility, anyhow.

The trolley clanged up. I paid my fare and an extra two cents for a transfer. I'd have to change cars at the Slauson station—the Slauson Tower, they call it, even if it's only two stories tall. I wasn't nobility to the guy who drove the trolley, just another damn passenger. I thanked him for the transfer all the same. He gave me a funny look; I knew that didn't happen very often.

Then he went, "Oh!" under his breath, realizing I wasn't quite what he'd figured I was at first. Negroes were more likely to do that than white folks were. He grinned a little. I nodded a little. I sat down under an ad for a crystal-ball reader who claimed she knew everything. If she did, how come she was fishing for suckers on a Red Line car?

Another clang on the bell from the motorman and away we went. I was the only one who got on at that stop. Vampire Village *is* a quiet place in the daytime. I got off at the Slauson Tower, ambled over to the platform marked SW, and waited for the next trolley. It pulled in a few minutes later. I hopped on, gave the driver my transfer, and perched under an ad that yelled WIZARDS AND DOCTORS KNOW IT WORKS! *It* was a hair restorer. The fellow sitting across from me was bald as an egg. If he'd tried the stuff, it was nowhere near as good as the ad said it was.

Southwest we went, and then straight south on Vermont. A lot of the land down there was still fig orchards and almond groves. Here and there, though, tracts of new houses sprouted amongst the greenery like toadstools pushing up through dead leaves. People keep flooding into Southern California. They have to live somewhere.

Vermont had some businesses on it, too, even when we'd gone as far south as Gardena. A variety store, a market, a Rexall. Across the street, a liquor store (it was called Squiggly's, God knows why), a hex shop, and a bigger building with a gaudy neon sign that said *Rainbow Club*.

And that was when I remembered what I knew about Gardena. It was the only place in the state where gambling was legal. There were four or five clubs like the Rainbow in town. You could eat and drink and play draw poker, which was politely said to be a game of skill, not chance. Gardena got something like a third of its tax money from them. Sure enough, the Monterey Club was only a few blocks south, just the other side of Rosecrans.

I thought about Oscar Ricks, and in my head I went, *Uh-oh*. You have gambling in a town, the city fathers won't be the only ones grabbing a cut of the profits. Not a chance. Not a prayer. The mob'll get its share, too, one way or another. If the mob was in the town, the clubs wouldn't be the only operations they were skimming from, either. How clean *was* Grampus Records?

A mile and a half later, I got off the trolley and got on a westbound bus. Gardena Boulevard was as much of a business district as Gardena boasted. A Bank of America. A little department store. A camera shop. A sorcerous-goods place called Ancient Egypt. A stationery store. Another Rexall.

And a Technocracy meeting house with a red yin-yang sign out front. There's one not far from my office, too. Some people have trouble figuring out when a ship has sailed. But wizards and slide-rule boys won't run a country any better than pols do. They'll just find different ways to screw it up.

The green-and-cream bus turned right on Normandie. It rumbled past the high school, which looked as if it had been there as long as anything in those parts. Two blocks farther on, there was Grampus Records. The sign had a smiling killer whale next to the name. I got off at the next corner, crossed the street, and walked back.

A Japanese man in a suit and a brown fedora came by me in the crosswalk. We nodded to each other. I'd seen other Japanese on Gardena Boulevard, too. The town seemed to have a lot of them.

Sure enough, one of the shops I walked past had only Japanese writing in the window. I had no idea how the cops would find it if they needed to, especially since the numbers on the address were tiny. A sign taped to the front door of the dive beside it was in letters I could read. It said WE RESERVE THE RIGHT TO REFUSE SERVICE TO ANYONE.

Nice, friendly place, huh? I wondered if that Japanese man could get a burger and fries there. I also wondered if I could, not that I aimed to give a joint like that my money. I suppose it would be a question of how quick on the uptake the guy behind the counter was.

As I got to Grampus Records, I saw the smaller print under the name: *A Whale of a Record Outfit*. Yes, I smiled. They were cute. How many businesses are cute? Not enough—I'll tell you that.

A bell rang when I went in. A secretary who was on the phone with somebody glanced my way, gave me a wait-a-second gesture with her free hand, and went back to what she was saying: "That's a dozen of 'West Coast Blues,' half a dozen of 'Cockroach on the Keys,' and another half dozen of 'Remembering'? Oh, and half a dozen of 'Since You Walked Away,' too? Hold on. I have to check on that one." She ran her index finger down a sheet of paper on her desk and nodded to herself. "Yes, they're all in stock. We can send them to you this afternoon—you should get them in three or four days. Shipping charges will go on the invoice. … Thank *you*, Mister Harmon. Goodbye." She hung up and gave her attention to me. "Hello! Can I help you?"

"I hope so. My name's Mitchell, Jack Mitchell. I'm a private investigator." I set one of my cards on the desk. "I'm looking into connections between record companies and, well, people who aren't exactly on the up-and-up."

"I'm sure we don't have any connections like that," she said primly. She picked up the card, looked at it, and set it down in a hurry, as if it were a scorpion that might sting her.

"I didn't say you did. I don't have any reason to think you do. But I need to do some checking so I can write a full report. Could I talk with your boss for a few minutes, please?"

I was pretty smooth, if I say so myself. I'm not a cop. Nobody has to talk with me. If you want to tell me to get lost, you can. I can't do anything about it. I can't do anything official, anyhow. I'm not allowed to threaten anybody, either. I'm not a mobster, and I don't want to be.

Of course, the folks I deal with don't always realize that straight off the bat. Having somebody like me come through the door flusters people, even when they haven't done anything. The secretary warily took my card again and carried it into a room behind her. She came out a minute later.

"Mister Jenkins will see you," she said.

"Thanks," I said. She sniffed.

I went in. The office was about the size of mine, and not a whole lot neater. My card lay on Jenkins' desk. He stood up and stretched out a hand. "Pleased to meet you, Mister Mitchell," he said. "I'm Kirk Jenkins. I run this madhouse, such as it is."

"Good to meet you," I answered. He was about forty, blond and pink to the point where he was only a couple of steps from being an albino. He was tall, too—a couple of inches taller than I am, and I'm six-two—and skinny, so skinny his clothes hung loose on him. He waved me to a beat-up chair. As I said down, I went on, "I'm looking into how small recording outfits manage to steer clear of the mob."

No suggestion I was looking into Grampus Records in particular. No suggestion I thought Grampus wasn't legit as legit could be. I'm careful about not giving away more than I have to, or I try to be.

Kirk Jenkins steepled his fingers. They were long and thin like the rest of him, and made a tall steeple. "Why are you doing that?" he asked.

"Because somebody's paying me to." I gave back the exact and literal truth.

"I don't have to tell you anything," he said, so he understood the rules of the game.

"I know you don't. Will you, though?"

"Sure. Why not? Everybody who knows anything about this business knows the boys you need to be careful about have their fingers in a whole bunch of pies. There are places where you have to deal with them if you want anybody to hear your platters."

"Jukeboxes." I didn't make it a question.

Jenkins nodded. "That's the big one, all right. They've got it sewn up tight. So they get a rakeoff from me—from the company, I mean—and we write it off our taxes as a promotional expense."

"What happens if you get audited?"

"We did, year before last. Nothing happened. It damn well is a promotional expense. Even the IRS knows records don't do a record company any good unless you get 'em out there. And the people you have to deal with don't call their outfit 'Mob Juke Boxes Incorporated' or anything like that. They look fine unless you start poking—or unless you get on the wrong side of them."

"Uh-huh." The Central Avenue clubs were like that, too. As long as you went along, everything was great. If you didn't, you'd be sorry … but not for long. Rubbing people out didn't bother Mickey a bit. "Are they trying to muscle in on other parts of your business?"

"They haven't so far," he said, and lit a cigarette.

I never waste an excuse to smoke, so I did, too. That bought me a few seconds to think. "Are you too small for them to care about you? Or don't they notice what goes on down here?"

"Could be either. Could be both. I don't have all the answers. Hell, I don't even have all the questions."

I chuckled in spite of myself. "Welcome to the world."

"Yeah." Jenkins looked at me. He looked away. Then his eyes came back. Not everybody white adds two and two about me, but he did. I could tell. I could also tell it didn't bother him much, if it did at all. There are people like that. Tell you the truth, I wish there were more of them. He went on, "Why did you know to come down here? Why did you pick here to come down to? Gotta be lots of outfits with more to talk about along those lines."

"I'm getting paid. Past that, it's nobody's business but mine."

"Okay, okay." He didn't get sore. He even held up a hand so I wouldn't. "I'm going to keep your card. In case those guys do come sniffing around, I may want to pay you myself. You never can tell."

"No, you never can." We shook hands. I took off. If Jenkins was telling me anything close to the truth, it looked as though Oscar Ricks could do a lot worse than Grampus Records. It also looked as though he'd never get rich signing with them, but that was his worry, not mine.

I took the bus south to 162nd Street, then walked west. A phone book had told me that was where the Gardena Police Department had its station. And so it did: a little toy cop shop next door to an only slightly larger city hall.

When I went into the station, the vestibule had a familiar smell. All police stations sing your nose the same old songs: stale smoke, staler coffee, old sweat, and—from the cells, wherever they were—sour puke. The desk sergeant's overflowing ashtray said he'd contributed a lot of smoke himself.

He eyed me. The way he growled, "Yeah?" told me he knew what I was right away. It also told me he wished I were something else.

I peeled another card out of my wallet and set it on his desk. He had to put on cheaters to read it. I said, "Can I talk to somebody from your racket squad, please?"

He wanted to tell me no. Try as he would, he couldn't find a reason. He pointed down the hall with a nicotine-stained finger. "Room Nineteen."

"Thanks." I'd been polite. As I headed for Room 19, I could feel his eyes boring into my back even so. Maybe it was because of what I was. Or maybe, like a lot of old cops, he despised all humanity impartially.

Room 19 was big enough for two desks. Nobody was sitting at one. At the other, a chunky young policeman with a pompadour was typing some kind of report. He just used his index fingers, but he was faster than most ten-fingered typists. The ashtray by his machine was pretty full, too.

The machine-gun rattle stopped when I came in. "What can I do for you?" he asked. I couldn't tell whether he knew what I was or how much it mattered to him.

Another card gone. I'd have to reload my wallet at the office. "I'm trying to find out whether the mob has its hooks in here, or how deep," I said. "With the card clubs and everything, you've got to be a tempting target."

"Think so, do you, Mister"—he looked at the card again—"Mitchell?"

"It's a natural thing to wonder about, isn't it, Officer Shaughnessy?" *Clyde Shaughnessy*, the name plaque on his desk said he was. "Somebody who wants to do business here does wonder. He doesn't need that kind of trouble."

"Nobody needs that kind of trouble," he said. "We try to keep it away as much as we can. I don't think we're perfect—"

"What is?" I said.

"Yeah, what is?" he agreed. "You expect miracles, talk to a preacher or a wizard. But the city needs the money the clubs bring in, and it doesn't need outsiders siphoning off any of that dough. So we keep a pretty close eye on things like that. I don't know all the details. Some of it's work for the bookkeepers, not for us. I do know we watch it, though."

"Okay," I said. He sounded as if he meant it. And maybe that meant something, maybe not. "Any other places besides the clubs where they might stick their noses in?"

He thought for a second. "Always the construction business. We have a lot of new houses going up. Oh!" He stuck a finger in the air. "There's a little record company over on Normandie. Music and the mob go together."

"That's a fact." I paused for effect. "What's a record company doing way out here? Uh, no offense."

"I know we're the back of beyond. Some people like it that way. It lets 'em keep their heads down and mind their own business."

"There are people who like to mind their own business?" I sounded amazed. Clyde Shaughnessy chuckled, for all the world as if I were kidding. I thanked him and left. He did have his fingers on the local pulse. How much good that did was anybody's guess.

I walked back up to Normandie and waited ten or fifteen minutes for the next bus. It took me to the Red Line stop on Vermont. Then I had to wait for the next trolley. Joys of travel without a car.

Passing the Rainbow Club on the way north made me thoughtful. I played my share of poker in the Army, especially overseas. Who didn't? What money we had wasn't good for much else. And even if we hung on to it, who could guess whether we'd get home to spend it properly? All that poker playing taught me something, too. It taught me I lost more than I won, and that cards and I weren't made for each other.

Most people who gamble lose. Most of the ones who do don't see they'll keep doing it if they keep playing. They're sure the next full house or four jacks is right around the corner, and it'll make up for all their bad luck. There's a word for people like that. How many of those suckers lost their shirts at the Gardena poker clubs?

After that, getting back to my part of town was a relief. It was till I saw Switchblade Sawyer leaning against a streetcorner light pole, anyhow. Switchblade's one of the neighborhood numbers runners. You don't have to go down to the South Bay to have money dribble out of your pocket as if it were a leaky cup.

I went over to my office to check my messages. Damned if I didn't have one. Hilda the answering-service lady told me Oscar Ricks had called early that morning. I took his number but didn't call back. It was the one he'd given me, which I figured was his home line. Chances were he was out doing whatever he did to keep eating when he didn't have any Central Avenue gigs.

While I was taking care of that, Old Man Mose was sniffing my shoes and the bottoms of my trousers. They interested him more than usual. "Where've you been? You smell funny," he said.

"How come you aren't laughing, then?" I said.

He looked at me. Cats don't laugh much, except maybe when they kill something. That tells you all you want to know about their sense of humor. "No, really, where were you?" he said. "You smell different."

"On the Red Line, and down in Gardena."

Mose knew what the Red Line was. He didn't like it. "Not the big clangy cat squasher," he said. "That mostly smells like cold iron. Some of that, but mostly you smell peculiar. Weird."

"Record company? Police station? Strange sidewalks?"

"Not sidewalks. Not polices, either. I know their stink, too. What's a record company?"

"A place that makes records so people can play music whenever they want to."

He gave a fine feline sneer. "Noise." I already knew his opinion of music, so I let that slide. He went on, "Is it connected with magic? It smells like magic."

Now I got interested. "It is, yeah. They use wizards to get the music from the people who're playing it to the records."

"That could be it. Smells like fishy magic. Or warmer and greasier than fishy."

For a second, I thought he was spouting nonsense. Cats see (smell?) the world in ways that seem crazy to mere people. But then I remembered what a grampus was, and I wasn't so sure any more.

He still might've been nuts, of course. I remember one time I went to the zoo, and an elephant stuck its trunk out between the bars of its enclosure and snuffled on my shoe. When Old Man Mose got a whiff of elephant snot, he wanted to go wherever that thing was, hunt it down, and have it for lunch. He wouldn't believe me when I tried to tell him how big it was. What does a cat know from elephants? He's still sure it would have been delicious.

So this could have been more of the same. Or he could have been on to something. "Good magic? Bad magic?"

"Greasy fishy magic," he said. So I'd have to find out for myself. I'd even have to find out if there was anything to find out.

Nobody came in. I fed Mose, gave him fresh water, and cleaned his sandbox. I fed myself, too—a burger and onion rings from a greasy (but not fishy) spoon around the corner. It was getting dark by then. A little past seven, I called Ricks' number. A woman answered. She put him on.

"Mister Mitchell!" he said. "What d'you know for sure?"

The older I get, the less I know for sure. By the time I get all gray and creaky, I expect I won't know diddly-squat. Meanwhile, I told him about my trip down to Grampus Records and the Gardena cop shop. I finished, "They aren't pure as the driven snow, if you know what I mean, but what is these days? The way it looks to me is, you could do plenty worse."

"I thought the same thing, but I wanted somebody else to look it over. Thanks, man. I'll probably go ahead, then," he said. "Sorry, but I can't bang my gums now. Gotta head out. I'm in a combo at the Basket Room till next Tuesday. Drop by if you have the chance." The phone receiver came down. Next thing I knew, I was talking with a dial tone.

On my way back to the apartment in Vampire Village, I ran into Rudolf Sebestyen. After a long day, I needed that the way I needed a hole in the head. Dora felt an obligation toward Sebestyen. She called him her half-brother, which meant the same vampire had made both of them what they were.

Okay. Fine. The trouble—one of the troubles—with that is, dear half-brother Rudolf's a bad item. He'd tried to find a way to rob the blood bank at County General, for God's sake. Not as if they wouldn't have let him have what he needed, but he wanted more.

The other trouble is, Rudolf had got sick and tired of being undead. Existence became a bother and a bore for him. So he took a fancy new dope called vepratoga. The fylfot boys came up with it during the war. They wanted super soldiers who could fight on and on without getting tired or needing to sleep or caring about wounds. They didn't have enough men, so they aimed to stretch the ones they had as far as they could.

Vepratoga didn't work the way they wanted. When you took it, you didn't care about *anything*, including your sergeant or your captain yelling orders in your ear. Sometimes that lasted weeks, sometimes months. Sometimes it was permanent.

There's a market for not caring. You could get hold of the stuff in our fair city. Not easy, not cheap, but you could. Sebestyen did. And, to make sure he never cared about anything again, he had himself turned into a zombie.

He didn't tell Dora about that. She felt more obligation toward him than he did toward her. She just knew he'd gone missing. So she hired me to help her find him, which is how we got together. I did it, too. And, with some other people, I got him unzombified, if that's a word.

But he didn't want to be unzombified. He'd liked the oblivion it gave him. To make matters worse, either vepratoga or zombification meant he could go around in broad daylight without the sun finishing him. He really loved that. Here he was, undead, with twice as much time on his hands.

So he was thrilled to see me. Oh, you just bet he was! His scowl showed long, yellowish fangs. Dora's benison meant nothing to him. I put one hand in my coat pocket, just to remind him I had a crucifix and an ampoule of holy water.

I didn't know for sure whether either of those would stop him. Evidently, he didn't, either, because he didn't try anything. He did say, "You will not always be so prepared. Neither will she." Yeah, he was a charmer, Sebestyen.

"We were doing the best for you we knew how to do," I answered.

"And which road is paved with good intentions?" he said. His accent was thicker, harsher, than Dora's. He sounded a lot like the guy in the movie, to tell you the truth. I didn't tell him so. Calling a vampire a lugosi is like calling a Jew a kike. Something only a son of a bitch would do, I mean. I try not to be one. Doesn't always work, but I try.

"You might have let your half-sister know what you were up to," I said.

"She might have minded her own business. She should have. Since she did not, one fine day she will find me minding hers. And you, when you are not carrying your toys."

If they were toys, he would have torn my throat out. I knew as much, and he was bound to know it, too. He didn't care to think about what they could do to him, though. He wouldn't have minded if the sun finished him. He tried to go up in flame and smoke after we brought him back to himself, in fact. It didn't work. There he was, undead night and day. But things connected with God still gave him pause.

"Take care of yourself," I said, and touched the brim of my fedora. "You know Dora and I were only trying to do what was best for you."

"I know you failed." He stared at me, trying to put me in fear or to charm me like a snake charming a bird. Whichever he was aiming for, he didn't get either. He said something in Magyar that should have set the sidewalk under my feet on fire.

I understood part of it; I was picking up bits and pieces from Dora. The rest? Well, if I had followed it, I probably would've had to try to finish him then and there. Since I didn't, I blew him a kiss instead. "Love you, too," I said, and came toward him.

He took half a step back before he could stop himself. That didn't make him like me any better, of course. "You are too stupid to know what you are fooling with, you … you Romanian, you!"

During the war, the Hungarians and Romanians had both sided with the fylfot boys against the Reds. But the bastards who followed the Leader found out in a hurry that they couldn't put Hungarian and Romanian units next to each other or they'd fight among themselves instead of against the folks they were invading. That ancient feud evidently went on among their vampires, too.

I just kept coming. Next thing I knew, Sebestyen wasn't there any more. I might have seen a bat flittering away. Or I might have imagined it. Either way, he wasn't bothering me any more.

Dora was reading—*The Egg and I*, of all things—when I let myself into the apartment. I made a beeline for the bottle of Wild Turkey. A good stiff knock would settle me down. I told myself it would do that, anyhow. If I needed some numbing against the world … well, it wasn't vepratoga.

I came out into the front room again. Dora's nostrils twitched. She didn't breathe, or I didn't think she did, but they twitched anyhow. "You have been afraid and ready to kill at the same time," she said. It wasn't a question, and Old Man Mose's nose couldn't have done a better job.

"Yeah." I nodded jerkily. I know what fear smells like. So does anybody who's gone to war. I couldn't smell it on myself, but what did that prove? Bupkis—a word I got from a fat, whiskery guy who sells dirty books. The other stink? Fury? I had to take Dora's word for that one.

"Tell me." She sounded gentle, like a mother calming a little boy. I'm sure that's how I seemed to her sometimes. It graveled me, but what could I do about it? Again, bupkis. To her, any mortal was but a walking shadow, a poor player that struts and frets his hour upon the stage, and then is heard no more.

Sorry. Didn't mean to shake a spear at you there.

"Tell me," she said again when I didn't answer right away. Gentle, yes, and irresistible.

"Rudolf." I gave it to her in one word. The bourbon was starting to build a glass wall against the slings and arrows of outrageous fortune (oops—I did it again). Not fast enough, though, dammit.

"Oh." She knew what that meant: trouble. "Are you all right?" She looked me over. She probably also smelled me over. I must've passed muster, because she answered her own question: "You *are* all right. What happened? Tell me exactly."

So I did, as best I could. I finished, "I think I scared him, too—some, anyhow. But probably not as much as he scared me."

Dora clicked her tongue between her teeth. I don't know how she didn't bite herself when she did that, but she didn't. "You are brave, which I knew. And you are foolish … which I knew. Have you any idea what he might have done to you? Any idea at all?"

"Maybe a little. But I have some idea what I might've done to him, too. I don't think I was the only one who did, either." My hand didn't move toward that pocket, much less go into it. You don't pull a gun on somebody you care about.

Of course she knew what I carried. That she let me come near her anyway, that she let me stay in the apartment while the sun was in the sky, told how much she trusted me. More than a vampire usually trusted a human, for sure. Even so, she said, "That might have done less good than you would have wanted. We are quicker than mortals believe, and stronger, too."

And sneakier. And all that good stuff. She was bound to be right. Most of the time, she was. When you're smart to begin with and you pile up way more experience than any live person can, that's what happens. Neverthenonetheless, I waved her words away. "Never mind, babe. I got through it. It's over."

"With Rudolf, it is never over."

Dora was bound to be right about that, too. Vampires play vengeance games the way mortals play bridge or chess, only they play them over centuries. They don't usually play them against mortals—try playing chess against a six-year-old—but that doesn't mean they never do. And, if Sebestyen was playing against Dora, he'd see me as a pawn to be taken off the board whenever that did him the most good.

"Ah, to hell with it," I said. "How'd you like to go up to the Basket Room Friday night? That Ricks fellow, the guitar player I'm working for, he's playing there. He invited me over. Want to hear what he's like?" Friday night was about as far ahead as a mere mortal could look.

"We can do that." Dora liked jazz. A surprising number of vampires do. The music of the oppressed hits them where they—mm, not where they live, but you know what I mean. She sniffed me one more time. "This Ricks personage, is he why you smell of sorcery and *gyilkos bálnák*?"

"Of what?" I said. She'd dropped into Magyar without noticing.

"Of killer whale," she translated. I started to ask what she was talking about, but then I remembered killer whale was another way to say grampus. She and Mose had both smelled the record company on me. That was interesting. Interesting in an unnerving way, but it was. I wondered what it meant, or if it meant anything.

Central Avenue. Friday night. Any night, sure, but especially Friday or Saturday. You go to Central after sunset, you throw on your glad rags and show the world you're somebody. Even nobodies want to look like somebody on Central.

My glad rags had gone up in smoke when the salamander torched the building where I used to live. That meant I looked more like a businessman than I cared to, though my bright blue silk shirt and the way I rolled my fedora's brim warned that I might be a businessman who'd slipped the leash.

Dora, now, Dora looked gorgeous. She made a point of that when she went out among live people. She had it, she was proud of it, and she flaunted it. The orange dress she wore could have come straight from the Academy Awards ceremony at the Pantages. I thought so, anyway, but what do I know about ladies' clothes? I'm just a guy.

I know she got wolf whistles as we strolled up Central toward the Basket Room. She didn't mind that. But when one fellow yelled something that was more filthy than admiring, she spun around and showed him her fangs. I've seen shells leave a 105 slower than he got the hell out of there.

She turned back to me and took my hand, as if to tell the world she belonged to me—or, more likely, to tell it I belonged to her. "I do not care for impolite men," she said.

"Yes, ma'am," I answered, deadpan. She sent me a sharp look, then smiled. I felt as if I'd passed a small test.

Everybody comes to Central on Friday and Saturday nights, to see, to be seen, to go to the clubs—best scene this side of Chicago—to drink, to eat, to find somebody who'll be friendly for a price, or to land whatever dope you're after. White people, yellow people, brown people, black people. People. All kinds of people.

And cops. The red lights on the roofs of black-and-whites spun round and round as the police cars rolled up and down the avenue. Two of LA's finest jumped out of their Ford—of course they bought cars from a bastard who hated unions—and grabbed somebody (yes, he was a Negro) on the sidewalk. I don't know what they thought he did. I didn't see him do anything. But they threw him in the back seat, where he couldn't get out, and zoomed away with him.

"I have seen occupying armies before," Dora said.

"Me, too," I answered. Hell, I'd been part of an occupying army, though most of the Italians welcomed us with open arms. The reason they did was, we chased off the fylfot boys who'd been occupying them before. The way the fylfot boys treated them .... Well, it would've made the LAPD jealous. I don't know how I can say anything worse.

No sooner had that crossed my mind than three policemen came down the sidewalk towards us. Cops in the Negro Belt had things happen to them if they were by themselves. Not often, but often enough. Two of these guys were white, the third black. The fylfot boys used Italian helpers, too. All three cops had faces like clenched fists.

Their eyeballs clicked as they went past Dora. They didn't hassle us, though. The white cops thought I was their kind of thing, not the other kind of thing. If the black man knew better, he didn't let on. That was lucky. White cops, they don't like guys with even one drop hanging around with blonds like Dora. I mean, they really don't like it.

We went past Club Alabam by the Dunbar Hotel and the Last Word. Right across the street from Club Alabam was an eatery called the Zombie, which always gave me the creeps. The Basket Room was another ten blocks farther north. More restaurants on the way, and barber shops and beauty parlors and churches and hex shops and anything else anybody could want.

Sometimes people still call the place we were going to Jack's Basket Room. Before I was born, Jack was champion of the world for a while—and didn't that set people's hair on fire! White people's hair, I mean, the hair on white people like those mean-looking cops. Jack liked blonds, too, which thrilled 'em even more. But he's been dead a few years now, and they don't use his name so much. The marquee said *The Oscar Ricks Trio*. He hadn't lied to me.

At the door, a man in a nice suit held out his hand for the cover charge. Two bigger guys in dumpier clothes stood behind him to make sure he got it. "I'm Jack Mitchell," I said, and nodded up at the sign. "Did Oscar leave my name?"

He pulled a sheet of paper from an inside coat pocket. His eyebrows jumped in surprise. Of course people would try to con him all the time. "I'll be damned—he did," he answered, stepping aside with an inviting wave. "Enjoy the show, Mister Mitchell." He was talking to me but looking at Dora. She looked through him, but didn't give him a vampire snarl.

When I told the maître d' who I was, he led Dora and me to a table near the stage. I slipped him two bucks. We came in between sets. The air was thick with the smell of fried chicken. It made my mouth water and my stomach rumble. They serve it to you in wicker baskets, which is why it's the Basket Room.

"Do you mind if I get some?" I asked.

"Of course not." Dora knew live people's eating habits were different from hers.

I waved to a waitress and ordered when she came up. She turned to Dora. "And what can I get for you, ma'am?"

"Nothing, thank you." Dora showed her teeth then, but only to let the girl know what she was, not to threaten her.

She didn't faze the waitress a bit. "Can I bring you some ice water or something better to drink?"

"Scotch on the rocks will do," Dora said. I ordered Wild Turkey to go with the chicken.

While we waited, I eyeballed the crowd without seeming to. People don't like you staring at them. Some of these people looked tougher than the bouncers out front—for whatever reason, a lot of mob guys really like jazz. Others were out to see and be seen, and to listen to the music, whatever it turned out to be.

The waitress came back with our drinks and my food. The chicken turned out to be damn good. So did the shoestring potatoes the drumstick and breast sat on. Dora smiled as I chowed down. "I remember the days when flesh satisfied me." She paused, then smiled again in a different way. "If you know what I mean."

I was taking a sip when she said that. I snorted so hard, bourbon almost—I mean *almost*—came out my nose.

About five seconds after the girl took away my basket, empty now but for bones, the fellow who'd let me in came up on stage and held up his hand to be noticed. "Folks, give a warm welcome to the Oscar Ricks Trio: Scar himself on guitar, Otis Jefferson on bass, and Jimmy Newcombe on drums. The Oscar Ricks Trio!"

People clapped as the curtain slid back behind him. I didn't know what we'd get; I put my hands together anyway. I was hoping for bebop. Even if Satchmo called it Chinese music, it spoke to me. It was weird. It had trouble fitting in with the bigger, wider world. But if you knew, you *knew*. Yeah, it spoke to me.

"How … interesting," Dora murmured, as if she was a long way from sure she wanted to be interested.

Well, the same thought was going through my head. Oscar hadn't told me he played electric guitar, all wired up and plugged into an amplifier. The bass man didn't have a big upright fiddle, either. He played an electric bass that looked like a guitar. He was all plugged in, too. The drummer's drums were, well, drums.

Then they started to play. You can do things with electric instruments you can't do with ordinary ones. They make sounds you can't get any other way. Oscar and Otis Jefferson were pretty damn good at doing just that. With the amps, they could also get as loud as a much bigger combo.

No, it wasn't bebop. I'm not even sure it was jazz. Jazz comes at you sideways, takes you by surprise. The trio took me by surprise, too—they surprised me by how they rode right over me till the sound filled my whole head and didn't leave room inside for anything else.

It's the damnedest thing. I wasn't sure what I was hearing. I was sure it took me out of myself, out of the Basket Room, off to somewhere far away. Where? It put me in mind of one of those pulp magazines with gaudy covers that are full of stories about wizards conjuring a man to the Moon and bringing him back in one piece.

We don't know how to do that yet, of course. One of these days before too long, though, you've got to figure we will. And when we do, everybody will be listening to licks that sound like the ones Oscar and his buddies were laying down.

Dora was frowning while she listened. She didn't approve. Every once in a while, she showed all the years she carried. She didn't look any older than I do, but she was. Oh, yes—she was. Her tastes had firmed long, long before I was born, and what she was hearing didn't suit them.

I'm not sure it suited me, either. But it intrigued me, not just for the sound itself but for the way it mashed music and engineering together. Yeah, it felt like the music of the future.

I wondered what the people who went to Technocracy meetings would make of it. Somehow, I couldn't see those cats getting down to the Basket Room to listen to it.

And then, in the middle of all that straight-ahead strangeness, the boys played half a dozen bars from "Relaxin' at Camarillo." Oscar didn't crack a smile. He didn't wink. He and Otis and Jimmy just did it, then slid back into their own groove. It might not have sounded like bebop, but it had that spirit. If you knew, you *knew*. If you didn't, they weren't about to tell you.

Me, I almost fell on the floor laughing. Dora looked at me as if I'd gone out of my gourd. I don't suppose she'd ever heard Bird do that. My record of it went up in smoke along with everything else in my place when the salamander came calling.

Here and there in the place, other folks got it, too. I could see the startled grins on their faces that showed they did. I could also see the set wasn't going down real well with most of the house. The goons were scowling. This wasn't what they'd expected to hear, and they didn't approve of anything they weren't used to. In their way, they were as conservative as Dora.

When the set ended, my ears were ringing. Every sound smaller than the ones that came from the electric guitar and bass seemed small and very far away. I'd had that happen to me after I stood too close to artillery firing fast, and after I'd done a lot of shooting with my Garand. After the Army turned me loose, no.

The hand the trio got was smaller than I thought they deserved. No, a lot of people didn't know what they were doing and didn't want to find out. Dora clapped enough for politeness' sake, not much more.

Oscar hopped down from the stage and came over to our table. I shook his hand. "That was crazy, man," I said. "I thought I was listening to, like, 1971."

If he'd grinned any wider, the top of his head would've fallen off. "Oh, good! *Somebody* can dig it, anyway. That's what we were aiming at."

"Very unusual music," Dora said, which might have been a compliment and, well, might not.

He looked at me. He knew what I was. He looked at her. As she had with the waitress, she let him see her fangs so he knew what she was. He took it in stride. Guys who play music take all kinds of things in stride. If they haven't done weird stuff themselves, their friends will have.

"We're hoping we can get people used to it," he said, and winked at me. "In 1971, you'll hear it all the time."

Before I could answer, one of the tough cats came over and growled at Oscar: "What the hell kind of shit were you playin' there?" It wasn't 1971 yet. Nowhere near.

Oscar plastered a smile on his face and nodded toward Dora, "Sir, maybe you don't want to talk like that in front of a lady."

He tried. He really did. He was black and the goon was white. That's a bad combination when things turn nasty. And the goon was liable to be connected to the owners. That's worse.

A second later, the fellow swung a haymaker that would've taken Oscar's head off had it landed. It didn't. The way Oscar ducked and sideslipped told me he might've been in the ring a time or three. I punched the tough guy in the nose. He went over backward. Then the fun really started.

The goon's friends came running. Oscar's sidemen jumped down from the stage to give the good guys a hand. Oscar himself threw a right that said I'd made a shrewd guess. But one of the clowns in the rumpled suits got him in the breadbasket, and he folded up like an accordion.

I hit that fellow before he could start stomping Oscar. Somebody hit me on the side of the head just above the ear. I saw stars for a second, but the way the tough guy yowled told me he might've ruined a knuckle or two. That didn't break my heart.

But things weren't going real well for us. One of the goons hit Jimmy Newcombe with a chair and knocked him sprawling. The bouncers ran in to join the other muscle men. Some of the people who weren't involved in the brawl screeched and ran like hell. Others dove under tables. And a few guys grabbed beer bottles by the neck in case they needed to use them.

The bouncers didn't need beer bottles. They had blackjacks. Jimmy Newcombe had just made it to his feet again when one of them laid him out. I decked him. His pal got me in the ribs. Hurt like a mad bastard. I hoped none of my slats was busted. I'd had that happen before, and hadn't enjoyed it.

Turned out that second bouncer made a mistake. Yeah, you might say so. Just a little one. Dora'd been sitting there till I got clouted. Letting the boys play? Call it whatever you want; she had been.

Then she wasn't sitting any more. She was on her feet. She picked up the bouncer—he probably went six-one, 230, something like that—and lifted him over her head without the slightest show of effort. I won't say without breaking a sweat, because she wouldn't have done that no matter what. She flung him in amongst the goons. I mean, she flung him *hard*. She knocked 'em down like a bowler making a spare.

That brought a lull. Not a hair out of place, she turned to me and said, "Perhaps we should go."

"Yeah, sweetie. Perhaps we should." I grabbed my fedora from the floor. It would never be the same; somebody'd stomped it. Damn! I liked that lid.

Exit we did, pursued by no bears. They were still untangling themselves from one another. Somehow, I didn't think the Oscar Ricks Trio would play its last set.

And we got out, got away, right in the proverbial Nicholas of time. We'd gone four doors or so south along Central (me trying to walk without bending anywhere) when a bunch of cop cars screamed toward the Basket Room, lights blazing, sirens wailing. L.A.'s finest piled out of them and swarmed into the club, hot to bust any heads that didn't already happen to be busted.

"What an interesting way to start the evening!" Dora said, merry as a grig, whatever the hell a grig is.

"Well, that's one way to put it," I answered. I could move—gingerly, but I could—without feeling knives in my chest. Maybe my ribs were just bruised, not broken. I could hope so, anyhow.

"Shall we go to Deacon's and see what is going on there?" she asked.

"Mm, maybe not," I managed.

"Oh. You are in pain." Dora sounded as if she needed to remind herself. No, she hadn't been a live person for a while.

"Some," I admitted. After a moment, I added, "You don't always show how strong you are."

"It is mostly safer not to. Sometimes, though, one must," she answered.

She understood the same thing Negroes and Jews do: when there aren't very many of your kind of folk, showing any sort of strength gets dangerous. Ordinary people start worrying about what else you may be able to do. And when ordinary people start worrying about you, bad things happen.

"I love you, babe," I said, mostly because, even though Dora was blond and beautiful and undead, she'd just shown that, in a really important way, she was a lot like me.

She sent me a reproachful stare. The idea that a mortal should love her always dismayed her. I knew I was only one link in a long chain of men who had, and that the chain would just get longer for years and years after I was looking at the grass from underneath, not from on top. I also knew she didn't love me back. By the nature of things, vampires can't. You know what else? I didn't care.

"You are a fool, Jack." She'd told me the same thing before, not always for that particular reason. Not always, but pretty often.

"If I am, I'm a happy fool." I was, too, except for the sore ribs.

"Happiness does not last, any more than love does," Dora said. I opened my mouth to explain how wrong she was. Then I closed it again, because I couldn't. We walked back to Vampire Village in silence.

I wondered whether the cops would come banging on the door to Dora's apartment over the weekend. People at the Basket Room knew who I was. Oscar Ricks had given the guy at the front door my name, and I'd given it to the maître d' myself.

But nobody from LAPD showed up. I wasn't that easy to find, not since my apartment—hell, my apartment building—got salamandered. Since other people besides the police were liable to want to knock me around a bit, or more than a bit, I didn't mind falling off the map for a while.

Still and all, if I was going to get any paying jobs, I needed to be at the office some of the time. I also needed to take care of Old Man Mose. He, of course, would put those in the opposite order.

I even went in earlier than usual Monday: I showed up a little past noon. Mose greeted me with, "The noisy thing was really noisy this morning. It made my head ache."

He meant the telephone. I could believe it had been ringing off the hook. The cops'd still want to talk with me. Again, they wouldn't be the only ones. I wondered what kind of delightful messages Hilda would have for me.

Before I could even pick up the phone to find out, somebody knocked on the door. Mose disappeared under the sofa. Like most cats, he took no chances with strangers. I sat down behind my desk. The chair creaked. It always does.

"Come on in. It's not locked," I said, thinking maybe it should have been.

The door opened. It wasn't one of our fair (if you're white or lucky) city's finest. It wasn't a goon or a bouncer from the Basket Room, either. It was Oscar Ricks, looking somewhat the worse for wear. Well, I did, too; I had a lump where that one son of a bitch hit me in the side of the head.

"Hello there," I said. We both chuckled; the other choice would have been screaming. I waved him to the couch. He'd get cat hair on the seat of his pants, but that was part of the price you paid for doing business with me.

"I didn't mean for any of that to happen," he said.

"What? You mean you went in there to play music, not to start fights?" I sounded astonished. Ricks chuckled again, sheepishly. I asked, "How did things go the couple of nights before we stopped by?"

"Not … too bad," he said after a visible pause for thought. "I know the music is different. Some people don't know what to make of it. Some people, they don't *want* to know what to make of it. But everybody stayed polite … till Friday night."

I hadn't known what to make of it, either. But I hadn't wanted to rearrange his face because I hadn't. I said, "You were having fun up there. I damn near pissed my pants laughing when you snuck in some of Bird's blues."

He grinned at me. "You do that stuff for the people who'll get it. The rest, it just flies over their heads. That's okay. I don't follow all the jokes other people tell, either."

"Is your drummer all right? He got decked pretty good."

"Jimmy's hurt, but he's not *hurt*, know what I mean? I came over to thank you for pitching in, y'know? You could've just let that sucker, like, beat on me."

"I wouldn't do that if I'd never set eyes on you before. You can't let people think they can get away with that crap."

"God bless you, man. And your lady friend. She let me know what she was, but I sure didn't reckon she could do what she done."

"Thanks. Um—if you see her again, you don't want to put it just that way."

"Huh? Oh! Right!" Oscar snapped his fingers, reminding himself. "I didn't think."

"It's okay. The name doesn't do me any harm. Have you made up your mind what you're going to do with the record deal?"

"I'll sign with Grampus. That way, I've got a chance to put something out there, anyhow, see what people make of it." Ricks gave me a rueful smile. "And if I get screwed, I get screwed, that's all. Happens to musicians all the goddamn time. Thanks for looking into 'em for me. They don't seem *too* crooked." Another smile of the same sort. "I'll find out."

"Luck," I said, as I would have to another dogface moving towards an enemy foxhole.

"We all need it." One more sweet-and-sour grin. "Next thing I need luck for is finding the next place for us to play. They said not to come back to the Basket Room if we knew what was good for us. You knew that'd happen, didn't you?"

"Afraid I did," I admitted. We shook hands again. He walked out. I wondered if we'd ever run into each other somewhere down the line. I also wondered if he'd get so famous, he wouldn't remember he'd wasted a hundred bucks on a down-at-the-heels private eye. You never could tell. He had something unusual going for him. If it caught on …

Mose came out from under the sofa. "What was that all about?"

"Business. Music."

"Oh. Noise," he said. I've never known a cat who cared for any human music but the dinner bell.

Another knock on the door. All of a sudden, no more Old Man Mose. "It's open," I said.

In came two cops. They were in plain clothes, but anybody—especially anybody from my part of town—would have made them in half a second. The older one looked at me as if he wanted to wipe me off the bottom of his crepe-soled shoe. "You're hard to find, Mitchell," he said, his voice raspy as a file from a million cigarettes.

"You found me, Sergeant Piskorski." I knew who he was. He was one of the Newton Division boys who kept the Negro Belt in line. I didn't bear down on the first syllable of his name. Tempting, but you have to know when you can't push it.

"You were in a brawl Friday night. We should've been able to question you Saturday morning," his friend said. Him, I didn't recognize. He sounded livelier than a zombie, but not much.

"I'm here now, Officer," I said.

"Detective," he said sharply. That flicked him.

Piskorski pulled a notebook and a stubby pencil out of a coat pocket. "Tell us what happened in the Basket Room," he said. So I did. He stopped me about three sentences in. "How do you know this Ricks character?"

"He hired me to look into something for him. I did."

He grunted and made a note. "Awright. Go on." He lit up a Camel. So did his boring partner. Piskorski didn't interrupt me any more. After I got done, he grunted again. "Yeah, that pretty much matches up with what I heard from other people. Nothin' to hang on you this time, but keep your nose clean, you hear?"

"I sure will, Sergeant." I sounded as if a Boy Scout wouldn't melt in my mouth, or whatever the stupid saying is. Piskorski looked disgusted. I'd been aiming for that.

Then the other cop—excuse me, the other detective—asked, "What do you think of the kind of music the Ricks Trio plays?"

"I liked it. It's going in a new direction," I said. "How about you?"

His face congealed into disapproving lines. "It isn't Benny Goodman," he said, as if that proved it couldn't be any damn good. Benny Goodman's bankroll shows way more people like him than Oscar Ricks. That doesn't mean there isn't room for both of them. Or I don't think it does. The other detective had other ideas.

Sergeant Piskorski didn't give a damn one way or the other. "C'mon, Webb. We've got his story now." They turned to go. The detective—Webb—opened the door. Before Piskorski went out through it, he rounded on me one more time. "Clean nose."

I'd look stupid with a dirty one, I thought. But I just nodded. The less you give them, the better off you are. Piskorski muttered and coughed. Then he and his friend left.

Old man Mose came out again. *He* had a clean nose. Sure he did—he could lick it. After he reeled his tongue back in, he remarked, "They smell even worse than you do."

"Thanks," I said. "I think you mean they smoke even more than I do."

"Same thing. The older one pours down even more of the stuff that makes people stupid than you do, too."

I hadn't caught the whiskey reek coming off of Piskorski, but what do I know? I'm not a cat. I don't have such a great nose for a human, either, no doubt because I do smoke. Mose has told me so more than once. So has Dora, whose opinion I actually value. I keep smoking anyway. Why? Because I like it.

I let myself be relieved that they hadn't dropped an assault and battery charge on me. Then I reminded myself they could if they ever decided they wanted to. Trust cops? In Los Angeles? Not me. Not anybody else in this part of town, either.

Later that afternoon, somebody else knocked on the door—three sharp, evenly spaced, dignified taps, not too loud and not too soft. Just right. The first one was plenty to send Mose under cover. By the second, I'd closed the desk drawer where the Wild Turkey lived. Yes, I'd been about to get into it. I hadn't expected anybody else. I never expect visitors, and most of the time I don't have any. Nobody becomes a private eye to get rich. Right then, I couldn't imagine why I'd got into this line of work. Stupidity, I expect.

"It's not locked," I said, and tried to look businesslike.

In walked a short, thin, prissy medium-brown man a few years older than I am. He was dressed to the nines, or maybe to the elevens. "Good day, Mister Mitchell. I have a matter of some concern about which I'd like to speak to you." He sounded the way he looked, fussily precise.

"Why don't you tell me about it … Mister Adams?" Yes, I named him a beat late; I recognized him only after I started talking. I don't think I'd ever seen him away from Deacon's till that moment. Deacon's was named for Deacon Washington, who ran the after-hours joint like his own little kingdom. Acolyte Adams was his partner, and you can take that however you want. Not only was the Deacon queer, he didn't care who knew it. A brave man, or a foolish one.

Adams hit from that side of the plate, too—they'd been together for years and years—but he didn't like to admit it.

I waved him to the sofa, but he kept standing. No cat hair for his backside, thank you very much. "I am afraid, Mister Mitchell, that someone is seeking to blackmail me," he said. He set an envelope on my desk.

I started to open it to see what was inside, then stopped when I noticed the postmark. "It's from Gardena!" I blurted.

"Yes. It is," he agreed, as if he were talking about a week-old halibut. "Why should that matter?"

"Mm, I don't know whether it does or not, but I've had other business down there lately. This makes twice more than I ever did before."

"Oscar Ricks," Adams said. It wasn't a question.

"And how do you know that?"

"His trio has played at Deacon's once or twice." Acolyte Adams screwed up his face. "Not to my taste, I fear, but Mister Washington finds them interesting. As, apparently, does a record company there."

"He told you about it?"

"He did. We are one of the few establishments to whose proprietors he felt he could speak freely."

I needed a few seconds to figure out what he was driving at. Then I got it. "Because you don't have connections to the guys with the ugly suits and the lumpy faces?" I had a lump of my own, but I didn't mention it, and neither did Adams.

"That's right," he said. "They tried to muscle in on us a couple of years ago, but Mister Washington stopped them."

"How did he do that?" If I sounded surprised, it's only because I was.

"He told them he paid the LAPD enough to make sure they would come after whoever did him harm. They must have checked and found he was telling the truth, because they haven't troubled us since." Acolyte Adams smiled a smile almost as thin as his mustache.

"A lot of money," I observed. Adams nodded. Well, Deacon's brought in a lot of money. I was sure of that. He couldn't have paid the talent who performed there if it didn't—or paid off the cops the way he did.

Then I read the blackmail letter. It was about what I expected. Whoever wrote it went into filthy detail about what Acolyte Adams and Deacon Washington did with each other. He said he'd prove it to the world unless Adams sent $5,000 to a post-office box in Gardena by two weeks from now.

"Uh-*huh*," I said.

"I would pay him if I thought he'd keep quiet once I did," Adams said bleakly. "But I fear he would only demand more." He didn't worry about laying out five grand for peace and quiet. I wished like hell I didn't.

"Seems pretty likely," I said. "Whom do you know in Gardena?" With anybody else except maybe Dora, I would've said *Who do you know . . . ?* With Acolyte Adams, *whom* won me a point.

"No one," he said. "But I know people in Inglewood and Hawthorne and Torrance, and they aren't far away."

"Okay. Different kind of question: have you taken the letter—or just the envelope—to a wizard who could use the law of contagion to trace it back to whoever sent it?"

"I did that, yes. The man told me it had been decoupled from the sender. That was the word he used, decoupled. I also had it dusted for fingerprints. Again, nothing useful turned up."

"Well, you tried. Good for you." Whoever was after him knew enough to be careful, which made my job harder. Happy day. And one more thing occurred to me: "I'm surprised this guy went after you and not Deacon."

"He did go after Deacon. Deacon wrote back to him that he could go ahead and print whatever he had on the front page of the *Sentinel*," Adams said. The *Sentinel* is the biggest Negro newspaper in town. I'd done a little work for its editor, though I didn't mention that. Adams sighed. "Some of my family would be very upset if my private life were to become public."

No, Deacon Washington didn't give a damn if the whole world knew he was queer. He positively reveled in it, and he made enough dough to pay off the Vice Squad so they wouldn't throw him or Adams in jail for perversion or anything.

Not everybody can live like that, though. I wondered how upset the Acolyte's *very upset* was. Horsewhip upset? Knife upset?

Forty-five-caliber upset? Somewhere in that range, unless I missed my guess.

As if reading my mind, Adams said, "Of course I rely on your discretion."

Bad things will happen to you if you aren't discreet, were the words behind the words. I answered, "You'd be a fool to deal with me if you didn't."

"Indeed." He licked his lips. "And what will dealing with you cost me?"

He would have laid out $5,000 without blinking an eye if he'd thought it would end the blackmail for good. After a moment's thought, I replied, "Most of the time, I'd say a grand." I wouldn't say that to anybody but him, which was something he didn't need to know. "Give me five hundred now, though, and let Dora and me into Deacon's for free for a couple of years. That'll be worth it to me."

"Agreed," he said at once. "Will you take a check, or would you rather I brought you cash tomorrow?"

"From you, I'll take a check," I said. He wrote me one, and I learned his real first name was Desmond. I stuck the check in an inside pocket. As he turned to go, I added, "Give Deacon my regards."

"I shall do that. Thank you so much, Mister Mitchell." Adams touched the brim of his hat and left. Old Man Mose didn't come out, so he'd probably gone to sleep under the sofa.

Dora hadn't been in her coffin long when I headed out the next morning. I knew where the Gardena post office was; I'd gone past it on the bus. I wanted to get there when it opened so I could wait around and see who used that post-office box. After that .... I didn't know what I'd do after that. Finding out about the blackmailer came ahead of worrying about it.

Rivke was standing on the corner as I walked toward the Red Line stop. We smiled at each other. "You are out early," she said.

"Yeah. Anybody would think I have to work for a living or something," I said. Her smile got wider. She was nice looking when she did that. After everything she'd gone through on the other side of the ocean, though, she didn't do it much.

I hopped on the trolley. We rattled south, slower than I would've liked. More cars on the road than usual. Well, it was closer to rush hour than usual for me. But more cars on the road any which way. They clog things up for the Red Line machines, make 'em fall behind schedule. If that goes on, I may have to think about getting one for myself. Of course, the more people who buy cars, the more trouble for the Red Line. I don't know what to do about it.

Things got better after I transferred at the Slauson Tower station. Fewer people live down south, which means traffic isn't so ugly. Orchards, groves, berry farms, those poker clubs, the new houses … I thought there were more of those than there had been even a few days earlier, but that must've been my imagination.

I made it to the post office before it opened. It looked like a WPA building, with little terracotta friezes over the front windows. They opened up at two minutes past nine, or maybe my watch was fast. I ambled in, bought some three-cent stamps, and then mooched over to the Federal wanted posters thumbtacked to a bulletin board.

One of the posters showed a photo of a tough-looking woman who was called, among other things, the Queen of the Yeggs. What a wonderful handle to hang on somebody! Under the photo were all, or at least a lot of, the things she'd been arrested for. She'd earned that name honestly. Or dishonestly, depending on how you look at things.

While I was eyeing the posters, I was also looking at the wall of boxes not far away. The one I was interested in was 446. Of course, nobody came near it. Hardly anybody came into the post office at all. I saw one of the clerks eyeballing me, wondering why I was hanging around. I smoked a cigarette, stubbed it out in one of those tall ash-trays full of sand, then went back to the wanted criminals. I really would have liked to meet the Queen of the Yeggs, but she seemed to hold court up in the Bay Area.

At ten o'clock, thumps and clumps and the waves-washing-in sound of shifting paper came from behind the wall of PO boxes: somebody was putting the day's load of mail into them. People came in right after that to collect whatever they'd been waiting for. Nobody opened Box 446. Nobody went near it. I swore under my breath and lit another Old Gold.

By eleven, the rush—such as it was—had thinned out. One guy stood behind the counter: the one who kept shooting glances my way. I wondered if he'd get antsy enough to call the police. That would be awkward. If they realized I had the proverbial one drop, it was liable to get worse than awkward.

I walked up to the counter. The clerk looked worried. Only desperate fools rob the post office. That's a Federal rap, and they land on you like a round from Anzio Annie. But he didn't know I wasn't a desperate fool. He didn't till I showed him my card, anyway. I said, "I'm investigating a blackmail case. Can you tell me who uses Box 446?"

"I'm sorry, sir, but under postal regulations I'm not allowed to do that unless you have a warrant," he answered.

I laid a double sawbuck on the counter. He looked at it, looked at me, and shook his head. I put another twenty on top of it. I hadn't cashed Acolyte Adams' check yet, so that was as high as I could go. If he proved honest or greedy, I was out of luck.

But he made the two portraits of Andrew Jackson disappear. "Let me check the records, sir," he said, as if it were an ordinary business transaction, the kind of thing he did four times a day. I couldn't prove it wasn't.

He went into a back room. If he stayed back there, what could I do about it? Not much, and I knew it only too well. He came back, though, with a small sheet of scratch paper in his hand. He set it on the counter upside down. I turned it over. It said, *Danny Becker, 145 West 154th Street.*

"That'd be just this side of Main Street?" I pointed east. Main is the street that divides East and West addresses.

"Yes, on the other side of the L.A. strip," he said. The few blocks from Vermont to Figueroa belong to the city of Los Angeles; they're a long, thin neck that connects it to San Pedro, which also belongs to it. Back before the first big war, L.A.'s city fathers decided they needed a port to make the town really sizzle. They got one, too, no matter how funny the map looks.

A bus took me over to Main, even if Gardena Boulevard magically transformed itself into 165th Street once we left the city limits. I took a different bus north to 154th Street. It was only two blocks long.

West of it lay a grove of olive trees; the bus had carried me past Olive Street on the way to 154th.

I found 145 without any trouble. I'd expected a house, but it was a business. The sign in front of two adjoining Quonset huts said BECKER SORCERY and, in smaller letters under that, WE PEP UP PRODUCTION! In still smaller letters, it added, PRINTING AND RECORD PRESSING OUR SPECIALTIES.

"Huh," I said thoughtfully, and whistled something tuneless between my teeth before I turned around and headed back to Main. No, I didn't go in there and beard Danny Becker in his den. You want to be careful before you start messing with wizards. Otherwise, they wind up messing with you.

That wasn't the only reason I didn't storm the castle then and there, either. Record pressing? Did Becker Sorcery work with Grampus Records? Did Danny Becker know, or know of, Oscar Ricks? Oscar'd gigged at Deacon's; Acolyte Adams'd said so himself. Were the two things I was looking at connected some way?

All kinds of interesting questions, weren't they? I would have liked answers. Answers are what the client's paying for. But even the questions were worth having. You don't find answers till you have the right questions.

On the far side of Main was a hamburger stand called Imperial Burgers even though Imperial was three or four miles north of there. I bought one. I don't know if it was fit for an emperor or even a king, but it made a decent lunch. Then I went back to Vermont and Gardena Boulevard and took the Red Line back to my part of town. And, as long as I was out and about during bankers' hours, I went to my bank and turned Acolyte Adams' check into folding money. Nothing like a bulging wallet to cure whatever ails you.

Saturday night. Central Avenue. Stepping out with Dora. I was proud to be seen with her, seen as part of the scene. I don't know if she was proud to be seen with me, but she seemed contented enough.

Turn off Central. Head down one of the little side streets. Never mind which one; you don't need to know. Everything changes once you leave the main drag. On Central, streetlights and neon hold night at bay. One or two porch lights along the side street. That's it.

Turn when you come to an alley. Keep walking, but be careful. If you don't know just what you're looking for, you'll go right past it. Even if you do, you may. It looks like a factory that made stuff during the war and got boarded up afterwards. A rickety staircase goes up to the second floor. Most people walk on—it looks as though nothing's happened there for a hell of a long time. But, once more, if you know, you *know*. We went up the stairs. They creaked under my shoes—not under Dora's—but they haven't fallen down yet.

Same goes for the walkway at the top of the stairs. Watch where you put your feet, though. There are gaps between the planks, and some of the ones that are there sit up higher than the rest. Oh—don't run your hand along the bannister, either. You'll fill it full of splinters if you do.

Assuming you make it to the end of the walkway, you come to some blackout curtains: war leftovers. If you push through 'em and past 'em, you come to another set. You push through those .... *And God said, Let there be light: and there was light.*

Standing in the light was Deacon Washington his very own self, collecting cover charges for Deacon's. Nobody ever tells him no, and not just because you won't get in if you do. He has other things going for him, Deacon Washington does. He's one of the biggest men I've ever seen. He's six-eight, six-nine, something like that, and massive, too. He's also one of the blackest men I've ever seen, which does things to some white folks.

"Twenty dollars apiece, if you please," he said, not looking up from his cash box. His voice isn't as deep as you'd expect. It's deeper. He has even finer diction than Acolyte Adams', which also does things to some white people.

I didn't tell him no. I did cough.

He looked up. He was working on a thundercloud frown, but it blew away when he saw who we were. "I beg your pardon," he said, and gave us a courtly wave towards one more set of curtains. "Go on in. Enjoy yourselves. That's what we're here for."

You pass through those last curtains and into Deacon's, you think you've fallen into one of those pulp-magazine stories where you can step between worlds. If it's your first time there, you probably think it's the world of the Arabian Nights. Thick, thick carpets. Cushions and couches—no chairs. More curtains separating spaces, only these are gauzy and gaudy. Lights of every different colors. Almost enough mirrors for a funhouse, and almost as strange as the ones in a funhouse, too. Around the edges, little dark cubbyholes where two or more people can do whatever they want.

Deacon's house quartet was up on stage. The piano player, I saw with some relief, was almost as dark as the man himself. I'd had professional entanglements with the white guy who'd filled that slot before. I didn't think this piano man knew that, but I didn't care to find out I was wrong.

After we settled ourselves on some cushions, a pretty girl drifted over and asked what we wanted. "Wild Turkey on ice," I said.

"A Bloody Mary for me, please," Dora added.

I had money ready when she brought them, but she waved it away. "On the house, Pablo told me," she said. Pablo's the boss barkeep there.

"That wasn't part of the deal," I said.

She and Dora both looked at me the same way: the way they'd look at any fool. "D'you want to go argue with him?" the girl asked.

"Mm, I guess not," I said. Now the girl's face showed that, while I might be dim, my bulb hadn't quite burned out. She went off to take care of somebody else, her backfield in motion. I touched glasses with Dora. "Mud in your eye." No point to wishing a vampire good health. They're either there or they're finished.

"Mud in your eye," she echoed, and sipped. As she swallowed, she nodded. "Horse blood. Deacon is considerate of all his guests."

He was black. He was queer, which affronted most whites and blacks. He was enormous. If none of that had taught him to watch out for folks who weren't just like everybody else, he wouldn't have been the kind of fellow who could run an after-hours club.

Before long, Acolyte Adams stopped by. Unlike his boyfriend, he sat straight up and down even on cushions. "I presume I may speak freely?" he said, his tone telling me he presumed nothing of the sort.

"If you can't in your own joint, where can you?" I asked.

But Dora got what he was driving at. "If you would like me to step away, I shall, of course."

He looked at her. He looked at me. "No, never mind," he said, concluding that, like most couples, we talked about things with each other. He wasn't wrong.

So I told him about my latest expedition to the South Bay, and about Becker Sorcery. "I don't know if they're connected to Grampus Records—I haven't checked that yet. But how many pressing operations would be running down there?"

"Grampus Records?" Adams looked puzzled for a moment. Then he realized what I was driving at. "Oh, yes, the company involved with Oscar Ricks. Isn't that interesting? If he's been telling tales out of school ..."

He didn't say what would happen then. He was a careful man. But I wouldn't have wanted to be Ricks if his mouth'd got ahead of his brain.

Then I remembered something else. "You didn't need to put our drinks on your tab. That wasn't part of the bargain, but I thank you for it."

"I didn't—" Just for a moment, Acolyte Adams looked humanly confused. Then he realized what had to be going on. "Deacon must have done that. I'll have a thing or two to say to him about it."

Which made me wonder which of those two lovebirds ruled the roost. I would've guessed Deacon Washington, on account of his size and on account of his noise. In public, Acolyte Adams was just his shadow. But behind closed doors, how much did any of that matter? I didn't know then; I don't know now. I do know we kept getting free drinks at Deacon's for a long time afterwards. Take it for whatever you think it's worth.

Somehow, I doubt the joint went broke.

"Enjoy the show for now. I must wander," Adams said. As he stood, he bobbed his head to Dora. "Always a pleasure to see you here, Miss Urban." Wander he did.

Dora leaned toward me. "He is a gentleman. A sad gentleman, but a gentleman nonetheless," she murmured into my ear.

"He sure is," I said, and let it go at that. Otherwise, I would've come out with something like, *He's a Negro. He's a queer Negro. How do you expect him to be anything but sad?* The outside world had what it thought were two terrific reasons for hating him. Sometimes I had trouble being with a vampire from Hungary. Of course, sometimes she had trouble being with a betwixt and between mortal. We both were what we were. We did our best not to let that rub us the wrong way.

Which is a fair part of what love's all about, isn't it?

The house combo left the stage. Some of the gauzy curtains slid aside so more of the club could get a good look. A few minutes later, the piano man who wasn't the guy I'd looked into came out. So did the bass player. He looked like a fellow without a care in the world; I wondered if he'd had himself a shot of whatever.

Deacon Washington walked out there. "Folks, tonight Wardell and Dexter are in the house. They may jam for us a little. Maybe just a little. Give it up for them, why don't you?"

I blistered my palms, let me tell you. They're two of the best alto men this town ever hatched, and when they face off against each other .... Chances are you've heard 'em on record. That's nice, but it's nothing like live.

They came out together. Dexter's the biggest man in any room that doesn't hold Deacon Washington. And he wears a hat to make himself look even taller. Wardell, I don't think Wardell weighs a hundred pounds soaking wet. He's not short, but he's the skinniest guy I ever saw this side of a skeleton. Whatever he puts on hangs on him like potato sacks. With a sax in his hands, though, he'll stand up to anybody, including Dexter.

They both use the junk. Honest to God, it makes you wonder.

Piano and bass started up, just noodling. Wardell and Dexter joined in. They were feeling each other out at first, each seeing what the other was liable to have in his pockets tonight. They kept on like that for a while, both waiting for the moment to take off—waiting like a dragonflier on a carrier getting ready to fly against the Knights of Bushido.

Wardell went first, sixteen bars of the most blistering bebop you can imagine. Most blistering except the sixteen Dexter threw back, I should say. And at the end of his, he gave Wardell the opening of Beethoven's Fifth: dadada *daah!* Dexter likes to quote that way. *Top that, sucker*, was what it meant.

Only Wardell blew it back in his face, all twisted and off key—Beethoven played by Spike Jones, Beethoven sneering at Beethoven.

The whole club fell out laughing. Even Dora grinned, and classical music's serious business to her. Eight bars this time. Wardell did things nobody except him would've dreamt a sax could do. And Dexter gave it back every bit as hot.

Four bars from each then. And two. And …. Somebody should have rung a bell. Like prizefighters, they'd finished that round. Dexter lit a cigarette. Wardell knocked back what looked like straight whiskey. They were both streaming sweat. No seconds in this ring to towel them dry.

The piano man began to play. The guy on bass gave that clever right hand some bottom. Dexter and Wardell went back to it with them. This time, Dexter soloed first and Wardell hit back. Shorter and shorter, harder and harder. Another round.

They could jam like that all night, and then all day. They have, plenty of times. By all the signs, they were going to again. But Dora said, "I must go. Soon the White Fire will burn the sky."

"I'll come with you," I said.

"You need not. I know this gives you much pleasure."

"You give me much pleasure, babe," I said, which made her smile. So we both got up and left. I don't know who won the duel that night, or whether anybody did.

There are no clocks in Deacon's. If you need to know what time it is there, you'd better wear a watch. Or be a vampire. Morning twilight was coming on hard when we got outside. Dora clucked to herself. "The music pleased me, too, and I stayed too long. I had better fly for safety."

She brushed her lips against mine. For a split second, I could feel the fangs behind them. Then she was gone, or her beautiful female form was. A bat flittered away, speeding south and west. She'd get where she needed to go. She'd cut it close before. Unlike her unloving half-brother, she wasn't ready to finish.

I went back toward Vampire Village on shank's mare, almost the only guy on the street. The night people had gone to bed. The morning people weren't up yet. The light got brighter as I walked. Things took on their true colors.

VV was even quieter than the live part of town. Vampires with any sense had already slammed the lids on their coffins. I could hear a car two blocks away, and the Red Line trolley from a good bit farther off than that.

I wasn't thinking anything much while I walked along. Then, out of the corner of my eye, I spied another flitter. A split second later, a vampire stood in front of me. He was nobody I'd ever seen before. The hungry—starving, really—gleam in his eye told me he didn't give a damn about Dora's benison. He didn't give a damn about anything but his undying appetite.

"Ach, Frühstück!" he said happily.

You fight the fylfot boys for a year, you pick up bits of their lingo. No matter how happy he was, I didn't want to be his breakfast. I knew right away he didn't play by any rules. He'd drain me dry as fast as he could and then find somewhere to hole up from the White Fire. I also knew I was in deep trouble. Hanging around with Dora, I didn't usually wear a crucifix or keep garlic cloves in my pocket. They would have been undeadly dangerous to her.

But I did have silver coins along with my pennies and nickels. I threw a handful of change at him. He laughed scornfully, dodging every flying dime and quarter and half with inhuman speed. Then he sprang at me.

I tried to slug him. Useless, of course, but you always want to go down swinging. Inhuman speed? Yes. He had inhuman strength to go with it, of course. He bent my head back as easily as if I were a baby and opened wide.

Before his fangs could pierce me, though, somebody behind him screamed something in a language that was almost *Deutsch* but not quite.

It made the vampire drop me like last year's girlfriend and whirl around. There was Rivke. She didn't have a crucifix, but the Mogen David she brandished blazed the same way a crucifix will if you use it against one of the undead. The one who'd dumped me on the sidewalk shrieked. Next thing I knew, he was a bat again, and going like a bat out of hell.

The sun came out while I was picking myself off the concrete. Did he burn up or get away? I had no idea. As I swatted at the seat of my pants to get the dust off (and to find out if I had a hole there), I mumbled, "Uh, thanks."

"Is *gurnisht*," she said, which I managed to figure out. She went on in a mixture of a little English and a lot of ... it had to be Yiddish, I realized. I understood maybe one word in five. I got that the vampire was new around here, and nobody knew where he lay during the day. If anyone found him, it would be his hard luck.

"Maybe he's gone for good now," I said hopefully.

"For bad," Rivke answered. Then she made a face. "He *nisht geendikt*." I heard the *end* in that and got it. "He too—" She tapped her forehead.

"Too smart," I said. She nodded. I feared she was right.

She said, "He have *Blitzrunen*."

And that knocked me for a loop. *Blitzrunen* was the right name for what we called Lightning Runes. They marked the fylfot boys' roughest, most fanatical fighters. I hadn't imagined there could be a Lightning Rune vampire. Only goes to show there are more things in heaven and earth, Horatio, than are dreamt of in my philosophy. "Is he that new, then? Or does he just like them?" I tried to decide which would be worse.

Rivke just shrugged. When I asked if she knew how he'd crossed the pond, she shrugged again. I realized I needed to thank her with something more than a mumble, so I did my best. She waved all that away, repeating, "Is *gurnisht*." And she went back on her Shabbas-goy beat, protecting the ordinary denizens of Vampire Village from people instead of saving a man from a not-so-ordinary vampire.

Me? I made it back to Dora's apartment. Sure enough, her coffin was closed. I lay down in bed and tried to sleep. I've got to tell you, though, I didn't have much luck.

I was not at my dynamic best by the time the sun went down and Dora came out of her coffin. That's putting it mildly. Aside from not sleeping, I'd got into the Wild Turkey. *It'll calm you down*, I told myself.

When Dora walked into the bedroom, she took one look at me and said, "What has gone wrong?" She knew right away something had. She would have smelled the bourbon on me, too, of course, but she was used to smelling bourbon on me. It's not as if I didn't put down a fair bit.

So I told her about the LR vampire, and about how Rivke'd stopped him from lowering my blood pressure in a permanent way. "One more thing to worry about," I finished, doing my best to sound as if it didn't matter all that much.

My best, I'm sure, was pretty bad. I'd learned in Italy that you don't get over almost dying right away. It stays with you. And I'd watched Dora's face get longer and longer while I talked about the new kid in town.

"You were very fortunate," she said when I finally ran down. Ran down—that's just what it felt like, as if I were a ticktock alarm clock somebody'd forgotten to wind and now I was a tick … tock alarm clock, and pretty soon I'd stop ticking at all. Dora went on, "I have not met this, ah, individual. But others have, and what they say of him frightens me. He is the kind who makes warm-blooded people, live people, want to finish us all."

"I believe that," I said. Anybody who belongs to a small group gets scared when someone else from that group goes off the rails. A Negro shoots three white guys robbing a jewelry store? The *Los Angeles Sentinel* runs a solemn editorial about wrecking the hard-won reputation of the race. A Jew's get-rich-quick scheme fleeces a bunch of gentiles out of their life savings? Jews remember the pogroms their fathers and mothers ran away from and worry that they *could* happen here. Of course it'd be the same way with vampires.

She set her hand on my arm. I noticed, as I usually don't, how cool her touch was. It reminded me of her true nature. And, when she said, "Yes, you would, of course. So many others might not," she might have been reminding herself that I also came out of one of those groups that great swarms of people love so much.

"I wonder how somebody like that managed to get away after the war ended," I said, as much to myself as to Dora. "We took special care of Lightning Rune guys we caught during the war and after the surrender. We knew how dangerous they were. A vampire who bought into what the fylfot boys were selling would be ten times worse." I didn't say *ten thousand times worse*, but it was in my mind.

"Yes. He would," Dora said soberly. "But you know you did not catch all the men who wore the *Blitzrunen*, not even all the ones who did the worst things during the war. Some of them got away by luck. Others, seeing they were likely to lose, arranged escape routes ahead of time. And some, ah, interesting personages and organizations helped them."

She waited to see if I understood what she meant. Being what she was, she had to talk about certain things because she couldn't name them straight out. Some newspaper stories talked about them, too, though the reporters who wrote those stories didn't have to do that. But I knew what she had in mind, all right. I said, "Not all priests are as holy as they make themselves out to be."

"Indeed." She seemed glad I did follow her.

"Would even one of those priests help an LR vampire, though?"

"One never knows, does one?" she said—not quite Fats Waller, but close enough. "It might not be necessary. Once some LR men get over here, they could assist without … those others. And, of course, LR men are not Reds."

"Yeah," I said, my tone sour as vinegar. Folks in Washington kept quite a few of the fylfot boys in clover for the sake of what they knew. They were the first ones who'd cooked up vepratoga, for instance. And, as Dora'd noted, the fylfot boys weren't Reds (which didn't stop Moscow from grabbing them, too).

Men who weren't Reds, people who emphatically weren't Reds, made the powers that be happy, especially in a year where the platter called *Are You Now or Have You Ever Been?* was topping the charts. A vampire who emphatically wasn't a Red might appeal to the powers that be, too. (How many vampires *were* Reds, here and in places like Moscow and Budapest, was another fascinating question.)

"Something ought to happen to that fellow," I remarked.

"If we can arrange it with enough discretion, something will," Dora answered. I followed that, too. First the vampires of VV would have to find out where the new vampire lay up by day. Then they'd have to make sure that finishing him wouldn't tick off anybody who could be dangerous to them. Only after that could he have an unfortunate accident.

"I sure hope you can," I said.

"So do we all. He is of great concern to us, for, as you discovered, he knows no restraint," Dora said. I nodded. Yes, the bastard belonged with the best of the bastards who wore the *Blitzrunen*.

Knowing no restraint was what the fylfot boys had been all about. Dora went on, "You are most fortunate your Rivke happened upon you so opportunely."

"I know," I replied, and then, when I really heard everything she'd said, "She's not *my* Rivke. I'm right here, where I want to be."

"Good." She left it there.

I started carrying a crucifix in my pocket again. I didn't like to do it, not in Vampire Village. Would you care to show off a fylfot in a Jewish part of town? This felt worse, even. A fylfot just makes a Jew want to punch you in the eye for wearing it. To a vampire, a crucifix is a dangerous weapon.

Dora knew I had it, of course. You don't keep many secrets from somebody you love, especially if her senses are vampire-keen. "Be careful with that thing," she warned me—she couldn't name it, any more than she could the sun. "If you are not, it will do you more harm than good."

"I will," I promised, and I was. I didn't want to use anything that drastic unless I needed to save myself.

Dora wasn't the only one who could tell it was there. I'd walk back from the office through VV long after sundown, of course. Every now and then, a vampire coming along the street toward me would sheer off and give me a wide berth, the way you would if you spotted a guy with the bulge of a .38 in a shoulder holster under his coat.

And I called Kirk Jenkins at Grampus Records. "I've got a question for you, if you don't mind," I said.

"Shoot," he said, which made me think of the crucifix and of a .38 in a shoulder holster.

"Who presses your records once you've recorded them?"

"There's a local company called Becker Sorcery. Well, just about local—they're over on the far side of the L.A. strip, but they've got a Gardena PO box. I really like the sound quality they have." Jenkins didn't hesitate. He just told me. A few seconds later, he asked, "Why do you need to know?"

"I just wondered whether they've got any connections like the ones I was looking for when I talked with you a little while ago," I answered, since I didn't want to tell him what I was looking into for Acolyte Adams.

"Oh, okay." He accepted that, or at least seemed to. "Not so far as I know. Anything else I can do for you?"

"Nope. Thanks." We said our goodbyes, and I hung up.

I still didn't know what all that meant, or if it meant anything. But Grampus did have a connection with Becker Sorcery. And Oscar Ricks had a connection with Grampus, and another one with Acolyte Adams and Deacon Washington.

That evening, I ran into Ricks at Allums Drugs. I was picking up some razor blades; he was buying toothpaste. The exciting life of the private eye and the jazz musician! We grinned at each other and shook hands. His fingertips were all callused—guitar player, sure enough.

"What's going on?" I said.

"Not much. Not enough, that's for sure." He looked unhappy. Scuffling for work is part of the exciting life of the jazz musician and the private eye, too. Isn't it just! He went on, "You know they'll never let the trio inside the Basket Room again."

"Sorry about that. I liked what you were doing there. A shame the goon didn't."

"Hell of a shame," Oscar agreed. "And I heard today Deacon's doesn't want us back, either. They didn't tell me why. We went over pretty well there, or I thought we did. They don't have goons who get their shorts in a twist when they hear something they haven't already heard a million times."

"You played Deacon's? I'm impressed, man!" No, I didn't let on I'd already heard that. The less you show you know, the better off you'll be.

"It's a nice gig. They treat you right, they pay good, and they *do* pay you." His face told of too many memories of places that had stiffed him. I recognized that expression; I'd worn it too often myself. He lit a Kool, blew smoke up at the ceiling, and added, "But when I talked to Adams, he just told me they weren't interested any more. I don't know why. I do know better than to argue with a guy who runs a club. This way, there's a chance he'll change his mind one day. If I piss him off, forget it."

"I hear that." We paid for our stuff, first him, then me. He headed north, back up to where he lived. I went down to VV. It was as lively as an undead section of town could be. Music came out of a few clubs. Not jazz—old-country music. Almost all the vampires came to America from somewhere else, and brought their taste with them. Strings and drums and piano, mostly. Have to be able to breathe to play horns or woodwinds. Whenever I heard a trumpet or a sax, I knew a live guy was sitting in.

I wasn't paying any real attention to the music. I was as jumpy there as if I were walking the main street of some village in Italy where the fylfot boys were still liable to have holdouts. I wondered if I had come up against that vampire with the Lightning Runes slogging my way up toward Milan. Whether I had or not, I didn't aim to let him get the drop on me now.

No sign of him, thank heaven. But here came Rudolf Sebestyen. What would the crucifix do to him if I pulled it out? Seeing for myself was tempting, but I didn't experiment. I wasn't sure it'd do anything at all. Since his stretch as a zombie, the usual rules didn't seem to apply to him.

He was as glad to see me as I was to see him. "What do you want, you son of a bitch?" he growled. Dora's accent turned English to music. Rudolf sounded more like rocks rolling downhill. Or I thought so, anyhow. I admit, I might have been prejudiced.

But that was the least of my worries then. "Call me an SOB all you want, but I ran into a real one." I told him about the vampire who'd worn the *Blitzrunen*, knowing as I did that there was a chance he'd like that bastard better than he liked me.

All he said when I got done, though, was, "Oh. Him."

"Yeah, him," I agreed. "He keeps running around like that, you'll have live people marching into Vampire Village with torches and stakes and priests and holy water. Isn't that what you came here to get away from?"

"Torches. Fire." Rudolf shuddered. He'd eagerly faced the sun after Rob Grau and Dora and I brought him back from being a zombie. That would have finished him all at once, though—it would have if it finished him at all, I mean, which it didn't. Ordinary fire took a while, and was sure to hurt every second.

"What do you know about him?" I asked.

"I have talked with him. I speak German, so he did not have to dirty himself with English," he said. I nodded; from what Dora'd told me, any educated Hungarian learned *Deutsch* as a window on the wider world. Rudolf went on, "He thought I might be useful to him, since I do not fear the White Fire. All he cared about was what I could do for him. He did not bother to hide it, since I was only *egy hülye magyar*."

"Only what?"

He realized he'd fallen back into Magyar. "A stupid Hungarian," he explained.

All vampires mostly care about what you can do for them. That's a big part of what being a vampire is about. They don't always show it so openly. Of course, if you were the kind of vampire who'd been part of the Lightning Runes gang, you weren't going to be the kind who pretended.

Something else crossed my mind. "You and Dora had a business for a while, bringing in coffins and graveyard earth."

"We did until the government made us stop, yes." Sebestyen bared his fangs in disgust. *Are you now or have you ever been?* again. The Feds wondered about connections with Red Hungary. They might have had good reason to wonder, too.

I was driving at something else, though. "Any chance this item could've crossed the ocean in one of those coffins?"

He started to tell me it was a ridiculous idea. I could see that. I could also see him change his mind. "There may be," he said slowly. "Those who followed the fylfot set up their own secret roads for escaping enemies who wanted vengeance. Surely they would have done the same for their undead. But if it is so, I knew nothing of it, nor did my half-sister."

"Okay." I hoped he was telling the truth.

He sneered at me. He must've heard I wasn't sure I believed him. "Do you want me to swear an oath by the One Who set the White Fire in the sky?" He couldn't name God, but he made me understand him anyhow.

"No, you don't need to," I said. "If you happen to find out where the *Blitzrunen* vampire lies up by day, though, you could do everyone a favor if you helped the White Fire take care of him."

"What would I get if I did?" Rudolf cared only about his own advantage, too.

"Enough blood to drown yourself, probably."

He thought about that. He might not have believed I could come up with anything he'd like, but I did. He ran his tongue over his lips. It was long and thin and pointed, the better to slip between his fangs. "Well," he said, and, a moment later, "Well, well." Then he walked past me as if I didn't exist. I'd given him something new to think about.

I asked Dora if she thought the LR vampire might have got out of Europe in one of the coffins she'd imported, too. "I hope not! That would be dreadful," she said. She didn't say it was impossible, any more than Rudolf had. Like him, she went on, "If it happened, it would have happened without my knowledge."

"Uh-huh." I nodded.

She also caught my doubt. "Do you imagine the Jews who ward Vampire Village while we lie quiet would not have finished Rudolf and me if they thought we had aided in such a vicious brute's escape?"

There she had me, because I didn't imagine any such thing. Of all the people the fylfot boys ground down, what they did to Jews stands out. If ever any group was entitled to revenge, they were. And the Shabbas-goy Jews in VV could have arranged it, simple as you please.

"A point," I admitted.

She inclined her head, as sardonic a thank-you as I'd ever seen. Yes, she'd been a noblewoman once upon a time. "Ask your Rivke what her view of this is if you have trouble believing me."

I hadn't cared to hear that once from Dora. I disliked hearing it a second time much more than twice as much. "She isn't my Rivke."

"Maybe she should be. Like you, she is alive."

I breathed hard through my nose, something I only do when I'm really ticked off. "Look, if you want me to leave, all you've got to do is say the word and I'm gone like Lutch Crawford and his Gone Geese. If I can't find anywhere else to stay, I'll sleep in the office."

"Myself, I prefer you to stay. But it will not end well for you if you do. You must know that as well as I do."

We'd already been round this particular barn too goddamn often. She was convinced I was wasting my time with her, and just as convinced mortals had no time to waste. "You didn't make me fall in love with you, babe. It just happened. And you know what else? I'm damn glad it did."

"But this is insanity. I cannot return what you feel. I can give you nothing."

Everything is a bargain with a vampire. Love doesn't work by those rules, or it'd better not—that's how things look to me anyway. "I'm happy now. Later on, I'll worry about later on if I've got to."

"You will never have children by me. Those days are gone forever. They were over a long time ago."

She kept going on about that. Children were the last thing on my mind, or else a few steps down from there. "When it bothers me, I'll let you know. Promise." I didn't say, *Cross my heart and hope to die*, not to her I didn't. I sure heard it inside my own head, though.

"Do you not understand you are mad?"

My Number One, Grade A crooked grin. "You bet I do, sweetheart, but I have fun." My best gravelly baritone, too. I went over and kissed her. I was taking a certain chance, you understand. If she was really and truly irked with me, she'd knock me across the room, and my Mr. Tough Guy act would fly out the window. She could do that if she chose to. I knew she could. Fall for a vampire and you learn such things.

For whatever reason, she chose not to. She kissed me back instead, laughing while she did it. She could be amused, even if most of the time her sense of humor was as dry as a martini wished it were. One thing led to another, and we wound up in bed. Dora might not have been able to love, but she could take pleasure as well as give it.

Afterwards, I touched my neck with my index finger. Yes, it was bloody. Of course it was. She always nipped me when we made love. The little wounds didn't hurt at all; her bite had something like novocaine in it. That was bound to be handy when she needed to sneak in somewhere and feed off somebody who had no idea when she was around. The bleeding had already almost stopped. I knew from experience the bites would heal fast and clean. They always did.

"There," I said. "Are you happier now?"

I made her laugh again. Twice in half an hour—a pretty fair night's work. She'd say things like that to me way more often than I aimed them at her. She was long past childbearing age, but I swear I brought out the maternal in her. And she poked me in the ribs, just hard enough to remind me of her undead strength.

"You win this round. There will be others," she said.

I kissed the end of her nose. "I thought we both won," I said. "That's how it's supposed to work, right?"

"How many things work as they are supposed to?"

"You got me there, toots." I yawned. "Now I'm gonna roll over and go to sleep, and you can laugh at me on account of it. I've got to get on down to Gardena again, and I'll do it pretty early."

"Not before the White Fire fills the sky with glare. That one who wore the *Blitzrunen*, you do not wish to meet him again."

"No, not before sunup. When you're right, you're right."

I must've been on edge, because the next morning the noise of Dora's coffin lid closing woke me. I don't usually hear it at all. Up earlier than I wanted to be, I took a shower, got dressed, and headed to the live part of town for a breakfast better than I could fix on my hot plate. Eggs over medium, crispy bacon, pancakes with maple syrup, and plenty of coffee resigned me to consciousness. The Waffle Shop's a good place, even if I go more for flapjacks.

Then I grabbed the Red Line trolley and headed south. I changed cars at the Slauson Tower. As I slid southwest toward Vermont, I saw they were starting to take out another fig orchard. A big sign that hadn't been there a couple of days before said, MORE HOMES

SOON! VETERANS WELCOME—VA FINANCING AVAILABLE! Fifty yards farther on, another sign said, THIS TRACT IS EXCLUSIVE AND RESTRICTED.

You go past Slauson, you see a lot of signs like that. They're illegal. *Restricted* means *segregated*, and the High Court's said you can't get away with that. But so far, nobody in California has paid any attention to what the High Court says. If you're a Negro and you want to buy a house south of Slauson, you can forget about it. Nobody will sell you one. Yes, that's filthy. Well, I'm here to tell you a lot of things have lain stinking under the warm, bright California sun for a long time.

One of these days, lawyers will put enough heat on the builders and the real-estate agents to change all that. One of these days, *all men are created equal* will mean more than *all men are created equal, except Negroes and Japanese and—what the hell?—Jews, too*. One of these days, court-mandated wizards will lay down a geas to make sure the country really tries to be what it claims it is. One of these days, *The land of the free, except ...* won't fly any more.

One of these days. But I'm not holding my breath.

I was still in a kick-the-dog mood when I got off the trolley at Vermont and Gardena Boulevard. Good thing I didn't see any dogs when I crossed the street. No dogs at the bus stop, either. For quite a while, no bus, either. I must have just missed the last one. Add the small annoyance to the big anger that damn RESTRICTED sign touched off in me and I felt ready to bite nails in half. Good thing nobody offered me any.

At much too long last, the bus did pull up, trailing a plume of fragrant diesel fumes. I got on, tossed my dime in the fare box, and rode east to Main. Then I waited for a different bus to take me north to 154th. It was about three quarters of a mile. I could have walked. I was too lazy.

I did walk down to Becker Sorcery. The Quonset huts made me think I was back in the Army again—not the kind of thought I wanted. Which one would Becker be in? The door at the end of the one to the left answered that for me. *Business Office*, it said. I went in.

Rat-a-tat-tat! Rat-a-tat-tat! That machine-gun noise reminded me of my Army days, too. It sounded like one of ours. The model the fylfot boys used fired so fast, it put you in mind of a buzz saw, not a typewriter. The noise in the Quonset hut, thank God, *was* a typewriter. The light brown secretary banging away at it stopped and gave me a professional smile. "Yes?"

"Is Mister Becker in?"

"What's this about?" she asked, in tones that suggested whether he was in or not depended on who I turned out to be.

"I'm a private investigator." I gave her one of my cards.

She looked at it, looked at me, looked at it again. This time, she asked, "What's this about?" in a different tone of voice.

"I'll be happy to tell Mister Becker," I answered.

She gave me a dirty look. She didn't tell me to get lost, though. They hardly ever do. Nobody has to talk with me, but people rarely realize that. "Hold on," she said, and got up from her desk. Carrying the card like a grenade with a loose pin, she went into the sanctum at the far end of the hut. When she came out again, she didn't close the door behind her. "He can give you a few minutes."

"Thanks." I went into the inner office and closed the door behind *me*. If I didn't offend her, it wasn't from lack of effort.

Danny Becker stood up behind his desk. He was younger than I'd expected—about my age. He was also darker than I expected—quite a bit darker than I am, as a matter of fact. He wore his hair very short, as if he'd got used to keeping it that way while he was in the service, and had a thin, neat mustache. He was a sharp dresser—not Central Avenue sharp, but business sharp.

After we shook hands, he waved me to the other chair in that cramped little space. "What's this all about, Mister Mitchell?" he asked.

The ashtray on his desk had several butts in it, so I fired up a cigarette. He did, too. I took a drag, blew smoke up at the corrugated iron above my head, and took another one before I said, "You press records for Grampus, don't you?"

"That's right." He was casing me the same way I'd cased him. After a couple of seconds, his left eyebrow twitched—not much, but it did. He'd worked out what I was. "What about it?"

"Every have any trouble with the guy who runs it?" I brushed the first two fingers of my right hand against the back of my left wrist to show what kind of trouble I meant. I wasn't going to show him my cards right off the bat.

"With Jenkins? Nah. If all the ofays were like him, everybody'd be better off. I mean, he'll try and beat my price down and he wants everything by day before yesterday, but he'd be like that even if I was green, or if he was. I'm like that myself a lot of the time. Little green man, that's me." His grin showed very white teeth except for one of the front ones, which was gold.

"Little green man, yeah." I grinned, too. Everybody was talking about little green men or Martians that summer. Astrologers and astronomers don't even know whether there's life on Mars, let alone whether Martian life is advanced enough to have night life.

"So, no, Jenkins is a pretty cool cat, like I said. Some of the other white folks I deal with …" Danny Becker used the same fingers-to-wrist gesture I had.

"Any mob connections you know of?"

He looked at me. "You've got a card. You've got a line. I don't know any more than that, who you are, who you really work for. If I lay a truth geas on you, maybe we can go on from there. Or maybe not, depending."

"I expect you wouldn't let a wizard I know lay one on you," I said.

"You expect right, my friend."

"Okay. Here's a different question for you. You ever get up to Central yourself, listen to some of the bands you make records for? If you do, we might have a drink or two together, talk about stuff that doesn't matter."

"I'm up there now and then. I live up there, after all." Becker looked at me again. "Where else am I gonna live?"

"There is that. I saw the new Restricted tract on my way down here. Happy days."

"Some stuff doesn't change quick. Some doesn't change at all." The wizard shook his head. "So yeah, I make that scene. The Dunbar, Club Alabam next door, Ivie's Chicken Shack, the Elks hall, the Downbeat, all those joints."

Every now and then, you've got to show a card. "Ever get over to Deacon's?"

He lit another cigarette. "I've heard of it. I don't go there. You must be richer than I figured you for. Richer'n I am, for sure."

"You've got a choice what you spend your money on, that's all. I heard Dexter and Wardell squaring off a few nights ago, hunting each other till the sun came up. If I eat pork and beans out of a can for a while after that, okay, I do. I just pretend I'm back in the Army, is all."

"That was one of the *good* cans, too," he said. "I was in the Blue Square Express myself." He mimed driving a truck. I nodded. Most of the drivers in the Blue Square Express were Negroes. Till just before the end of the war, the powers that be didn't want to trust us in combat, so a lot of us hauled supplies across Gaul.

"They didn't put you in the Thaumaturgy Corps?"

"I was the wrong color for that."

"Even with wizards, they were that way?" I thumped my forehead with the heel of my hand. We always needed wizards; we never had enough. But I guess we didn't need 'em bad enough to put Negroes in those slots.

"Especially with wizards. Wizards were officers, like doctors. They didn't want to find out what would happen if a corporal from Arkansas had to salute a black man." Danny Becker eyed me. "What did they do to you?"

"Dogface in Italy," I answered. He lifted that eyebrow again. I laughed, not that it was funny. "On my papers, it says I'm white. White folks can't always tell. So they gave me a rifle and stuck me in the line. Lucky me! I didn't lose the war all by myself, and the fylfot boys didn't quite kill me."

"Why didn't you tell 'em they screwed up? You would've been safer, man."

"It tickled me then. And I was patriotic, know what I mean?" I laughed again, on the same note. "First bullet that cracked past my ear taught me patriots are people who haven't got shot at yet."

"There you go," he said.

"Here I go, yeah. Thanks for talking to me." I got up. We shook hands again. I walked out. I didn't have anything I could take back to Acolyte Adams. Becker could have been the guy who was squeezing him, but I needed more than *could have*. I wondered whether Adams did.

When I got back to the office, Old Man Mose wasn't sleeping on the sofa. He might have been out hunting, hoping—like me in Italy—for food that didn't come out of a can. He might have been, but he wasn't. A few minutes after I sat down behind my desk, he came out from under the couch and jumped back up onto it.

"Why did you hide?" I asked him. "You knew it was me. Who else turns the key in the lock?"

"I don't take chances." Old Man Mose hoisted one leg in the air and started polishing his nuts with his tongue.

The pose didn't encourage conversation. Neither did the wet, squelchy noises he made.

I looked at the mail that had come through the slot. A light bill. A phone bill. A money order from Edna Terwilliger, whose cheating husband I'd trailed in one of my very first jobs after I got out of the service. She'd owed me a couple of hundred bucks then. I hadn't expected I'd ever see a dime of it, but I was wrong. Whenever she could scrape a little money together, she sent it to me. This time, I got the grand sum of $11.14. She was within forty dollars or so of paying me off by now. She was as honest as she was broke.

Having finished his personal grooming, Mose said, "I killed a rat while you were out in funny-smelling places."

"Good for you!" I said. But, on second thought, it might not've been so good. "In here or somewhere else?"

"Out in the alley. I wouldn't even say anything about it, only it smelled funny, too, kind of like that thing you keep hanging around with." Mose twisted his face into a fine kitty sneer. Cats don't like vampires. It's mutual.

Vampires and rats do hang around together, though. Everybody's known that at least since Bram Stoker's day. "Did this one say anything before you killed it?" I asked. Rats don't talk so people can follow them, but cats mostly understand what comes out of their nasty little mouths.

"Just rat noises." My red, fuzzy friend and accomplice—when he felt like it—sneered some more. "I mean, what's an Oberf, anyway?"

"Oberf? You're right. A rat noise—a funny one," I said, but it bothered me. I'd heard that funny noise somewhere before, only not from a rat. Where? When? I worried at it the way you worry at a piece of gristle stuck between two back teeth. And, like a stubborn piece of gristle, it didn't want to come loose.

I was walking to the place Dora let me share with her when I suddenly stopped short—so short, the woman behind me almost walked up my back. When I just stood there as if I were a new tree planted in the middle of the sidewalk, she made her way around me, giving me one hell of a mean look while she did.

"Sorry," I mumbled, half meaning it at most. I'd finally pushed the miserable bit of gristle out. *Oberf* was short for *Oberführer*, a rank the Lightning Rune soldiers had that didn't exactly match any pay grade in the fylfot boys' regular army—or in ours. Trust the LR to go and do something like that. An *Oberführer* wasn't a colonel, and he wasn't a one-star general (our system), either. Somewhere in between there. A high rank, however you looked at it.

Next interesting question was why a rat in the alley back of my office knew what an Oberf was. I started walking again while I chewed on that. I didn't need more than three or four steps before it crunched. Not so long before, I'd met a vampire who'd worn the *Blitzrunen* during the war. Somebody like that would have had a high rank, wouldn't he? Would he have been an *Oberführer*?

I heard Bugs Bunny in my head. *Nyehhh—could be!*

By the time I got back to the apartment, I was tired—I'd been up quite a while. I was also thoughtful: so full of thought, I hardly talked to Dora at all while I fixed myself a can of Dinty Moore beef stew. "What's wrong?" she asked as I spooned it up.

"Not wrong, exactly, but ..." In between bites, I told her about the rat.

"You think it was spying for the vampire?"

"I don't know what else it would have been doing. Can you think of anything?"

"Nothing that seems likely." Dora frowned. "Not good that the rat came so close to finding you out. Also not good that the *Blitzrunen* vampire cared enough about you to try to look for you."

"Yeah, I had the same thought. If it occurred to you, too, chances are there's something to it. Happy day. Happy—" I broke off. She wouldn't have appreciated *happy goddamn day*.

"I wonder where he is lying up during the day. Finishing him seems more urgent than ever now," she said.

I nodded, rinsed out my can, and threw it in the wastebasket. I made much more garbage than Dora did. Fixing food will do that. "I wish your half-brother liked us better," I said. "I told him about it, but I don't think he cared much."

"I wish he liked us better, too. I made a mistake when I had him brought back from zombiehood. I know that now, but how could I have known it then? I thought I was doing what he would have wanted."

"You weren't the only one, babe. Who would've figured anybody'd *want* to be a zombie?" I went to the window and looked out, wary about Rudolf Sebestyen and about the LR vampire. I didn't see anything at all for the first minute or so. As my eyes got used to the darkness, I saw the shadows the building and its neighbors cast on the street; the moon was a few days before full. Its light didn't show me any vampires in bat form. I hadn't expected it would, but I wanted to do *something*, no matter how futile.

That's the story of mankind, huh?

"It is not just that Rudolf himself is sly and can face the White Fire. He also has connections, undead and living, who could help deal with … the other one."

Rudolf was thoroughly unsavory, no matter whether Dora wanted to call him that. Even if he'd been on good terms with her and me, I'd've kept an eye on him. But I'd also seen he was liable to be useful against the vampire who'd worn the *Blitzrunen* if he wanted to be. If.

"Hell with it," I said. "We'll muddle along somehow or other."

We muddled along by going up to Central Avenue Saturday night. The moon had got full by then, and glowed in the southeast. Musingly, Dora said, "I know the White Fire also burns the moon, and yet I can bear the reflected blaze. What could the moon be made of to let this be so?"

"Gotta be green cheese," I answered, which started us down a new rabbit hole. For all the time Dora'd spent in the States speaking mostly English, she'd never heard that one before. She wanted to know why I said it and why people ever thought it was true. Since I said it because it's an old silly saying and had no idea how it got started, I wasn't much help.

We drifted from club to club. It was disappointing. No sign of Danny Becker. Nobody big was in town that weekend, either. The house combos were nothing to write home about. I looked at my watch after we walked out of another dive. "Deacon's will open up pretty soon," I said. "It's fun no matter who's playing."

"We can do that." Dora sounded less enthusiastic than usual. Most of the time, she enjoys herself at Deacon's, as much as an undead person can enjoy herself. I wondered how much of her sour mood was on account of dear Rudolf and how much because of the vampire who'd worn the *Blitzrunen*.

Before I could say anything, we both heard a howl that made the hair on the back of my neck stand up. Dogs will howl at the full moon, of course. So will coyotes, and every now and then you'll see one, usually skinny as a rail, trotting down a city street looking for cats or possums or garbage. But this didn't sound like a dog or a coyote to me.

It didn't to Dora, either. She stood statue still for a moment—all but her lips, which skinned back from her teeth so she showed off those fangs. I don't think she knew what she was doing. In a low, throaty voice, she said, "*Vérfarkas.*" That last letter's an *s* in print, but sounds like *sh* when you say it.

"English, please, dear," I told her.

"Oh." She hadn't realized she'd fallen back into Magyar, either. "It means *werewolf.*"

My turn to say, "Oh." As soon as she told me, I knew she was right. I'd heard them before, though not that often. Every day but once a lunar cycle, a werewolf's as human as anybody else. When the full moon comes up ... well, you know about that. Werewolves can't help themselves, not on that one day. Blood banks help ordinary humans.

They also help vampires get along with the majority. Nobody's found anything that eases werewolves into café society, not yet.

"It is not good," Dora said. "A pogrom against werewolves can easily turn into one against vampires, too."

I squeezed her hand. One more time, I knew she was right. People who hate Negroes hate Jews, too. They do most of the time, anyhow. They're also the kind of people who screeched loudest for all the Japanese to get locked into camps after the Knights of Bushido jumped on the Sandwich Islands with both feet. Pure American patriots, they'll tell you they are. And if you believe that, my friend, I've got a bridge to sell you. Cheap.

The werewolf howled again. That's a scary sound, all right. I've heard from people who were there that the fylfot boys tried to use werewolves against us even after they said they'd given up. Didn't work—a Tommy gun with silver slugs'll make any werewolf say uncle. But the bastards tried.

I didn't want to think about that. "Deacon's?" I said again.

Dora didn't tell me no, so we drifted over there. When Deacon Washington waved us in, he asked, "Did you hear it?"

"We heard it. Twice." I didn't need to ask what he meant. Dora nodded somberly.

Free cover. Free drinks—that still held, too. Helped my wallet, even if I still tipped as if I were buying. Wasn't really good for what ailed me, though, even if I drank a fair bit. When we finally did head back to Vampire Village, Dora had to keep me steady. She'd matched me, but booze didn't hit her the same way.

Morning twilight was just coming on. The moon still gave more light. Tomorrow, the werewolf would be a solid citizen again. What he'd done tonight … was liable to make the *Times'* front page.

We turned down our street. I stopped short. Somebody'd painted a white fylfot on the asphalt, one that stretched almost from curb to curb. Underneath, upside down but big enough so I had no trouble reading it anyway, was one word—WERWOLFE! I don't *sprechen* much *Deutsch*, but I didn't need much to work out what it meant.

"I wonder who did that." Dora didn't sound as if she wondered at all.

I thought of the LR vampire. I also thought of Rudolf Sebestyen. Thinking of Dora's half-brother made me ask, "Can you be a vampire and a werewolf at the same time?"

"I have never heard of such a thing," Dora said. After a moment, she added, "Who knows what may have happened that I never heard of, though? The world moves faster than I do. Soon the White Fire comes, and I shall not move at all until it leaves the sky again."

When I went out to head for my office the next day, that big old fylfot and the *Werwölfe!* under it were still there. I'd hoped they were just a bad dream, something spawned by all the Wild Turkey I'd put down at Deacon's. I wasn't nearly hung over enough to believe that, you understand, but I'd hoped. You can hope without believing. It's easy. People do it all the goddamn time.

Vampire Village is pretty empty in the daytime, but a woman stood across the street from me, staring at that stinking fylfot with her hands pressed against her cheeks, the way you're more likely to see in a horror movie than in real life. This was much too real, though. She raised her hands a little higher, to her eyes, then bent and started crying as if her heart was breaking.

A woman .... Maybe I ought to get my eyes checked, 'cause it wasn't till she started bawling that I realized it was Rivke. Well, whose heart was more likely to break than somebody who'd found out exactly what the fylfot boys could do?

You see somebody hurting like that, you want to help whoever it is. I hurried across the street without even thinking about it. Then I stopped, because I had no idea what to do next. "Hey," I said, and "Hey" again, letting her know I was there.

She flung herself into my arms. I was a floating chunk of wood, that's all, a tree trunk or something, and if she hung on to me as hard as she could, maybe she wouldn't drown. She cried herself out against my chest.

When she finally pulled away, I had a big wet spot on my left lapel. Rivke stared at me as if she had trouble remembering who I was—or much of anything else, come to that. She looked like hell, if you want to get right down to it. Her cheeks were all red and blotchy, still with tear streaks running down them. Whatever makeup she'd put on had given up the fight. Her eyes were red, too, but that was the least of it. The look in them was a million miles and a million years away. I'd seen and done some horrible things in Italy, but the number and the fylfot branded on her arm told me what a piker I was.

She gave a herky-jerky nod toward the big fylfot, the one in the street. "All this, all this I think *kaputt*," she said. "You know *kaputt*? You understand?"

"I know *kaputt*," I answered solemnly. And I did. It was one of the words dogfaces like me picked up from the fylfot boys. It sounded much more final than something like *done*.

I'm not sure Rivke even heard me. She went on, "I cross *yam*—ocean. I cross America. I go far far far from—" She touched her brand with two fingers from her other hand. "Far as I can. And here—" She started crying again, not so hard as she had before.

"It'll be okay," I said. "The bastard who did this can't do anything to you. Not here, he can't. If he's the one I think he is, you scared him away from me with your Star of David."

"That one? The *vampir*?" It wasn't quite English, but close enough. They say the same thing about grenades.

"Yeah. Him."

"Gevalt!" Rivke said, which wasn't English at all. I followed it anyway, thanks to that fat, sweaty Jewish guy I know who runs a dirty-book shop downtown. Rivke pointed at the fylfot on the street again. "What to do about that?"

"I'll call Street Maintenance when I get to the office. I bet they don't like fylfots any better'n we do."

"Hope not." She sniffled. "Thank you." Then she seemed to notice the blot on my lapel. She turned red, not the way she had before but from embarrassment. "Thank you," she repeated, on a different note this time. "I sorry."

"It's nothing. What are friends for?"

"Friends." By the way Rivke said it, it came from a language far more foreign to her than English. But, after she thought it over, she nodded. "Friends." This time, she might have halfway meant it.

I didn't call Street Maintenance as soon as I walked into the little place I don't call home, even if I do stash bourbon there. *Care and Maintenance, Feline, for the Benefit of* came first. Catbox. Water bowl. Food. All the important stuff.

Once Old Man Mose was stuffing his furry face with mackerel in gravy, I dug out the White Pages and flipped to *City of Los Angeles*. I ran my finger down the phone numbers till I found the one I wanted. When I called, I wondered if they'd stick me on hold. But they didn't. I told a nice man named Ralph Evans what my trouble was.

"Oh, for crying out loud!" he said when I got done. I had the feeling he might've used bluer language if he weren't a civil servant. "That's the third different place we've got reports of those today. Somebody needs to … have something happen to him." Yes, he was holding back.

"No kidding!" I said. "I didn't go through the mill to have something like this show up over here." I held back, too. What a good boy I was!

"Me, neither," Evans said. "We'll get on it as fast as we can. I don't know about today, but tomorrow looks good."

"Thanks. I've got a Jewish friend who was even more upset about it than I was. Jewish from over there, I mean. She knows what the fylfot was all about—from the inside out."

"Yeah, I bet she would. I saw some things myself, but if she lived through that …. Thanks for calling, Mister Mitchell. We're on it now."

And maybe they'd take care of it as fast as Ralph Evans said, and maybe they wouldn't. In Los Angeles, you never know for sure. But they would take care of it sooner or later. That was as much as I could reasonably expect.

"What's a fylfot?" Mose asked. "You keep talking about it. Can I eat one?"

"No. It's a human symbol, a nasty one." I drew a fylfot on a sheet of scratch paper and showed it to him. Cats don't read or write. A good thing, too, or they'd sit behind desks and we'd be their pets. If we're not already, that is. They don't make much sense of pictures, either.

"What's it a symbol of?" Mose asked, and licked his nose.

"Bad things. Bad men marched behind it and killed a lot of people because they followed it. It made them hate the people who wouldn't follow it."

"Humans are crazy." The red tabby spoke with great conviction.

"We think the same thing about cats."

"That's just stupid. Cats are fine. We're normal. Well, except for Siamese. I've got to admit, they're pretty stinking peculiar."

"See? You do it, too. If all the regular cats set out to kill all the Siamese because they act funny and have blue eyes, that'd be like what the people who followed the fylfot did."

"Cats wouldn't listen to anybody who tried to get them to do anything like that. Or they'd start out and then forget what they were doing and curl up somewhere and go to sleep."

I sighed. "You don't know how lucky cats are."

"Of course I do. I could have been born a human." Old Man Mose had had enough of talk. He curled up somewhere—on the sofa, where else?—and went to sleep. Even though I sometimes put my feet up on the desk and dozed in the office, I was jealous.

I should have done that then. Nothing was going on. After night came down, I headed back to VV. The moon was just rising. It was still plenty bright, but it wasn't full. *Good*, I thought.

Rivke wasn't around when I turned on to my street. Well, of course she wasn't. After sundown, vampires could take care of themselves. I walked past the house at the end of the block before I even noticed the sawhorses in the roadway blocking it off to traffic. May I be cut in thin strips and popped into hot oil for French fries if Street Maintenance hadn't painted over the fylfot that very afternoon.

I didn't jump in the air and click my heels together like an Irishman dancing a jig, but that was how I felt. Something had worked! Something in the City of Angels, in the government of the City of Angels, had actually worked! That doesn't happen every day, and you'd better believe it.

So I was all smiles when I let myself into the apartment. Dora sent me a suspicious stare. Okay, I sure hadn't been smiling the last time she saw me. "What is this good news?" she asked, as if she didn't believe there could be any such thing.

I pointed to the window. "You must not've looked out, babe. They've already got rid of the stinking, rotten fylfot. If that's not good news, what is?" I threw my arms wide. "C'mere and kiss me!" I wasn't drunk, but I felt as if I were.

Dora went to the window instead. She was always the kind to make sure for herself. When she turned back to me, she was smiling. "It is as you say. How remarkable!" Did she mean it was remarkable the city had moved so fast or remarkable I'd told her the truth? Sometimes you'd rather not know such things.

Luckily, I didn't have long to dwell on it, because she did kiss me then. She's always careful doing that. She'll bite my neck when we make love. I've already talked about it, yeah. It seems to be something she needs to do, for whatever vampire reasons she has. But she never uses her fangs by accident.

I wanted to go on from there. We had something to celebrate, after all: if not a victory, a counterattack, anyway. But the kiss didn't last as long as I hoped it would. Dora dropped her head to my chest. I needed a moment to realize what she was doing. She was sniffing my lapel.

Then she wasn't in my arms any more. "That one. Again," she said. Her voice didn't sound undead, just dead. Vampires are creatures without hopes, without expectations. She kicked me in the teeth with that.

"Oh, for—" I stopped short. *For God's sake* was right out. *For Christ's sake* likewise. Even *For heaven's sake* was pretty iffy. "She was out there crying on account of the fylfot this morning. She cried on me some. What was I supposed to do? Kick her to the curb? I wouldn't do that to a puppy, let alone a person."

"We both knew this would happen sooner or later," Dora said.

"Nothing happened. Nothing is happening. That's what you're getting upset about—nothing." I meant it. She had ways, ones that likely had to do with her sense of smell, to be sure I did.

She looked at me. "So you say now."

"I say it because it's true. You've got to know it is."

She didn't call me a liar, which went a long way toward proving my point. Of course, when you're having a fight with somebody you love, proving your point may do you more harm than good. Dora asked a different kind of question: "Does the poor little dear one have any idea what you are?"

"I don't know. It's never come up. I do know she can tell me more about the shitty end of the stick than I can tell her, and that's really saying something." I knew something else, too: I'd have to tell Rivke about myself first chance I got. If all of a sudden she didn't think I was a friend after that, well, I'd learn something. Sometimes you've got to find out.

Dora understood which way my thoughts were going. "It may not even mean anything to her. Chances are she has never imagined there are people who could be more despised than *zsidók*."

I knew what the last word meant; she'd used it before. I said, "The fylfot boys went after queers and gypsies hard, too, but.... Yeah, she'd have a hard time believing that."

"If what you are does not trouble her, you might do better to—" Dora stopped short, something she hardly ever did. She knew her mind and spoke it.

I set both hands on her shoulders and pulled her close to me. She let me do it, though we both understood she could throw me across the room if she felt like it.

"Listen up, babe," I said roughly. "I love you. For better and for worse, I love you. For better and for worse is what love's all about, right?"

"What do I know of this? I have memories from the days when my blood ran warm, but that was in another country; and besides, the wench is undead," she said. I wanted to give her a hand. The way she talked said she'd learned English after she got here, but she was still able to do that to Christopher Marlowe. Yeah, she deserved applause.

"If you don't know, how's about you listen to me?" Had I watched Humphrey Bogart a time or three—dozen—too often? Oh, I might have. But half the guys in the country've done that.

Dora knew who Bogie was, but he cut no ice with her. "Love invites marriage. Marriage invites children. Children I can never give you. I know we have spoken of this before, but tonight you seem to need reminding."

"If I worried about it, honey, why would I be here now?"

"Because men are very stupid, very simple creatures." This time, Dora pulled me to her. Yeah, she's a lot stronger than I am. She's a lot softer than I am, too, and as she pressed me close her body molded itself to mine in that miraculous way women's bodies have. Very stupid? Very simple? I'll cop to those. But I have fun.

I had fun, and did my best to give Dora some, on the floor, not six feet from her coffin. Not counting the casket, I hadn't done anything like that since the night after we chased the fylfot boys out of a small town most of the way up the Italian boot. Nice when they show you they're glad to see you.

Afterwards, I pushed back and up on to my knees. I do try to be a gentleman with my weight. "Happier now?" I said, and winked at Dora. Yes, I was throwing her own line back at her.

She could have given Queen Victoria not-amused lessons. "Pleasure and happiness are not the same. Pleasure is a thing of the flesh, happiness one of the spirit. Being what I am, I find the flesh is willing but the spirit weak."

Willing flesh. Willing beautiful flesh. If that's not a young man's dream come true .... I was still pretty goddamn young, pretty stupid, pretty simple. I reached out and set one hand on the soft inside of her thigh. "I'm one lucky fella, let me tell you."

She didn't let me tell her. She didn't let me leave my hand there, either, dammit. She twisted away, got lithely to her feet, and went into the bathroom to clean up. When she came out, I went in there myself. Want to know how young and stupid and simple I was? I thought making love solved things instead of just papering them over. How simple is that?

I didn't run into Rivke for a few days. Like a cop but more honest, she had a Vampire Village beat she patrolled, and didn't happen to be on the part near my building when I came out. All things considered, that might have been just as well. It gave Dora and me the chance to get easy with each other again after the spat.

Then I headed up toward my office when she was on my block. We waved to each other from opposite sides of the street. Where I'd trotted across to her the last time, she trotted across to me now. She was smiling, not bawling. She pointed to the paint that blotted out the fylfot. "Gone!" she said.

"Yeah." I nodded. "The guy I talked to in Street Maintenance said there were three of them, not just this one."

"*Blitzrunen vampir mamzer*," she said, which wasn't English or hard to decipher. Then she looked down at her shoes. "Thank you."

"Believe me, I was glad to do it. I fought the fylfot boys in Italy. I don't want to have to do it again." I did pantomime and played charades to make sure she understood what I was saying.

Her smile told me she did. Then that smile turned embarrassed. "Thank you also for—" Instead of finishing, she studied her shoe-tops some more.

"It's okay. That was nothing. I knew you were upset. I knew why, too. Like I said, what are friends for?" Now it was my turn to hem and haw. "I don't want to bother you or anything, but, um, you ought to know …" I ran dry.

"Vus?" Rivke sounded as confused as she looked, and who could blame her? I was botching it.

I tried to finish what I'd started so badly: "I don't know whether you know or not, I don't know whether you care or not, but I think I ought to tell you I'm a *shvartzer*." One more word I could thank—well, sort of thank—Al Harris for.

She gave me a head toe-to-toe once-over. I think part of her surprise was that I'd come out with a Yiddish word. "*Nu?*" she said. "So what? You, me, we both peoples. What else matter?"

If I'd sagged any harder, I would've turned into Jell-O on the spot. I'd never felt so relieved at passing a drill sergeant's inspection in basic. Those bastards could've given me a week of KP or sent me on a four-mile run for screwing up. Rivke, though, could have decided I wasn't a people, or not one she wanted anything to do with. She could have, but she didn't. Unless you've been in a spot where somebody could easily decide you aren't a people, you haven't felt that kind of relief yourself.

Lucky you, in that case.

"Thank *you*," I said. I *am* husky, but I don't usually sound husky. Right then, I did.

And I confused her again. *"Fur vus?"* she asked. But then she got it. "Fylfot *mamzrim* do. I not one of they. You neither."

That's how it's supposed to work. If it did work that way more often, America'd be the country it says it is, not the country it really is. People just a little darker than I am wouldn't need a guidebook telling 'em where it's safe for them to buy gas or get dinner or have a drink when they're on the road. New tracts of houses wouldn't be restricted, either. And don't even get me started about *some* places.

But never mind that. Rivke hadn't flunked the test. She'd passed it as well as anybody was ever likely to. I swept off my fedora and bowed to her. Not Bogart this time—more like Tyrone Power buckling a swash. Hollywood has a lot to answer for.

She giggled, so I produced the desired effect. "I'll see you later," I said. "I've got to go to work now." If her English had been better, I would've told her I was off to slay some metaphorical antelopes, or maybe cantaloupes. She's bound to be lucky her English wasn't better.

As soon as I got to the office, I made sure Old Man Mose had a bowl full of what looked like Dinty Moore only with more beef, fresh water, and a cleaned-out catbox. He accepted my worship at the Shrine of Bast as no less than his due. Looking up from his Chunky Beef (the can said), he told me, "This is okay, but I like the fish stuff better."

"The fish stuff is more expensive, so I get this sometimes," I said.

Mose just looked at me. Trying to explain money to a cat is as useless as, well, trying to explain money to a cat. "You don't love me," he said.

"Think about when you were chasing mice and grasshoppers on the street, Greedyguts. Think about how scrawny you were before you started hanging around with me. Think about how you were sleeping under cars instead of on the sofa. Then tell me all about it."

"Chasing your dinner is fun. This just sits here."

"How much fun is chasing your dinner when you don't catch it? The stuff out of a can won't disappear into a mousehole or get away."

He thought that over for a few seconds. Then he started stropping my ankles and purring like a diesel motor. Anybody who didn't know him would've been sure he was grateful. Me, I tagged it for kitty sarcasm.

The phone chose that moment to ring. Sometimes the noise makes Old Man Mose run under the sofa. He's not scared of it, but he hates it. This time, though, he went back to eating. I picked up the handset. "Mitchell Investigations."

"You better watch where you're stickin' your nose, Mitchell." Whoever was on the other end of the line sounded as if he'd watched too many movies, too, only he leaned toward George Raft. He went on, "You'll be sorry if you don't."

"Sorry about what?"

"Everything." He hung up.

I was chiefly sorry he didn't tell me more. If I'd known what he was threatening about me, I'd have had a better idea which nerve I'd struck. Now all I knew was that I'd hit one somewhere.

Which meant I was doing something right, anyway. That was nice to know. A compliment, if you want to call it such. When this guy and his pals whaled the living snot out of me, I'd know they were doing it on account of I was so damn smart.

Smart about what? If they were smart, they wouldn't tell me.

Old Man Mose finished eating and used the catbox. He didn't care that I could see him do it. Well, I didn't care if he watched me using the people box, either. Sometimes he strolled in there and helped me. That's what he called it.

He covered up his mess. He was good about that. I've known more than a few cats who weren't. He hopped off the box and asked me, "What was the noise all about?"

"A threat."

"Like this?" Mose puffed out his fur, bottlebrushed his plumy tail, laid his ears back, and showed off his fangs as if he were a vampire.

I went over and scritched him under the chin. His fur went down, his ears came up, and he started to purr. He meant it this time. "Yeah," I said. "Just like that."

Whenever I came through Vampire Village on the way home after dark, I made sure I was ready for trouble. I had a crucifix in one pocket and an atomizer full of holy water in another. I wished I had a revolver loaded with silver bullets, too, even if the moon was nowhere near full. Dora also gave me her benison more often than she had been in the habit of doing.

The vampires knew I was loaded for—not bear, but you know what I mean. To them, I was as conspicuous as a GI lugging a BAR down the main street of some Italian town. "Does Mistress Urban know you've got all those nasty things?" one asked. They respected her, and put up with me because they did.

"She thinks it's a good idea," I answered. Word must have spread fast, because that was the only time they called me on it.

Whatever worries Dora'd had about Rivke, she stopped showing them. The time rolled around when I'd got enough new blood so she could safely feed on me again, and she did. As she was finishing, I came out with what I'd thought the last time she'd done it: "Some ways, this is more intimate than making love, isn't it?"

"Yes, I think so," she answered. "Not many mortals would see that—but then, not many mortals are so closely connected with a vampire as you. But pleasure, while pleasant, is not necessary and may be delayed. Nourishment? No."

"There's more to it than that. Part of me is part of you. Some little part of me will always be part of you." Having some little part of you also be part of a vampire is about as close to immortality as you'll come if you're a childless guy like me.

The idea seemed to startle Dora. "That … is true," she said slowly. "I had not looked at it so." She hoisted an eyebrow like a warning flag. "It does not make you unique, you understand."

Don't think you mean too much to me, she meant. To be fair, she'd never made any bones about that. "I didn't say it did. I don't think it does."

That must have been the right answer, because she said, "All right, then," and pushed me down flat on the bed with effortless strength. A lot of the time, she let me pretend I was the big strong man, but that's what it was: pretending. Once she had me where she wanted me, she gave me my reward for letting her take what she got from me.

When you donate blood at a blood bank or the Red Cross, they feed you cookies and orange juice to help you come back to normal again. Dora's way is a lot more enjoyable, even if it made me want to roll over and go to sleep instead.

I woke up just after sunrise feeling emptier than empty. I staggered out of bed and lurched to the bathroom. The lid to Dora's coffin was already closed when I went to the kitchen, of course. Instead of cookies and orange juice, I made myself coffee with Pet Condensed Milk and lots of sugar and scrambled three eggs on my hot plate.

Getting outside of that improved my attitude, you bet. I took the stuff I'd used back to the kitchen and cleaned up. I always did that right after I fixed myself food. Dora put up with my eating mortal chow in her place, but I knew she didn't care for the smells from what I cooked up.

I raised the venetian blinds in the front room. With my love in her coffin, with the lid down, that was safe enough. All the same, I wished I hadn't. The fylfot in the street was back, this time without WERWOLFE under it. Maybe the *Blitzrunen* vampire hadn't had time to finish.

"Well, shit," I said, and probably some other things I'd better not set down on paper. I looked up and down the street, and didn't see Rivke. That was good, though I didn't think she'd burst into tears this time. I figured she'd be furious, the way I was.

I'd meant to go back to bed after I got myself some sustenance (thank you, Mr. Fields), but that goddamn fylfot changed my mind. I headed for work instead. If I needed to doze there, I'd doze, that was all.

When I got to the office, I fed and watered Old Man Mose and cleaned up after him. The essentials first? Now that you mention it, yes. Then I called Street Maintenance and asked for Ralph Evans. Better to deal with him, I figured, than to have to start from scratch with somebody else.

They put me through to him when I told them what I was reporting. Once they did, I had to tell him, too. "Godfrey Daniel!" he said when I got done, so he might've appreciated William Claude himself. That crack sure didn't come out of left Fields. "Right on top of where it used to be, you say?"

"Afraid so." I nodded, even though he couldn't see me do it.

"If we paint it over again, what's to stop him from coming back and redoing the stinking thing again? The vampires in VV ought to take care of this themselves."

"They're working on it. They haven't found his day lair yet—that's the problem. But I've got an idea, if you want to hear it." I'd been thinking hard while I rode north and east.

"I'm all ears," Evans said.

"Suppose that next time you send your crew over there, they dump some garlic powder into their black paint. The vampire'd have to stand right on top of it if he wanted to put the fylfot in the same place. How much would he enjoy that?"

He didn't answer for a little while. Doing his own thinking, I suppose. He chuckled before he said, "I like it, and then again I don't. I bet you're right—that LR bastard wouldn't care for it one bit. But what if we get a whole block, or maybe all of Vampire Village, sore at us? That'd be like blasting a whole village to get rid of one lousy sniper."

During the war, we'd blown more villages than I can count to hell and gone to kill or drive off a few fylfot boys. Ralph Evans had to know that as well as I did. I said, "Talk to your wizards. They'll tell you how much is too much and how much is just right. Or if it won't work, they'll say so."

"Okay. I'll do that. It's a better idea than anything I thought of. How'd you like to start working for the city? We could use a guy who thinks left-handed."

"Thanks for the idea. If I ever decide I want to do that, I'll call you. You can tell me how to get through the paperwork minefield." I didn't say that sitting behind a desk eight hours a day in a big room full of desks just like mine with people doing the same thing I was, and all of us doing the same thing over and over, would have made me need a Section 8 in nothing flat. I stayed polite, though. You never can tell. Sometimes you get so desperate, you'll do something that drives you nuts as long as it keeps the wolf away from the door.

"Okay," Evans said. "It isn't really as awful as you think it is, I'll tell you." He knew what was going on inside my head, all right. I got off the phone as soon as I could. People who can read my mind like that scare me.

"Fylfots," Mose said when I hung up. "Stupid lines. If you can't eat it or screw it, if it can't eat you, what difference does it make?" Sometimes I wish I were a cat.

Three days later, they were painting over the fylfot when I went to work. I waved to the crew. They waved back. One of them gave the half-effaced symbol the finger. I sent him a thumbs-up. He grinned at me.

I sniffed as I walked along. I couldn't smell any garlic, but what did that prove? Diddly-squat. My nose is only human. Even for an only human nose, it's not that great. Smoking ruins your sense of smell. Old Man Mose and Dora have both told me that over and over. But I enjoy it, so. …

Acolyte Adams stopped by to find out how I was doing with his blackmailer (I'm sorry, but I can't make myself call him Desmond). I had to tell him I hadn't got as far as he would have wanted. "Has the guy got in touch with you again?" I asked.

"No-o-o," he said, plainly wishing he didn't have to admit it. "But I don't like living with the sword of Damocles hanging over my head." His expression asked if I knew what the hell he was talking about. Mine told him I did, and that my mama would have warmed my fanny if I didn't. His tight nod said I'd passed the quiz. He added, "I wish you had more."

"Well, I understand. I'm sorry. But a lot of stuff's going on now." I told him about the *Blitzrunen* vampire, and about the fylfots on the street in VV.

"That's disgusting," he answered, which it was. He didn't say anything about his own time helping Uncle Sam win the war, if he'd had any. I wondered if he'd got drafted and picked up his own very real Section 8. They used them a lot to sweep queers out of the service. A Section 8 wasn't suppose to count against you on Civvy Street, but of course it did. If Acolyte Adams'd tried to land a regular job instead of being part of Deacon's, he'd've had himself a tough time.

"It sure is. You can imagine how happy the Shabbas-goy Jews in the Village are about it." I kept quiet about Rivke in particular. She was nobody's business but mine (not that Dora agreed with me there).

"Indeed," he said. From him, it sounded natural. He stood up to go. "I hope you have something of interest to report to me in the not too indefinite future." What he hoped was that he hadn't wasted half a grand and extraordinary privileges at Deacon's.

"I'm doing my best, Mister Adams," I said, which was … within shouting distance of being true, anyhow.

We shook hands. Out he went. He'd got his message across. I'd have to get down to Gardena and the adjacent area sooner than I'd thought I would. Sometimes this miserable job looks too much like work.

I wondered whether Oscar Ricks would also show up and complain that I wasn't looking hard enough for mob connections in the music racket. And I wondered if the phone would ring and somebody who *was* a mob connection would tell me I'd better quit looking for people like him. If I was really lucky, somebody like that would call while Ricks was in the office with me.

Nobody showed up. The phone didn't ring. Except for Acolyte Adams, no one seemed to give a damn whether I was working hard or not. I smoked Old Golds. I took a nip or two—but not three or four—from the bottle that lived in the desk drawer with my brass knucks and the .38 I seldom carried. I scritched Old Man Mose till he got happy enough to roll over and let me rub his fluffy tummy. That I did warily. Mose likes it and then, without warning, he doesn't. He'll go from purring his silly head off to making you bleed with no in-between at all.

Since I'd gone to work earlier than usual, I headed back to VV not long after sunset. A little twilight was still fading from the western sky when I set out, in fact. And I got punished for being less diligent than I might've been, too; I was still several blocks from the apartment when I crossed paths with Rudolf Sebestyen.

He seemed to hate me less than usual, which was, well, interesting, anyhow. All he said as we came up to each other was, "What do you know, Mitchell?"

"Not a whole hell of a lot," I answered. "How about you? Have any luck tracking down that vampire who used to wear the *Blitzrunen*?"

"No, and I have been looking, too, by night and with the White Fire in the sky. Since I can do that, I should have found his den, but he has hidden it better than I imagined he could." Rudolf sounded disgusted, whether with himself or with the other vampire I can't say. After a moment, he went on, "Someone like him is dangerous. He makes live people want to finish every vampire they can catch."

"Oh, man, I hear that." I hadn't expected to sympathize with Dora's half-brother—Sebestyen was not anybody who inspired sympathy most of the time, which is putting it mildly—but I did then. Negroes wince when a black man gets nailed for molesting little white girls because they know that endangers every colored person. Same deal. Bad apples make people who aren't part of your group want to roast your whole barrel.

"Yes, you would, eh?" Sebestyen knew what I was. I have to say, he'd never come down on me for that. He despised me for reasons personal, not racial.

"You'd better believe it," I answered. "Listen, if you do find him and you can't finish him yourself, let me know right away, okay? I'll help or I'll get other people who will."

"That I shall do," he said, and went on his way. It was the most civil encounter we'd had since I helped unzombify him, not knowing that was the last thing he wanted.

I was going to tell Dora about it as soon as I got back to the apartment, but she started complaining before I could even take off my fedora: "It is horrible outside! Why does everything reek of *fokhagyma*? Horrible!" Her nose wrinkled. Her mouth twisted in revulsion.

"I don't know, babe. What's—what did you call it?—*fokhagyma*, anyway?" I pronounced it as well as I could, which probably wasn't very. When you start from English, you have to go a long way before you bump into Magyar.

Again, she hadn't realized she'd fallen into her birthspeech. "Garlic," she translated, and made that sound as loathsome as the other.

"Oh." A light went on upstairs. Ralph Evans must've listened to me, and his wizards must've told him how much powder to mix into the paint to make the stuff effective without poisoning half the vampires in VV. I spread my hands in apology as abject as I could make it. "I'm afraid that's liable to be my fault."

"What?" Her hair stood on end. Her eyes got enormous, and I was their target. Old Man Mose can do that when he spots a mouse or a moth. Ordinary mortal humans? No.

"Sorry, honey." I explained as fast as I could, before she ripped my throat out and left my bleeding carcass on the floor because she wouldn't deign to taste me any more.

I must've been just barely in time. I'm still telling this story, aren't I? Dora's pupils shrank; her hair lay down into its usual waves. "Very well," she said, though I got the feeling she was giving me the benefit of the doubt. "I see why you did what you did. In its way, it is even clever. But you have no idea how dreadful the air is to me now. No idea at all."

"Sorry," I said one more time. I don't think it did me much good.

VI

No, I didn't go down to Gardena again the next morning. Yes, I know I should have. But I just couldn't face it. Rattling past that new tract with the RESTRICTED sign, and to hell with what the High Court had to say ... I was tempted to go down there with a couple of gallons of gasoline and a Zippo on a night when the wind blew hard out of the east: let them see how they liked that.

Tempted or not, I didn't do it. A private eye like me knows how good forensic sorcerers can be when they're trying to track down somebody who's cost a fat cat a big chunk of change. You're looking for a hero, look somewhere else. The less those people notice you, the better off you are.

So I went north and east instead, up to County General. Yeah, the shining hospital on the hill. It really is, when the smog and fog let you see it. The blood bank is one of the new buildings in the massive complex. When the hospital first went up, nobody knew how to transfer blood safely, and nobody wanted to let vampires use blood banks.

Every day, it seems, we make progress. Transfusions. That High Court ruling. Sometimes, though, it's two steps forward, one step back. That goddamn RESTRICTED sign. No, I couldn't get it out of my head. I expect an old-country Jew who had to be back inside his ghetto by sundown would have understood.

Of course, most of the ghettos are wrecked now. Most of the old-country Jews are dead. The fylfot boys weren't playing around.

I walked out of a warm, smoggy morning into the blood bank's sterile chill. Sure, cold is good for keeping blood fresh longer. But that's only part of why it feels like that in there. One of these days, we'll have air conditioning that will cool the inside of a building without turning it into an icebox. One of these days, but not yet. The ice elementals still don't get it. That's a bit of progress we're still looking for.

"Hi," I said to the receptionist who gave me a bright, meaningless smile. "Could you ring Doctor Berkowitz and tell him Jack Mitchell would like to see him when he's got a few minutes?"

"Okay, Mister, uh, Mitchell. Hold on, please." She picked up the phone. As soon as she did, a small spell kept me from overhearing what she said into it. I can read lips, but don't tell the people who set up that system. It might make them unhappy. When the gal put the handset back in the cradle, she turned audible again: "He's drawing some blood right now. If you care to take a seat and wait …"

I took a seat. I waited. I leafed through a magazine. What is it with medical places and old mags? This one didn't quite date back to the year the Browns won the pennant, but it came close.

With nothing better to do, I looked at it anyway. An article talked about the inflation that followed the end of rationing. Let me tell you, article, you ain't heard nothin' yet.

I was about to throw the magazine across the lobby when an elevator's doors opened and Izzy Berkowitz stepped out. Yeah, as Jewish as his name, with curly red hair and a hell of a schnoz. I hopped to my feet and hurried over to him. We shook hands and thumped each other on the back. We'd been through some stuff together, Izzy and I.

"Good to see ya!" he said.

"Good to be seen. It's been too long."

"It has, yeah. You still hanging around with that pretty little vampire?"

"Dora? You better believe it."

"Figured you were. You got a good thing going there. Funny—on account of that, I was gonna give you a call some time in the next few days, and now you went and beat me to the punch. Of all the nerve!" He winked at me.

"What's going on?"

Instead of answering, he turned around to check the clock above the elevators. "Half past eleven. Early for lunch, but what the hey? You wanna walk over to that little Mexican place and get some tongue tacos or something?" A quick gesture said he didn't want to talk here.

"Sure, we can do that." I love tongue tacos. So does Izzy. The folks who run that little hole in the wall—it's called El Burro Loco—think we're nuts. As far as they're concerned, gringos don't eat tongue. But it's not Mexican food. It's poor-people food. My folks weren't all *that* poor, but they got the taste for the stuff when they were, and passed it down to me.

As soon as we got off County General grounds—but not till then, I noted—Dr. Berkowitz asked me, "Ever run across a vampire who calls himself Lothar Kreuzbach? Ever hear any of the vampires you know talk about him?"

"I don't think so. Name doesn't ring a bell."

"Ah, hell. I was hoping you would have." He kicked at the sidewalk. We ducked into El Burro Loco then. The woman behind the counter grinned at him; he was a regular there. In his shoes, I would've been, too. It was better and cheaper than the hospital cafeteria. Instead of talking about vampires, he started talking about *tacos de lengua*. He pointed at me. "*Por los dos.*"

"*Sí, Señor,*" the gal said. Even I understood that one.

We sat down at one of the four or five rickety tables in the place. A bunch of people came in, got something, and walked away munching. Our tacos came in jig time, brought to us by a twelve-year-old who looked a lot like the counter lady. It was still summer vacation, yeah, but I bet he helped out other times, too. When the family needs a hand, what are you gonna do?

For a while, we were too busy to talk. That joint gives you a ton of food for not much dough, and it's always good. After a bit, once we'd polished off the tacos and were grabbing shreds of lettuce and onion from the bottom of the basket, Izzy asked, "So what brings you up to this part of town?"

"I've got my own vampire problem." I told him about the *Blitzrunen* bastard, about how I met him for the first and almost last time, and about the later fun and games he was probably behind.

"Yeah, some of that made the *Mirror News*," he said. I hadn't seen anything about it in the *Times*. But then, during the war the *Times* was halfway rooting for the fylfot boys. More than halfway. They're like that. Izzy added, "The past is never dead. It's not even past."

"Faulkner could write some." I left it right there. It was either leave it or go off like a round from a 155. I hadn't come to see Izzy for that.

He surprised me—he caught what I didn't say. "Sorry," he told me. "I was dumb."

"Never mind. It's not like he was wrong. Not there, anyhow." I got back to what I *had* come to see Izzy for: "Have you ever heard of somebody being a vampire and a werewolf at the same time?"

He looked at me. "Where d'you find 'em?"

"I don't know if I have. But that first fylfot on my street showed up at the end of a full-moon night, and it had *Werwölfe* written under it. Made me wonder."

"I don't know of any cases like that," he said carefully. "But I don't pay as much attention to werewolves as I do to vampires. Werewolves are more interested in spilling blood than feeding on it."

Not quite realizing I was doing it, I touched one of the scars on my neck. When I did realize, I jerked my hand away. I'm sure Berkowitz noticed; he didn't miss much. I tried to jerk the subject away, too: "What's up with the vampire you're interested in? Lothar—something." I couldn't come up with the last name.

"Kreuzbach," he said. Then he didn't tell me what was up with, not straight out, anyway. His eyes got wide. "You know what? I bet Kreuzbach and your *Blitzrunen Oberf* are the same guy!"

"Oh, yeah?" Now I was all ears. "How do you figure that?"

"He came in wanting a feed not so real long ago. It was the first time he'd shown up, so the nurse on duty called me down to look him over. He had a driver's license and a Social Security card. They both looked legit."

"The fylfot boys were good at forging papers," I remarked.

"Yeah. That occurred to me later. At the time, I didn't see any reason not to get him a unit, so I started to go do that. He'd been eyeballing me while we talked, and he asked if the nurse—her last name is Svensson, just so you know—could bring it instead. When I asked him why, he said, 'I don't want it polluted,' just like that."

"Ouch!" I said, in lieu of something stronger. "That's pretty raw. What did you do?"

"I said I'd bring it to him, and I'd be happy to stick it up the other orifice if he liked. I know I shouldn't have—we took care of Lightning Rune POWs during the war—but I lost my temper. For some reason, he walked out then. Oh, and Susie Svensson kissed me as soon as he was gone. I haven't even told my wife about that."

"I think I would've done my goddamnedest to drive a stake through his heart," I said.

"Don't believe I wasn't tempted. Wanna hear something funny?" Berkowitz laughed in a way that suggested he knew Queen Victoria.

"I'd love to hear something funny."

"Okay. I'm Isidore, right? My folks called me that 'cause it sounded more American than Isaac. That happened all the time when I came along. There are lots of Morrises who aren't Moseses, too, and Sheldons who aren't Shmuels. Fat lot of good it did me, huh? Loathsome Lothar Kreuzbach took one look and knew right away I was a damn Jew."

"That's not much of a joke."

"I'm getting there, I'm getting there. You happen to know what 'Isidore' means?" He waited till I shook my head, then went on, "It means 'gift of Isis,' that's what. My Jewish mom and dad, they tried to make me seem American, and what did they wind up doing? Putting me under the protection of an ancient Egyptian goddess! A pagan goddess! And if that's not funny, Jack, what the hell is?"

"Maybe you had to be there." Some bebop cats talk about black humor, where you play something that shouldn't be funny for laughs. You see enough combat, you start doing that a lot, too. It keeps you from going as nuts as you would otherwise.

"Maybe so." Berkowitz didn't get mad. He was a pretty cool cat, Izzy was. And then, out of the blue, I laughed in his face. He still didn't get mad. He just said, "Okay, now you've got a joke. C'mon—give."

"You aren't the only one with a name that doesn't fit so well. I don't know what *Bach* means, but isn't *Kreuz* 'cross' if you're talking to the fylfot boys? Hell of a handle for a vampire to have, isn't it?"

His eyes glowed. "Damned if you're not right. And a *Bach* is a stream. When you study medicine, you've got to soak up more *Deutsch* than you ever want. And I heard and spoke a good bit of Yiddish when I was little, so I had a head start. I guess Kreuzbach'd mean a stream with a cross by it, probably someplace near where Lothar's great-granddad or whoever took the name growing up."

"See? We've got it all worked out! Only things we don't know are whether Lothar's really the *Blitzrunen* vampire and where that SOB hides during the day whether he's Lothar or not."

"Details, details. You're gonna piss and moan about every little thing …" Izzy dug in his pocket and plopped change on the table.

I'd meant to buy, but he beat me to the punch. "Thanks," I said, and not another word. He would have got sore if I'd tried to take it away from him. People say Jews are cheapskates, so he goes out of his way not to be.

We both got up. As we walked out the door, he waved to the lady behind the counter. She smiled back. He and I went to the blood bank. We shook hands in front of it. He hurried on in, ready to do whatever needed doing. Much more slowly, I ambled over to the trolley stop. Pretty soon, a car pulled up. I hopped on and headed down to my part of town.

"Took you long enough to get here," Old Man Mose said when I unlocked the office door and came inside.

"Yeah, yeah." I looked at his bowl. Empty. I hadn't needed to deduce like Sherlock Homes to work that out before I checked. He was obviously starving to death, all fifteen pounds of him. I fed him. I gave him fresh water. From the state of the catbox, I suspected something was still going through him.

He made a good start on his C-ration—uh, beef with gravy—then looked up, licked his cute pink nose, and told me, "That's more like it."

I bowed. "Always happy to serve you, Your Majesty."

"Good. You'd better be." Mose knows what sarcasm is, but doesn't recognize it unless he's using it himself. He's a cat, in other words, not that there aren't people like that, too.

"Anything interesting happen before I got here?"

"Nothing *very* interesting. A ghost showed up. Then he went away." Mose yawned to show how that excited him.

"Was it Eb?" I asked. Ebenezer's the ghost I know best. He was a New Englander who'd been a Pinkerton till he stopped a Minié ball during the Civil War. These days, his incorporeal remnant works for the LAPD Missing Individuals unit.

But my chunky red fluffball only yawned again. "I don't know. What difference does it make, anyhow?" Ghosts can't do anything to cats. Cats can't catch ghosts, and ghosts don't have enough of a scent to let cats track them by smell. No wonder cats don't care about them.

"Was he going through my files?" I pointed to the cabinets. They were locked, though that wouldn't have stopped a ghost. If you have any sense, you don't keep all your important stuff in obvious places.

"I quit paying attention to him when I realized what he was." Old Man Mose started eating again. Talking to me wasn't very interesting, either, especially not with food around.

I called the answering service and asked Hilda, "Any messages for me?"

"Yes, there was one," she said, sounding vaguely surprised—it's not as if my phone rings off the hook. I heard her shuffling papers. Then she came back on the line. "It's from a Daniel Becker. He wouldn't leave a message with me, but he wants you to call him back." She gave me the number.

I wrote it down. "Thanks," I said. It was a FAculty phone number, which fit with where Becker's place was. I dialed it. His secretary answered—I recognized her voice. I told her who I was.

"Oh, Mister Mitchell. Yes, he did want to talk with you," she said. "Hold on and I'll put you through."

"Hello, Mitchell," Becker said once the secretary connected us. "You some kind of psychic or something?"

"Jesus, I hope not!" I said, which made him laugh. But I meant it. I've talked about the ads for psychics above the windows in Red

Line cars. You see 'em on bus benches, too. The people who buy them're trolling for suckers, nothing else but. I'm not saying there aren't real psychics, smart psychics, too, 'cause there are. But they don't need to advertise. They do fine all by themselves. Oh, do they ever!

"Anyway," Becker said once he'd had his little chuckle, "you know how we were talking about getting shaken down by the mob?"

"I do remember that, yes."

"Well, yesterday this fellow walked in and told me Mickey'd just noticed I was around. He was pretty smooth—smoother than I expected from somebody doing what he's doing—but the long and short of it is, Mickey needs some cash every month if I don't want my business to start having accidents. Or maybe I'm the one who'd start having 'em. He wasn't real plain about that. You know the guy I'm talking about, right?"

"Mickey, you mean?"

"Uh-huh. The fellow who saw me was just a flunky, a soldier."

"I don't know Mickey real well." I wanted to be real plain about that. "I've seen him on Central Avenue a time or three. He dresses pretty snappy. That doesn't make him a nice guy. They say he's got hooks in some of the clubs there. I think they're right for a change." That brawl at the Basket Room might've given me a hint.

"They say he kills people. I bet they're right about that, too." Becker sounded pretty bleak, and who could blame him?

"What are you gonna do? Call the cops?"

He snorted. "It'd be the sheriffs out here. This is L.A. County, not the city of Los Angeles. The sheriffs aren't as crooked as the LAPD, but—?"

"Who is?" I broke in. There'd been a huge LAPD scandal not so long before. The smell got so bad, the chief had to quit, but juries acquitted all the policemen who were arrested. They got their old jobs back, too. And the honest cop who turned them in? The powers that be threw him off the force. Sometimes you can't win for losing.

"Yeah, who is?" Becker agreed, so he knew what I was talking about. He went on, "I like to think I can take care of myself. I'm pretty good at that, if I do say so myself."

He sounded like a hotshot wizard, sure as hell. Those guys can do a lot of things ordinary people can't, so they think they've got the world by the short hairs. Sometimes they're right, at least for a while. When they bump up against people like Mickey …

"You'd better be careful," I said. "If you don't think those people have sorcerers working for them, too, you're making a big mistake."

"That crossed my mind." He sighed. "You wonder how anybody could do something like that. The pay's gotta be good, but even so—"

I interrupted again: "Mister Becker, the fylfot boys had wizards working for them. So did the Knights of Bushido, or they never would've caught us flatfooted at Pearl Harbor. D'you really want a salamander burning down your business, or maybe your house?"

"A salamander …." The way Becker said it, he must've thought first of Hiroshima and Nagasaki. But there are smaller ones, too. He didn't need long to remember that. "Somebody used a salamander to torch an apartment building not that far from me a little while ago."

"Somebody sure did. It was my apartment building. Would've torched me, too, only I wasn't home."

"Oh," he said, and then, "Jesus!"

"Uh-huh." I nodded, even if he couldn't see me do it. "If you want to be a hero, you can do that. But I think you're smart enough to know they don't find babies under cabbage leaves."

He didn't say anything for close to a minute. He might've expected me to tell him his strength was as the strength of ten because his heart was pure and his cause was just, or at least hoped I would. But I'm only a private eye trying to get along in a world I didn't make. And, because of what else I am, I know too damn well what happens to you if your heart is pure and your cause just. It doesn't matter if your strength is as the strength of ten, either. They'll beat you down all the same, and beat you harder because you made trouble for them.

He knew that stuff, too; as I say, he's darker than I am. At last, he sighed. "Thanks for calling me back, Mister Mitchell."

"Any time," I answered, but he'd already hung up.

Saturday night, Dora and I went to Santa Monica Beach. I would sooner have gone while the sun was up, but that wasn't practical for her. One Red Car transfer downtown was all we needed. When we got there, we could see the lights of the *John Smith*—you know, the gambling ship—where it was anchored out past the three-mile limit. We kicked off our shoes and walked through the sand like a couple of kids.

I wondered if there were merfolk out in the water. The tide was coming in. We got our feet wet, and the bottoms of my trousers. It was silly fun. Dora said, "I have flown over the beach, but never walked it before. I did not think the water would be so cold."

"Everybody says that about the ocean here," I answered. Los Angeles is nice and warm. The Pacific off Los Angeles will freeze your nuts off if you have any.

I hadn't been to the beach myself for a while. Not because the water's cold, but because people just a little browner than I am find the welcome they get isn't any warmer. I'd never had that trouble myself, but I knew I might. Going at night, and going with a green-eyed blond, cut down the risk.

Dora snuggled against me. I put my arm around her shoulder. That made her snuggle tighter, grateful for the warmth. Vampires aren't like lizards. They don't slow down to a crawl when they get cold. But they don't like it, either.

We walked along, so close together our feet got tangled up a couple of times. I might've swallowed a mouthful of sand once if she hadn't held me up. "Thanks," I said, grinning like a silly fool. I was about as happy right then as a man is likely to get.

Happiness isn't part of the vampire condition. I know that. About the closest they come is the satisfaction they get from drinking their fill. But Dora seemed … more than usually content with my company, is the best I can put it.

Not many people were on the sand after sundown. I stopped, turned toward her, and kissed her. Yes, I could feel the fangs when I did. "What was that for?" she asked after I let her go.

"Because," I said. Even in the darkness, I could see her lift an eyebrow. So I tried again: "Because I love you, that's what."

"It is a mistake. I keep telling you it is a bad mistake." She did, too. She'd never thought my loving her was anything but a stupid idea. She'd never tried to hide that. I didn't listen. When you're in love, you don't.

We walked on. I heard music, even though nobody was there. That wasn't on account of I was in love, though. It was because we were getting close to Ocean Park Pier, which was full of rides and honky-tonks and I don't know what all, every bit of it designed to separate marks from cash as painlessly as possible.

I pointed toward the entrance. "Want to?"

"Well, why not?" she said, as if humoring a little boy. She took that tone with me a lot. Considering how much longer she'd been around than I had, I suppose she had the right. Sometimes it got on my nerves anyhow. That night, I didn't care.

We put our shoes back on. I had sand between my toes—I could feel it. If any grains had the nerve to stick to Dora's elegant feet, she didn't let on that she noticed.

I smelled creosote from the planks, and popcorn, and stuff frying, and the ocean under all of it. We walked right past the Bug House. It's a funhouse with a mirror maze, and what good is a mirror maze to somebody who doesn't have a reflection? The Chute the Chutes was a different deal. You go up enough stairs for a half-grown skyscraper, then get into a boat and slide down a steep ramp into a pool at the bottom. You get wet, but you're too busy screaming to care. I was, anyway. Dora's cool had nothing to do with her body temperature.

After the boat, we went flying on the Strat-o-Liner, which had airplane-shaped cars that went round and round on the end of long arms. When the ride first opened, people said it went so fast, the cars would get thrown off the arms. Just because they said it didn't make it so. The Strat-o-Liner's never had an accident. Real airplanes should be so lucky.

After we were back on solid ground again—and after I stopped being dizzy—I asked Dora, "Is that anything like what you feel when you fly by yourself?"

"I am sorry, but it is nothing like that," she said. I must've looked stricken, because she gave me a quick kiss and added, "But it was very interesting, no doubt of that." See what I mean? Like a little boy.

The honky-tonks on the pier kept their doors open so you could listen to the music coming out from inside. They hoped that would draw people in. The first three joints we walked past, the noises I heard made me want to run away instead. When you're used to

Central Avenue, Ocean Park Pier is a longer drop than the one on the Chute the Chutes.

Or I thought so till we came to a little place called I Like It Like That. What was coming out of that door was coming straight from the future. The sign by the entrance said, *This weekend only—The Oscar Ricks Trio!* But I didn't need the sign. By their licks shall ye know them.

"Let's go in," I said.

"Try not to get into a fight," Dora told me.

"I'll do my best."

Two-buck cover, two-drink minimum. The price of admission wasn't any better than it would've been at a top-end Central Avenue club. The crowd was a lot smaller, though. I looked around. I didn't see any obvious tough guys, which was good. All the same, I picked a table where I could watch the stage and the way in without being too obvious about it.

Oscar nodded to Dora and me when we sat down. He and his electrified accomplices went right on playing. Not everybody in there loved what they did. A couple walked out just as we got our first drinks. As I had at the Basket Room, I kinda dug it.

When I said so, Dora answered, "If they turn their amplifiers up enough, they can pin us to the wall like butterflies with their noise. Is this what you call music?"

She had a point. She commonly did. Even so, I said, "Yeah, it is. Music isn't just about thinking. It's about feeling, too. That's part of the reason you play it loud."

"This is … possible," she said after a small pause. "When I became what I am, I was divorced—*severed* might be the better word—from all that. I still think as well as I ever did, though. Better, perhaps, thanks to the experience I have."

I didn't know how to respond to that, so I kept quiet. Oscar's trio ended their set a minute or so later. He said, "We're gonna take fifteen, folks. Hang on. We'll be back." Not everybody did hang on. Several people beat it, one guy digging a finger into the ear that had pointed toward the little band. I hoped Ricks didn't see that.

He came over to our table. I waved to the waitress and bought him a drink—poor man looked like somebody who could use one. "How you doing?" I asked while we waited for it.

"Hanging in there. Hanging on, or trying to," he said. "The word's out about me on Central. Nobody there wants to hire the trio. I told you, I got turned down at Deacon's, for cryin' out loud, and they swear they aren't mobbed up." The whiskey arrived. He drank half of it.

"Sorry to hear that. They aren't, not as far as I know." His troubles there had nothing to do with the mob, but I didn't want to be the one who told him so.

"Yeah, well ..." He shrugged. "I'm here. Pay's not great. Nobody who matters will ever hear me here, either. But it beats sitting around gathering dust. I guess it does."

"Speaking of mobbed up—" I did tell him what I'd heard from Danny Becker.

"Great!" Ricks gulped the rest of his booze. "If the bastards' right hand knows what their left is up to, they'll work out that he's pressing for Grampus and Grampus is recording for me. I'll be up the creek without a paddle then, won't I?"

I didn't want to say yes, but I couldn't lie well enough to say no. And it turned out the I Like It Like That had a bouncer. He walked up to the table and spoke to Dora and me as if Oscar weren't there: "Sir, ma'am, if this fella's botherin' you, I can send him on his way pronto."

He didn't say *this colored fella* or anything even sweeter, but I knew what he meant. So did Oscar Ricks. I said, "No, it's fine. We all know each other." The thick-chested guy shrugged as if to say there was no accounting for taste.

"Jesus! I'm sorry about that," Oscar said.

Dora flinched, and he fell over himself apologizing. She waved it off. "No great harm done."

"Life in L.A., man," I said. This isn't Mobile or Little Rock, no. It isn't heaven on earth, either. Ain't no heaven on earth, far as I can see. Dora and I drank our minimum fast and got the hell out. I couldn't stand to stay another minute.

Monday morning, down to the South Bay again. That's what they call all those dinky suburbs south and west of the big city. Down past the RESTRICTED sign, too. The tract was going up fast. I muttered under my breath. Especially after what had happened in the club on the pier, I really felt like paying it a late-night call. If you aren't pink-and-gold enough to make the fylfot boys happy, I've got no idea how you can make it through a day without feeling that way at least once. And I can pass, so I miss a lot of it. If you're brown; if you're black …

I got off the Red Line at Vermont and Gardena Boulevard, then took two buses over to Main and 154th. A block and a half west to Danny Becker's Quonset huts. "Oh, yes, Mister Mitchell. Of course I remember you!" the secretary said, for all the world as if I hadn't had to remind her of my name. "Let me see if Mister Becker can talk with you now." She went in. She came out. She gestured. His Majesty had time for his lowly subject.

That's how I read it, you understand. Maybe I was on the sensitive side right then, especially since Becker went through all the same crap I did. After the usual social nonsense, he said, "I wondered if I'd see you after we talked."

"Here I am, seen," I said. He chuckled and waved me to a chair. When he lit a cigarette, I did, too. He blew a smoke ring. I can't do that for hell, so I aimed a stream of smoke at his. Shot it down, by God! I took another drag, then asked, "You know a fellow named Desmond Adams?"

"I don't think I know anybody named Desmond."

"Sometimes he goes by Acolyte Adams."

A light came on in Becker's eyes. "Oh, him! The sissy! He's one of the pair who run that after-hours club, right?"

"That's him," I agreed.

"I've been to Deacon's a few times, so I know who he is. That's about as far as it goes. It's not what I thought you'd want to talk about. What's up with him?"

"Somebody's blackmailing him," I said. He started to answer. Before he could, I added, "Somebody who's using your box in the Gardena post office."

Well, I got his attention. He pointed a finger at me, moved it in quick passes, and muttered under his breath. Something glowed green in the air above his hand. He looked surprised. "You aren't lying."

"I've got better things to do with my time than come all this way to tell lies, thank you very much."

"Okay, but what's it got to do with me?"

"Well, the obvious question is, who's more likely to use your post-office box than you?"

He started to get sore. Then he stopped again. I admired him for that. "A point," he said. "But it isn't me. I don't care what Adams does, as long as he doesn't try doing it with me."

I felt the same way. The law, of course, has a different idea. So do a whole lot of other people. That's why guys like Acolyte Adams got blackmailed so often. You need a big helping of I don't know what—arrogance? not giving a damn? big brass ones?—not to worry about such things. Deacon Washington had it, and then some. His partner didn't.

None of which had anything to do with the price of beer (which, at Deacon's, was four bucks a glass). I said, "Okay, if it isn't you, who's it most likely to be?"

"Helen out front makes post-office runs for me sometimes. So do a couple of the supervisors on the production side, to get orders moving out to customers," Becker said slowly. "I don't know if they'd do anything like that. I'd sure hope they wouldn't. Hell, I don't even know if they have any idea who Acolyte Adams is."

"Everybody hopes the people who work for them wouldn't do anything like that. And everybody finds out some of those people damn well would. I'd be out of work if they wouldn't." I eyed the wizard. "And if they've never heard of Adams but you have, what does that make me think about you?"

"You've got your nerve, don't you?" He eyed me right back.

I didn't care for the way he did it. "Somebody always knows where I'm going. If I don't come back, this is where the investigation starts." I hoped he didn't use his truth spell on me. It would tell him I was lying through my teeth.

I got lucky—he didn't. He must have thought I was only doing what anybody with an ounce of sense would have. That leaves me out, I'm afraid. "Take it easy, man," he said. "I'm not going to mess with you. I've got no reason to. I'm just trying to make a buck and not give too much back to Uncle Sam—or anybody else."

Remembering what we'd talked about a few days earlier, I asked him, "How are your charming friends? Have you made arrangements, or are you still holding out?"

"I've made arrangements. What you said made more sense than I wish it did. They even let me dicker them down from what the goon said they wanted at first—not a lot, but some." Becker laughed sourly. "Just like any other businessmen, right?"

"Sure." Except other businessmen wouldn't break his leg if he got behind on his payments. Most of 'em wouldn't, I should say. I noticed he didn't tell me the mob had let him jew them down. He also hadn't called Acolyte Adams most of the things a regular guy commonly calls a queer. *Sissy* was as nasty as he'd got, and that's weak tea.

Which proved nothing, of course. But it made me a little more likely to believe him. I should say, it made me want to believe him, and I hadn't when I was riding down there. "Okay," I said. "I'm not going to stop poking around. You may want to do some of that on your own, too. If you find anything, and if you want to let me know about it, you've got my number."

"You've got mine, too. I have enough worries with the … businessmen. I don't need any more trouble rolling down on me. If you find something interesting, let me know."

I nodded. "I'll do that." And maybe I would, and maybe I wouldn't. That would depend on what it was, and on what it said about Danny Becker. If he had the brains I thought he did, he'd work that out for himself.

After I stubbed out the latest Old Gold I'd been smoking, I stood up. Becker and I shook hands. As I walked through the outer office, I glanced over at Helen. I think she thought I was giving her the eye, because she preened without moving, the way women can. She wouldn't have done that if she'd known what was in my mind.

Back to my part of town. It's a lot more crowded than the South Bay, older, more rundown. But it's my part of town, and I get reminded of that every time I stick my nose outside it.

I was walking from the trolley stop to my office when a scrawny street kitty trotted up to me and asked, "Hey, buddy, got any mice you need killed?" It stropped itself against my ankle. Old Man Mose would smell that on me and give me hell on account of it, as if I had a jealous girlfriend and came back smelling of cheap perfume.

"Sorry, I've got a friend who takes care of that for me," I told the furry optimist still weaving around my feet and trying to make me fall on my face.

"Bet I'd do it better," the cat said. Then it stopped and did some serious sniffing of its own. It made a horrible face, as if I'd just given it nasty medicine. "A *vampire*?" It ran away as fast as it could.

So I got to tell that to Mose when he did catch the odor on my trousers. "I used to feel the same way," he said. "But the one you found for yourself, she's not *too* bad. For a vampire, I mean."

"Thank you so much," I said, and startled myself at how much I meant it.

VII

I was heading back to Vampire Village from the office some time between ten and eleven one night. The weather was of the kind that makes people who live in places like Minnesota or Nebraska or Massachusetts pack up and head west. It was October, getting on toward time to trick or treat, but my jacket was unbuttoned. About half the guys I saw were in shirtsleeves. The sky was full of a million stars despite the city lights.

Despite the city lights and despite the full moon, I should say. When I looked to my left, there it was, shining on the getting-toward-midnight blue like a gold double eagle. I'm old enough to remember when you saw those passing from hand to hand. Not too often, because twenty dollars is a lot of money, but you did. They aren't legal tender now, of course, which doesn't mean they don't still circulate.

These days, though, the full moon meant other things to me. I kept swiveling my head around, trying to catch a werewolf's howl. Was that fellow who'd been a *Blitzrunen Oberführer* also the fellow Dora and I'd heard when the moon got as round as a big coin before?

To tell you the truth, I didn't want to find out, not just then. I didn't want to hear any howls. All I wanted was to get back to the apartment, fix myself something to eat, and kiss my sweetie, those last two not necessarily in that order.

A police car slid down the street. I felt the cops' eyes on me. You always do—they want you to. But the car kept rolling. It wasn't late enough and I wasn't dark enough for L.A.'s finest to jump out and start grilling me me about who I was and where I was going … and to pull out their nightsticks and whale hell out of me if I gave them any lip or if one of them happened to be in a lousy mood.

Things like that happen all the time in what the LAPD calls the Negro Belt. Cops hold it down the way the fylfot boys held down the part of Italy they still occupied. I doubt I would have thought of it like that if Uncle Sam hadn't shipped me to the Mediterranean and let me see such things for myself. I wasn't the only one who'd seen things like that and drawn my own conclusions from them, either. Oh, no. Nowhere near.

There'd also been partisans in the hills in Italy. One of these days, the LAPD may need to worry about partisans, too.

As soon as I got into Vampire Village, my dark mood lifted. The streets were crowded and lively, as lively as they could get when most of the folks walking along were undead. The cops didn't hassle them at night. Vampires make cops nervous. That happens when you aren't so sure you've got the whip hand.

They do werewolf howls in the movies. Those aren't like the real thing, though. The one I heard from not nearly far enough away made me freeze in my tracks. I mean freeze literally; ice walked up my back. Some part of you far deeper than thought knows, *This beast wants to kill you and eat you.*

And I wasn't the only one who felt it. It also got to the vampires. Either they remembered the days when they'd been warm or they figured the werewolf wouldn't be fussy. I can't tell you. I can tell you they stopped in midstride, same as I did.

Then I heard a cry—no, a shriek. It unparalyzed me in a hurry. The most lethal weapons I had against a werewolf were the dimes and quarters in my pockets. I ran toward the scream anyway. You do, or else you don't.

Some of the vampires ran with me. Some went the other way. Some just stayed where they were. It happens with soldiers, too. You can put somebody into combat, but you can't make him fight. He has to do that for himself.

I tore around a corner. A man was down. Something crouched over him, biting and tearing. No, the creature didn't crouch. It went on all fours. "Hey!" I shouted. The vampires started yelling with me.

The werewolf snarled. It loped toward me. I threw pocket change as if it were a grenade—whatever silver I had, plus pennies and nickels that wouldn't do me one goddamn bit of good. Something must've connected, because the werewolf howled on a different note, one of sudden pain, and twisted to snap at its shoulder.

A vampire tackled it. The guy wasn't very big, but by that tackle he would've been a star for the L.A. Dons in the All-America Football conference.

Of course, vampires are much stronger and faster than live people. I know I've said so before. Dora could have knocked the snot out of me if she ever decided she wanted to. We both knew that; neither of us ever brought it up. But the werewolf threw the vampire off it as easy as you please, then went after him with a set of chompers that looked as if they could've beavered through a big old redwood in nothing flat. It bit the vampire, then spat. The flavor wasn't to its taste.

Against several vampires, it would've been in trouble. Animal cunning or what was left of human intelligence must have told it as much. Snarling and snapping, it broke through them and ran away. Undead or not, they didn't seem eager to go after it.

Me, I went over to the poor bastard the werewolf had pulled down. He lay unmoving in a spreading pool of gore. I knew right a way I couldn't do a thing for him; he was already gone. Once in Italy, because I was very, very lucky, I went past a foxhole where a mortar round had gone off right in front. The guy in it must've been standing up when it hit. He didn't have any face left. I still see him sometimes, in the dreams where I wake up all drenched with sweat.

This fellow looked like that. Worse, I think, and I wouldn't have dreamt that was possible. Toss in the iron stink of all the blood he'd spilled, and for a few seconds I wasn't on the streets of Vampire Village any more. I was back in that muddy farmyard, hands clutching my rifle tight enough to hurt.

Then something snapped me out of it. Two sirens, different notes: a police car and an ambulance. The cop car was closer. I got the hell out of there. I couldn't face dealing with the LAPD then. Most of the others anywhere close by also lit out for the tall timber. The cops could talk to the handful of natural-born innocent rubberneckers who stuck around.

The first thing I did when I got to the apartment was kiss Dora. The next thing was to lower the level in the Wild Turkey bottle, and I mean lower it a good bit. I needed the glass wall bourbon builds between you and the bad things out there. Even before the first knock hit hard, I sent reinforcements after it.

"Are you all right?" Dora knew I drank. She knew I didn't usually drink like that.

"No," I explained.

"Tell me." Her voice was soft and resistless.

So I did. Sometimes getting it out helps. Sometimes not, too. I didn't want to go back to that farmyard, but I did. She needed to hear all of it if she was gonna hear any of it. I thought so, anyhow. By the time I got done, I was sweating as hard as I did in one of those dreams.

Then she kissed me. It wasn't maternal, not even slightly, but it soothed me just the same. "It will fade," she said, which was what I most wanted to hear.

"I love you. Lots," I said. I'm sure that wasn't what she most wanted to hear, but I said it even so. *In* Wild Turkey *veritas.*

I slept late the next morning. No, let's stick with the *veritas*, okay? I knocked myself on my can with the bourbon. I felt it, too. I've had more mornings after that were worse than I care to recall, but I felt it. Aspirins and coffee and a couple of scrambled eggs for grease to coat my stomach helped as much as they ever do, which is to say, some but not enough.

Dora knew nothing about that. She slept the sleep of the undead, there in her closed coffin. Somewhere not real far away—I wished I knew where—the vampire who had been *Oberführer* Lothar Kreuzbach slept that sleep, too. Was he dreaming of his days—well, his nights—of glory bearing the *Blitzrunen*? Or of biting a man's face off the night before?

Or was he as dark and useless as a lamp that wasn't plugged in? I wasn't sure I wanted to know.

Out into the cold, cruel world I went. I've done braver things, but not a whole bunch of them. I really wished I could jump into a hole and pull it in after me. Out I went even so. Yeah, hero stuff. Only nobody'd pin a medal on my pocket for it.

There was Rivke, standing on the corner. We waved to each other. Well, she waved first, and I wasn't rude enough not to answer in kind. She came across the street, looked me over, and stopped short in a way she wouldn't have if she'd liked what she saw better. "You are all right?" she asked, sounding as doubtful as Dora had the night before.

"I've been better," I answered. I would have loved to lie, but I knew I couldn't bring it off. I'm sure my eyes were the pissholes in the snow the poets sing about. I'm also sure I looked generally the worse for wear. That's how I felt.

"*Vus iz* … wrong?" She gave me the word I needed in English.

"The werewolf. The werewolf who may be the vampire. He killed a man near here last night. He almost killed me." I'd nearly forgotten about that. God knows why. Sure, I've been in danger before. But the guy with no face had hit me way harder than the notion that I could've been a guy with no face to bring back bad memories in someone else.

"Gevalt! Vey iz mir!" If Rivke'd been Catholic, she would've crossed herself. She wouldn't have wounded any vampires if she had, not at that time of day.

"Yeah." I took out my cigarettes, stuck one in my mouth, and then remembered I ought to offer them to her. When I held out the pack, she nodded eagerly, so I gave her one and lit it for her. We stood there sucking in smoke together. Cigarettes let you keep company with somebody without needing to talk. Even with yourself.

After the Old Golds went into the gutter, Rivke said, "He needs ending, that one."

"Or they both do, if the vampire isn't the werewolf," I said.

She shook her head. Her curls bobbed. "Same one, I think. Same bad."

"Yeah," I said again, because it felt that way to me, too. "I wish we could end him. He's not done making trouble."

"*Ikh vayss*," she said. "Still bad."

"Yeah." My mouth was a one-trick pony. "Maybe we'll get lucky. Maybe."

"*Alevai omayn*," she said. When Al Harris came out with that, it meant something like, *I sure as hell hope so*. I tipped my hat to her and headed off to work.

I was almost there when a cat came up to me. I needed a moment to recognize her: the scrawny kitty I'd sent away with a flea in her ear not long before. "Somebody's in your office!" she said.

"Sure—Old Man Mose. I already told you I had a cat," I said.

She looked at me as if I was even dumber than your ordinary, run-of-the-mill human. "No! Somebody like you!"

Nobody had any business being in my office when I wasn't around. Not even the landlord—I hadn't got behind on the rent for a while. Were the cops coming around to shake me down? They'd got careful for a while during the scandal. Maybe they figured the coast was clear now. Maybe they were right.

Or maybe it was friends of the goon who'd given me that heart-warming phone call, ready to deliver a different kind of message. I hoped not. Trouble with the mob was as bad as trouble with the law. But that seemed all too likely.

I bent down and scritched the skinny stray under the chin. She didn't quite snap at me. "If I get out of this in one piece, I'll take care of you. Promise."

She sniffed. I must not have smelled like a liar, because she said, "Deal." Then she scooted away. If I didn't get out of it in one piece, she didn't want anybody knowing she'd tipped me off.

I walked up to my door as if everything were normal. In fact, I whistled a tune to let anybody inside know I was there. What do you do if you want to jump somebody coming into an office? You hide in back of the door and hit him from behind. I've done it myself. Most of the time, it works like a charm.

Not always. I unlocked the door. When I opened it, though, I flung it back as hard as I could, and put all my weight behind it. Sure as hell, it didn't slam against the wall. Two squashed guys yelled in dismay. No, that kitty didn't steer me wrong.

I jerked the door open again. One goon was perfectly set up for a kick where it would do him the most good, so I gave him one. He folded up like a clasp knife. The other guy still had some fight in him. Some, but not enough. When he went down, I kicked him in the head so he wouldn't get up. I gave the first one the same treatment. Never let 'em think, *Hell, I almost had him*. Losers gotta know they lost.

When they were in no shape to do anything about it, I relieved them of a pistol, a knuckleduster, a blackjack, and a couple of blades. If they'd got started on me .... Well, they damn well hadn't.

I waited till they came around. It took a while; kicks in the head will do that to you. They'd feel them for days, maybe weeks. When they were sitting up and could make sense of words, I told 'em, "Get the hell out of here. I got into a fight with one of your boys 'cause he didn't like the music a guy I work for was playing and tried to rough him up. It was personal. It didn't have anything to do with the organization. Go tell your people I don't have any quarrel with them. Far as I'm concerned, it's over."

They needed a bit longer to get to their feet. I let 'em splash cold water on their faces and clean up a little in my john. One of 'em said, "Our people ain't gonna think it's over." That worried me, but I didn't show it. I stood there watching them lurch down the street till they turned a corner and disappeared.

And that skinny tabby loped up and ran into the office before I could shut the door. She made a beeline for Mose's food dish and started chowing down. The noise got him out from under the sofa, you betcha. "That's mine!" he yowled, and puffed out his fur so he looked as big as three cats.

She went right on eating. I said, "She's earned a place. She warned me those plug-uglies were in here. I can get enough tuna and mackerel and what-all to make you both fat." *And another water dish, and another box*, I thought. I asked my new friend, "What do I call you?"

She looked up from the glop long enough to answer, "Me? I'm Mehitabel." Then she went back to eating.

I packed up the goons' troubles in an old kit bag—well, an old shoe box that I tied up with string. Then I took the Red Car to Hollywood Boulevard and Highland. Not a part of town I get to much, but I needed to that afternoon. A bus carried me down to Highland and Melrose. I crossed the street, walked back a few doors, and there it was—the Rhum Boogie.

The Rhum Boogie was Mickey's club. If I was gonna find him anywhere, I'd find him there. It was still sleepy when I went in. A couple of guys sat at a table nursing beers, that's all. They got very alert very fast. "Waddaya want?" one of them growled.

"I need to talk to Mickey," I said. Sometimes you've got to stick your head in the lion's mouth.

"Who the hell are you?" the other tough guy asked.

"Jack Mitchell."

By the way they both jerked, I might've stuck 'em with hatpins. "You got your nerve," the second fellow said, "comin' over here right after—"

"That's what I wanted to talk to him about." I stood there. I waited. If I didn't show nerve, whether I had it or not, they'd make me sorry.

They put their heads together. One of them stood up. "We'll see if he wants to talk to you, pal. If he don't ..." He let that hang as he lumbered through a door behind the bar. If Mickey didn't feel like talking to me, the tough guys would get to have their fun. But when the bruiser came back, he looked surprised and disappointed. Jerking a thumb toward that door, he said, "C'mon."

The door opened onto a narrow hallway with cramped dressing rooms on either side. My escort led me up a flight of stairs. Another doorway waited. The bruiser jerked his thumb again. I went in. He stayed right there.

Mickey's office would've suited a hotshot Hollywood lawyer. Big, airy, everything in it right up to the minute. But behind that battleship of a desk sat that dapper but tough little Jew. He had people rubbed out as casually as he took the foil off a stick of gum.

"Close the door, Mitchell," he said, so I did. He went on, "Have a seat." I did that, too. He pointed at my shoe box. "What you got there?"

I set it on the desk. "Bringing back some things the boys who visited me left behind."

He opened a desk drawer. If he pulled out a .45 …. But all he had was a scissors. He cut the string, took off the lid, and looked inside. An eyebrow jumped toward where his hairline had been once upon a time. He put the lid back on. "Not a bad haul. Okay. What now?"

So I told him about the stupid fight at the Basket Room, about the phone call I'd got, and about the fun earlier in the day. "I don't go out of my way to mess with your people. I wish you'd tell 'em not to mess with me," I finished.

He thought for a few seconds, then asked, "How'd you know they were in there waiting for you?"

"A crow tipped me off." I try not to deal with crows; you can't trust a word that comes out of their beaks. But I wasn't going to let him know about Mehitabel.

"How about that?" he murmured, his eyes as blank and shiny as glass. Some of the birds around my office were liable to be in for a hard time. I felt bad about it, but what can you do? Mickey's attention came back to me. "Well, okay. You didn't want anybody messing with your guy. I get that, even if the noise Ricks makes with that electric contraption is only fit for chasing dogs away."

"I kinda like it." I seemed to be saying that to everybody who'd heard Oscar play. He might've been making the music of the future, but he sure wasn't making the music of the present.

"Feh," Mickey said: more a disgusted noise than a word. Then he quit worrying about what the electric guitar sounded like. "Awright. Get on out of here. Nobody'll give you any more grief about that."

"Thanks. Appreciate it." I tried to sound like somebody entitled to an answer like that, somebody who hadn't looked for anything else. It felt more like moving forward right after a rifle round cracked by not nearly far enough over my head.

When I walked out of the office in one piece and happy with the world, the wide-shouldered fellow still waiting at the top of the stairway grimaced. He and his friend wouldn't get to have fun with me after all. Life was tough sometimes.

He took me downstairs. I nodded to him, nodded to his buddy, and headed for the door. "See ya," I said. Out on the sidewalk, I allowed myself a sigh of relief. I'd stuck my head in the lion's mouth, and he hadn't bitten down. This time.

When I got back to my office, Old Man Mose and Mehitabel looked about ready to bite down on each other. Bits of cat fuzz here and there said they'd already squared off a time or two. They both started telling me stories about how each of them was right and the other one was a monster.

"Knock it off. I don't want to hear it," I said. "You're both good kitties. Why don't you see if you can get along?"

"She tried to *wash* me!" Mose sounded as if that was an unforgivable sin. And, for him, it might have been. One of the things a cat means by washing another cat is *You aren't the boss here. I am.*

"Mose has been here for years. You'd better remember that," I told Mehitabel.

"Yeah, yeah," she said. Cats remember exactly what they want to remember, of course. Anything else, they cough up like a hairball.

"I mean it. You did me a favor. I'm paying you back. If you wear out your welcome, though …"

She daintily strode over, rubbed her head on my shin, and started to purr. Not to be outdone, Mose rolled over on his back on the sofa. I rubbed his tummy. Sometimes he tries to murder my hand when I do that. He decided he liked it now. The idea of having a couple of cats on their best behavior for a little while, each keeping an eye on the other and both watching me, held a certain appeal.

I sat down in the creaky chair behind the desk and waited for the phone to ring or for someone to knock on the door. As usual, I had a long wait. Mehitabel jumped up into my lap. Old Man Mose never does that. He's not a lap cat. Never has been. Never will be. Mehitabel curled up there. I stroked her. What else was I gonna do? She purred and then she went to sleep.

"What a phony," Mose said.

"It's nice," I said. He made a revolted noise. He knows what he thinks about laps, Mose does. He also had an opinion about Mehitabel—and the sense to keep quiet about it. I wondered what I'd do when I needed to stand up. Hey, you can have worse problems. And I'd already got a start on warming the chair for Mehitabel.

"You have cat hair on your lap," was the first thing Dora said when I walked into the apartment.

Before I said anything at all, I kissed her. That was always worth doing. Then I looked down at myself. Mehitabel had more white fur than Old Man Mose, and yes, it showed up against the dark brown slacks I was wearing. Then I realized what a busy day I'd had.

"Mehitabel saved me from a lot of trouble this morning," I said, and told her the story of the cat, the muscle boys, my trip to Hollywood to see Mickey, and how Mose and Mehitabel were and weren't getting along.

When I got done, she said, "Mickey worries me. He cares no more for ordinary people than one of us would. If he had decided you were a nuisance—" She mimed rubbing a spot off a mirror.

"Yeah, I know. But I had to take the chance. If I didn't, the ordinary thugs'd keep coming after me. Sooner or later, they'd either hurt me bad or punch my ticket for good. This way, he'll put a flea in their ear."

"He says he will."

"When those guys say things like that, they usually mean them. They've got to. You bargain with them, it's on their word and yours. Nobody'll sue anybody for breach of contract. They don't play by those rules."

She considered. "It could be. I have known such here and on the other side of the ocean. But if you change your mind, you can do less to him than he can to you if he changes his."

"So?" I shrugged. "I've always been on that end of the stick." I used the neighborhood's two-fingers-against-the-wrist gesture. I never would've done that with somebody darker than I am. I'm not entitled to, even if I understand it. I wasn't sure Dora did.

But she said, "You could get away from all that. Your looks would let you. Surely you must know as much." She followed me just fine.

"I could, yeah." My mother'd wanted to do that. She might well have passed. She couldn't try, though, not without leaving my darker father, and she wouldn't. She soured his life instead. Which made me go on, "I wouldn't be able to look myself in the eye if I did, though."

"You have pride." Dora said it as if reminding herself.

"I guess maybe I do. Pride is one of those things you can have when you don't have anything else."

This time, she kissed me. "What a Hungarian thing to say!"

We went out after that. We had a couple of drinks at a bar not far from the apartment. When she didn't drink Bloody Marys, Dora liked scotch. I stuck to Wild Turkey. Bourbon and beer have got me this far. I expect I'll stay with 'em a while longer.

Most of the folk in the bar were vampires. Dora gave me a fresh benison before we went in, to remind them I was hers. She carried weight in Vampire Village. All the same, I would've worried more in the days before blood banks. Bedford Tyler bared his fangs at me. He has an apartment in Dora's building, and he's, well, a piece of work: an undead, unreconstructed antebellum Southerner, God help us all.

I smiled back, not meaning it for a minute. But you can't let them know they scare you, especially when they do. He said, "Once upon a time, in the good ol' days ..." His drawl was thick enough to slice.

"Good for whom?" I asked. I tried not to think that he might have owned some of my relatives once upon a time.

"Foah the South. Foah the Los Cause, before it was lost."

I turned my back on him. Staying close to Dora, I could do that. He didn't push it. I hadn't thought he would. And I had had plenty of trouble for the day.

Vampires drink hard. They need to, to feel anything at all. And, by their lights, they have to hurry up with their boozing. Vampires and barkeeps in VV hate the two a.m. closing time. Customers leave when they're nowhere near ready to lie down in their coffins. That costs the bars money, but they haven't been able to get an exemption to the law.

After we left the bar, we went to a place that sold women's clothes. Dora bought a reddish brown linen dress that went with her green eyes and blond hair. She looked damn good in it. She looks damn good in anything, or nothing. Still, I couldn't help thinking the crayon makers would've called her dress burnt sienna.

As we were leaving, her with one of those bags with handles on her arm, I suddenly stopped short. "I need to see Mickey again!" I said.

"Why?" she asked, in lieu of *Are you out of your ever-lovin' mind?*

"Because if anybody can find out where that Lightning Rune vampire hides in the daytime, the mob can."

We walked on for a couple of steps before she said, "I ought to tell you this is the worst, the filthiest, thing I ever heard of. I ought to tell you mortals have no right to hunt my kind while the White Fire is in the sky. I ought to tell you we take care of our own."

"But … ?"

"But that one does not follow the rules of civilized behavior. He would have fed from you, would likely have glutted himself on you, even though you wore my mark. He would bring an *üldözés* down on all of us with his greedy madness."

"A what?" The word that mattered was in a language I didn't speak.

Dora had to think back to remember what she said. When she did, she laughed. "A pogrom, I should have said."

"Oh." Now I got it. I wasn't sure Rivke would have thought she should have said that, but I took the point. If anybody from a small group got out of line, or if people from a big group thought somebody from a small group did, those people would land on the small group with both feet.

After another few steps, Dora said, "This being so, your seeing Mickey may not be the worst thing in the world. If it causes inconvenience here in the Village, I will make certain no one takes it out on you."

"No one like Bedford, you mean," I said.

"Yes. Like him."

"Thanks, babe," I said from the bottom of my heart. Having vampires, especially that one, sore at me was the last thing I wanted.

We kept strolling along till we passed a secondhand bookshop. Like the clothing store, it was open. Places that weren't bars could keep vampire hours and stay busy sunset to sunrise. Dora paused to look in the window. Vampires love to read; VV is full of bookshops. When you have an unlimitedly long existence stretching out before you, nothing makes time go by like a good book.

When Dora stopped, so did I. I saw my reflection in the window. Not hers, of course; she didn't have one. I'd wondered why before. Who hasn't? Now—in a reflective mood, so to speak—I wondered again, more seriously. Our wizards and engineers, and no doubt the Reds', too, were bound to be trying to harness that effect and turn it into a weapon or a defense against a weapon.

She went in, and I followed. I grabbed one of those magazines with a wizard saving a pretty blond girl from a demon out of another dimension on the cover. I had time to kill myself. She bought a copy of John Gunther's *Inside U.S.A.* It was fat enough to keep her busy a while, for sure.

We took our booty, spoils, and plunder back to her place. She started in on the Gunther. I settled down to the story about the blond and the demon. It wasn't bad, but halfway through I wondered why she couldn't have been brown instead. Then I wondered why I'd needed so long to wonder. That was a while ago now. I still can't tell you.

Before I went to Hollywood, I stopped at the office to make sure Old Man Mose and Mehitabel hadn't murdered each other or wrecked the place. They had knocked an ashtray off my desk and spilled butts on the already-decrepit rug.

"Knock this off!" I told them in my fiercest voice as I cleaned up the mess. "You keep it up, you can both go out and hunt grasshoppers and sleep under cars, you hear?"

"Yes, sir." Mehitabel took me seriously.

"Yeah, yeah." Mose knew better. Pretty soon they'd both have me wrapped around their claws. But that'd be pretty soon. Meanwhile … Meanwhile, I rode the Red Car to Hollywood. Part of the route ran down the middle of the Hollywood Freeway, which kept pushing north and west toward the Valley. Some of the workers pushing it that way were zombies, dammit. I'd rescued one guy who'd been shanghaied into zombiehood, but how many more were still slaving away without any idea who they were or even that they were?

I didn't like to think about that, so I was glad when the trolley car went west on Hollywood Boulevard. I got off at Highland and rode the bus down to Mickey's Rhum Boogie. One of the guys I'd run into the afternoon before was there. "You again!" he said.

"Yeah, me again," I admitted. "I need to talk to your boss one more time."

"What about?"

"A vampire," I said. I don't know what he expected, but that wasn't it. He muttered to himself, but he went back to see if Mickey needed to talk to me. When he came out of that door behind the bar again, he gestured for me to go with him, so I guess Mickey did.

Into that fancy office. Mickey waved me into the chair. "Siddown. A vampire?"

"Uh-huh. A vampire. A vampire called Lothar Kreuzbach, who I think was an *Oberführer* in the *Blitzrunen* during the war."

He leaned forward. His chair didn't creak when he did. "Okay. I'm interested. Tell me more."

I told him what I knew. I told him what I suspected. I told him what I was guessing about. That the vampire might also be a werewolf was still a guess. I admitted as much.

He sat there thinking for a little while. Mickey was mean, but he wasn't anybody's dope. The mob sent him out here because he wasn't. Bugsy, who was here before him, had a lot more charm, but he didn't bring in the dough the way he should have. Mickey had an adding machine where most people keep a soul.

"You're liable to be right," he said when the wheels and cogs inside his head stopped spinning. "I know about the werewolf. Full-moon nights, people are scared to stick their noses outside. It hurts business for the clubs on Central—here, too. One day a month, sure, not a big bite, but a bite. If he's a vampire, too, that's double trouble. I've been thinking about getting silver bullets for some of my boys."

"Like the Lone Ranger?" I said, even though I'd had the same idea.

"Uh-huh, like the Lone Ranger. Hadn't thought of that, but yeah." Mickey chuckled. "Don't remember him fighting werewolves on the radio or in the movies."

"No, neither do I. There was that one two-reeler with the ghosts, but I can't think of any werewolves."

"Me, neither. They missed a trick." Mickey gave me maybe the chilliest once-over I've ever been on the receiving end of. "You seem to follow weird things around, Mitchell. A vampire girlfriend. A clown with an electric guitar. And now a werewolf? What is it with you, anyway?"

He knew about Dora. Well, he'd have ways to find out things like that. It made me nervous, though. But I had to answer the question. "Beats me," I said, no more than a heartbeat slower than I might have. "I guess the guy who's writing my story has it in for me."

He looked up at—no, through—the ceiling. I hadn't tabbed him for pious, but I could've been wrong. "We all wonder about that, I bet," he said, then went back to business: "Okay, we'll see what we can do. Dunno how much that is, but we'll find out. Happy?"

"You took me seriously. Sure, I'm happy. I didn't know if you would."

"You got balls coming here once. Coming back for this other thing …" He nodded at the door. "Go on now. Scram. I have my own fish to fry."

Scram I did. The bruiser outside eyed me with a certain respect as he took me downstairs: now I'd stuck my head in the lion's mouth twice, and got away with it both times. I nodded to him and touched thumb and forefinger to the brim of my fedora. Then I got the hell out of there.

Back at the office, my ashtray was on the floor again, and some other stuff, too. Old Man Mose and Mehitabel both radiated innocence so hard, I almost needed sunglasses. Ever been in a house with two-year-old twins? Cats are like that, only with pointy teeth and sharp claws. It's what makes them fun. And it's why they drive you crazy.

"I told you you'd better knock this off," I said, in my meanest, fiercest voice. I knew they wouldn't, not right away. But it only makes things worse if you let them think they can get away with stuff.

When I fed them, I gave them canned kidneys. I don't put that one out very often; it stinks up the office even worse than fish. I hoped they'd figure out I was punishing them. No such luck. They loved it.

"Give us this one more often!" Mose said when he came up for air.

"It's good!" Mehitabel agreed with her mouth full. One thing you learn if you're a baseball fan is, you won't win every game you play.

The cats might've been chasing each other around, but they didn't seem to want to kill each other. I counted my blessings, here where Dora couldn't hear me do it. Then I paid some bills. I wasn't rich, but I wasn't hiding from people I owed money to, the way I had been not so long before.

Of course, if the office stayed as quiet as it did for the rest of the day, I'd be back to stiffing folks and telling lies sooner than I wanted to be. "Play nice," I told the cats when I headed down toward Vampire Village. They were both sleeping, but they wouldn't've listened to me if they were wide awake. Cats don't. You have to try anyhow.

I ran into Rudolf Sebestyen on the way back to the apartment. By the way he came up to me, I don't think it was an accident. He greeted me with, "I saw that fellow who does not like anyone last night."

"Did you?" I said, and waited till he nodded. Then I asked, "Why didn't you do something about it?"

"He is too strong." He sounded embarrassed. "But he has not forgotten you, or how you burned him. He wants to repay you." Rudolf wanted to repay me, too. He didn't sound brokenhearted or anything.

"Burned him?"

Dora's half-brother shrugged. "His words."

"Oh." I left it there. But I'd burned a werewolf with silver, not a vampire. Which meant …

VIII

Gardena. Gardena meant getting up too goddamn early. It meant changing trolleys at the Slauson Tower. It meant rattling past that stinking RESTRICTED sign … and past the tract of houses going up like nobody's business behind the sign. It meant poker clubs on Vermont, and it meant getting off the Red Line car at Vermont and Gardena Boulevard.

Gardena. A town where nothing had ever happened and nothing ever would. A tinpot business district surrounded by acres and acres—hell, by square miles—of orchards and groves and all the other things you did with land when you didn't have enough people to live on it. Want to buy some strawberries? Figs? Christ, I missed Central!

A bus ride west to Normandie, then north past the high school. I got out, crossed the street, and headed for Grampus Records. I'd forgotten the restaurant with the WE RESERVE THE RIGHT TO REFUSE SERVICE TO ANYONE sign on the door. Forgetting it hadn't made it disappear, worse luck.

And then the record place. When I walked in, the secretary smiled. This was the second time I'd visited, and we'd talked in between, so we were practically old friends. "Good morning, Mister Mitchell," she said. "What brings you here today?"

"The Red Line," I answered.

She laughed more than the joke deserved. That she laughed at all was more than the joke deserved. "Let me tell Mister Jenkins you're here." She hurried into Jenkins' sanctum. I watched her hurrying. She was nice to look at, even if I knew I'd never do anything abut it. She came out a moment later, still smiling, and held the door open for me. "Go on in."

"Thanks." I smiled, too, as I walked past by her. None of it meant anything past *You're here and I'm here and we're both polite*. But that counts, too. When you aren't polite with strangers, you're liable to try to kill them, and they you. I'd had a bellyful of that in Italy. I was glad I came home in one piece. Too many guys didn't. Too many guys didn't come home at all.

Kirk Jenkins came out from behind his desk to shake my hand. More than Mickey did, but he didn't have Mickey's clout. "Morning, Mitchell," he said. "You're too early."

"Huh?" I said brilliantly.

"Oscar and his trio had a great session last night. They're pressed to wax, but I haven't started the clay, let alone the metal masters. That's for this afternoon. Then they go over to Danny Becker for duplication."

I hadn't had any idea Ricks had gone down to Gardena to record. I also realized I knew less than I should have about how the noises musicians make get turned into records you can play at home or in a jukebox (a mob-controlled jukebox, 'cause there's hardly any other kind). But I did know enough to say, "That's where the magic comes in—the sympathetic magic, I mean."

"There you go!" Jenkins beamed at me, the way anybody will when he finds out you understand at least a little bit about his racket. "Becker and his assistants will transfer the pattern from the master to the blanks that way. Untouched by human hands, you know."

"Uh-huh." I nodded. "I didn't come to talk about the recording session, though."

Jenkins seemed to realize all of a sudden we were both still standing up. He waved me to a chair, then sat down himself. When he lit a cigarette, so did I. He sucked in smoke, blew a stream at the ceiling, and asked, "What is on your mind, then?"

"Ever gone to an after-hours place called Deacon's?"

"I've been there once or twice. Crazy joint."

"Isn't it, though?"

"Yeah." He grinned at me. I grinned back at him. It's like bebop. If you know, you know. If you don't, telling you won't help. He went on, "Haven't been there in a while. Most of the time, the tariff's too steep for me." So either he was tight with his cash or running a record company wasn't a sure-fire highway to fame and fortune. I would have bet on the second choice. He blew out more smoke. "What brought that on?"

"Somebody trying to blackmail the guys who run the place."

"Oh. Mm, I can see how that might happen." Yeah, he knew about the Deacon and the Acolyte. He seemed to take them in stride, though, the way he took me. For a white man from that neck of the woods, he was pretty cool, Jenkins was. He asked the next reasonable question: "Why are you bringing it up with me?"

"Because the blackmail letters want answers sent to a Gardena post-office box. This isn't New York or Chicago, you know? I wondered if you could point me toward somebody who might want to do something like that."

"Nothing occurs to me off the top of my head," he said, stubbing out his coffin nail. Then he thought for real, and thought hard. I could practically hear the gears working inside his head. But he didn't give me a name. I'd hoped he would finger Danny Becker or somebody who worked for him. No such luck. My job is like baseball. You get a hit one time in three, you're a star.

"Okay. Thanks for letting me bend your ear," I said.

We shook hands again. I walked out of Grampus Records, past the restaurant where I wouldn't eat if I were starving to death, and down to the corner to wait for the southbound bus. When it stopped, I climbed aboard, thinking I'd take it east on Gardena Boulevard all the way to Main and then go north to 154th so I could visit Becker, too, and maybe see how his magic turned blank records into groovy ones.

But I got off before the bus went all the way from Normandie to Vermont. I was interested in the magic-supply place called Ancient Egypt the same way Dora was intrigued by the shops like that on Central. Magic is magic, but people from different places get where they're going by different roads.

Ancient Egyptian magic—if that's what the store dealt in, if the name wasn't just a lure—might be interesting. I'd bumped up against Assyrian magic when I was trying to find out what had happened to the poor guy who'd got shanghaied into zombiedom. I hadn't enjoyed that even a little bit. But Egyptian magic was older yet and—I hoped—less bloodthirsty.

A bell rang when I opened the door. The first thing I did, before I went all the way in, was sniff. Old Man Mose thinks people's noses are bad in general, and my smoke-filled one bad in particular. He's bound to be right, but one thing I've found is that every magic shop smells different.

Ancient Egypt was no exception. It smelled … how do you put smells into words? Not very well, that's how. It smelled as old as the Pyramids. The odor was partly earthy, partly meaty, partly spicy. I couldn't recall smelling anything like it before, but then all at once I did. One hot summer day, right after I'd gone into the line in Italy, I'd had to dig a foxhole in the middle of a graveyard our artillery and the fylfot boys' had churned up pretty well. When my entrenching tool dug into the dirt I'd smelled something close to this, only minus the spice.

"Good morning, sir," said the man behind the counter. "How may I help you today?" He was middle aged, heavyset, with a hairline that hadn't budged a quarter of an inch since he was twelve and a proud, formidable nose. He had brown skin—he was darker than I am—but not the kind of brown you usually see up in my part of town.

"What am I smelling?" I asked.

He smiled. His teeth were very white. "That would be mummy."

"Mummy? Isn't that taking the Ancient Egypt bit a little far?"

"You don't think I mean it," he said. It wasn't a question. I nodded because I didn't. But he went on, "It *is* mummy, sometimes human, sometimes from a cat or crocodile or other creature, mixed with myrrh and white pitch."

I started to call him a liar. I remembered that foxhole again. My nose told me he was liable to be telling the truth after all. So I took a different tack: "Where d'you get mummy?"

"From the Two Lands, of course, when I can." He paused till he was sure I understood he meant Egypt. "That is the most ancient, and of the highest quality. But it has been hard to come by since the war. Sometimes I must make do with supplies from the Canary Islands."

"Isn't that interesting?" I said, instead of something like *I'll be damned.* "What do people use it for?"

"It is sovereign against toothache and fluxes of the bowels. It also aids against consumption and pains in the stomach—ulcers, modern doctors would call them." By the way he spoke, he didn't have much use for modern doctors or modern anything else. After a moment, he added, "And artists use it for the warm shade they call mummy brown, though it will fade if left under bright light."

"How about that?" I said—one more phrase unlikely to land me in trouble. I came all the way into the shop, letting the door swing shut behind me. I paused again in front of a case full of scarabs. Some were of stone, others of faience, still others of brass; a few were actual dead beetles. Some of the stone and brass ones were upside down to show the hieroglyphs on their flat bottoms. "Can you read those?" I asked the shopkeeper.

"Not well, though I continue to study," he said. "I am Shenouda Youhanna. As my name will tell you, I am a Coptic Christian, which gives me a head start. The Coptic language, which we still use to pray to God, comes down from the old speech, but we write it in an alphabet mostly borrowed from Greek, so the ancient writing is not natural to me."

His name didn't tell me any such thing, but I nodded as if in wisdom. I pointed to an upside-down faience scarab whose shape and turquoisish color appealed to me. "Are you able to make out what that one says?"

"Let me see." He came out from behind the counter and plucked the scarab from the case. He frowned as he tried to decipher it. "I think it is a prayer to the goddess Isis. You have heard of Isis?"

"I have, yes. That's perfect. I've got a friend called Isidore. How much?" I didn't see any price tags on the case. Maybe Shenouda enjoyed haggling.

"This one? A dollar and a quarter," he answered. "Plus sales tax, of course."

I laughed. "Of course. But I wondered if it was an ancient relic. A buck and a quarter tells me no."

"I have ancient things here. This is not one of them, though. Over centuries, faience fades and turns brownish. This is a modern reproduction."

I laid out a paper Washington, a silver Washington, three Lincolns, and an old Indian-head penny I'd forgotten I had in my pocket. Shenouda put the scarab in a little paper bag. I stowed it away and turned to go. Then I swung back. "Does Danny Becker ever come in here?"

One of his eyebrows jumped. "Why do you want to know?" he asked, which meant *yes*. It also meant Shenouda would tell Becker about the snoopy guy inquiring about him the next time the wizard dropped by.

"Just curious," I said, bland as oatmeal without sugar. "I know him a little, and I know he's a very modern magician. I wondered if old sorcery interested him at all."

"To a student of the thaumaturgic arts, all aspects connect with all others," Shenouda replied. Since I'd had a similar thought not so long before, I didn't try to argue with him. I touched the brim of my hat and left.

Out on the sidewalk, I discovered one of my shoes needed tying—or I made as if it did. While I knelt, I glanced inside Ancient Egypt. Sure as hell, Shenouda Youhanna was using the telephone. I got to my feet and headed up Gardena Boulevard toward Vermont.

Somehow, it didn't seem like a great time for me to visit Danny Becker.

When I got to the office, Mose and Mehitabel were both asleep on the couch. That looked promising. I ran a sheet of paper into my old upright Underwood. I needed to tell a dry-cleaning place payment would be late—uh, later. The typewriter was massive enough to stop an antitank round from one of the fylfot boys' 88s and go on working. I've got a touch like a tap-dancing rhino on account of it, but it does the job.

What I wanted to say was *Dear Sirs*. What I saw on the paper was *DEAR SIRS*. I frowned. I know damn well I hadn't left the shift lock down last time I typed something, so I impersonated the Belgian guy with the silly mustache and the hairnet. My little gray cells didn't have to overheat or anything. "So," I asked the cats, "who's been jumping around on the typewriter?"

Old Man Mose stretched out a paw. "She did it."

"Capitals at last, Mehitabel?" I said.

"You cockroach!" Mehitabel said, not to me but to Mose for squealing on her.

"They're fun to chase. Don't taste real good, though." He missed the point, odds are accidentally on purpose.

As long as the cats weren't biting or clawing each other, they could bicker as much as they wanted. I took the letter I'd messed up out of the Underwood, crumpled it up, and flung it in the wastebasket. Some clever wizard ought to invent a way to fix a mistake you've typed if it's too big to erase without letting the whole world know what a fumblefingers you are. Come up with a spell like that and I bet you'd get rich.

My second try would do. Oh, I banged down an *e* on top of an *r* I'd hit instead, but everybody does stuff like that. I put the letter in an envelope, licked a stamp and stuck it on, then took it to the mailbox and dropped it in. If the dry cleaners got shirty, I'd give 'em what I owed. I would if they didn't, too. Eventually. I always pay my debts. Eventually.

That done, I took a nip of Wild Turkey—only a little one, only for to taste (I got that from an Italian who thought he spoke more English than he did). Wild Turkey makes the world a nicer place. It makes you not care so much when the phone doesn't ring. And it didn't. I put my feet up on my desk, pulled my hat down over my eyes … and Old Man Mose jumped onto my stomach before I could doze off. If Mehitabel could do it, he could, too. *He* fell asleep. Me? I couldn't. Life isn't fair.

The sun went down. I took Mose off me, got up, and closed the venetian blinds so nobody could snoop. Maybe something would happen if I hung around longer. Or, as I discovered, maybe not. I gave up and left, hoping the shift lock was the worst thing the cats could find to do.

Nobody much was on the street. Central is where things happen. Avalon, a few blocks west, can cook, too, especially when the Angels are at Wrigley Field. My office is on San Pedro, the next fair-sized street west. San Pedro has other things wrong with it, too. One is, it's dull.

I didn't let dull lull. I had one hand in my jacket pocket, ready to grab crucifix or holy water. My head was on a swivel, the way it would have been moving toward an enemy outpost line. I didn't know Kreuzbach was on the prowl, but I wanted to be ready in case he was.

More folks came out at night in Vampire Village. I saw several vampires I knew, and nodded to them the way I would have if I ran into an acquaintance on Central of a Saturday night. They nodded back the same way.

Things might not have been so friendly if I hadn't had Dora's benison on my forehead. People—live people—are of course vampires' preferred prey. Blood banks have blunted that brute fact without overturning it. If vampires had their druthers …

Every now and then, I wondered what life was like on the other side of the Blood Curtain, in the countries the Reds run. How much of a hold vampires have on those lands is something live people argue about all the time. Dora and Rudolf Sebestyen, having come out of Hungary and still doing business there when they can, know better than anybody live is likely to. They say very little.

Vampire horrors, though, are old and familiar. The whole civilized world joined the Moscow Reds to take on the new horror the fylfot boys' Leader called up—and if that doesn't give you a measure of the Leader's damnation, nothing ever will. Then again, Loathsome Lothar and a good many other vampires went with the fylfot boys against the Red regime. So did thousands and thousands of live people who thought they were a better bet than Moscow—and if that doesn't give you a measure of the Reds' damnation, nothing ever will.

Trying to work out all the complications made my head ache, and made me wish I'd drunk more Wild Turkey back at the office. Well, I could take care of that when I got to the apartment.

I wanted to kiss Dora when I got back, too, but the place was empty. She'd taped a note to the inside of the door. *Blood bank*, it said: short and to the point. It was too soon for her to take another pint from me, so she'd gone out and got pot luck, as it were.

With only myself for company, I heated up a can of spaghetti and meatballs. Had the meat in the meatballs neighed or barked before it went into the can? You know what? I hardly cared. Eating endless cans of Army rations will do that to you. So will eating endless tin bowls of whatever the cooks threw in the stewpot.

I washed supper down with bourbon. Then I cleaned up my mess. Thanks to going through the service, I knew how. Thanks to staying there with Dora, I knew I'd better.

Since I'd finished my pulp magazine, I was flipping through *Inside U.S.A.* when she came through the door without bothering to open it. "Hey, sweetie!" I said. I was glad to close the book; Gunther doesn't pull any punches when he talks about the South. Los Angeles isn't a great place for folks like me to live. What goes on in Dixie … reminds me why my folks got the hell out. The distance from bad to worse is a lot better than the one from good to better.

After we kissed, Dora said, "Doctor Berkowitz told me to give you his best."

"You saw Izzy? I wondered if you would when I read your note. I found a present for him down in Gardena this morning." I dug the little paper bag out of my inside jacket pocket and poured the scarab into the palm of my hand.

"Why would he care about this? He is a Jew." Back when she was alive, Dora'd been a Hungarian noblewoman. She'd thought of Jews the way any other Hungarian noblewoman would have—she hadn't thought much of them. But she knew Izzy and she knew America played by different rules, so she made an effort to get past her old feelings. Sometimes the effort was better than others. Pretty good tonight.

"Why?" I explained about Isidore and Isis.

"Oh." She thought for a moment. "Do Jews really believe a different name will protect them? It will not change their nature."

"It's not about protecting them, exactly. More about fitting in. When I was a kid, Al Simmons was a great ballplayer. Only his real name isn't Al Simmons. It's Aloysius Szymanski. Like that."

Dora cared nothing for baseball. For one thing, it's not the Hungarian national pastime. For another, till Al Simmons' career was winding down, they always played it during the daytime. She took my point even so. "Protective coloration," she said, as a predator would.

"Well, yeah," I said. Names like Simmons or Isidore weren't just protective coloration. But they weren't *not* protective coloration, either.

She noticed what I'd been reading. "What do you think of it?"

"I think I'm glad I don't live in Alabama," I answered from the bottom of my heart.

"I can understand that. Gunther also talks about a Pennsylvania coal-mining town that still has, next to city hall, an iron stake where they can chain the vampires they catch till the White Fire finishes them. Against the law now, but they have not taken the stake down."

A Pennsylvania mining town would be full of Hungarians and Poles and Bohemians and other people who loved vampires to death, and of their children whom they'd brought up in the old ways. The vampire equivalent of a sundown town, I guess, where if you were the wrong color you'd better not be there after dark.

"It's a club," I said. "You're a member. So am I. Izzy Berkowitz, too."

"What kind of club would take all three of us?" Dora asked. I don't think she had any trouble about belonging to a club with me. Whether she felt like being in one with Izzy .... That might've been a different story.

"A club where all the fine, ordinary people want to jump on the folks who're in it, that's what kind," I answered.

"Oh." She sounded thoughtful. She didn't try to tell me I was wrong, either.

I got nervous as the moon started fattening in the sky again. I didn't know I'd have werewolf trouble when it turned full, but I knew I could. That's a bad feeling. Say you're going along a road with buddies. You see a little stand of pines up ahead, a couple of hundred yards off to one side. You don't know that the fylfot boys have set up a couple of machine guns in among the trees, but you know they could. Like that.

One afternoon, I went downtown to check on something I haven't even bothered talking about till now. This silver-fox gal named Janine thought her lover boy was spending some of his cash on another cutie instead of her. He ran a numbers parlor out of the back of a laundry up there. More mob stuff, because of course they get their rakeoff from that kind of action. Or if they don't, you start having accidents.

Well, I can't tell you how much of his cash good-time Lester was laying out for this other lady. But it didn't take much digging to find out he was real friendly with not just one but two women who weren't paying me to check on him. Nice when you can earn your money fast. I mean, he didn't even bother hiding it. One of 'em worked in the laundry. He stashed the other in an apartment a couple of blocks away.

I had some time on my hands after I nailed that down, so I paid a call on Al Harris. His little shop wasn't far away. It was at 231-3/4 Hill Street. With an address like that, take two steps too many and you've walked right by it.

It doesn't go out of its way to show off, either. A tiny little sign says BOOKS, and under that MAGAZINES. If you don't already know it's there, you'll never find it. That suits Al fine.

A guy was coming out as I was about to go in. He'd bought something; he had a flat paper bag under one arm. He didn't meet my eye. I didn't meet his, either. Places like Al's have their own etiquette. Everybody pretends no one else is around. Officially, there are no places like Al's. Nobody goes to them, either. Not officially.

Inside, the place smells of pulp paper and of Al's cigarettes. He built the shelves and cases himself, to hold the stock with as little waste space as possible. That lets him cram in more of it. Al has something for everyone. Everyone who's a guy, I should say. I've never seen a woman in his joint. I don't expect I ever will.

One fellow in there was eyeballing a paperback called *Sailor Boys at Play*. He might have been a sailor boy himself, not in this last war but the one before. Another man, younger, was ogling a publication called *Two on One*. By the cover, the people in it were violating every commandment except maybe remembering the Sabbath day. They did seem to be having a good time doing it, I will say.

Yeah, that kind of bookstore. I looked at this and that myself, to keep from standing out. Some of it floated my boat, some I put back on the shelf in a hurry. Whoever liked *that* kind of thing ... was just another customer, as far as Al Harris was concerned.

The younger fellow bought his dirty magazine. The other guy put the book back and slid out. *No, I wasn't here. I never come here, not me*, his manner said. With nobody else in the place, I went up to the counter.

"Waddaya know?" Al said. He's a fat guy with a Brooklyn accent. He usually needs a shave. He did that day. He needed a shower, too. Hell of a nice guy, though. A sweetie. We've done this and that for each other for a while now.

"I know Lester's gonna catch it from Janine," I answered.

"On account of Brenda, you mean? Or Susie?"

I looked at him. "I just wasted three hours running all that down. I should've come here first."

He shrugged. His extra chins bounced up and down. "Lester stops by. Every so often, I waste a little dough with him. A buck, two bucks, nothin' that'll hurt if I lose it. He likes to talk, Lester does."

"He ever buy anything?"

"Blonds. He likes blonds."

"Well, who doesn't?" I said, thinking of Dora. Lester was as black as you can get. Janine, Brenda, and Susie were different shades of brown.

"If you're smart, you don't pick 'em for hair color." Al shrugged again. "*Nu*, some people ain't smart."

"I've got a question for you."

"Shoot."

"What do you do on full-moon nights, especially when a werewolf's on the loose? You stay open pretty late, so. ..."

"I don't worry about me. If it gets somebody, law of averages says it'll get somebody else. I tell Margie to stay inside, and to keep Skeeter in unless he's really gotta go out, and to get him back in as soon as he's done his business." Margie is Al's wife. Skeeter's their dog. I've seen pictures of him. He's fatter than Al. Imagine a friendly, furry bratwurst with short legs—that's Skeeter.

"Okay. That makes sense. You probably ought to keep doing it for a while." I lit a cigarette of my own. After a drag or two, I tapped the end in the ashtray on the counter. Then I said, "Ask you something else?"

"You're full of 'em today, aincha? Anybody'd think you snooped for a living or somethin'."

I took that for a yes. If it turned out to be a no, he'd tell me. "Where do you get the stuff you sell, anyhow?"

He didn't answer right away. Just when I started to think he wouldn't answer at all, he said, "Well, there's a lot o' little businesses like that out here. Photographers an' all, y'know. The girls come out to Hollywood sure they're gonna be stars, and then they ain't. They gotta eat some kinda way, so they do that an' hope nobody who knows 'em ever finds out. Biggest problem the guys who take the pictures have is finding people who'll print their mags for 'em."

"Thanks," I said. "I sorta figured it worked like that."

But Al hadn't finished. "The other folks I get my merchandise from, they're the same guys Lester gets his numbers from every day."

"The mob?" I don't know why I should've been surprised, but somehow I was.

"Right the first time. They charge more than the little outfits, too, even though their stuff mostly ain't as good. For them, it's just a business, y'know? Some o' the little guys, they think they're makin' art. Hell, they may even be right. But you don't wanna tell the mob to go take a hike. It's a cost o' doin' business, like payin' off the vice cops to leave me alone."

"Do you write it off your taxes?"

"Bet your butt, I do. Business expenses, right? I got receipts. They say books. They say magazines. What kind? The tax guys don't care. I collect sales tax for the state, too. All those bastards make money offa me."

He sounded offended, the way any upstanding small businessman would have. St. Al the Dirty Book Dealer. I'm sure he would've joined the Chamber of Commerce if they'd let him. As things were, some of the members probably came to him … as long as their wives didn't find out.

Before I could find anything else to say, his bell rang. Somebody else who would loudly tell you he never visited places like this was visiting a place like this. I stubbed out my Old Gold. "See you," I said. "Take care of yourself."

"You, too," Al answered. "Give Dora my best."

"I'll do it." I headed for the door. The new customer didn't look at me. I didn't look at him, either. I eased myself out onto the grimy sidewalk and headed for the trolley stop.

Since I'd taken care of Mose and Mehitabel before I went looking into Lecherous Lester, I rode the Red Car all the way down to Vampire Village. I didn't feel like sitting in the office waiting for the phone not to ring. The sun was sinking toward the Pacific by the time I got to VV. The place would get moving pretty soon. That was more than I could say about what would go on at the office unless the cats started brawling.

Dora's coffin hadn't opened yet when I walked into the apartment. I sat down and started looking at *Inside U.S.A.* It's a book where you can go straight through or hop around. Hopping, I chanced on the story of that Pennsylvania mining town Dora'd mentioned. The folks who did things like that were sure they were fine, upstanding Americans. So were the gentlemen farther south who liked to put on hoods and burn crosses.

Colored guys who'd been in the service had found out that people in Albion and Gaul treated them like human beings, not like—well, you know. They wondered how the hooded crossburners were any different from the fylfot boys. Damn good question when you get down to it, eh? There'd already been trouble about that down South. There was liable to be more.

A noise made me set the book down. Dora'd opened the coffin and was sitting up inside. Being undead wasn't like sleeping; she hadn't been there at all during the day. "I did not look for you to be here before I returned myself," she said.

"For once, I had some work that was easier than I expected. Oh—and Al Harris says hello."

"He is polite. I do not think we have ever met in the flesh."

"You'd remember if you had. Al's got a lot of flesh to meet. And he knows Rudolf—I can't tell you how, but some kind of way."

"It seems unlikely that Rudolf would stop at his establishment for the sake of what he sells—although, with men, one never knows about such things." Dora's scorn covered every single member of the human race with a member. I started to get huffy. Then I realized, first, that she had considerable experience of men; and, second, that she had to be hoping to get a rise out of me.

So all I said was, "Men seem to like to look more than women do. I don't know if that's true with vampires, but it sure is with ordinary guys."

"You are the one who leaves the light on in the bedroom," she ... agreed? But then she decided that wouldn't quite do. She added, "And, little by little, you begin to learn."

"Thanks, babe," I said from the bottom of my heart. From somebody I still didn't know how much older than I am, that was no small compliment.

Her mouth twisted, the way it usually did when I called her babe or sweetie or honey or anything like that. It bothered her. But not saying those things bothered me, because I felt them. I kept coming out with them, and she kept wincing. She wasn't annoyed enough about it to fight, not this time. Instead, she asked, "What do you want to do tonight?"

"Let me fix myself some grub, and then we can do whatever you feel like." I didn't aim to fight, either.

Dora nodded, so I did up a can of corned-beef hash. Afterwards, I made a salad with half an avocado, a cut-up tomato, and some green onions; it let me pretend I was eating something good for me. After I cleaned up, I looked a question at her.

"Let us go out," she said. I came to attention and gave her my best salute. Her smile showed off her fangs.

She headed north and east instead of staying in VV. Even on a weeknight, Central Avenue is the place to be. Oh, yeah, Hollywood Boulevard. The Sunset Strip. I can go to places there and probably not get thrown out. Doesn't mean I want to. Passing always leaves a bad taste in my mouth. I know that isn't true for everybody like me. I'm not telling anybody else how to live; I'm just saying what I do. For me, it's Central.

We stopped at Margot for a drink or two. It's just north of Vampire Village, a few blocks down from most of the clubs. They see vampires in there all the time, and take them in stride. I got myself a Wild Turkey. Dora ordered scotch. She mostly does in places where the Bloody Marys come with tomato juice.

"Do you really like that stuff?" I asked her.

"It is liquor. It is what the Hungarian aristocrats would drink to show how sophisticated they were." Dora paused. "I would expect the new Red aristocrats in Hungary also drink scotch, and for the same reason. They will be lying, too. They are even more provincial than the old nobility." She didn't bother hiding her contempt.

"How many of them are vampires?" I asked. For the *Are you now or have you ever been?* crowd, that is *the* question, way more than *To be or not to be?* They use vampires the way the guys with hoods who burn crosses use Negroes, the way the fylfot boys used Jews: somebody to point at to make ordinary people angry and scared.

"A fair number," she answered after a noticeable pause for thought. "A fair number are Jews, too, no doubt for the same reason: to make most Hungarians fear and hate." Yeah, we were thinking along with each other. She went on, "This is as Moscow arranged it. The Reds there want their puppet regimes to remember on whom they depend for power."

I hadn't taken that extra step, not by myself. But it fit. Good old Uncle Joe stopped being good old Uncle Joe the minute the fylfot boys surrendered. After that, he was in it for himself, nobody else. Before that, too, I'm sure. But after that it was obvious.

"Is Uncle Joe … ?" I didn't finish the question.

Dora understood me anyhow. "I cannot tell you that. It is a matter for debate among my folk, just as it is among the warm. I hope not. There are individuals with whom one would rather not be associated."

"The *Blitzrunen Oberf*," I said.

"Yes, he is one. So much of what he wished to accomplish, though, they have achieved in Moscow. Next to the Red rulers there, he is only a model or a toy. That must gnaw at his liver the way the eagle gnawed Prometheus'."

"I thought it was a vulture."

"An eagle," Dora said firmly. For all I could prove, she'd known Prometheus personally, or known others who'd known him. I didn't have the nerve to try to tell her she was wrong.

We went to a few of the clubs. The jazz didn't do what I needed, not that night. It should take you out of yourself, make you forget your troubles while you listen to the hep cats blowing. It should, but it didn't, not for me, not then. The goddamn world was too much with me. Or maybe I just felt the eagle's beak in my own belly, assuming there's any difference between those two.

IX

Janine stopped by the office the next day to see what I'd found about her two-timing boyfriend. Old Man Mose disappeared under the sofa when she knocked, the way he does. Mehitabel stayed on the arm of the sofa to find out what was going on. That was interesting.

As she had when she hired me, Janine wore her silver fox jacket over a nice dress. Silver fox ain't mink. I'm sure Janine understood that. But along Central Avenue, it's just about as good. It's what you put on to show the world your man knows how to treat you right.

Which, of course, Lester wasn't doing. He wasn't two-timing Janine. He was three-timing her. She listened to what I had to tell her, then said, "You sure about all that?"

"Afraid I am. I'm sorry," I answered. "I dug all this out myself, and then later on I ran into somebody who'd heard it on the street."

"Probably heard it from Lester his ownself. That man, he does like to run his mouth," Janine said, as Al Harris had before her. She shook her head, more in anger than in sorrow. "Brenda *and* Susie? Really?"

"Afraid so." I tried to show as much sympathy as I could. She still owed me fifty smackers, and I didn't want her storming out of there without paying me.

"Separate or together?" she demanded.

That caught me by surprise. "I'm sorry. I didn't try to find out. Do you need photos?" I hoped like hell she didn't. She wasn't married to Lester, so she couldn't very well divorce him. Evidence in a divorce case is mostly why people want those pictures. I'd got them a few times; any private eye will have. It's one of the most dangerous parts of the job, though. Folks don't *like* getting interrupted at a moment like that.

But Janine shook her head again. "Nah. I just wondered, is all." She unsnapped her little handbag—all sequins and rhinestones—pulled out two twenties and a ten, and threw them on my desk. "Here. We're square."

"Thank you very much." I meant it. Getting money after you've given a client bad news isn't usually so easy. "Uh, what will you do now that you know?"

"Me?" Janine got to her feet. She was a nicely made woman, a bit on the chunky side. The way she stood there made me realize most of that was solid muscle, not fat. "I'm gonna tear that cheatin' bastard's head off an' piss in the hole, that's what I'm gonna do."

She didn't sound like somebody who was kidding. "If the street knows he's running around on you, the cops won't need long to work it out, too," I said quickly.

"Screw the *po*lice!" Janine said with magnificent contempt. But then she saw I was serious. "Yeah, yeah, Mister Mitchell, I ain't gonna do that for real. You better believe I'm gonna make him sorry, though. And Brenda. And Susie."

"Separate or together?" I asked, straight-faced.

She looked at me. Instead of getting angry, she started to laugh. In fact, she laughed till tears gullied her powder and paint. "You're a devil, you are!"

"At your service, ma'am."

Still laughing, she left. I didn't think Lester would be laughing once she got done with him. Or Brenda. Or Susie. Even without homicide on her mind, Janine was nobody you'd want sore at you.

I gathered up the money and put it in my wallet. Mehitabel asked, "Why do people get so excited about those little pieces of paper? You can't eat them."

Talking with cats about money is hopeless. I knew that; I'd gone round the barn with Mose a good many times. Maybe it'd be different with Mehitabel. "No, I can't eat them. But I can give them to a storekeeper and get food for myself from him—or food for you."

"Well, food for me is important," Mehitabel said. "But what does the storekeeper do with the papers, then? Can *he* eat them?"

"No. But suppose it's cold outside and he needs a coat to stay warm. He can give those papers to the person who sells coats and get one for them."

"People skins," Mehitabel muttered. Like Old Man Mose, she thought humans were strange for not looking the same all the time. But she knew I was me because I always smelled like me and sounded like me. Looking different mattered less to her than either of those. She asked, "Can you use any old papers for that?"

"No, only special ones," I said. Cats don't understand reading, either. And they really don't understand governments. Trying to imagine a government of cats is like trying to imagine hot snow. The words are there, but the thing can't possibly be real.

Mose came out from his foxhole. He washed himself for a little while, then said, "You see? Humans are crazy."

"How can they be crazy when they know how to open the things with our food on the inside?" Mehitabel said.

"There is that," Mose admitted.

Instead of laughing at him for admitting such a thing, Mehitabel said, "I feel funny. I feel … different."

"Funny how?" I asked. If I needed to take her to the vet, he'd want cash up front. I'd stiffed him as long as I could with a couple of bills for Mose. Oh, I'd eventually paid him—I eventually pay everybody—but I'd been slower than usual, and usual isn't fast. So was I apprehensive? Oh, maybe a little.

"You smell different." Old Man Mose studied Mehitabel with a new intensity. "You smell … interesting."

Was she coming into heat? Would she be yowling in my cramped office? Would there be kittens down the road? If there were, on whom could I palm them off? All good questions. I had answers for exactly none.

And I did what I'd done a time or two in Italy when the fylfot boys hit a soft spot in our lines with mortars and machine guns. I retreated. Fast. Whatever the cats got up to, I didn't want to know about it. I didn't even want to think about it.

So Hilda and the answering service took care of whatever calls I got for the rest of the day. I bought something to eat on San Pedro instead of heating up a can of stew or hash on my hot plate. Then I went back to the apartment.

Dora was just out of her coffin. When I told her what was going on with Mose and Mehitabel, she said, "No kittens here."

I sighed. Kittens are enormous fun before they turn into cats. They're fun afterwards, too, but not the same way. "I wish vampires liked cats better," I said, because I knew I couldn't win an argument about that.

"Then change the way they taste. Change the way they smell," Dora said.

"You don't have to feed off them."

"I still smell them. If you must have them at your office, you must, but not here," she said. No, no give at all, not that I'd expected any.

A couple of nights later, we were walking up Central Avenue, the full moon bright and golden in the east, off to our right. Dora said, "It reminds me of a ducat in the sky."

"You pick your goldpiece, I'll pick mine. Most of the time, I'd say it looked like a double eagle," I answered. "Right now, though, I'm afraid it looks like trouble."

"Yes, there is that." She looked worried. "I wish the werewolf would go and torment some other part of town and leave us alone." Live people aren't the only ones who prefer their troubles at a nice, convenient, safe distance.

"That would be good, yeah." I didn't think it was likely, and I'm sure Dora didn't, either. To keep from thinking about it—and to keep from thinking about much of anything—I put my arm around her shoulder, which was always worth doing. "I love you, babe."

Okay, I made her stop thinking about werewolves. "I wish you would not say that," she told me in a voice like Himalayan winter.

"How come? You know it's true."

"And you know I cannot love you back. A wise man—a live man—once defined love as that state where someone else's happiness is more important to you than your own."

"Whoever he was, he sure sounds like a wise guy—uh, a wise man."

"You always joke when things are serious." She sounded exasperated. "Caring for anybody more than myself is not something of which vampires are capable. I cannot love you. I cannot love anyone."

"However you want to put it, we've done fine so far."

"And what will happen as the years go by? You will change and find someone else, someone alive." She didn't say Rivke's name, but it hung in the air between us all the same. "Or you will grow old and die, and I … I will go on. That is what vampires do. We go on until we finish. We do not change."

"I'm not worrying about years going by. Sufficient unto the day is the evil thereof," I answered.

For me, it was just a saying. Dora, though, Dora flinched as if I'd slapped her. "I know Who said those words. I know from which Book they come. They pain me to my heart."

"Oh, honey, I'm sorry!" I felt awful, or whatever's three steps down from that.

"I have borne worse," she said. "Usually, you are most careful."

"I wouldn't hurt you for anything."

"I shall recover." Of course she was brave. That made it worse.

When we got to Central, we went past a couple of parked police cars, their overhead lights flashing. Two cops were using their nightsticks on a colored kid. Two more stood by, pistols drawn and ready. "Move along!" they shouted in ragged chorus. "Everybody move along! Keep moving!"

And, God help me, I did. And that pained *me* to the heart. What had the kid done? Anything? If you're brown enough, you don't have to do anything to get worked out on like that. As I looked back over my shoulder, the cops who'd been pounding on the kid grabbed him and threw him into the back of one of the police cars. They banged his head on the top of the door frame, but that didn't bother them. They laughed about it, in fact. Then they zoomed away. The other two LAPD men holstered their revolvers, got back into the second car, and started patrolling again.

All that's part of the Central Avenue scene, too. The white folks who come there enjoy it as much as they dig the jazz at Club Alabam. The people who live around there .... Well, what can they do? This arrest probably wouldn't even make the inside pages of the *Lookout*. If you hadn't seen it with your own eyes, you'd never know it happened.

But I had.

So had Dora. She set a cool, pale hand on my arm for a moment. Quietly, she said, "This is how an occupying army behaves. I have seen a few in my time, or more than a few."

"Yeah, I know." I was holding in as much as I could. As I say, I'd seen how the fylfot boys occupied Italy. Oh, the LAPD wasn't quite that bad—not this time, anyway. The kid wouldn't die. Sooner or later, he'd get out of jail. The cops didn't leave his bleeding body on the sidewalk to make people who saw it thoughtful. Not this time. But the difference between the one set of occupiers and the other wasn't nearly so big as it should have been.

"Maybe we ought to have a drink before we go any farther," Dora said.

"Maybe we should." I was keyed up and jumpy and ready for trouble, so ready I looked forward to running into the werewolf. I wanted to kick its butt. I needed something to take the edge off.

We ducked into the first bar we came to. Everybody stared at us. I saw right away it was a place for locals, not one where people who weren't from there stopped in very often. They saw ... two white people. A big guy asked me, "Man, what you doin' here?"

"Getting the taste of watching cops kick the snot out of a kid down the street out of my mouth," I answered. I was ready to take him on, too, and everybody else in there.

He had another look at me. Then he looked at Dora again, too. Just for a second, she let him see her fangs. After a deep breath, he said, "Couple o' open stools at the bar."

And after that, we were among friends. They liked that I drank Wild Turkey. A lot of them were drinking bourbon, too, the ones who weren't drinking beer. If Dora hadn't been a vampire, they might have rolled their eyes at her scotch. As it was, they didn't let it bother them.

I told the story of the LAPD and the kid several times. "Maybe he did something. Maybe it was something bad," I said. "But even if it was, they could've just put him in the car and taken him away. There were four of 'em."

"This here's supposed to be the United States of America," the big man said. His name was Henry.

"This *is* the United States of America. The part they don't talk about so much," I replied.

We had a couple of drinks there. Henry bought for us the second time. I got him a fresh boilermaker when he ran dry, too. I didn't have to watch my back when we left.

"That could have been trouble," Dora said once we'd got a few doors north of the place.

"I know." The I-want-to-fight-everything had dribbled out of me. "They had to figure out we weren't what they thought we were at first." I stopped and kicked at the concrete under my feet. Much good it did me. "Only we *are*, dammit. Or we can be. What the cops did to that fellow, they'd do to anybody in that bar. And they'd laugh while they were doing it, too. Anybody but us. With us, they'd think twice."

"A policeman who laid a hand on me would regret it very quickly." Dora still had the hauteur of the noblewoman she'd been while she was alive—and, I gathered, for a long time after she became a vampire.

Me, I studied at a different school. You never argued with cops. You always did what they told you to. You weren't safe that way, but you were safer. If you grew up anywhere near Central Avenue, your mama and your daddy made damn sure you learned that lesson. They beat it into you if they had to.

We kept walking. I paused at a familiar corner. "Deacon's?" I asked.

"Deacon's," Dora agreed. So we turned away from the bright lights and into the darkness.

Up those rickety stairs. Along the even more rickety boardwalk. Through the blackout curtains—probably the only working blackout curtains in L.A. since the second year of the war, when everybody realized the Knights of Bushido couldn't fly their dragons far enough to burn down the city.

On the other side of the curtains stood Deacon Washington, big as life—which, for him, was saying a lot. He smiled a peculiar smile when he saw us. "Look what the cat dragged in!"

"Listen, if you want us to start paying you again, we can do that," I said. I didn't want to get on his bad side, not for anything.

He shook his head. "Desmond made the deal. I'll live with it. If you don't understand that some things matter more than the bottom line, are you really a man at all?" He eyed Dora. "Excuse me. A person, I should say."

As a noblewoman would, she graciously inclined her head. "Thank you. I appreciate that."

"I don't want to offend anybody unless I want to offend somebody," Deacon Washington said, tacking on a rumbling chuckle. He was queer as all get out, but he never played at being a girl. That wasn't his style. He waved us through another set of blackout curtains. "Have yourselves a time, friends."

Cigarette smoke. Cigar smoke. Pipe smoke. Reefer smoke. Incense. I don't know what all else. Your nose worked overtime at Deacon's. Your eyeballs, too, what with the lamps with different colored bulbs and the mirrors and the curtains. The house combo was noodling away to give everyone's ears something to do. Deacon's is a lot of things. Dull it isn't.

Dora and I planted ourselves on a low divan nobody else was using. A pretty girl came by to find out what we wanted to drink. I asked for Wild Turkey. Dora got a Bloody Mary. The girl seemed to expect money, so I forked over.

But when she brought us the drinks, she gave me back my double sawbuck. "Pablo says you're on the house." Pablo couldn't see us from where he was, but what we wanted must've told him who we were. The girl swayed away. She was something else to keep your eyes amused.

Wild Turkey is Wild Turkey. You can't mess it up. "How's yours?" I asked Dora. "Is it the McCoy?"

"Yes, it has blood in it. Deacon Washington knows how to please his clientele. That is one of the reasons I enjoy coming here. Being an outsider—doubly an outsider, I should say—he cares about people no matter of what sort they may be."

That *doubly an outsider* hit home. Of course being a Negro put the Deacon on the outside looking in right from the stop. Being a queer on top of that, or alongside it .... You can't hide your color. The other, you can. Most queers do, black or white. But hiding had never been Deacon Washington's MO, maybe because he was too big to hide, maybe because he was who he was. *This is how I work,* he might as well have shouted to the world. *You don't like it? Too damn bad.*

He paid off the Vice Squad so they didn't give Deacon's a hard time. As far as I knew, he didn't pay them off to leave him alone. I can't tell you whether Acolyte Adams did.

We had another drink. Then we found one of those dark, quiet almost-caves that didn't have anybody else in it right then. Anything can happen at Deacon's. Exactly what did happen in that little niche is nobody's business but ours. That Dora can see in the dark at least as well as Old Man Mose helped us make ourselves presentable again before we left the place to someone else, or to another friendly couple.

We came out just in time to hear the Deacon go, "Folks, fronting the boys tonight will be L.A.'s own Art Pepper! Let's hear it for him!"

I blistered my palms but good. I'd heard Art Pepper playing on Central before either one of us went into the Army. Bird is the only cat I know who can blow a meaner sax than Art Pepper, and when Art's on he can give even Charlie a run for his money. On his game, I mean, not on junk. He and Bird have that in common, too. Is there a connection between the needle and how they play? That's for God to answer, not me.

"Why does he not get a bigger hand?" Dora whispered to me.

"Your guess is as good as mine, babe," I answered, also quietly. Oh, I knew why, but I didn't feel like talking about it. Thing is, Art Pepper's a white guy. Some people will say that means he can't match colored jazzmen because he didn't get the music through the titty, if you know what I mean. Even some jazzmen say that.

Thing is, though, if you listen to Pepper with your eyes closed, you won't know he didn't grow up right around this part of town. Mezz is like that, too. I won't lie; most white fellows who play jazz sound like people speaking a foreign language. They may speak it well, but you can hear the accent. Not Art Pepper. I don't know how he knows, but he knows.

He was on that night, too. I can't say if he shot up before he came out. He wasn't nodding or anything, but that might just mean he'd gauged the dose right. Or maybe wishing he'd stuck more in put the sorrow in his sax. One of these days, he'll land in prison. Being white won't save him, not when it's H. I hope I hear him a lot before he does.

I will say the applause he got after his set was louder than the crowd gave him when Deacon Washington introduced him. He looked happy and surprised. He knew he didn't always get the respect he deserved. I'm sure he knew why, too. He soldiered on anyhow, the way you do when the music has you as hard as the junk does.

Once things quieted down a bit, Acolyte Adams came over to me and asked, "Have you got anything new?"

"Not much," I admitted. "Have you heard anything new from your friend?"

"Friend!" He spat the word. "No, thank—" He remembered Dora. "Thank you very much."

"Thank *you* very much," Dora said quietly. Not everyone would have recalled how hearing God's name wounded her.

"Er, yes. Of course." Acolyte Adams sounded embarrassed. As was true of many a self-made gentleman, failing at the role upset him more than it would have bothered somebody born to it.

"What do you think of the Pepper kid?" I asked him, as much to distract him as for any other reason. Art Pepper was three or four years younger than I am, so naturally he seemed like a kid to me.

"He feels it. You have to give him that, in spite of ..." He didn't finish the sentence, or need to.

And he got it right. Pepper did feel it, and never mind he was white. You can't get away from black and white, not even on the piano. On the sax, though .... Sometimes, if you're lucky, maybe you can. For a little while, anyhow.

Now our moonshadows stretched east of us, where they'd stretched to the west when we went up to Central. Deacon's is an after-hours joint. It doesn't close down at two in the morning, the way regular bars do. Twilight turned the eastern horizon pale when we left, and began washing out even the shadows the full moon cast.

"Will you need to fly back to your coffin?" I asked Dora. "If you have to, just go. Don't take chances on account of me."

"I should be all right. If I am not, you may be certain I shall not endanger myself." She sounded amused and indulgent—yes, she was mothering me again.

Sometimes, being treated like a short-pants brat made me sore. This time, for whatever reason, it didn't bother me so much. "Okay, babe. I worry about you, that's all," I said, and then, "Must be love or something."

"Or something," she echoed, not indulgently at all. "Believe me, I am quite capable of managing my own affairs."

I couldn't very well tell her she was wrong. I did the next best thing—I changed the subject: "At least we haven't heard the werewolf tonight. Maybe the *Oberführer*'s on vacation." Yeah, I joked about him. If you don't joke, you start going crazy pretty damn quick.

Dora didn't think it was funny. "If that person is both vampire and werewolf, he endangers the living and the undead alike."

One more time, I couldn't argue with her. And then, as if on cue, I did hear the werewolf howl, somewhere not nearly far enough away. At the end of that dreadful noise, others came in: a small chorus of yips and yaps and yelps.

"Those are the strangest-sounding coyotes I ever heard," I said. "I didn't know there were such things as werecoyotes, anyway."

"Not coyotes." Dora's voice couldn't have been any flatter if she'd run over it with a steamroller. "Those are jackals. We have them in Hungary—the golden kind. They also live in Egypt. The deity called Anubis takes his form from them."

Naming Anubis didn't faze her one bit. That meant something, but what? That Anubis wasn't a real god? I don't think so. If any god is real, all gods are real. Some are more powerful than others, that's all. And the yips and yaps made the hair stand up on the backs of my hands.

"Maybe you'd better fly," I said. "If Loathsome Lothar's a werewolf, he won't be able to come after you—or I sure hope he won't." I tried to imagine a werewolf with a vampire's batwings. The picture didn't want to form. A Hollywood special-effects man might've managed, but I couldn't.

Had she been a live person, Dora probably would have said something like, *I don't want to leave you.* But she was a vampire, as she kept reminding me. She nodded and answered, "That is a sensible suggestion." Next thing I knew, she wasn't in human form any more. A second after that, she flew away.

Which left me all by myself. I'd been as ready as I knew how to make myself. I pulled a bunch of silver dimes out of a pocket and threw them on the street behind me. They jingled sweetly and rolled every which way. I grabbed some more and kept them in my clenched fist, all nice and ready to fling. Then I started moving faster myself.

I didn't look back. Carpetbag Booker had it right—something might've been gaining on me. And old Carpetbag—and he *is* old, somewhere between forty and fifty: damn old for a baseball player—is pitching for the Tribe these days. That never could've happened before the war. One thing the fylfot boys did was, they showed us what hate was when you let it run wild. Some of us, I hope, got the message. The ones who didn't … might've been the jackals following the werewolf.

Then I heard another howl behind me, a howl of pain. I did look back for that. The wolf and four jackals all looked to have hotfoots? Hotfeet? Whatever you wanted to call the injuries, the werebeasts didn't like stepping on dimes.

I let them hear I had more dimes in my hand, too. Nothing rings like silver. The wolf snarled horribly. One of the jackals howled. None of the creatures felt like coming after me, so I went on my way.

When I walked into the apartment, Dora was about to climb into her coffin. She paused long enough to say, "I am glad to see you again, Jack."

"I'm glad to be seen, too," I answered. She shut the lid on me; I don't suppose I can blame her. The sun came up for real a few minutes later. Out on the street, those dimes would be shining. Scroungers would have fun. I didn't care. I'd never spent money better.

I got a spicy shrimp salad at El Burro Loco. The shrimp were big enough to be lobsters in training. They don't stint there, not even a little bit. Izzy ordered tongue stewed with cactus leaves and pepper and I don't know what all else.

Before I started making a pig of myself, I dug the scarab I'd bought at Ancient Egypt out of my pocket and slid it across the table to him. "Here. I found this for you," I said.

He looked at the beetle, then turned the scarab over and eyeballed the hieroglyphic inscription on the flat side. "Thanks—I think," he said. "Any particular reason?" That translated into English as *Are you all the way nuts or just mostly?*

"The guy who sold it to me said it was a prayer to Isis. I don't think he was lying just to make me part with a little dough."

"If this thing is as old as it looks, you spent more than a little."

"It's not, and I didn't. It's a modern copy of an ancient one. From what he told me, faience fades or gets discolored when it's as old as it'd have to be to come out of an Egyptian tomb."

"Well, what do you know? Okay, I've learned something today. Thanks." Izzy Berkowitz put the scarab in his jacket pocket. "I don't think I'm gonna tell my dad I got this, but I like it. Whatever else you can say about it, it's pretty."

"Uh-huh. The shop had a little case full of 'em. Some really were antiques, or the fellow said they were. He priced 'em that way, too."

Izzy grinned at me. "Was he an ancient Egyptian himself?"

"Pretty close. He was a Coptic Christian. By the way he made it sound, you won't come any closer than that these days."

"From the little bit of poking around I've done 'cause I've got the name I do, I'd say he's right." Izzy started eating. A slow smile spread across his face. "That's so good, it might be illegal."

I cut one of my shrimp in thirds—that's how big it was. Lime juice, garlic, enough in the way of peppers to make you start sweating and to clear out your sinuses whether they needed clearing or not. "Yeah!" I said, and grabbed a bottle of Mexican soda to help put out the fire. Beer would have worked better, but the place didn't have a liquor license.

For a while, neither one of us said anything much. We were too busy chowing down, first because we were hungry and then because we were enjoying what we had. After a while, once we started to be able to see bottom, Izzy paused long enough to ask, "So what brings you up to this neck of the woods?"

I told him about my adventures on the night of the full moon. He looked at me. "Werejackals?"

"That's what Dora said they were. They didn't sound like coyotes. I saw 'em well enough—it was getting light out—to say they didn't quite look like coyotes, either."

"Werejackals," he repeated, and smacked his lips almost the way he had over the stewed tongue. "I haven't checked the literature, mind you, but as far as I know werejackals have never been reported in Southern California before, or anywhere else in this country west of the Mississippi. Up in Canada once or twice, but Canada has more of a connection to parts of the Albionese Empire where jackals live than we do. You're positive they were were-?"

"They sure didn't like stepping on the dimes I threw into the street to slow 'em down."

He nodded, more to himself than to me. "Okay, they were were-, all right. Hard to get more diagnostic than that."

"The other thing that brought me up here was to find out whether you'd been able to learn whether dear *Oberführer* Kreuzbach can be a vampire and then a werewolf on the same night, or is he a vampire most nights and a werewolf all night when the moon is full?"

"Oh. Kreuzbach. Yeah." Izzy looked unhappy. The werejackals intrigued him so much, he didn't feel like shifting gears. "*Ma nishtanah halailah hazeh, mikol ha laylos?*" he said, or something like that. I'm afraid I just looked at him. He smiled crookedly. "It's the first of the Four Questions you ask at the Passover Seder. It means, 'Why is this night different from all other nights?' "

"Oh, okay." Once I got it, it was funny.

Funny up to a point, anyhow. Izzy said, "I sure wish some folks in Vampire Village could find out where Kreuzbach beds down while the sun is in the sky. If we could get rid of him, we'd solve a lot of our problems."

"They haven't had any luck with that, and they really want him gone, too. The things he does put them in danger, too. And I've tried to get some other help on that." I told him about my latest visit to Mickey at the Rhum Boogie.

"That's right, you have all kinds of interesting friends, don't you?"

"You mean like you?"

He laughed more than the crack deserved. "Mickey's like me some ways, maybe a little less some others. He's what we call a *shanda fur die goyim.*" His gaze sharpened. "Kreuzbach would sure as hell be a *shanda fur die goyim* for vampires, wouldn't he?"

"I'd be able to answer you better if I knew what you were talking about, but you keep throwing foreign languages at me."

"Sorry about that." Izzy's grin told me just how sorry he was. "A *shanda fur die goyim* means a spectacle for the gentiles—a Jew who robs or steals or kills or rapes so all the folks who aren't Jews can go tsk-tsk-tsk and say, 'See? That's the kind of thing *those* people do!'"

"All right." If I'd heard that one from Al Harris, I didn't remember it. "Now that I understand you, he would be, yeah. They worry about that kind of thing. It scares the crap out of them, to tell you the truth. When a colored guy goes off the rails, we worry about it, too."

"You don't get lynchings here." Izzy wasn't grinning any more.

"No, not here. But a lot of Negroes who live here came from places where they did happen. My folks did—I know that. They didn't talk about it much: mostly to make sure I always remembered how careful I needed to be around white people. And people do still get lynched in the South. You don't see the stories in the *Times* or the *Mirror News* or the *Herald* or the *Examiner*, but—"

"Especially not in the *Times*," Berkowitz broke in.

"You got that right," I said. If the *Times* ever ran a story about a lynching, it'd be one cheering the lynch mob on. That's the kind of rag the *Times* is, the kind it always has been, probably the kind it always will be. I went on, "But the *Lookout* and the other colored papers let people who care about things like that know what's going on."

" 'People who care about things like that' means 'people who know they're liable to get lynched,'" he observed.

"Well, sure. And water is wet, and you need air to breathe, and nobody turns into a werewolf except on the night of a full moon." I shouldn't have been that snotty. Most white folks wouldn't have had any idea what I was talking about. But Izzy's people had got kicked in the teeth, too. I remembered the fylfot and the number Rivke'd wear on her arm as long as she lived.

"One of these days, maybe we'll have a country where nobody needs to think something like that can ever happen to him," he said.

"One of these days, maybe we'll have one where nobody ever thinks it'd be fun to string someone else up on account of what he looks like or what he believes or whether he's alive or undead," I said.

"That'd be good, too," Izzy answered, his voice not much above a whisper. "That'd be better, in fact."

"It would, wouldn't it? But I'm not holding my breath. How about you?"

"I wish I were. I'd be mighty blue if I tried, though, wouldn't I?"

"Funny, you don't look bluish," I said, and flicked away a little beetle that was strolling across the table as if it owned the joint. Hell, for all I know, it did.

After that, we didn't seem to have a whole lot left to say to each other. I grabbed the check this time. We got to our feet and headed out. The woman behind the counter called, "*¡Hasta la vista!*" It's not *Goodbye*; it's more like *Till I see you again*. I like that better. I was sure she'd see Izzy again in the next few days. And I figured I'd be back myself before real long.

"Thanks for the scarab, Jack," Izzy said as we ambled back toward County General. "Thanks for thinking of me."

"That's what it's about, huh? If we think of each other, with luck we won't have to think about stuff like lynchings and numbers branded on arms and … well, and like that."

"With luck. With a lot of luck." He put his arm around my shoulder for a second, even though he had to reach up to do it: I'm taller than he is. I'm damn glad he did.

Mehitabel went out prowling. She did that a lot; she was still used to being as near wild as made no difference. Old Man Mose went out, too, but not so often. He'd hung around with me ever since I opened the office after the Army gave me my Ruptured Duck. He'd come to enjoy living soft. No fool, Mose.

"So," I said to him, "are you happier having a lady cat around now that you're screwing her?"

"While I'm doing it, sure," he said. "Any other time? Forget it. She eats my food. She makes trouble. She gets me into trouble with you."

They had a bad habit of chasing each other all over the office, and of pingponging off anything pingpongable while they were at it. They'd pingponged off me now and then, sometimes with claws in, sometimes not. Have you ever tried to put Merthiolate on that spot right between your shoulder blades? I have. I don't recommend it.

I did my best to discourage that kind of pingponging. Up till then, my best hadn't involved felicide. I gave Mehitabel and Old Man Mose to understand that this pleasant state of affairs might not go on forever if the pingponging continued. I may have exaggerated for effect, but I made them thoughtful.

"Humans make too big a fuss about screwing," Mose told me. He had no idea what he was talking about, which made him no less sure he was right. Cats are always convinced their vagrant opinions are worth their weight on gold.

"It's more complicated with us," I said. "Women don't go into heat the way female cats do. You can't tell by looking—"

"By smelling," Mose broke in.

"By smelling. Have it your way." Smelling matters more to cats than it does to us. But I also remembered a guy in my company who used to swear his nose let him know whether a gal would or wouldn't. I can't say whether he was telling the truth. A couple of weeks later, he stopped a machine-gun burst with his chest. Almost cut him in half. That gave me one more reason not to want to think about him. I went on, "Because we can't tell, a lot of what goes on with us is trying to find out who will and who won't. Even if somebody will, you don't know ahead of time whether you'll be able to get along afterwards."

Old Man Mose looked up from a delicate bit of personal housekeeping. Okay, he was polishing his balls with his tongue, if you really want to know. "Is that why you keep hanging around with the dead thing?"

Cats like vampires every bit as much as vampires like cats. "She's not dead. She's undead. Zombies, now …"

Mose didn't exactly have an upper lip. He curled it anyhow, showing off his canines. "I bet it wouldn't stop some of you nasty things," he said.

By a few of the publications Al Harris carried in his literary emporium, Mose was right. "It would stop me," I said. Thinking about it was plenty to make my stomach want to turn over. Doing it? Not this boy, no indeed.

"Doesn't seem like much difference between the one and the other, not to me." By the way Mose talked, I might've been a mouse he was tormenting to work up an appetite before he finally killed it and ate it.

"Fat lot you know it. You're just a stupid cat," I said.

"I must be. I'm arguing with a human." He went back to what he'd been doing, as if to tell me it was more fun than that. If I'd been limber enough to do it myself, I might've thought he had a point.

I went through the *Lookout*. If Janine had murdered three-timing Lester, it hadn't made the paper it was most likely to. The

Times didn't care what Negroes did to each other, only if they did it to white folks. The *Herald* and the *Examiner* weren't much better. You wouldn't expect anything else from Hearst papers, would you? The *Mirror News* might've been earnestly concerned. People there meant well, but.... C'mon, you know what paves the road to hell as well as I do, right? Sure you do.

The sun set. Even though it wasn't anywhere near full dark yet, Vampire Village would be stirring. The Shabbas-goy Jews and other daytime watchers would go on home and leave the place to the ones who only came out at night. I still don't exactly understand how vampires could look so sharp when they couldn't primp in front of a mirror, but they managed. Dora's makeup was almost perfect; she never had a hair out of place. The same held true for most of her folk. I was sure those who didn't bother with such fripperies—Rudolf Sebestyen, for instance—could have had they chosen to.

Mehitabel came in. Old Man Mose woke up enough to hiss at her, then went back to sleep. I'm not certain he heard her hiss back. "Catch anything interesting?" I asked her.

"A lizard. Well, his tail. The rest of him got away. How come the tail keeps wiggling even after the lizard's gone?" The way she eyed me told me humans were supposed to know such things. That was part of what they were good for—that and feeding cats.

I disappointed her: "No idea. Sorry."

"Fat lot of good *you* are." A drill sergeant couldn't have sounded more disdainful.

Since I'd had a bellyful of cats mocking me and an empty bellyful of nobody coming in demanding my services while waving large-denomination bills in my face, I left Mehitabel and Old Man Mose to their own furry devices and headed on down to Vampire Village. A police car cruised by me ... then pulled over and stopped. Both cops got out. The guy who was driving said, "Let me see some identification, pal."

You don't have to give it to them. The law says you don't, anyhow. It doesn't say what will happen to you if you don't, though. You find out about that all by your lonesome. Since I'd already found out, I said, "My wallet's in my left front trouser pocket. I'm going to reach in there and take it out. That's all I'm going to do, Officer."

I must have sounded properly meek. My folks had trained me well. Coming from the South, they knew the need. Neither LAPD man drew his pistol. I walked up slowly, letting the cop who'd given me orders see my hands all the time. I showed him my driver's license and my business card.

He grunted. "Oh. You're that Jack Mitchell," he said. His tone might've meant anything or nothing. I'd done a few things that annoyed the cops, but they're mostly on the same side as private eyes.

If he and his partner grabbed their nightsticks and tried to knock the crap out of me, I promised myself they'd get a surprise. That meek act goes only so far. But he handed my stuff back and waved me on. The two cops slid into the patrol car again.

"Keep your nose clean, Mitchell," said the one who'd been quiet up till then as the driver put the Ford in gear. It pulled away, belching a little smoke from the tailpipe.

I imagined going back to the apartment with a dirty nose. Cops seem to think it happens all the time. That wasn't as satisfying as imagining stomping both of them to within an inch of their lives. It was nowhere near as satisfying as imagining living in a country where things like that never happened. Imagining such crazy things is dangerous. If you aren't careful, you may start believing they can happen.

Yes, I got into the bourbon after I sizzled some canned hash to grease up the inside of my stomach. Naturally, Dora noticed. She paid more attention to me than I paid to myself. "What is wrong, Jack?" she asked.

So I told her. I hadn't said anything about it till then, but it all came pouring out of me. I finished, "What the hell good did it do to whip the fylfot boys when we've got our own Lightning Rune troops riding around with flashing lights on top of their cars?" Bitter? Who, me? Why would anybody think I was bitter? What could I have to be bitter about? Yeah, what?

Her dress was of an orange two shades darker than Old Man Mose. It had pearl buttons down the front. She touched the top one. "Do you want me to help you feel better?"

I wasn't drunk enough to grab at anything like a stupid, horny fool. I wasn't drunk enough to fail if I tried, either. I was just drunk enough to see things clear. I shook my head. "Thanks, honey, but it isn't a good idea right now. I'd better not. I'd just be mean."

She gave me an appraising stare, the kind that reminded me how much older than me she was. Slowly, she said, "You may be starting to grow up."

"That isn't what this feels like. It feels like …" I ground to a stop then, because I didn't know what it felt like. Not the Wild Turkey's fault. I'd started drinking to blunt whatever it was I felt. It just hadn't worked.

"You want a revenge you have not the power to take," Dora said with her usual precision.

Damned if she wasn't right. Vampires understand revenge. They understand it better than live people do, I daresay. Well, they have more time on their hands than we do. They can wait and spin plans for decades or even centuries, plotting the perfect payback. Mostly, they play those games against one another. Every so often, mere mortals get in the way, poor bastards.

"You're right!" I exclaimed. I couldn't find the thing myself, but I recognized it when she pointed it out to me. Revenge on the cops, who could've got away with killing me if I gave them even a little lip. Revenge on the city, for hiring cops like that. Revenge on the country, for being full of cities and towns and no-account little burgs that hired those cops.

Revenge on the world! Of course, that was what the fylfot boys wanted, too, for losing the war before this last one. Life stinks when you hold up a mirror and see your own worst enemy in it, looking back at you with your face.

Vampires don't show up in mirrors, not even to themselves. As I've mentioned, that can be a problem. Till that moment, I hadn't realized they might also be lucky.

"I love you, sweetie," I said.

"You have not finished growing up," she answered.

"I guess not. Somebody smarter than I am said, 'You're only young once, but you can be immature forever.'"

She smiled wide enough to show off her fangs, which meant I'd tickled her. "And whoever that was probably was not even thinking of vampires."

"I bet he wasn't. Me, though, I was thinking of Bedford Tyler." Damned if I didn't make Dora laugh out loud. As I've said, Bedford inhabited Dora's building. Before he was a vampire, he'd been a Southern gentleman. An aristocrat. A slaveowner.

He still thought he'd been robbed on account of emancipation. As far as he was concerned, he had the God-given right to do whatever he wanted to colored people. The God Whose name he couldn't stand to hear thought a hell of a lot like him. Ever notice how most people's Gods think just the way they do? I wonder why that is.

Bedford would've loved to drain me dry, for instance. I'm sure he would have tried it if I weren't Dora's toy. Dora scared the piss out of him, the way she did with most vampires in VV. It wasn't because she was an aristocrat more authentic than he ever could be, either. She could've been a pigkeeper while she was mortal and she would have had the same effect. It was because she was her.

Bedford would've loved to drain me dry.... I came back to that. It wanted to take me somewhere. The Wild Turkey I'd taken aboard helped smooth the path. I said, "If anybody in Vampire Village wants to give the *Blitzrunen Oberf* a hand, five gets you ten it's good old Bedford Tyler."

All of a sudden, Dora wasn't laughing any more. She grabbed me and pulled me close and kissed me hard enough so she drew a little blood just from the pressure of her teeth against my lips. "That is a very clear thought, a very penetrating thought. You may not have finished growing up, but never let anyone tell you you are foolish."

"Thanks." I meant it. She threw praise around the way Jack Benny threw money. (Jack Benny in his act, I mean. Jack Benny for real is one hell of a generous man.)

"You deserve it," she said.

"It does make a crazy kind of sense, doesn't it?" The more I ran my mouth, the better and less crazy the sense it made, too. "Not just the butternut gray and the *Feldgrau*, either. Those Southern white slaveowners wanted to keep Negroes property forever. The fylfot boys wanted to enslave the whole stinking world for the next thousand years—the whole stinking world except for them, I mean. They were a perfect match, if only they'd been around at the same time."

"As Bedford Tyler and Lothar Kreuzbach are," Dora said.

"Yeah." I nodded, even though some of what I'd said wasn't quite true. The fylfot boys didn't want to enslave *everybody* who wasn't blond enough and pink enough to suit them. If you were a Jew or a gypsy or a queer, they didn't waste time with that. They just killed you.

The fylfot and the number on Rivke's arm .... Bastards hadn't rubbed out everybody they wanted to, but nobody could say they hadn't given it their best shot.

"Do you suppose you could get into Bedford Tyler's apartment while the White Fire is in the sky and see if it holds more than one coffin?" Dora asked.

"I can try. Depends on what kind of lock he has on the door." I'm not the worst lockpick in the world. I'm also not the best. A really good piece of hardware, especially one backed up by a solid spell, will beat me. Or, if it doesn't, it will make me leave tracks, you might say, which wasn't really something I wanted to do.

"That might be worthwhile," she said.

"If I can do it. You're right. I should find out." I paused. "I don't hate everybody as much as I did a little while ago. Are you still interested, babe?"

"I could be. How persuasive are you?"

Her arched eyebrow was a challenge. I did the best I could. It must've been good enough, because I'm not going to tell you about the rest of the night.

Breakfast the next morning was scrambled eggs, coffee, and aspirins. Whiskey *will* get even with you. The jimjams weren't galloping. I hadn't drunk that much. More of a brisk trot, I'd say.

Instead of going down to Bedford Tyler's door and trying to pick up a breaking-and-entering rap, I decided to see whether I could find some help from a friend who had abilities I didn't. That meant a trip to LAPD headquarters, dammit. I wasn't thrilled, but what can you do?

One thing I could do was stop at the office first. The cats had knocked down everything they could and a few things I hadn't thought they could. "Have fun?" I asked them.

"It's her fault," Old Man Mose said. "She smells wrong."

Mehitabel hadn't been to the vet or anything. That can do it. But she knew what was bothering Mose even if I didn't. "I'm going to have kittens, you idiot. I smell the way I'm supposed to."

"Oh, kittens! Kittens are tasty," Mose said.

Mehitabel hissed at him and bottlebrushed her tail. He wasn't kidding, and she knew it. Cats enjoy becoming fathers. They don't enjoy being fathers. To them, kittens are nothing but nuisances that grow up to be young cats who'll run them out of town.

"Mose, you aren't going to murder Mehitabel's kittens," I said.

"Sure I am." He had all the confidence in the world.

"No. You aren't. Get used to the idea. She won't let you, and I won't, either."

He said something impolite. Mehitabel said something impoliter. Her tail got fatter yet. All her body fur puffed out. She wasn't as fluffy as Old Man Mose, but you never would have known it then. And she hadn't even started looking as if she'd swallowed a basketball yet. The next couple of months were going to be fun. Then she'd have the kittens, and that was liable to be more enjoyable still.

I wanted to put my head in my hands. Old Man Mose didn't help when he said, "It's all your fault. If you hadn't let that walking fleabag live here, this never would've happened."

No, I didn't reach for the Wild Turkey. A man of stern moral fiber, that was me. I said, "Mose, remember how much you used to enjoy finding places to sleep when it rained and eating crickets and lizards and whatever you could scrounge from garbage pails?"

"Those were the days," he said happily, which wasn't the attitude I was looking for.

"Well, if you want them back again, keep going the way you're going."

He thought that over. Then he flowed under the couch, growling as he went. And when I say flowed, I mean flowed. Cats are liquid. Everybody who's ever had anything to do with them knows it.

"I can take care of myself. And of the kittens, when there are kittens," Mehitabel said.

“I’m trying to keep trouble from starting. That’s better than stopping it once it does start. Easier, too.”

She looked at me, her eyes two green lamps of incomprehension. “Humans are crazy,” she said.

“That must be why I took you in, huh?”

“I guess so.” She hopped up onto the sofa Mose was under, curled into a circle, put her tail over her eyes, and went to sleep. I wished I had such a nice way to get out of arguments. Hell, I don’t even have a tail.

All things considered, I was glad to leave the office that night. I figured Old Man Mose would get used to Mehitabel’s new aroma in a couple of days. Then we could go back to business as usual till the kittens arrived. That would be a whole new act in the shambolic circus of my life.

I’d just got down into Vampire Village when I saw the fellow I least wanted to run into coming up the street toward me. Yes, there was Lothar Kreuzbach, big as life but not nearly so warm. “I have a crucifix. I have holy water. I have garlic powder and goofer dust,” I said. “You want trouble? I’ll give you some.”

He held up his right hand. “Let it be a truce, then. Not peace, but a truce.”

We’d given the fylfot boys in Italy truces so they could pick up their wounded. They’d done the same for us every now and then. And after the truces ended, we got back to the serious business of killing each other. So I held up my hand, too. “Okay, truce, but don’t come too close. What’s on your mind?”

“Nothing much. I merely pay my respects to a brave opponent.” He sketched a salute.

“Yeah, and rain makes applesauce.”

He came closer—not close, but closer. As he stood under a streetlamp, I saw he had a bandage on his left hand. That surprised me. Not much will hurt a vampire. They heal as fast as they get wounded. Oh, a stake through the heart will do for one, but a bullet won’t—the damage it makes disappears as soon as it happens. Fire, now, they’re afraid of fire. They don’t get over that. And …

I started to laugh. Kreuzbach drew himself stiff and straight, all affronted dignity. “You find me risible?” he asked, as if I’d slapped him in the face.

"Oh, I might. I just might, buddy. Anybody'd guess you might've walked on a dime the last time the moon was full."

He bared his fangs. They were thicker than Dora's, thicker than those of any vampire I'd seen. Funny how that works, huh? Yeah, hilarious. It had to have something to do with being part wolf, or part-time wolf. He had a better start on fangs than vampires who used to be ordinary people could.

"You have no idea what you are talking about," he said, but for once he didn't sound so sure of himself.

"No, huh? Tell you what, though. Next time I see you when you've gone werewolf, I'll leave you a nice can of Dr. Ross dog food." And I started singing the stupid jingle they plug the stuff with.

That did it. He didn't turn red; vampires aren't equipped for that. But he showed every other sign of being as mad as I could have wanted. Voice thick with fury, he said, "This truce is now ended!"

"Okay." I took out my bottle of holy water. It was an old perfume bottle with an atomizer. I let him see it. "Come on, if you're so eager." I didn't tell him God was on my side or anything like that. Holy names stop vampires, yes, but if you use 'em when you don't really need to, they have a way of rebounding on you.

He showed me his teeth again, and very impressive they were, too. I just stood there waiting. If looks could kill .... But they can't, not unless you're Medusa. "There will be other times," he said.

"Jawohl, Herr Oberführer!" I took a couple of steps toward him.

Next thing I knew, he wasn't there. I might have caught a glimpse of a flittering bat, or I might have imagined I did. Not for the first time, I wondered if the son of a bitch could turn into a bat while he was a werewolf. If I was real lucky, I decided, I wouldn't have to find out.

Dora looked at me when I finished telling her about my adventures on the way home. "You were tempting fate," she said. "Mortals who do that do not commonly come to happy ends."

She was bound to be right. "Yeah, well, I got away with it," I said, scuffing my feet on the rug like a second-grader when the teacher caught him doing something nasty.

"I thought you had better sense," she said. That stung worse than a teacher's swat on a nasty second-grader's backside would have. After letting it sink in, she added, "Had you sung that jingle at me, I believe I would have tried to tear your throat out in spite of the holy water you carried."

"I wouldn't have done that to you, honey. For one thing, it's cruel and unusual punishment. For another, you aren't part werewolf, so I wouldn't have any reason to."

"You did not sing it to me now, but your mentioning it makes me sing it to myself. It is more adhesive than any glue. Horrible little song!"

She was right again, of course. "That's why it makes Dr. Ross a ton of money," I said. *It's got more meat*, the jingle goes. Some things you hear, you don't know whether to believe 'em or not. I've heard Dr. Ross uses seal meat and whale meat in their dog food. I can't swear it's true, but the guy I heard it from sure thought it was. That may be why the glop is so cheap.

After I fixed myself something to eat—no matter what you do to Treet, it still tastes like Treet, even with no seal meat involved—we went out into Vampire Village. We stopped at that bar not far from the building. I wondered whether Lothar Kreuzbach would be in there drinking to drown his sorrows (though alcohol doesn't hit vampires nearly so hard as it does live people). I also wondered whether Bedford Tyler would be holding court, which he liked to do regardless of whether anybody else was listening to him.

I didn't see either one of them. I didn't miss them a bit, either. Dora ordered a shot of scotch. I had my usual. "Here you is," the bartender said as he gave us the drinks. He was no vampire; he was a warm one like me. He wore a long-sleeved white shirt, so I didn't know if he had a fylfot and a number branded on his arm, but the way he talked and the haunted look in his eyes told me it was a fair bet. I wondered if he knew Rivke.

"Would you like another?" Dora asked when we got to the bottoms of our glasses.

"One's okay for now, unless you do."

"No, never mind. I have the taste in my mouth now. For a while, it will linger."

"Okay." I set down an extra quarter. The barkeep put it somewhere unofficial. Neither his boss nor the Infernal Revenue Service would ever hear about it.

Dora and I went on out. I thought about a movie, but I didn't feel like going back uptown to watch one. There are no theaters in VV. They put one in before the war, but it went bust fast. Vampires make lousy movie customers. Don't get me wrong—they like movies as much as everybody else does. But they don't buy sodas or candy bars or popcorn, which is where a theater operator makes a lot of his dough.

When I remarked on that, Dora said, "Do you know what else we lack here?"

"Tell me."

"A blood bank. Would you not say that is rather more important than a moving-picture house?"

"It is, yeah. Maybe you ought to talk with Doctor Berkowitz the next time you go up to County General to feed."

"I have spoken with several people there. They fear robberies if they place the supply in the midst of those who need it." By the way she curled a lip, she didn't care a fig for what they feared.

"Isn't that interesting?" I said, and kept on walking. She knew as well as I did that her own charming half-brother had made plans to knock over the County General blood bank. They probably wouldn't have worked—Rudolf Sebestyen was always better at talking than doing—but he had tried. Dora knew, but chose not to remember. Of course vampires act that way, too. Didn't they used to be people?

All the time we were ambling along, I kept looking this way, that way, every which way, and especially behind me. Dora would've needed to be blind not to notice. She finally had enough of it. "What are you doing?"

"Checking six," I said automatically. You can take the guy who's been through combat out of the Army. I had that Ruptured Duck to prove they'd done it. What I needed longer to realize was, you can't take the Army out of the guy who's been through combat. Bad dreams. Jumpiness at sudden loud noises. Brawling as if you don't give a damn, because a lot of the time you don't. Being wary enough to worry a cat.

"Excuse me?" Dora spoke excellent English, but she had no idea what I was talking about. Lucky her.

I tried again: "Keeping an eye out for Lothar Kreuzbach so he doesn't take me—us—by surprise."

"Oh. You do not think my senses adequate for this?" She sounded offended.

Well, too bad. "One never knows, do one?" Poor Fats. He didn't even make it to forty, but he left behind a bunch of fine music and some plain common sense. After a couple of steps, I added, "I didn't have you along when I was in Italy. I got used to taking care of myself."

If that offended her, I was ready for the argument, the fight, whatever it turned into. But she walked along for a little while, then said, "All right. Let it pass."

Part of me was disappointed we didn't have a row. The dumb part, you'll tell me. I already know that, thanks. You've got to be dumb to want to quarrel with somebody you love. I'm sure you've never been dumb like that, not once in your whole entire life. Oh, you bet I am.

I tried to drive a stake through the dumb part's heart, though I knew I couldn't kill it like that, the way I could a vampire. "Hey," I said. "Thanks."

"You are welcome. As I have mentioned, I think you are beginning to grow up, whether you can see it for yourself or not."

"I'll try not to do it in public, if that's all right with you."

Her smile showed dimples, which it didn't always do. "However you please, of course."

And after that everything was okay between us. I felt like one of those combat engineers who look for mines—sometimes with a sorcerous detector, sometimes just with a stick—and defuse the ones they find. They're some of the bravest troops in the Army, because they have to know their life expectancy in that job gets measured in weeks, not months. Everybody else sure knows it.

We headed back toward the apartment. No, we didn't tear each other's clothes off to make up, nothing like that. She read a book. I listened to the radio for a while, but it was dumb even for radio. Changing stations didn't help, though I did manage to pick up one from Denver through waterfalls of static.

"Mind if I go to bed?" I asked.

"Sleep well," she said, so I guess she didn't.

I had my feet up on the office desk. Another exciting evening at work. Maybe somebody gorgeous would walk in and offer me ten grand to find her missing cocker spaniel. Maybe I'd flap my arms and fly to the moon, too.

Old Man Mose was out and about, tomcatting around somewhere in the neighborhood. Mehitabel was sleeping on an old blanket I'd folded up and set near the bathroom door. She didn't always feel like using the sofa; it smelled too much like Mose.

If I took a slug of Wild Turkey from the bottle in my desk, I might go to sleep myself. Not as if I'd never done that there, not even a little bit. But I was doing it less than I had before I started hanging around with Dora. Somebody nice to go home to will make you not want to hang around the office.

All of a sudden, Mehitabel woke up, rolled over onto her belly, and stared intently at the ugly wallpaper between my filing cabinets. "What is it?" I asked. She didn't answer. She just kept staring. The fur on her tail started to stick out.

I stared, too. I didn't see anything. I didn't hear anything. I didn't smell anything, either, though that proves next to nothing. I'm a human to begin with, and a human who smokes to add insult to injury.

But then I thought I might see, or might almost see, something between the file cabinets after all. That wallpaper looked as if I was seeing it through curdled air. And, if I looked off to one side of it, I could make out a kind of a shape that included a long nose and a long chin.

A ghost. Probably a ghost. Fairly probably even a ghost I knew, as much as you can know a ghost. "That you, Eb?" I asked, and waited.

You don't hear what a ghost says to you. The words form inside your head without going through your ears first. I can't explain it any better than that. "Ayuh, it's me." Eb had been a Pinkerton from New England before he stopped a Minié ball during the Civil War. Now, a lifetime later, he was still snooping, only for the LAPD.

"What brings you here? Is this a friendly visit, or are you looking for something I've got?" I asked.

"Friendly, I reckon," he answered, followed a moment later by a ghost of a ghost of laughter—again, I don't know how better to put it. " 'Course, I'd say the one even if it was t'other. Don't want you exorcisin' me or nothin'."

"Like I would!" I dug the Wild Turkey bottle out of the drawer and poured a couple of fingers' worth into a glass. "Here you go. Out yourself knock!"

"Don't mind if I do." The curdled air came over to my desk. Mehitabel scuttled out of its way. She'd never met Eb before, unlike Old Man Mose, who took him in stride. Eb stood over the bourbon and … inhaled? One more thing I don't know how to describe. He couldn't drink, obviously, but he got something from the stuff any which way. As if to prove as much, he said, "Mighty nice. Mighty smooth."

"Glad you like it." You know how Jews take care of the glass of wine they leave out for Elijah on Passover? I dealt with the material spirits I'd poured for Eb the same way. They must have set fire to my brain, too, because the next thing out of my mouth was, "D'you know anything about a vampire by the name of Lothar Kreuzbach?"

"That feller? Heard o'him, ayuh. Nothin good. Makes your friend Sebestyen look like a saint in heaven next to him, don't he?"

"Rudolf's no friend of mine, but he's Dora's half-brother, so I'm stuck with him." Imagining being Rudolf Sebestyen's buddy was harder than imagining him at God's right hand. Everything else Eb said, I agreed with.

"I wouldn't want to admit it, neither." The ghost gave me another ghostly horse laugh.

"Yeah, yeah. Listen, we can argue about it later. Or you can ask Rudolf what he thinks of me. But stand back when you do, or he'll scorch your ectoplasm for you."

Eb disappeared, or at least the air in the office uncurdled. "What a horrible thing!" Mehitabel said. "I can't smell it or feel it, but I know it's there." She shuddered.

"Old Eb's all right," I said.

"No, he's not! Things you can't smell or feel aren't natural." Well, Mehitabel had that straight.

Before we could start arguing about it, Eb came back. "You was right. He don't like you for beans."

"How did you find him so fast?"

"I kept lookin' till I knew where he was." Eb made it sound simple. Trying to understand it has driven live people way smarter'n I am clean around the bend.

"Could you find Kreuzbach the same way?"

"Reckon I can give it a try." Eb stopped manifesting in the office again. This time, he didn't reappear so fast. When he did, he was … puzzled? worried? "He don't seem to be nowhere, consarn it."

He hadn't had any trouble with Rudolf. It was nighttime; Kreuzbach should have been going up and down in the world. I had another rush of brains, or possibly bourbon, to the head. "Can you check Bedford Tyler's apartment? Same building I live in, Number 23."

"I'll do it." Eb wasn't there any more.

Me, I was so happy, I wanted to hug myself with glee. I hadn't been looking forward to breaking and entering, which was the only way I could get into Tyler's place. Even in the daytime, it was dangerous. But a ghost, now, a ghost could do the entering without any breaking.

Or I thought so, till he … mm, *reappeared* stretches a point, but I'll use it anyway. Ghosts don't have crests to fall, but he was one crestfallen spirit any which way. "What's the matter?" I asked. Something sure as hell was.

"I couldn't get in. Ain't that the goldarnedest thing you ever heard of in all your born days?" Eb went over to the glass and found something dreadful had happened to it. "Can you give me another snort o' them corn squeezins?" he asked plaintively.

"Comin' up." I poured. He did whatever he did with the Wild Turkey. "Why couldn't you get in?" I imagined him slipping through the keyhole or sliding up between a couple of floorboards that didn't join perfectly. Ectoplasm can do all kinds of things real matter can't.

"Dog my cats if I know. It was like the place had glass around it, only I could've got through glass."

"How about that?" I whistled tunelessly between my teeth. Had Bedford Tyler, the old dog, found himself a new trick? Or was Kreuzbach in there with him after all? The fylfot boys came up with lots of nasty tricks during the war, most of 'em, luckily, so near the end that they didn't get the mileage from 'em they could have earlier. It wasn't impossible, or even unlikely, that a *Blitzrunen Oberführer* knew about one when Washington and Moscow didn't.

"Goldarnedest thing," Eb said again. "Obliged for the popskull." He was gone.

I took care of the Wild Turkey's mortal remains. "Disgusting," Mehitabel said. I don't know whether she meant the booze or the ghost. I didn't try to find out.

All right, I would have to break into Bedford Tyler's apartment to find out what the hell was going on in there and why Eb couldn't get in. The idea appealed to me at least as much as a root canal would have. "Gotta be done, though," I told Dora, trying to talk myself into it.

"It is dangerous," she said. "If you leave traces behind, or if he has sorcerous wards in place .... And he probably does, or else the ghost would have had no trouble seeing what lay behind that glassy shield."

"I know, I know," I said. She wasn't making me more enthusiastic, let me tell you. "But getting rid of Kreuzbach has to be worth it. I wouldn't *mind* getting rid of Bedford, either, you understand, but he's not what Eb'd call a big thing. The *Oberf* is. If he's there, I've got to know it."

"Kreuzbach is important, yes. But you underestimate Tyler at your peril."

Dora kept being right, dammit. I didn't want to take Bedford Tyler seriously. Somebody who might have owned ancestors of mine? I wanted to think that business was behind us forever, and that we'd keep moving further and further away from it. Nobody, though, nobody could pretend we're that far removed from what the fylfot boys had in mind. Some of them still do—Lothar Kreuzbach, for instance.

"You will do this while the White Fire blazes, is it not so?" Dora persisted.

"That's what I had in mind, yeah. Bedford won't be able to stop me then."

"On the other hand, I will not be able to assist you at need."

"Would you?" I was surprised. More than surprised, in fact. I was amazed.

"I would not bother if it were only Tyler. Like so many of us, he longs for days that can never return. But the *Oberführer*'s dreams still lie unquiet in their graves." Dora's thoughts echoed my own. And I was sure she included herself in that *Like so many others*. She might not like it, but she had to understand she wasn't going back to Hungary to lord it over an estate full of frightened servants.

"If I can get in and out during daytime without Bedford knowing, I'm golden. If I find Loathsome Lothar there, I'd like to finish him. One good chance is all I'm going to have."

"You may not have even one." A frown line appeared between her eyebrows, then smoothed out again. "I will accept your judgment, though. I have no recent experience with life under the White Fire." The frown line came back, though one of her eyebrows quirked upwards. "I have no recent experience with life."

I kissed her. "You're plenty lively for me, babe."

That eyebrow jumped higher. "You are a man. I am your lover. So long as I please you, your objectivity is suspect."

Men are stupid. Men are simple. One more time, Dora wasn't wrong. "Must be love, wouldn't you say?"

"In a word, no. I can be your lover, as you can be mine. Being what I am, I cannot give you love. That is not the same as the other."

No point to arguing with her. We'd already gone around that barn too often. Odds were we'd keep doing it till she got sick of me or I died of old age, whichever came first. And if she stayed around five hundred years after I started pushing up daisies, every once in a while she'd think, *He was the specially silly one.*

Instead of arguing, I went to bed. Some of the things I needed to get into Tyler's place were up at the office. I wanted to go up there, grab 'em, and come back while it was still morning. Then I'd see what I could do about breaking and entering.

I got up at eight—the alarm clock made sure of it. That felt like the crack of dawn to me; I'd got used to keeping something close to vampire time. It wasn't, of course; Dora would have closed her coffin more than an hour earlier. I made coffee, scrambled a couple of eggs, and fixed toast with cherry jam. The toaster was new. Step by step, inch by inch, I was getting domesticated. It amused Dora.

Down the stairs. Out to face the morning sun. No matter what hours I kept, Old Sol didn't make me burst into flames. I did smoke, though. I lit an Old Gold as soon as I got to the sidewalks.

Rivke stood at the corner, keeping an eye on things while the vampires couldn't. She waved to me. I waved back. "I do not long time you see. Glad I do now," she said.

"Your English gets better all the time," I said.

She made a face, but I could tell she liked that. "Maybe better. Not good."

"It will be." I meant it. When I first met her, she could hardly string two words together. Not very long ago, that. Now she was making herself understood even if she did seem stuck in the present tense.

"I hope yes," she answered. Not something anybody who'd grown up with English would say, but she got her meaning across. She looked me over. "Why you out so soon? So *early*." She corrected herself.

You know what? I told her why. Then I wondered how come I was doing that and what she'd think about it. After all, she was in VV to protect vampires from live people like me. But that was after I'd got started. I couldn't very well stop in the middle. As usual, my mouth ran half a lap ahead of my brain. You bet it's happened before. You bet it'll happen again, too.

So I got to the end and waited to see what she'd do or say. If she ran off to get some more Shabbas-goy Jews to stop me, what could I do about it? Not much, not right then, not that I could see. And if they put somebody inside the building to guard Bedford Tyler's door during the day, I couldn't do anything about that, either.

After, oh, half a minute's thought, Rivke said, "Whatever happen to Kreuzbach, he for himself make it. Not because he vampire. Because he *Blitzrunen Oberführer*."

I wanted to kiss her. *Dora wouldn't like that* jangled through my mind like a fire alarm. I just said, "Looks that way to me, too."

"You need help? You want help?"

Dora really wouldn't like that, I thought. But Rivke'd saved my bacon—a hell of a thing for a Jew to do, huh?—once. Trouble didn't panic her. After what the fylfot boys put her through, chances were nothing panicked her. I nodded. "If you're crazy enough to want to."

Her smile was carnivorous. "For this one, I that *meshuggeh*, yes." I understood her. Al Harris used that word, even if he pronounced it *meshiggeh*.

"Okay," I said, "you're on. I've gotta go up to the office and get some stuff. I'll be back in half an hour, an hour at most."

Up at the office, Old Man Mose and Mehitabel were snarling and hissing at each other. They weren't biting each other's faces off or trying to rip each other's guts out, so I left them to their games. Anyway, fresh food in their bowls distracted them better than anything else I could've done. I gave 'em fresh water and cleaned their boxes, too.

The important stuff taken care of, I went to the closet and put on greenish brown work pants, a work shirt the same color (it had *John* embroidered over the pocket), and a brown-green cap that said GVS above the bill (no, I don't know what GVS stands for, either). I had dull black crepe-soled shoes in there, too. I grabbed a tool chest off the shelf, took some stuff out of my desk and stuck it in, then went on my merry way.

When I got back to Vampire Village, Rivke didn't recognize me. I wasn't the guy she knew any more. I was just a workman looking for the right address. Or I was till I said, "Ready?"

She laughed in startled delight. "Yes!"

We went into the apartment building a couple of minutes apart, first her, then me. There was a chance the manager—a live person—might ask me questions before I could head upstairs. I didn't have great answers for questions like that. Luckily, I didn't have to try any.

Up to the second floor. The hallway was quiet as the grave. Fair enough, since the tenants lay in their coffins, not dead but not alive, either. No noises from the kitchens. No radios playing. No nothing.

Only my footsteps, and those were almost silent, too, thanks to the work shoes I wore.

Rivke stood in front of the door to apartment 23. I set down my tool box, opened it, and took out the lockpicks that usually lived in one of my desk drawers. Rivke made a small, pleased sound, so she knew what they were. I got down on my knees and set to work.

Right away, I knew the lock wasn't a cheap one that had been in the building since it was new, the way Dora's was. But I kept at it—not likely anybody would stick his head out and ask what the hell I was doing. After what seemed like forever, the last pin rose. I felt like cheering. Rivke clapped hands without making a sound.

I opened the door very, very carefully. Sure as the devil, it went in a couple of inches and then stopped. Along with his fancy lock, dear Bedford had a chain securing his door. I'd wondered if he might. The tool box held wire cutters, too. The last time I'd used a toy like that, I'd been snipping the fylfot boys' barbed wire in the middle of the night with cold rain pouring down on me. Anybody who calls war romantic never fought in one.

"But—" Rivke's voice was the tiniest thread of whisper.

"It's okay," I whispered back. I knew what she was worried about. I could take care of it, or of most of it.

The chain snipped, I tried the door again. It opened. I took the two pieces of chain out of the mount and stuck 'em in one of the pockets on the work pants. They had pockets the way Joseph's coat had colors. I stepped into the apartment. Rivke followed, closing the door behind us.

The place was a mirror image of Dora's. Bedroom *this* way, kitchen *that* way, instead of the opposite. Furnished-apartment furniture—well, except for the bookshelves and the big coffin.

Only one coffin, dammit. "Crap," I muttered, or words to that effect. I'd hoped for two. Bedford didn't seem to have a roommate after all. Unless … I checked the bedroom and the kitchen and even the tub. Nope. No second coffin.

I came back to the front room. Rivke looked a question at me. I shook my head. She made a face. Then, evidently lacking the English to tell me what she had in mind, she mimed opening Bedford Tyler's coffin, carrying him to a window, and chucking him out. Which would have finished him nicely, because the sun was shining, nice and bright, on the grass down below. Winter, sure, but Southern California winter.

Not without regret, I shook my head again. My biggest worry wasn't finishing Bedford. It was that, if he went up in flames, he might set the building on fire. And, since none of the other vampires could get away during the daytime, the flames would likely finish them, too.

When I got that across to Dora, her eyes went wide. She pressed both hands to her mouth in melodramatic horror. "Uh-huh," I said. So we left Bedford where he was, sleeping a sleep that was more than sleep.

Well, you can't be smart all the goddamn time. Half the movies ever made revolve around people doing really stupid things. Movies are pretty stupid themselves most of the time, but they're dead right about that.

Next reasonable thing to do was get the hell out of there. Before we did, though, I reached into my tool box one more time and fished out another brass chain with those grooved things on the ends that fit into the slots on the door and wall mounts. It wasn't quite identical to the one I'd snipped, but it came close.

I stuck one end piece into the wall mount and screwed it into place. The chain dangled down, of course. When Bedford Tyler came back to himself, I hoped he'd figure he'd just forgotten to use it when he shut down for the day.

We slipped out of the apartment, quiet as a couple of cats that weren't bickering with each other. I was ready to beat it then, but Rivke set a hand on my arm, so I stopped. Very softly, she started a chant whose rhythm sounded familiar, even if the language didn't.

I recognized it after a few seconds. Damned if it wasn't the spell for the Indian Rope Trick, the same one wizards who operate elevators use millions of times every day. I'd never heard it in Yiddish before, though, let me tell you.

And, through the door, I heard a few faint clanks as the links rose. She made a couple of passes. A small scraping noise came through the door: the other grooved waddayacallit going into place where I couldn't put it.

Rivke grinned at me. "Okay!" she said. *Okay* was one bit of English she'd got down solid.

"Better than okay!" I agreed. One more time, I wanted to kiss her. One more time, I didn't. We went downstairs and out.

Not many people on the street in Vampire Village in the middle of the morning. A police car slowed down so the cops inside could give us a long look. But what did they see? An obvious Shabbas-goy Jew and an obvious repairman. Hard even for cops to decide either one of us was a suspicious character. The car sped up again.

"I didn't know you could work magic!" I said.

Rivke shrugged and smiled at the same time. "Little bits." She held her thumb and forefinger a millimeter apart. "Help keep me live when … when times bad." The smile blew out like a candle flame. She touched the fylfot and number burned on to her upper arm with her other hand.

Going to war against the fylfot boys was bad enough. But, in Italy and Gaul, they'd mostly played by the rules, even if their LR troops sometimes murdered prisoners and civilians for the fun of it. (It was a whole different story in the East. There, the fylfot boys hadn't even pretended war had rules. Neither had the Reds.)

But to be a Jew in their hands … I knew the kind of dreams and waking memories I still had. What were Rivke's like? I didn't want to imagine.

"I'm sorry." I meant it. Of course I did. That only goes to show what worthless things words are a lot of the time.

"Here now," Rivke said. "Them? *Kaputt!*" She tossed her head in a gesture of magnificent contempt.

But some of them weren't *kaputt*, dammit. Lothar Kreuzbach, for instance. Him I would have defenestrated. In a heartbeat, I would have. I bet I could've flung him far enough from the apartment building so he wouldn't take it along with him when he burned. If I couldn't have managed it by myself, Rivke would've been glad to lend a hand.

"We keep on. All here, we keep on," she said.

"You betcha," I told her.

"Having the chain was clever," Dora said when I recounted the day's adventures. "But leaving it hanging down was risky."

"I know, but I didn't see anything else to do. Then—" I explained how Rivke had got it to go where it needed to.

Dora heard me out with no expression at all on her face. "She is a paragon of virtues, that one," she said tonelessly.

I knew that would happen. It ticked me off anyway. It ticked me off more, in fact, *because* I knew it would happen. I breathed out through my nose, trying not to show what I felt. "She helped me. We're friends. I'm here. With you. Because I love you and I want to be here with you. You'd smell it on me if I tried lying to you, right?"

"That is so," she said, her voice still empty of, well, everything.

I've never heard anybody admit to anything, murder included, with more reluctance. Reluctantly or not, though, she did admit to it. "Okay, then," I said. "In that case, how come you sound like a jealous high school sophomore?"

She'd made me angry. I'd bet all I own plus another ten bucks on the side she meant to. Now I'd infuriated her, and I had no idea how or why. Had she been a live person, she would have turned red as a beet. But vampires don't do that. They can't.

"You idiot." Now Dora's voice had something in it: winter. Winter colder than any I'd ever known, and trying to fight a war in the north of Italy while the number turned over on the year odometer was no fun at all, take it from me. She went on, "Of course I am jealous. What else can I possibly be? We are always jealous of the living. We cannot be anything else. They still have—*you* still have—what we gave up. Do you not understand that?"

"You've gotta be kidding me," I said. "Don't *you* know how jealous live people are of vampires? In forty or fifty years at most, I'll be dead. Gone. Off the map. Forgotten. *Kaputt.*" Yeah, that was a handy word. I first got it from the fylfot boys. "You know vampires who've been around for forty or fifty centuries. You can do that yourself."

"Time weighs heavily on us. The more of it that piles up on our shoulders, the heavier it gets. Ask my half-brother if you doubt me."

I winced. Time weighed so heavily on Rudolf Sebestyen, he got himself turned into a zombie so he could forget it and everything else.

"Besides," she added, "there is always the belief that live people go Somewhere Else when they die, a place where they continue forever. We are quite sure there is no forever for us. When we are finished, nothing is left. Whatever the thing you have is, we gave it up to become as we are."

I can't remember the last time I worried about or even thought about what'll happen to me after I die. I figure it'll be like going under an ether cone, only you don't wake up afterwards. I know other things can go on: look (out of the corner of your eye) at Eb, for instance. But they mostly don't, or don't seem to.

"You take that stuff way more seriously than I do," I said.

Dora's eyes were even less readable than usual. "Perhaps I have reason to," she said. "And that is not the only reason I have to be jealous of mortals. You know as well as I that I can never give you children."

"One more thing I never cared about," I answered. But I might have been the only one in the whole country who didn't. You see stories in the papers all the time about how the dogfaces back from the war and their wives and sweeties are having kids like you wouldn't believe. The Baby Boom, the guys who write that stuff are calling it.

"You have not yet. This does not mean you never will. Believe me, I know what I am talking about."

Which meant she'd had another lover—other lovers?—who went down that road … and who made a pain in the backside out of himself—themselves?—doing it. I said, "Maybe we should burn that bridge when we come to it, not beforehand. In the meantime—"

In the meantime, I took her in my arms. She felt like one hell of a woman, and you can take that to the bank. She wasn't as warm as a live woman would have been, but I'd got used to that. Unlike a live woman, she could fling me across the room if she didn't like what I was doing. But I'd got used to that, too, and I didn't think she would.

I turned out to be right. She knew mortal men needed to feel they were stronger even when they weren't. And she let me take her back to the bedroom. Before we lay down, though, she said, "This will not solve anything, you know."

"Nothing ever solves anything," I said roughly. "For a little while, though, I won't have to think about that."

"Ah." She nodded. "A thought that could have come from one of us."

And so I did my sweaty best. She didn't sweat along with me, but she wasn't made for that role. As far as I could tell, my best was good enough. How far could I tell? I didn't ask; she might have told me. Besides, if you have to ask, you won't like the answer.

It ended too soon. It always does, for everyone. I lit an Old Gold. The one afterwards is the best one of the day. Unless that's the one right after dinner. Or the first one in the morning. Or …

Dora moved away from me in bed. "I know this is a common habit, but I have never understood it."

"Old Man Mose says the same thing," I answered cheerfully.

That annoyed her. I knew it would. She didn't want to be on the same side of anything as the cat. I grinned and opened my mouth to say something else that would irk her even more. As long as we were giving each other grief about silly stuff, we wouldn't be fighting over things that really mattered.

Before I could bring it out, somebody knocked on the door.

I jumped. Dora's eyes widened and her pupils got big—that amounted to the same thing. The next minute and a half were like something out of a comedy movie, or would have been if those could get away with showing naked people. Army life had taught me things about dressing in a hurry I'd never dreamt of before Uncle Samuel grabbed me. I don't know where Dora learned, but she threw on her clothes as fast as I did.

Quick as we were, though, whoever stood out there in the hall knocked again—sharp, harsh, angry knocks—before we got fully sheveled, if that's a word. We hustled to the door. Dora asked, "Who is there?" Her apartment, after all. I was just a pet.

"Bedford Tyler."

She opened the door. "I will talk with you," she said. "You are not welcome to come inside." Invitations matter to vampires. I'd had to tell Dora to come into my office before she could hire me to look for her missing half-brother. What happened afterwards … just happened, that's all.

Bedford gave her a venomous look. Everything about him screamed *The South shall rise again!* His hair came down over his ears. He had a mustache and a little chin beard. And he wore his nondescript jacket as if it were a frock coat.

"Don't reckon I want to talk with *you* anyways." He didn't sound like Foghorn Leghorn, but something in his voice made me think of the bigmouthed chicken. His gaze swung my way. He didn't eye me any too sweetly. "My bet is, this son of a bitch here was the bastard who snuck into my place while the White Fire kept me still."

I looked back at him. "Bedford, my bet is, you're full of shit."

He rocked back on his heels. He *really* didn't fancy that. Not only was I tainted with the tar brush, I was tainted with it and uppity at the same time. His expression told me what he would have done to me in the good old days.

But the good old days were dead and gone—and Dora stood there beside me. He said, "Go on, you lying skunk. Make me believe you."

"I can do that. Easy as pie."

He folded his arms across his chest. A cavalry colonel in gray might've struck a pose like that. "Go ahead. I'm waiting."

"You can't see it for yourself? Are you honest to Something that stupid?" No, I didn't throw God's name at him. I wasn't in desperate need, not with Dora there. I went on, "Think straight, Bedford. What would I do if I got into your place while the sun was shining? I'd open your box. I'd open your window. I'd throw you out. And I'd laugh while you burned."

Now he stared at me with horror in his eyes. He took hating me and people like me for granted. Somehow or other, though, it didn't seem to have crossed his mind that I might hate him right back. He didn't have a cape that he could swirl dramatically around himself while he made his exit, but he seemed offended enough for all ordinary use.

"Close the door again," I told Dora. "You'll let flies in."

She did. After a moment, she said, "But you were in there. You did not finish him."

"Rivke wanted to. I talked her out of it. We would have done it if we'd found Kreuzbach. I didn't think dear Bedford was nasty enough to deserve it. Looking back, I may have been wrong."

"You put him in fear. I did not think you could do that."

"The same way a tough Jew would scare the *Oberführer*. They think they can do whatever they want to us, with us. When we hit back, they don't like it so much."

"How are you different from a Red?"

"I'll tell you a secret, sweetie. I don't know if I am. I don't care, either. What I do know is, nobody's gonna step on me any more."

That was what had got to me when the LAPD cops stopped me and put me through the mill. I was somebody walking along minding my own beeswax in a particular part of town. I hadn't done anything. They had no cause to suspect I had. They stopped me anyhow, for no better reason than that they could get away with it. Something like that never would've happened in Westwood or any other part of L.A. where white people live.

"You had better be careful, too." Dora's voice was soft and serious.

I'd been careful with the cops. With cops, you've got to be. With scumbags like Bedford Tyler? I was done with that. After a moment, I managed, "I'll do my best."

"I hope so," she said. "I would not wish anything … unfortunate to happen to you." That was about as close as she ever came to talking about love.

"Believe me, babe, I don't want anything unfortunate happening to me, either. You can take that to the bank," I said.

"Good." She left it there. I did, too. I don't know what she was feeling. Me, I hated fighting with somebody I loved more than I hated going up against the fylfot boys. If something they threw at me hit, it was all over. That's simple. Stuff you get hit with in a lovers' quarrel comes back to bite you again days, weeks, months, even years later. It can hurt even more then, too.

Stuff you get hit with in a lovers' quarrel is like a vampire, I guess. It's undead.

I was coming back from the office a couple of nights later when—surprise!—I ran into Bedford Tyler. *Surprise like snow is black*, Al Harris would say. I carried the crucifix and holy water and garlic powder to protect myself from the *Oberführer*, but they'd also work against Bedford.

"We need to talk, Mitchell," he said. "I don't care for your attitude. I don't care for it one bit. You are presumptuous for a mortal man. Quite presumptuous."

"Why don't you just say uppity and get it over with? There's another word you can say, too. We both know what it is." I could have come out and called him a lugosi. That would have done to him what his using his pet name for colored folks would have done for me. It would have made him want to kill me.

Of course, he already wanted to kill me, so I'm not sure how much good staying polite did.

"You brought it up, sir. I didn't. Unlike you, I'm a gentleman."

"That's why you came upstairs and said I did things you know I didn't do." If you're going to lie, revel in it.

"I can't prove you did. If I could ..." Bedford showed off his canines. I'm not sure many gentlemen, Southern or otherwise, would have done that.

I laughed at him. He drew back in overacted dismay. Maybe you aren't supposed to laugh at gentlemen. I don't know. I said, "Those aren't anything special."

One of those perverted guys who like to wag what they've got at women did that to the sister of a friend of mine. *Do you know what this is?* he yelled. She looked him in the eye—not farther down—and said, *It's something like a dick, but much, much smaller.* The way she tells it, he's running yet.

Vampires don't keep their vanity in their crotch. Their fangs? That's a different story. "Where have you seen better?" Bedford Tyler demanded haughtily.

"On that guy who was in the Lightning Runes during the war, just for starters." I didn't say *Blitzrunen*; I didn't think Bedford understood German. Hell, I wasn't sure he understood English.

"You know not what you speak of," he said, and his voice went soft and deadly. "Like the heroes of the South, those who followed the fylfot have a proper understanding of how the various tribes of men should stand in relationship to one another."

"Killing off the ones you don't like, you mean?" I said. There under a streetlamp, his eyes glittered. That was just what he meant—as if I didn't know already. I went on, "I always thought the gray of the Stars and Bars and the gray the fylfot boys wore had a lot in common. Thanks for showing me I was right."

He sprang for me. Fast as he was, he wasn't fast enough. I gave him garlic powder in the face. Why not holy water? Why not the crucifix? Either one would have done more damage. Why not?

Because my right hand happened to be wrapped around the garlic powder jar, that's why. I didn't have time to shift it.

The garlic got him off me. That was plenty good enough. He reeled back, choking and coughing and wheezing and rubbing at his eyes. Tears streamed down his face. Now I advanced on him, seasoning bottle in hand. "C'mon, buster! Want some more?"

He didn't want any more. He ran, faster than I could go after him. He didn't turn bat and fly away, which was interesting. Maybe he couldn't, not with all that garlic messing him up. What do I know?

One thing I know is, not a single vampire in VV wanted to get anywhere near me as I went back to Dora's apartment. I might have been carrying a skunk that had just let go. Hell, I might have *been* a skunk that just let go. I had the garlic closed by then, but the memory lingered on. And I was sure I still had garlic powder on my clothes.

I found out I had reason to be sure of that when I tried to go into the apartment. Dora recoiled from me, revolted. "Gah! Stop! *Fokhagyma!*" she exclaimed.

"What do you want me to do? Stand out in the hallway all night?"

"Yes!" she answered, which wasn't what I wanted to hear. She went back into the bedroom and returned with my old Army duffel bag. "Put your clothes in this. Tie it tight after you do. Then come in and wash the filth off you. Hideous!"

"You want me to undress out here?"

"Yes!" she said again, even more emphatically this time.

"What if somebody comes out? What if somebody comes down the hall?"

"Do you think you have anything a vampire has never seen before? Even if you do, do you think a vampire will want to come anywhere near you while you reek of *fokhagyma*?" Dora still wouldn't say it in English.

So I shut up and got out of my clothes. Yes, all of them. No, nobody came out and embarrassed me more than I was already. I stuffed my duds, shoes and all, into the duffel, then yanked the drawstring as hard as I could. I threw the bag into a corner of the kitchen, where Dora didn't go much. Then I scurried into the bathroom, turned the water in the tub up as hot as I could stand it, and flipped the knob from bath to shower. I soaped myself down not once but twice.

When I came out, I was clean enough to squeak. Or I thought so, anyway.

Dora was less impressed. "That is better," she said. "Better, but not good. The nasty stinking rose still burns my nose."

"It's not me. It's the clothes. I'll take 'em to the office with me when I leave tomorrow. Then I'll take 'em to the cleaners. Well, I'll shine my shoes. That should do the job for them." I didn't say anything about her rhyme scheme. I don't think she came out with it on purpose, and she was in no mood to get teased on account of something like that.

She sure wasn't. "Most of it is the clothes. Some is still you." She sighed like the martyr I'm positive she thought she was. "I suppose I can bear it till I go back into my coffin to hide from the White Fire. I suppose. But why did you do such a dreadful thing?"

"Because Bedford Tyler tried to jump me, that's why. You think I throw garlic around in Vampire Village for the fun of it?"

"Who can guess why mortals act as they do?" she said cryptically. Then she came back to the other part of what I'd told her: "Why did Bedford do that?"

"The two of us just don't get along for some reason." I brushed the first two fingers of my right hand against the back of my left wrist. I knew she understood the gesture.

"Bedford is what he is," she said.

"Ain't that the truth!"

"He can do nothing else." Dora sounded like a vampire Martin Luther. "Were he a live man, he might change. We, though, we go on as we were when we left living behind. From then on, the only change we have is finishing."

"I dunno," I said. "Bedford was real clear on how the Stars and Bars and the fylfot boys had the same lousy ideas about a lot of things. He sounded as modern as a few years ago, anyhow."

"Only because the followers of the fylfot happen to hold to certain beliefs he already agrees with."

I grunted. That sounded as if it might be true, anyway. I said, "How come *Oberführer* Kreuzbach liked the crap the Leader spewed so much?"

Dora just shrugged. "You would have to ask him. Perhaps because he was a son of a bitch before someone made him one of the creatures of the night." She brought out the insult with the precision and relish of someone whose first language wasn't English.

I noticed that, yeah. But I noticed her quoting the movie even more. I hadn't called Bedford a lugosi. Live men who do that all of a sudden stop being live. Dora hates the movie. What vampire doesn't? Quite a few of the undead got finished on account of it. But she's seen it. And she'd used lines from it before.

Go figure.

Don't ask me. I've got no answers. Stuff doesn't have to make sense. It just has to happen. Then folks put it into patterns. But they make the patterns. The stuff doesn't.

Now ask me if I was hungry. Why, yes, as a matter of fact I was. I threw on a bathrobe—cooking naked isn't a good idea, not when hot grease spatters—and sizzled something up for supper. I ate it. I cleaned up. Dora kept her distance from me, and from the duffel bag that might have escaped from an Italian diner.

"I'm gonna hit the hay," I told her when the chores were done.

"Good night," she said. I blew her a kiss. After a very visible pause for thought, she blew one back at me.

Next thing I knew after I put on pajamas, the sun was up. Dora's closed coffin lid looked even more like a KEEP OUT! sign than usual. It looked like an *ACHTUNG! MINEN!* sign, if you really want to know. I made coffee, fixed a breakfast at least as thrilling as dinner had been, took another shower, and got the hell out. I slung the duffel over my shoulder like a freshly discharged swabbie.

When I got to the office, first thing out of Old Man Mose's mouth was, "What stinks in there?"

"Oh, shut up," I said. For a wonder, he did.

XII

I finally decided I had to go down to the place that made records and talk to the shift supervisors. If they could use the company post office box, they could use it to blackmail Acolyte Adams. I felt guilty because I hadn't given him his money's worth yet. He had to know I hadn't, too. That was liable to get me blackballed from Deacon's one fine day. And if getting blackballed from the best after-hours joint in town isn't a fate worse than death, what would be?

Seeing the swing-shift guy—his name, I remembered, was Gus Friedrichs—would snafu when I got up and when I went to sleep less than heading south early in the morning would, so I decided to do that first. "Would you like me to go along with you?" Dora asked.

"It's okay, babe," I said. "I'm not expecting any trouble."

"The trouble you do not expect is the worst kind."

"I'll be fine," I said. *I'm a big boy and you're not my mommy anyway* was what was in my head. Some other time, I might have come out with it. We were still walking on eggs after the last time we'd snapped at each other on account of Rivke, though, so I kept quiet. Sometimes—a lot of the time—the best thing you can say is nothin'.

"Be careful," she said, as if I weren't old to go out after dark by myself.

"Bedford Tyler thinks I am," I said. She made a face. Even after I got that garlicky suit cleaned, she didn't want it in the apartment.

I had to scrub myself with a brush to get the last of the stink off my skin. Then I had to throw the brush away. Two bits, straight into the trash. I mean straight—I had to take it out right away.

I rode the Red Car down to Vermont and Gardena Boulevard. A lot of the way, especially after people got off at the poker clubs, I had the trolley car all to myself. They must roll up the sidewalks in the South Bay after the sun goes down. Even Gardena Boulevard seemed quiet as the tomb. The only thing that was open was the Rexall catty-corner from the trolley stop. The big city, it's not.

And I had to sit around and wait for the bus to take me over to Main Street. They cut the schedule at night down there, too. When the damn thing finally did show up, it was empty till I got on.

I waited even longer at Main and 165th for the northbound bus. No lights at all on that corner. Somebody came toward me while I was sitting on the bus bench. My silhouette must've been bigger than the guy mooching my way expected, because he turned around and made tracks.

When the bus came, it wasn't all mine. Two drunks on the back seat were passing a fifth of rotgut back and forth. They didn't care about me at all, and it was mutual. I just hoped they wouldn't start puking till after I got off.

They didn't—lucky me! The corner of Main and 154th was as black as the inside of a fylfot boy's heart, too. How can it be Main Street if it isn't Main enough to have streetlights, for cryin' out loud? But I knew the answer to that. I was a long, long way from downtown.

While I waited to cross the street, a quiet car went by. Just before the light changed, so did another one, older and noisier. Neither driver had any idea I was there. Walking west, the only thing I heard was my own footsteps. I paused a couple of times to make sure I didn't hear anybody else's. Nope. I might've been the only guy awake for a mile in any direction.

I might've been, but I wasn't. There were the Quonset huts that held Danny Becker's enterprise. The parking lot in front of them had lights. It had cars in it, too. The hut on the left, the one with the boss' office, was dark. Not the other one. Even at—now that I could see a little, I checked my watch—a quarter to eleven, work there went on.

When I tried the knob on the front door, it opened. No more than two steps inside, a colored guy was putting a stack of records into a cardboard box. "Who the hell are you?" he said, and grabbed a pry bar in case he didn't like my answer.

"My names's Mikkelsen," I said, which it wasn't. "I need to talk to Gus Friedrichs for a few minutes."

"About what?" The guy didn't set the pry bar down, but he didn't look so ready to rearrange my face with it, not after I came out with a name he knew.

"That's between me and him," I said. To ease the sting, I held out a fin.

He grabbed it. Candy is dandy, but liquor is quicker. So is folding money. He turned around and yelled, "Hey, Mister Friedrichs! Fella wants to talk with you!"

"I am busy. Ten minutes!" came from some place I couldn't see.

"Ten minutes," the guy repeated for me, as if to say it wasn't his fault.

"Yeah, I heard." I pulled out my Old Golds. After I stuck one in my mouth, I held out the pack to him.

"Don't mind if I do. Thanks." He took one. I lit up for both of us. We smoked together. It's a thing you can do that makes you feel like buddies. You don't have to say a word. Sometimes not talking somehow makes it better. I didn't know most of that till I put on olive drab.

An ashtray sat on the work table next to the box the guy was filling. It was already loaded with butts. Before long, two more went in there. The fellow started putting platters in the box again. He didn't want his boss catching him goofing off. Who would?

All of a sudden, the night-shift supervisor was there. I thought I should have heard him coming up, but I didn't. He wore a funny kind of cap: no bill, but with a slightly bulbous crown that made me think of a mushroom in training. "Yes?" he said.

Then we looked at each other again. We both said the same thing at the same time: "You!"

This time, I didn't pull out the garlic powder. I grabbed the holy-water atomizer and squirted it in Lothar Kreuzbach's direction. Which did me no good at all, because the *Oberf* got out of range as fast and as silently as he'd approached.

I ran after him. "What the hell?" yelped the workman I'd smoked with. I ignored him. He could damn well figure it out for himself.

Three guys, two white, one Negro, were doing whatever they were doing in the back half of the Quonset hut. Magically stamping the master's grooves on blank records, I suppose. Another time, it might've been fascinating. Just then, I had other things on my mind. "Where's Kreuz—uh, Friedrichs?" I barked.

One of the white men crossed himself. "He turned into a bat! Right in front of me, he turned into a bat! Jesus Christ!" The other two guys nodded, eyes wide. Whatever they'd been looking for—a nice, quiet shift, probably—this wasn't it.

The sign of the cross and the holy name would have hurt Kreuzbach if he'd stuck around. But he hadn't. The hut's windows weren't very big, but they were open, letting in chilly night air. It would have got stuffy and foul in there if they weren't. As it was, the cigarette smoke was thick enough to slice.

"I thought Gus was a prick. Never reckoned he was a vampire." That wasn't the fellow who'd crossed himself. The black man had found his tongue.

"Goddamn squarehead." The third fellow spoke up, too. "He drove us like he was one of the fylfot boys and we were Hebes, that's for sure." His friends nodded. To me, he went on, "What in blazes was that all about, Mister?"

"Blackmail. And other things. You aren't so far wrong, I'll tell you that." I turned around and walked out of there.

Only after I got outside did I stop to wonder whether that was such a hot idea. Dear, sweet Lothar, *Blitzrunen Oberführer*, vampire, werewolf, and everybody's pal, was somewhere out there, too. Vampires are at home in darkness; live people aren't. If I wanted to keep on being a live people, I needed to be careful. Extra careful. Super-duper extra careful.

I walked back to main with the atomizer in one hand and my crucifix in the other. I tried to look every which way at once, too. While I was at it, I wished I could turn my neck as far as an owl can. For some reason, wishing didn't get me what I wanted.

When I got to the corner of Main and 154th, I kept walking: south now instead of east. I guessed I could get back to Vermont and

Gardena Boulevard faster on shank's mare than I could if I waited for the next bus. In case I was wrong, I hoped I could flag it down.

I turned west on 165th, which would become Gardena Boulevard when L.A. County and L.A. city became Gardena. And I got lucky: a westbound bus chugged up just as I came to a corner. I hopped aboard and put a grateful dime in the fare box.

The Red Line took me back up to my part of town. I was nervous in Vampire Village, too. After all, if Kreuzbach didn't hang around near Danny Becker's place, where was he likely to go? VV, where else? Say the secret word and win a hundred dollars!

But I made it. I'd had strolls through Italian towns, or what was left of them, where I didn't sweat as much. As soon as I walked into the apartment, Dora said, "What *happened*?" I don't know whether she saw my fear or smelled it. Both, chances are.

When I got to the office the next day, Mehitabel and Old Man Mose were glaring at each other, ears laid back. "Knock this crap off," I told them. "I don't have time for it now."

"Why should we?" Mehitabel snarled.

"Because I'm bigger than both of you put together. And because I'm the one who opens the cat food," I said. She shut up.

I called my answering service. "You have three messages from a Danny Becker," Hilda told me. "He wants you to call him as soon as you can."

"Give me his number." I had it written down, but Hilda needs to feel useful. After she gave it to me, I thanked her, hung up, and then picked up the handset and dialed it.

"Oh, yes, Mister Mitchell. He wants to hear from you," Becker's secretary said. "Hold on. I'll put you through."

"That you, Mitchell?" he said when she did.

"No, but I should be here pretty soon," I answered.

I got five seconds of dead silence, then a couple of desiccated chuckles. "One of those, are you?" he said. "Listen, wise guy, what the hell happened here last night?"

"Well, for starters, I found out your swing-shift supervisor is likely the guy who's been blackmailing my client," I said. "I also found out he's a vampire who was an *Oberführer* in the fylfot boys' Lightning Rune troops during the war."

"Jesus Christ!"

"Somebody like that, yeah."

"No wonder he didn't want to take the day-shift slot."

"No wonder at all," I agreed. "Wait, though. It gets better."

"Better how? Do I want to know?" Becker sounded apprehensive. Well, he had reason to, didn't he?

"The other good news is, one night a month—guess which one—he turns into a werewolf, too. Oh—and he's got a pack of jackals who run with him. Werejackals, I should say. I know they are, on account of silver hurts them."

More silence. Then he asked, "How do you know that?"

"Because I threw down a bunch of dimes to slow 'em down while they were after me, and they yipped and limped when they stepped on me. Kreuzbach did, too."

"Who?"

"Sorry." I knew how I'd confused him. "The guy you call Gus Friedrichs, I know him as Lothar Kreuzbach. That may be his real name, but I wouldn't swear to it."

"Uh-*huh*." He chuckled again, more dryly yet this time. Then he asked, "You don't happen to be a wizard yourself, do you?"

"Who, me? Hell, no. Not even slightly. How come?"

"Because you found an elegant solution for dealing with were-beasts. Dimes! I might not have come up with that one myself."

"Sometimes you'd rather be lucky than good."

"Sometimes you'd rather sandbag than take credit when you deserve it," Becker said. I had no idea how to answer that, so I kept quiet. He went on, "Never mind. You told me what I needed to know. Thanks—I think. But one thing I don't know is where to find another supervisor as good as he was."

"Sorry about that." I lied without hesitation. I was just sorry I hadn't been able to finish Kreuzbach for good.

We said our goodbyes. Then I took care of the cats. For one thing, if they had their noses in their bowls for a while, they wouldn't want to fight each other so much. And, for another, it was still too early to go over to Deacon's. Deacon Washington and Acolyte Adams kept vampire hours, even more so than I did.

Old Man Mose and Mehitabel attacked the beef in gravy as if they hadn't seen food for weeks. Mehitabel had an excuse. She was eating for … four? five? six? For several, anyway. Mose? Mose was just a pig.

When the sun was about to set, I headed over to Deacon's. I stopped on the way for a hamburger and fries and a Coke. I would have got a beer instead, only the stand didn't have a liquor license. All the same, it was better than anything I would've made for myself.

Twilight had started by the time I tossed my paper basket and cardboard cup in the trash. I turned off Central where you do and went down the alley. I climbed those rickety stairs and made my way along the walk. Good thing nobody else was around to see me do it. Who shows up at Deacon's at that time of day?

I went through the first set of blackout curtains. When I pulled aside the second set, the door behind them was closed and locked. Nope, they weren't open for business yet. I rang the bell next to the door and waited.

After a bit, I thought I heard noise on the other side of the door. It didn't open right away, though. That was when I noticed the fisheye lens set into the door. Whoever was on the other side could check me out without letting me do the same to him.

I must have passed muster, because Acolyte Adams did open up. "What can I do for you, Mister Mitchell?" he asked. *This better be good*, he meant.

I gave him the same story I'd told to Danny Becker, with assorted embellishments and cuts to take into account what he already knew. I ended, "So I've found who's been shaking you down. That's the good news. The bad news is, this side of finishing him, I don't know how to make him stop."

"A vampire *Blitzrunen Oberführer*?" Adams is as self-contained as a K-ration can. He still sounded gobsmacked—a lovely word I got from an English sergeant not far south of the Po.

"A vampire werewolf *Blitzrunen Oberführer*," I amended.

"Yes, that's right. I forgot that part. How on earth did he pick the Deacon and me as targets?" But that question answered itself. Or, in case it didn't, Adams took care of it: "He would have been here at one time or another!"

"Probably at one time *and* another," I said. "You and your, ah, friend aren't exactly secret about what good, ah, friends you are."

He sighed. "I've asked the Deacon to be more discreet. I've begged him to be more discreet. I've even told him to be more discreet. He is a marvelous man. He is gifted, truly gifted, at any number of things. Discretion, alas, is not one of them. Neither is listening to me."

Deacon Washington loomed up behind him. Till you see the Deacon at close range, you can easily forget just how enormous he is. "I listen to you all the time," he rumbled. "Then I go ahead and do what I want anyway."

"I know," Adams said sadly.

"Hello, Mitchell," the Deacon added. "What brought you here? You don't show up for the fun of it, not at this time of day you don't." By the way he sounded, I might've shown up at the a.m. six, not the p.m. one.

So I gave him the abridged edition of what I'd told his partner. I wound it up with, "Lots of people, living and undead, are looking for Kreuzbach. Sooner or later, we're bound to catch up with him."

"Nobody's bound to do anything." The big man spoke with great conviction. "I'm not worried for myself, anyway. Everybody knows what I am. Everybody knows what I do. That means everybody knows about Desmond, too." He set a hand on Adams' shoulder. "He knows everybody knows, too, but he gets nervous just the same."

Quietly, his longtime lover said, "My mother and father don't know. They … wouldn't be happy if they found out."

Deacon Washington scowled. "It shouldn't work that way. What we do with each other is every bit as natural as what Mitchell does with his pretty vampire girlfriend. Or even what he'd do if he had a live girlfriend." He winked at me, then went on, "We are what we are, that's all. Giving us grief for being queer is as stupid as giving us grief for being black."

"Well, thank heaven *that* never happens!" Adams said, his voice so sour I was amazed he didn't pucker up as if he'd bitten into a persimmon that wasn't ripe yet.

The Deacon laughed like a loon. So did I. I bet we would've laughed harder still if Acolyte Adams hadn't been kidding.

A couple of days later, I had lunch with Izzy Berkowitz at El Burro Loco and brought him up to date. He clicked his tongue between his teeth when I got done. "You like to take chances, don't you?"

"Now that you mention it, no. I didn't know that Friedrichs guy was gonna turn out to be Kreuzbach. He didn't know the guy who wanted to talk to him was gonna be me, either. I can't tell you which one of us got a bigger surprise."

"Okay, Okay. But you couldn't do much to him. He could've torn your throat out—or just broken your neck if he was in a hurry. Vampires are *strong*."

"I do know that. I live with one, remember? But I came loaded for bear—if the bear sleeps in a coffin."

"Vampires are *fast*, too," Izzy said. "How'd you yank the holy water out quick enough to shpritz him before he got you?"

"Combat reflexes," I answered. "And luck. But mostly combat reflexes. I didn't know what kind of trouble I'd be walking into, but I knew I was liable to be walking into some."

He nodded. "Fair enough, I guess. A lot of the guys who went through the mill have that kind of hair trigger these days."

"Yup. Did you see the story in the *Mirror News* the other day?"

"I sure did," Berkowitz said. "That's what made me answer the way I did."

A couple of punks, one with a knife, had tried to rob a fellow about my age. He had a pistol, too, in his jacket pocket. He didn't even take it out; he fired through the pocket. One punk was deceased, the other in the hospital in serious condition. The story said the guy who dealt with them had won a Bronze Star and a Purple Heart on Sulfur Island, out in the Pacific. He would've had his own set of combat reflexes.

I said, "I really hoped Kreuzbach would be in Bedford Tyler's apartment. That would have solved a whole bunch of problems. But only one coffin, dammit."

"Too bad," Berkowitz said. "He's dangerous. Smart, nasty .... I know I'm not telling you anything you don't already know."

"That he's a werewolf on top of everything else only makes it worse, you ask me," I said. "And I really, I mean *really*, don't like the werejackals who run with him. He's bad enough without help from his friends."

"That's pretty peculiar, all right." Izzy stopped talking and made a face that was, well, pretty peculiar. After a moment, I realized he was trying to extract a shred of shredded pork from between two teeth. God, or Somebody, was taking revenge on him for not keeping kosher. Then he grunted and smiled—he had wrestled with the Lord (or at least the pork) and prevailed. He pulled the scarab I'd given him out of a pocket. His smile got wider. "This is a nice little piece. Thanks again."

"Glad you like it," I answered. I meant it, too—Izzy's a good guy. I wanted to do something nice for him. He deserves it. I hadn't done anything very big, but what the hey, what the hey, as Mehitabel would tell you.

"Jackals," he went on in musing tones. "There's an Egyptian god called Anubis. He's got the head of a jackal, you know."

"Uh-huh. Dora talked about him, too, right after I met them."

"Anubis and Isis, they don't always get along." Izzy still sounded musing.

I hadn't known that, but I answered, "Nobody's worried about whether they do or they don't for a whole bunch of years."

"Well, no, but didn't somebody who looks a lot like you help get those Assyrian *lamassus* off the walls of the US Rubber factory a little while ago?"

"Can't imagine who you might mean." The same way I didn't care to remember a lot of what I'd been through during the war, I tried not to think about what had happened on that dark and dreadful night.

Dr. Berkowitz snorted. "Tell me another one, why don't you? But I'm not sure gods and demons ever go away, know what I mean? Most people may stop paying attention to them, but that doesn't mean they aren't there."

"You're full of cheery thoughts today, aren't you?"

"Who, me?" He grinned. "I'll tell you something else, too. People were worshiping my God at the same time as others were worshiping Isis and Anubis and their buddies. And my God may just be the same as yours. He may." Damned if he didn't wink at me.

"He may, yeah." I wasn't going to let him agitate me.

"Only we don't break Him up into three pieces." He was out to agitate whether I wanted him to or not.

My father and mother were believers, I mean serious, church-every-Sunday believers. They raised me that way. Of course they did. Only you know how sometimes you get a smallpox vaccination and it doesn't take? Religion was like that for me, even before I went into the Army. Afterwards? I dare anybody with a working nose to walk across a battlefield three days after the killing stops and then sing a hymn to the greater glory of God.

And yet .... And yet ... "I carry a crucifix. I carry holy water, too. They work."

"Yeah, I know. But didn't you tell me your Jewish friend got Kreuzbach off you with a Star of David? That works, too. I don't know whether both calls go through to the same phone number, though."

"I expect Jesus thought they did, even if He never heard of telephones."

"What did He know, though?" Berkowitz winked again. "And what do preachers nowadays know about what He knew?"

"I won't touch that one. You're still trying to rattle my cage."

"Would I do something like that?"

"Probably. Some people would be happier if there weren't any gods or magic in the world at all and we figured out all the answers with slide rules."

"Wizards have special slide rules, too," he pointed out.

Which they do. So do artillerymen, come to that. I saw some when I got far enough back of the line to notice what the gunners were up to. One sergeant even tried to show me how his gadget worked. Since my trade doesn't involve adjusting for windage and weather, there's one more thing I've forgotten.

I grabbed the check again—another use for combat reflexes. "I don't want God thinking I'm taking charity from a blasphemous cactus like you," I said.

"Bound to be a smart move," Izzy replied. "Now you're giving me charity instead. What will He think of that?"

I shrugged. I had no idea. Then I said, "Dora would flinch if she could hear us talking like this. Kreuzbach, too, for that matter. Vampires take sacred things more seriously than live people do. It makes you wonder."

"That it does." He stood up. "But maybe that's what we're for. Wondering, I mean, not believing."

"Maybe." I got to my feet, too. The lady behind the counter waved goodbye to us. We were good customers, especially the doctor. We walked out. It was nice and warm. Not hot, but warm. It can do that any month of the year. And it was nice and smoggy, which I enjoyed less.

We went back to the blood bank. We shook hands there. He went in, while I headed over to the Red Car stop to take the trolley down to my part of town. The trolley eventually pulled up. I paid my fare, found a seat near none of the other six or eight people already on it, and got ready to be bored for the next little while.

Trolley rides *are* boring, and are supposed to be. When they aren't boring, it's mostly because something horrible happens: a nut pulls out a knife or a gun, the Red Car runs over a pedestrian or gets hit by a speeding De Soto, or the earth elementals trigger a quake and a building falls on you. You hope you're bored. Every other choice is worse.

Except, this once, it wasn't. I'd picked a seat on the west side of the trolley car for no reason I could find except it wasn't close to anybody else. But that seat gave me a glimpse of Bunker Hill in the distance, and of Angel's Flight. Just at that moment, the angel was carrying somebody up to the top of the hill.

The angel's wings and body flashed golden in the sunshine. He's big enough to be easily seen, even from so far away. I've taken Angel's Flight myself. You have to give the angel something valuable, or he won't fly. What you give doesn't have to be *very* valuable; a penny will do. The angel's never dropped anybody yet, not since Spanish explorers found him more than a hundred fifty years ago and probably not before that, either.

Trusting myself to him still makes me have the willies. I keep thinking, *There's always a first time*. Doesn't mean I don't shell out for him when I need to. Just means I worry about it. So, yeah, maybe I'd rather've been bored after all.

When I was going home that evening, I ran into Bedford Tyler. No, not literally. He stopped in his tracks when he saw me coming. I had plenty of time to take out the holy-water atomizer before I got close to him. I wasn't messing around with garlic this time.

Not that the garlic hadn't done a job on him. He looked halfway between somebody with the worst hay fever you ever saw and somebody who'd been mustard-gassed in the first big war. Most of the time, vampires heal as fast as they get hurt. Bedford looked as if he'd be a while getting over this, though.

He greeted me with, "You son of a bitch."

"Hey, I love you, too." I made sure he could see what I was holding. "I love you this much."

"You skunk, you ruined me."

"You've been ruined a lot longer than that. I already told you once, there's no difference between the Stars and Bars and the fylfot boys."

"I don't care what you told me."

"As long as you care enough to leave me alone, I don't care what you care." I took a couple of steps toward him. I had the atomizer ready to squirt, too. If an LAPD car had cruised by right then, the cops could've hauled me off to jail for assault with an undeadly weapon.

Bedford Tyler knew I'd use it, too. And he knew I'd enjoy using it. He almost fell over his own feet getting the hell out of my way. Once upon a time, he might've bought and sold and owned some of my relatives. Once upon a time, before he became a vampire, he might've been part of the reason I could pass if I wanted to.

Dora told me once that vampires cared only and always about themselves. I wasn't a hundred percent sure that was true for all vampires all the time. But I was damn sure it had been true for Bedford long before he started hopping into a coffin when the sun came up.

Now I scared the piss out of him. That got me higher than the finest reefer, higher than chugging a pint of Wild Turkey. "Come on up to Central one of these days," I told him. "Everybody there'll want to give you a big kiss, same as I do."

He bared his fangs at me. Even his gums were all swollen. Sure as the devil, some of the garlic must've got into his mouth. For some reason, I felt less sympathetic than I might have.

I held up the holy water. "If you see Kreuzbach again, tell him this is waiting for him. This or the White Fire."

Under his blotches and blisters and bumps, he all of a sudden looked as reverent as a vampire's ever likely to. "You don't know what you're talking about," he said. "When some of us speak of the South rising again, we understand it's only wind and air. Alas, that ship has sailed."

Even the metaphor he used was as outdated as the Stars and Bars. But he hadn't finished yet: "Those who follow the fylfot, though, they know they can still bring the Leader's vision to fruition—if not on the far side of the ocean, then here. Lothar Kreuzbach sees clearly how to make this come to pass. You fool yourself if you imagine such a worm as you can make him turn aside from the true path."

I almost squirted him then, just to see what it would do to him. We smashed what the fylfot boys believed in, smashed it flat and stomped on the pieces. To hear him spout that crap in America made me see red, let me tell you.

"If you live long enough, you'll see how right I am. And if you don't, no one will care," he said. "I expect to be here. I expect I'll help guide the ship of the New Order into safe harbor right here in the United States."

He laughed then. Vampires have a way of laughing when they wound. The wounding is what they find funny. This goes a long way towards explaining why, however long they may exist and however frightfully wise they may grow, they've never come close to ruling the world.

I don't believe they have, anyhow.

There on the street, I tch-tched at Bedford. "You honest to Pete *are* that stupid, aren't you?" No, I didn't say *honest to God*; I was remembering how doing that unless you had no choice didn't usually have a Hollywood ending. Maybe I should have, just on the off chance. Oh, well. Too late to worry about it now.

"What do you mean, tiny crawling worm of a mortal?" Yes, I'd offended him. He already thought he was better than people like me; no wonder the fylfot boys, who thought they were better than everybody else, appealed to him so much.

I smiled my sweetest smile. "You keep your coffin somewhere inside your apartment." I didn't tell him Rivke and I'd walked right past it. He couldn't prove that, and I wasn't about to admit it.

He flinched. I figured he would. Vampires know too well what's liable to happen to them when they can't do anything about it. They're strong, they're clever, they're undying. All that stuff. Yeah. But they have their weaknesses, too, and laughing at hurtful things isn't the biggest one.

Then Bedford wasn't there any more. I got the briefest glimpse of him in bat form. I did use the atomizer when he transformed—one puff, to keep him from going for my throat. But that wasn't what he had in mind. All he wanted was to get the hell away from me.

For once, he and I felt the same way. Me, I also felt all wrung out, like a sponge squeezed dry. I'd felt like that when Rivke saved me from the *Oberführer*, too, and before that following some of the nastier scrapes in Italy. After those, a lot of the time I'd found a foxhole or a haystack, curled up, and gone to sleep. Get down to that level and every goddamn one of us is only an animal.

But I couldn't curl up on the sidewalk a couple of blocks from Dora's apartment. I kept putting one foot in front of the other one, the way I did during the war when my lieutenant wouldn't let me stop. I hadn't fallen over then, however much I wanted to. I didn't now, either.

For my sins, though, I did come across Rudolf Sebestyen before I got to the building. If he wanted trouble, too … I didn't know what I could do about it. After everything he'd been through, the sun didn't finish him. Would my weapons do any good?

Luck was with me—I didn't have to find out. He laughed when he saw me. "So that was you, was it?" he said.

"What was me?"

"Scaring Bedford Tyler into shitting blood was you." He laughed some more. It wasn't at any wound I bore, not this time. No, Bedford's terror was what tickled him. One more reason vampires don't—or I think they don't—rule the world is how little loyalty to their own kind they have.

"Yeah, well, he scared me, too," I said. "He's fallen in love with the fylfot boys. If that's not scary, what is?"

One more laugh from Sebestyen. "The imbecile does not realize that to Kreuzbach he is the same as me, just another *emberalatti*."

"Another what?"

"*Untermensch*," he translated. That wasn't English, either, but I understood it. The propaganda posters and leaflets the fylfot boys left behind talked a lot about how we followed capitalist Jewish *Untermenschen* and were cat's-paws for Red Jewish *Untermenschen*. The leaflets were too scratchy to be good for anything when you crumpled 'em up. A shame, but what can you do?

"He's white," I pointed out.

"He is American." Sebestyen made a horrible face. "To the *Blitzrunen Oberf*, even I, a cultured European, am beneath contempt. How much more so a barbarian from this side of the ocean, eh? But Tyler imagines himself Kreuzbach's equal."

"Americans run on equality." Even as I said it, I caught the black humor. Bedford Tyler was sure he was better than I was, but had no idea anybody could think *he* was inferior. He was equal to anybody, regardless of whether I was. And yet he wasn't any more American than I was. Funny. Yeah. Sure.

"I know." Dora's half-brother burned the Declaration of Independence's magnificent poetry with two dry words rubbed together. And, when you remember how the guy who wrote that magnificent poetry owned slaves and didn't turn 'em loose, maybe Rudolf had a point.

XIII

Dora said, "You should have the sense to understand what happens when you frighten a little man. He will kill you if he can."

"Bedford already wanted to kill me." I sounded sulky, like a third-grader when a teacher tells him two and two make four. He's thinking, *I already know that, for crying out loud. Let's get on to the hard stuff, like how much are sixteen and twenty-eight?*

She stayed patient. Well, why not? Unlike live people, vampires have all the time in the world. Most of it, anyway. "Yes, of course he did," she agreed, like that same teacher wondering if I were even ready for two and two. "But now you have made it more urgent. He may not be sure you were in his apartment before. Now you have threatened that you will go in there and harm him while he is helpless. And he may also be afraid for Lothar Kreuzbach's sake. He may."

I understood her hesitation there. I'd just been thinking about how vampires cared only for themselves. Dora understood that better than I ever could, because I saw it from the outside in, if you know what I mean. She … I was going to say she lived it, but that's not quite right, is it? She experienced it.

"He is all excited about what the fylfot boys bring to the table, yeah," I said. "Almost like he's bought himself a new religion, isn't it?"

"A convert's zeal. That may be some of it. I would not have put it in those terms myself, for reasons you will understand."

"Oh, I may," I allowed.

Dora looked at me again, this time with amusement mixed with annoyance on her pretty face. A look I was used to from her, in other words. But something more serious lay underneath it. If hearing the name of God can harm you, you bet you'll think about religion as little as you can.

"Bedford *is* like a convert, whether he realizes it himself or not," I went on. "Kreuzbach's given him a whole bunch of fancy new reasons to believe the crap he already believes."

My beloved eyed me one more time. "Every so often, I must remind myself that you can be dangerously perceptive," she murmured.

"Talk dirty to me some more," I said. She stuck out her tongue at me. It seemed longer and more limber than a live person's was likely to—the better to lap up blood, I suppose. I added, "Being able to size people up helps with the racket I'm in."

"Yes, I suppose it would. You would do well to remember, though, that to Bedford Tyler this is neither a racket nor a game. It is not played for points or for anything as trivial as money."

" 'As trivial as money'? Them's fightin' words, babe!"

"Next to continued existence, what is money?"

And, of course, Dora had a point. But she might have had less of one than she thought. Sure, a lot of people put life ahead of lucre. Quite a few don't, though. You hear stories all the time about the guy who jumps off a tall building because ending it all seems better than going broke. And I thought about the fylfot boys, and especially about *Blitzrunen* troops. They all carried daggers with *My honor is called loyalty* etched on them. And they kept fighting long after they must've known they had not a prayer of winning. A good many killed themselves instead of surrendering, too. As far as they were concerned, life without the Leader wasn't worth living.

Why couldn't *Oberführer* Lothar Kreuzbach have been considerate enough to stand there and face the rising sun when he saw the war was lost? That would have saved everybody a lot of trouble. *It sure would've saved* me *a lot of trouble*, I thought selfishly.

Things are different for vampires, though. Ordinary—I should say, live—Lightning Rune soldiers still had the hope of heaven if they killed themselves. Considering some of the things they did, not much hope of heaven, or it looked that way to me, but they would have seen it otherwise.

To hell with them, and to hell with how they saw it. In his second Inaugural Address, Honest Abe quoted Matthew: *The judgments of the Lord are true and righteous altogether.*

The Lord doesn't waste His time judging vampires, though. When they're gone, they're *gone*. Again, unlike me, Kreuzbach would have known that from the inside out.

I didn't want to think about him, or about little Bedford Tyler. I drank some Wild Turkey so I wouldn't have to. And I made love with Dora. Making love doesn't solve a goddamn thing. I'd reminded myself of that before, not very long ago. But it's sure as hell worth doing for its own sake.

Just as I came out of the building the next morning to head for the office and try to keep the cats in line, a moving van pulled up in front of the place. One of the guys in the cab hopped out to open the truck's rear gate. "Who's leaving?" I asked.

He looked down at the paper on the clipboard in his left hand. "Some damn lugosi called Tyler. Bedford Tyler. We're hauling the coffin, an' we gotta be extra careful with it." He sounded disgusted.

For some reason, hearing dear Bedford called a lugosi didn't offend me nearly so much as, say, hearing Dora called one would have. I can't imagine why. Anybody might suspect I was a human being or something. But let's not get carried away. I have to tell you, I thought about slipping the mover twenty bucks not to be extra careful with the coffin. I didn't do it, though. Call it my good deed for the day.

I did ask, "Where's he moving to?"

"We ain't supposed to say nothing about that," the guy answered. I wasn't a double sawbuck interested in knowing. I will admit, I was a couple of bucks interested. I held them out all casual-like. Next thing I knew, they were in the mover's pocket. He was smooth, that fella, even if he had to look down at the clipboard again before he told me, "Gardena. One of those little South Bay burgs, y'know?"

"Uh-huh. How about that?" I said tonelessly. Up. Down. All around. I wondered whether houses there, like the tracts farther north and east I'd seen from the Red Car, were restricted. I wouldn't have been a bit surprised. The builders didn't want people like me—well, people more obvious about what they were than me—buying any of those nice, new houses. They might not want people like Al Harris or Rivke buying them, either.

But vampires? They didn't care about vampires. Most—almost all—vampires are white. And most—almost all—aren't Jewish. That the name of God, sincerely and desperately uttered, would wound vampires didn't bother builders a bit. Chances are the name of God, sincerely and desperately uttered, will also wound builders who use restrictive covenants. They've given up at least as much of their humanity as vampires have.

"Thanks," I told the mover. He nodded and went back to what he'd been doing. I headed for the office. What he'd told me made me thoughtful. I'd sooner've been thought-empty. If Bedford had a house in Gardena, would he take in Lothar Kreuzbach? Lothar would have time on his hands now that he wasn't running Danny Becker's swing shift. And Becker's outfit was near Gardena, and worked with firms from Gardena. *How about that?* I thought. I kept walking.

Yes, of course the cats were squabbling again when I came in. Toddlers with teeth and claws. One of them a pregnant toddler with teeth and claws. Enough to drive you crazy? More than enough.

Like any other toddlers, though, easily distracted. Food and fresh water did the trick. Just to make things even more exciting, I dumped the old litter in the catboxes and chucked it in one of the trash cans in the alley behind my building. (The fellow two doors down never had rented a new zombie to replace Rudolf Sebestyen, who'd swept that alley before we swiped him and unzombified him. Maybe the guy was afraid he'd lose another soulless tool that still walked like a man.)

Fresh litter thrilled Old Man Mose and Mehitabel. It always does. He took a dump in one box. She peed in the other one. They did cover well; I give them that much.

And a good thing they did, too. Not fifteen minutes later, somebody knocked on the door. I'd smoked an Old Gold or two by then, which put other odors in the air. So I didn't worry too much when I called, "C'mon in."

Acolyte Adams did. One of the most fastidious men in the world? Of course. Did his nostrils twitch? Of course. The cats themselves were nowhere to be seen. People who came in to talk with me were presumed felicides till proved otherwise.

He set a flyer on my desk. "These are up on telephone poles and walls and I don't know where else, all over the neighborhood." He didn't sound happy.

No wonder he didn't, either. The flyer looked professionally printed. At the top, it said, DO YOU WANT FAIRIES IN YOUR NEIGHBORHOOD? It named Deacon Washington and Acolyte Adams and went into filthy detail about the kinds of things they did with each other.

"Oh, hell," I said. I wanted to put my head in my hands. I wanted a slug of Wild Turkey, even if the sun wasn't over the yardarm yet. I believed those flyers were all over the neighborhood, too. What had Lothar Kreuzbach been doing for Danny? He'd been sorcerously duplicating records. If you could use magic to make lots of records from one original, of course you could do the same damn thing with flyers. Only the original changed.

"I paid you a considerable sum, Mister Mitchell, to make certain this kind of thing would not happen," Adams said. "Now it has. I'm not a satisfied customer."

"You paid me to stop a blackmailer. I've done that, I think. He must have realized he wouldn't get anything from you. This side of finishing him, how was I going to stop him from putting out this kind of garbage once he did realize that?"

He noticed I didn't say *murdering*, and knew why I didn't. "That's right. You told me he had been working for a wizard who specialized in duplication. How convenient for him." *How inconvenient for me*, he meant.

"Afraid so," I said.

After a moment, he said, "About that cap you told me he was wearing …"

"Funny-looking damn thing. What about it?"

"It sounds like a Deutsch forage cap from the first war, not this one. My father went Over There and brought back a cap like that for a souvenir. I saw it a lot when I was still a boy. As far as I know, he still has it, but he doesn't show it off the way he used to."

"Mm, I believe that." A lot of water's gone under the bridge and over the dam since they ended the War to End War on the eleventh hour of the eleventh day of the eleventh month. Somehow or other, war didn't magically end after that, either. Or what the hell was I doing in Italy? Why the hell did I still have nightmares about it?

"Indeed," Acolyte Adams said. As far as I know, he never got drafted. I can't tell you whether that was because he was queer or for some other reason. He went on, "However interesting all this may be, it does nothing to solve the problem of these stinking defamatory flyers."

I don't think I ever heard anybody trot out old man *defamatory* in conversation before. I admired him for it. But that wasn't what made me answer the way I did. Wondering how and why the draft had passed him over was. I said, "Mister Adams, do you mind if I say something that may offend you?"

"Go ahead," he replied. "You're polite about it, anyhow. More than I can say about these damned flyers. They've already offended me right up to the waterline. You can't add much to that."

"Okay. Thanks, even." I reached out and tapped the one on my desk with the tip of my index finger. "This is foul, yeah. But how many people who know you and the Deacon don't already know you're both queer? You may keep quiet about it, but he sure doesn't."

The Acolyte opened his mouth, then closed it again. "Mm, a point," he said at last. "However much I wish it were, it isn't exactly a secret. But, as I've told you, my father and mother don't know. She keeps trying to set me up with nice girls." The look on his face …. I'd never seen fond annoyance before, but I did then.

I thought about trying to explain to my mother that I was sharing a beautiful vampire's apartment. She would have gone after Dora with a stake and a big old hammer to pound it into her heart. "Mothers aren't reasonable," I said.

Adams' gaze sharpened. Up till then, I hadn't said much to make him think I deserved to be taken seriously. Well, queer men get shoved into their own little box a lot of the time, the same way black men do in a white men's world. If you're queer and black at the same time, it has to be twice—more likely four times—as bad.

But everybody has a mother. And, just as I read his face, he must have read mine. "You've got your own … irregular living arrangements, don't you?" he murmured.

"I sure do. At least mine aren't illegal, though," I said. "Do you think the LAPD will shake you down if they see one of these stupid things?" I tapped the flyer again.

"As if they need the excuse. Of course, the Deacon pays off the Vice Squad so they don't bother us for running the club. If they see that—and if they happen to be able to read—the monthly bill will probably go up." Adams sighed. Deacon Washington spent money for the fun of spending it. He wasn't like that himself.

He also wasn't ready to spit in my eye any more. I took that for a win, the way I would have if the fylfot boys pulled out of a village we wanted without making us spend blood to take it away from them. He even shook hands with me before he left.

I started to crumple up the nasty flyer and chuck it in the wastebasket. Then I stuck it in Acolyte Adams' file instead. Sometimes I'm so goddamn professional, I scare myself.

Old Man Mose came out from under the couch. "What was that all about?" he asked. Cats don't understand blackmail. That's lucky for us—they'd be good at it if they did.

"People business. People business about screwing," I said.

"Stupid stuff. You do it and you forget about it." Cats don't understand lots of things.

A couple of days later, I had to go up to downtown. Janine, the gal whose boyfriend had been three-timing her, wanted me to check up on him. She wanted me to do it enough to cross my palm with greenbacks. "I heard tell he done skipped town," she told me with a certain vindictive relish. "I bet I ain't the only one after him."

She heard right. Or Lester wasn't running numbers from the back of that laundry, anyhow. One of the women who worked up front (no, not a girlfriend of his) said, "Yeah, he pulled up stakes.

The boys, they's lookin' for somebody new to take care o' their business for 'em."

"Mickey's boys, you mean?"

She shook her head. "Nah, the numbers, that's still Dragna's territory."

"You're right. I forgot," I said. Mickey'd come out from back east to get L.A. organized the way his bosses wanted. Jack Dragna and his outfit were here already. They went running the numbers racket, but they had to pay him a rakeoff.

So exit Lester, pursued by a bear. Pursued by a bunch of bears, in fact: at least three ex-girlfriends, and maybe the mob with them. If I had so many people after me, I wondered where I'd wash up. On the seacoast of Bohemia, I bet. When you're in that kind of jam, it's the only safe place.

Since I'd found out what I needed to know, I could've just gone back to the office. Or I could've headed over to the downtown cop shop and talked with Eb in Missing Individuals to see if he knew more about where Lester had gone or was going. I could have, but I didn't. Janine hadn't asked me about that. She'd just wanted to know whether he'd bailed out. If she wanted me to dig up where, too, she could pay me again.

Instead, I wandered over to the little shop on Hill, the one with the half-invisible sign that said BOOKS and, underneath it, MAGAZINES. Nobody ever went into that shop. Nobody ever came out, either. Somehow, Al Harris made a pretty fair living from it anyway.

When I opened the door, a bell rang. Even it sounded muffled and apologetic. The inside of the place smelled like old paper and cigarettes. I admired a brunette on the cover of one of the magazines in there. She showed a lot to admire. I wondered what she did when she didn't pose for pictures like that. Aside from pretending she'd never done any such thing in all her born days, I mean.

One of the men who were already in there rounded a corner and started to come up my aisle. As average a guy as you could want. He saw me, turned around, and went back the way he'd come. Nobody wants anybody else to see him looking at dirty pictures or skimming dirty books. An awful lot of guys do it, though.

I waited. I looked at this and that. None of the literature in there was the kind that would've made Hemingway worry he'd have to work for a living instead of sitting in front of a typewriter with a drink at his elbow. After a while, I was the only guy in the joint except for Al. I came up to the counter.

"Hey, Jack. How ya doin'?" he said.

"Could be better, could be worse. How's by you?" Whenever I talk with him, Brooklyn rubs off on me.

The corners of his mouth turned down. "*I'm* okay. Stuff ain't so great, though."

"What's the matter?" Honest to God, I had to work not to make that come out *Watsamatta?* The only time I was ever in New York was when I got on the troopship that took me to beautiful, romantic, chewed-up Italy.

"Margie was out walkin' Skeeter the other night." He shook his head. His chins wobbled. Yeah, he's porky. Margie, too, but it looks better on her because she doesn't look as though she needs a shave all the damn time. Skeeter I've already talked about.

"Okay," I said, just to keep Al going. "What happened then?" I knew something must have.

"These four skinny, sharp-nosed dogs—or they might've been coyotes, I dunno; Marge wasn't sure—they all came runnin' up and started biting Skeeter. Bit the hell out of him." He said it *ky-otes*, two syllables, which nobody from L.A. does. "They woulda killed him if Margie didn't grab a board outa the gutter an' start beatin the crap outa them. The vet says he'll heal up, but it'll take a while. Cost a ton for medicine an' everything, too."

"That's terrible!" I said, the way anybody would. Then three more words came out of my mouth: "Not coyotes. Jackals." I pronounced *coyotes* with three syllables.

"Jackals?" Al's eyes are pouchy and red-tracked, but they're almighty shrewd. He focused on me like an overstuffed sniper. "You know somethin'."

"I've had jackals after me, if that's what you mean. Werejackals."

"Werejackals?" The way he said it made it sound like a brand new filthy word, filthier than anything in his emporium. He counted on his fingers, trying to work out just when it had been. "Yeah, the moon woulda been full then, wouldn't it?"

"I think it would." I hadn't had any trouble from Kreuzbach then, in wereform or as a vampire. Maybe he *was* down in Gardena with Bedford Tyler. Or maybe he'd lit out for the seacoast of Bohemia himself with Lester the numbers-running loverboy.

Al kept studying me. "Werejackals with that *Blitzrunen* vampire werewolf *mamzer*?"

"Uh-huh."

"Why would they wanna go after Skeeter, though? He didn't do nothin'."

"He was with me. She knows you. You know me." I spread my hands. "I can't prove anything, but I can make chains like nobody's business."

Before he could answer, the sad doorbell announced another customer. I turned around and leafed through a magazine called *How Many Ways?* Quite a few—I can tell you that. For some of them, though, you needed a contortionist. For others, you needed two. Like any adventure, probably more fun to look at from a distance than to try.

The guy grabbed something, came to the counter, paid, waited for Al to put his prize in a brown bag, and got the hell out of there. Once you've put your money down, you don't hang around at that kind of bookstore.

I set the magazine I'd been looking at back on the shelf. It wasn't as sleazy as some of the stuff there. You might even argue it was educational. Or your lawyer might, if the cops caught you with it.

Al said, "I don't want trouble from nobody."

"Who does?" I answered.

"Maybe you better not come around here so much for a while. Not till that miserable son of a bitch is archaeology."

"Archaeology?"

"Hell, yes. You know. Deader'n history."

"Oh." Once he explained it, I got it. That's too late, of course. I touched the brim of my hat and left almost as fast as if I had one of those flat paper bags under my arm.

Yeah, I should have got Bedford Tyler's address when I had the guy with the moving van right there. Since I hadn't, I went down to

Gardena again. If he'd bought a house, there'd be a record of it. The small-town city hall, I remembered, was next door to the small-town cop shop.

A pretty clerk—a little plaque told me her name was Dolores Yoshino—looked through the recent mortgage files for me. "No one by that name here, Mister Mitchell," she said. As soon as I'd set down my card with *Private Investigator* on it, she'd turned eager to help. She seemed to think she'd fallen into a movie. A surprising number of people do.

"Okay," I said, even if it wasn't. But I hadn't expected to hit the jackpot there—Bedford Tyler'd got out of his apartment too fast to have bought anything. "How about rentals?"

"I can look, but not all of those get reported. They should be, but they aren't. We won't find out about that unless the new tenant gets in trouble."

"Would you see what you can find, please?" I was ready to lay out some cash if she said no.

But I didn't have to. "I'll check," she answered. She went to a different file cabinet and poked through it. When she turned around again, I knew what she'd say before she said it: "I'm sorry, but no luck here, either."

"Ahh—phooey." She was pretty enough so I didn't want to cuss in front of her. Then something else occurred to me. "Does Gardena have a policy against letting vampires live here? Because he is one."

"No, sir. Gardena doesn't do that kind of thing. People like me had less trouble here than almost anywhere else when we came back after the war."

"No *Restricted* signs?" I couldn't keep an edge from my voice. I did hope it wasn't a serrated edge.

Miss Yoshino was nobody's dope. She'd been all wide-eyed and admiring before. Here she was, helping a private eye! Her second look was more measuring. When she added two and two, she got four. But, to be fair, it didn't seem to bother her. "Those are up in the unincorporated area or in Los Angeles. Builders can't get away with them in Gardena."

So there, I thought. Out loud, I said, "Good. That's good." Sad when a little town is more decent than the big city, but then, a whole great big swarm of places are more decent than L.A. I'm not saying hell is one of them, but I'm not saying it isn't, either. If you get the chance, ask Satan what he thinks.

I thought about going over to Grampus Records, but I didn't do it. If messing up swing-shift production at Danny Becker's outfit meant records weren't getting made, Kirk Jenkins wouldn't want to see me. I headed east instead, to Becker's Quonset huts.

When I walked into the one where he had his office, his secretary recognized me. "Mister Mitchell, isn't it?" she said. I admitted it was. She checked to see if the boss was willing to let me honor him with his presence. Since he was, she gestured me in.

We shook hands. Becker waved me to a chair. "How are you gonna make trouble for me today?" he asked.

"I dunno. I'll think of something."

"The trouble is, I believe you. I found somebody for the swing shift—I promoted everybody one rung, and hired a new fellow for the bottom slot. And we're moving about two thirds as much product as we were with Friedrichs there."

"Kreuzbach. *Oberführer* Kreuzbach."

"Yeah, you told me. He was a hell of a foreman, though."

"Very Prussian, I bet. Efficient," I said. Danny gave me a dirty look. Know what? I didn't care. Now that the war is over, people on the far side of the Atlantic are complaining about how things there have gone to pot because we aren't letting guys who were in the *Blitzrunen* or were proud followers of the fylfot get their fancy jobs back. Poor dears! Oh, the poor dears!

But you know what the real bastard of it is? A lot of the people over there who were serious followers of the fylfot were the sharp ones, the ambitious ones, the go-getters. That was the train to ride, so they rode it. Some of them really believed all the stuff the Leader spouted; the rest made like they did for what they could get out of it. Whether they believed it or not, they still rode that train. All the horrible things the fylfot boys did—I thought of Rivke and her branded arm—they did because they were on the train. And without those people, what had been Fylfotland didn't run as well as it would have if they were pitching in. Ain't that a kick in the head?

It's such a kick in the head, some of our generals—and some of the Reds, which only goes to show what goes around comes around—are letting more of the ex-fylfot boys do their stuff after all, regardless of how we thought things would work right after the fighting stopped. One more time, efficient.

Nobody asked me, but I know how I feel about that. Betcha Rivke feels the same way, too.

All that woolgathering made me miss something Danny said. "I'm sorry?" I said.

He was polite. He didn't even remind me he was repeating himself: "If you're a good foreman and a son of a bitch, being a son of a bitch counts for more."

I grinned at him. "Okay. We're on the same page." He gave me a look. He couldn't know what was going through my head while I wasn't listening to him. Mm, I take that back. He was a wizard, so he probably could have if he'd put some work into it. But he didn't. I told you he was polite.

He asked, "Have you got any idea where he went after your, uh, encounter?"

"Wherever his wings could take him. Or do you mean, where after he wasn't working for you any more?"

"Either one."

"I don't know where he flew to. But the other ..." I told him about Bedford Tyler, and about how Tyler had all of a sudden decamped for Gardena. "I came down to see if I could find out where in Gardena he was staying, but I struck out at city hall. Can you do any better?"

"I'm not sure. If you've got anything that used to belong to him, the law of contagion may help me locate him. Once in contact, always in contact, you know."

"Uh-huh." I did know that much. I mean, who doesn't? But I'm no sorcerer, so it does me as much good as a plaster-of-Paris apple. It wouldn't do Danny Becker any good, either: "No, I don't have anything like that, dammit."

"Finding anyone by magic is harder without a link. Finding a vampire without a link is much harder. There's no life force to connect to, not with the undead."

"Where does that leave me?"

"Where you started, I'm afraid," he said. I was afraid of that, too. I tipped my hat to him and left.

"I want to have these kittens," Mehitabel said. I couldn't blame her. She looked like a football with legs, her belly dragging just about down to the ground. And when I put my hand on that belly—when she didn't try to murder my hand because I put it there—it felt as if she had a football game going on inside her.

"I bet they taste good," Old Man Mose said helpfully. Mehitabel's ears went flat against her head. Her tail puffed out.

"Knock it off, Mose," I said. He bared his teeth at me. He's bitten me a few times—okay, more than a few—but I'm enough bigger than he is that even he understands he can't win a real fight against me. So I told him, "Knock it off," again.

"Don't you eat people-kittens when you can get 'em?" he asked.

"There's a modest proposal!" I exclaimed. He just looked at me with those copper-green eyes of his. I don't suppose you can expect a cat to know about Dean Swift. Since you can't, I added, "The only people who do that are cannibals."

"Catnibals!" he said, and it was my turn to stare at him. For the life of me, I couldn't remember why I'd started hanging around with a cat who made puns like that.

"If you try to hurt my kittens, I'll eat you." Mehitabel sounded very sincere.

"Nobody here is gonna eat anybody," I said to her and to Mose. They both glared at me. They would have glared more—or else run away—if I'd told them about the time I asked for rabbit stew at an eatery in a village the fylfot boys had pulled out of. I ate rabbit when I was little. We had a garden in the back yard, and my father did his best to keep the bunnies from helping themselves. My mom would cook up the ones he caught. The more we fed ourselves, the less we spent at the grocery.

But I'll swear till the day I turn a hundred and twelve that the rabbit that Italian gave me meowed instead of hopping. Roof rabbit, I've heard it called. And I'll never eat rabbit again, not till that hundred and twelfth birthday.

"I'll make sure there's enough chow here so you won't even want them," I promised Mose.

"Of course I will." Mose wasn't making things any easier. Making things easier isn't in the job description God—or Old Scratch, more likely—gave to cats. Mehitabel's tail got big again. She hissed at him. He hissed right back.

I banged my hand on the desk. Old Man Mose jumped in the air. Now his tail poofed out. Mehitabel would have jumped if she hadn't been in a delicate condition that made her look like the aforementioned football with legs. Since she couldn't jump, she hissed at me.

"Knock it off, both of you!" I snapped. I did know how to get their attention. How to keep it for longer than half a minute .... That was a different story. So I made the message short and sweet: "Nobody's gonna eat anybody. You got that?"

Mehitabel said, "I won't eat anybody unless somebody messes with my kittens." She showed Mose her teeth.

"Mose won't do that," I said. "*Will* you, Mose?" He didn't answer right away. "You *do* know what's good for you, don't you, Mose? You *do* know where your cat food comes from, don't you, Mose?" I spelled out what was good for him in case he had trouble figuring it out for himself, which he probably did.

"Yeah, yeah," he said sulkily.

"Then tell Mehitabel nothing—nothing orange and fuzzy, I mean—is going to happen to those kittens. Sound like you mean it. Make her believe you do. Make *me* believe it. Remember, they're your kittens, too."

"Orange," Old Man Mose muttered. As far as he was concerned, most people colors were just lies humans told to confuse cats. He had a notion of what blue and yellow were. Past those, everything was hit and miss.

That mutter also kept him from doing what I wanted him to. "You expect I *will* keep feeding you, right?" I said.

If looks could kill, Mose would've been up for Murder One. But he wasn't a cockatrice or a basilisk, so I didn't fall over. I did keep waiting for him to do what he needed to do—always a gamble when you're dealing with an annoying damned cat.

He let out a long feline sigh and eyed Mehitabel with a gaze that was ... well, less lethal than what he'd aimed at me, anyhow. "As long as the big guy keeps me full out of what comes out of a can, your kittens are safe from me," he said.

"You'd better keep feeding this slob," the mother-to-be warned me.

"Why did you follow me here, if not for the grub?" I answered. "Do I let you guys go hungry?"

"You better not!"

"I won't and Mose won't. There! Are you happy now?" I walked over to her and scritched the side of her jaw. She let me get away with touching her. After a while, she decided she liked it and started to purr. Queen Victoria knighting a grubby commoner who'd invented something useful couldn't have been more gracious—or more condescending.

The phone rang. Mose disappeared under the sofa. He disapproved of loud, unexpected noises. I picked up the handset and said, "Jack Mitchell, private investigator." I sounded so suave and debonair, I should've been up on a movie screen in bigger-than-life black and white.

"Hey, Mister Mitchell!" The voice on the other end of the line was familiar—and excited. "Oscar Ricks."

"What's cookin'?" I asked, because I figured something was.

"We got another gig at Deacon's this weekend!" he said. "You have anything to do with that? I know you're tight with him, and with the Acolyte, too."

"I wish I could take credit for it, but no. Chances are Dora and I will show up and listen to you." I didn't tell him Deacon Washington and Acolyte Adams were tight with each other, but probably with nobody else on God's green earth.

He laughed. "You should've lied, man. I wouldn't've known the difference."

"I would."

That made him pause a few seconds before he said, "You're okay, you know? Oh—Deacon's still steers clear of the mob, right?"

"As far as I know, but I don't know how far I know. You'll see mob guys there—I've seen Mickey there a few times—but they're customers like anybody else. Or I think they are." I let the other stuff slide. I never know what to say when somebody tells me I'm good. Well, it doesn't happen all that often.

"See you 'round, then." He hung up.

"Who's that guy?" Mehitabel asked. She hadn't been around when Oscar first came around.

"He plays music on Central Avenue and anywhere else he can. Strange music, but I like it."

"All music is strange," Mehitabel said. Cats understand notes even less than they know from colors.

Central Avenue is made for strutting. If the suit you put on to go to the clubs is the same one you put on to go to the office, you're wearing the wrong clothes. And you're too dumb to know you're wearing the wrong clothes. But if you see people there laughing at you, that's why. Or maybe you're just a mullion.

I wasn't as decked out as I would've been before the salamander sent my apartment up in smoke. Then again, I had Dora on my arm. As long as I did, nobody'd pay much attention to me. Yeah, she looked that good. She enjoyed looking that good, too. It showed. You'd best believe Central is for strutting.

Hemlines have been going down. Dress designers must hate men. Dora didn't care what fashion designers did. She'd seen more twists of style than I can't tell you how many mortals all lined up in a row. Her dress stopped closer to her knees than to her ankles. With her legs, she'd have been a fool to hide more of them than that.

A guy in a shiny new Hudson honked at her as the car crawled by—traffic struts on Central, too. She smiled at him. It would've been a c'mere smile, only she made sure he got a good look at her fangs.

He hit the gas and almost, I mean *al*most, locked bumpers with the Ford in front of him. Dora smiled at me, too. I already knew she had fangs, so she didn't show 'em off. I grinned back. "You enjoyed that," I said.

"Only a small amusement," she answered.

Then an LAPD black-and-white blew two blorps from the siren and pulled the Hudson over. The fellow behind the wheel was a Negro. You never would have guessed, would you? All of a sudden, it wasn't funny any more—not to me, anyhow. "L.A. cops don't like it when a colored guy comes on to a white woman, not even a little bit," I said.

"I am not exactly a white woman," she said.

"You know that, and I know that, but those policemen don't." I'm not exactly a white man myself, of course—one more thing L.A.'s finest didn't know. A good thing they didn't. I hadn't just come on to a white woman. I'd caught one, or she'd caught me. They purely hate that.

As soon as we turned off Central, it was out of the bright lights and into the rest of the Negro Belt. Yeah, I had cops, and cop talk, on my mind. Central makes everybody enough money so the police and the mob try not to mess it up too much. Off of Central, the mob doesn't care and the cops do whatever they damn well please. Who'll stop them? Who'll even notice?

Even though I knew how much sharper than mine Dora's senses were, I didn't take anything for granted. Who knew what all hid out there in the darkness away from the streetlamps? Rogue cops? Vampires? Ordinary robbers and strongarm men? You never could tell.

Something howled, not far away. It wasn't a werewolf; the moon hadn't swung back to full. Maybe a coyote. Maybe a lonely dog. Wherever you go, you always find a lot of lonely dogs.

Away from Central, it was as dark as the inside of a Vice Squad sergeant's heart. I missed a curb, put my foot down farther than I expected, and damn near fell on my face. I did manage to catch myself before Dora grabbed me, which was something. Not much, but something.

"You are all right?" she asked.

"Yeah. Graceful as usual, that's all."

"Good. Down this alley here, yes?"

"Uh-huh," I said. She knew where Deacon's was. In darkness like that, she knew better than I did. But she pretended she needed answers from me. Why? I don't think it was to make me feel better; vampires aren't big on buttering live people up. Before she became one, though, she would've been raised to do things like that. Hell, plenty of women still are. When Jefferson wrote about all men being created equal, he didn't worry about his slaves or his wife.

"Here we are," Dora said, a split second before I found the stairs with my foot. Up we went. I was careful. She just went. Well, she could turn bat if she started to have a bad fall. I couldn't.

Along the rickety walkway to the first blackout curtains. I held them open for her. She went ahead of me as if that were only her due. I'm sure she thought it was. I followed. The heavy black cloth fell into place behind me.

Deacon Washington was sitting with the cash box. "Hello, free-loaders," he said, and waved us on.

The air changed once we went through the last set of curtains. Cigarette smoke. Reefer smoke. Several warring perfumes and colognes. Sweat that said some people who'd used perfume or cologne should've showered instead. Everybody was talking at once. The lights weren't much brighter than they had been outside. I didn't feel any too bright myself.

The house combo was playing in the background while Dora and I grabbed a bunch of cushions of all different sizes, built ourselves a nest, and flopped down into it. The combo had another new guy on piano. He was white, but he wasn't Jonas Schmitt. As soon as I made sure of that, I forgot about him. It took a bit, what with the dim lights and the curtains between us and the little stage.

He was pretty good, maybe as good as Schmitt as far as talent and skill went. But Schmitt was more at home in jazz than this fellow was. He sounded more as if he'd come out of an oompah band from Milwaukee or Cincinnati.

A bar girl brought us drinks. I got my usual Wild Turkey. Dora'd asked for scotch. She did that a lot, but not usually at Deacon's. "Why not a Bloody Mary?" I asked her.

Her nostrils twitched. "Because the blood they put in them would distract me tonight. Others of my kind are here."

"Your half-brother?" I knew Rudolf Sebestyen came every now and then.

"I do not think so," she said. "I ought to be able to pick out his particular scent—although with everything in the air tonight, it is harder than it should be." She sounded troubled.

"Okay." I had to hope it was.

Not far away from us, another couple was making out. Deacon's has nooks and crannies and caves for people who want to do that in private, but this pair didn't give a damn. I needed longer than I should have to realize they were both of the female persuasion.

Dora noticed them, too. "Elegant variations," she murmured.

"Yeah, well, the Deacon and the Acolyte are an elegant variation themselves. They wouldn't get all huffy about another one, would they?"

"I suppose not. You are not 'all huffy' yourself, either, are you?" Dora quoted me as if what I'd said were another foreign language to her, not English.

I shrugged. "Nope."

"I have seen this with you and the pair who run this place, but you know them. Why does it not trouble you more?"

"I've known some fruits. I've known some dykes. Far as I can see, they're just like anybody else except for who they go to bed with. And there's this—" I used the two-fingers-on-the-back-of-my-wrist gesture. "Don't we have enough other things to do without coming down on people who aren't quite the same as we are?"

"One would hope. More often than not, one would be disappointed." Dora swallowed the rest of her drink. I thought she'd leave it there, but a couple of seconds later she grabbed me. For the next little while, we put on a show of our own, probably wilder than the one from the friendly ladies. I was ready—no, I was eager—to look for one of those caves.

But Dora didn't seem to be, not yet. Things slowed down again. "What was that all about?" I asked. "Not that I didn't enjoy it, but—" It wasn't her style. Most of the time, she let me take the lead in such things. Here, she'd reminded me she was, among other things, a hunter.

She didn't answer for so long, I thought she wasn't going to. At last, she said, "It could be that you truly are a decent human being."

I whipped my head around to look over my shoulder—I figured she had to be talking to somebody behind me. "Don't worry, babe.

I'll call the girl to fetch you another scotch. You'll feel better once you get outside of it."

"Alcohol does not affect me much. I drink it for the taste. You know that perfectly well, too. I have noticed before that you have no idea what to do when someone speaks well of you. Why do you think you do not deserve it?"

"I dunno," I said, in lieu of, *You never met my mother*. Nothing ever measured up to her standards, including my father. If she could have got out into the wider white world ... I bet she would have looked down on it, too. But she'd married Dad before she realized he was too brown to let her even try. That was one of the reasons he didn't measure up. Not the only one; also not a small one.

As for me? I did well enough in school, but well enough wasn't good enough for her. Neither were my manners. Or the girls I hung around with before she died. Or my taste in books. Or a bunch of other things.

That made me wave for the bar girl, all right. Dora might not've needed another drink, but I did. The Deacon and the Acolyte were giving them to us on the house, but I tipped the girl anyway. She was still doing the work.

Then Deacon Washington loomed over us. He looked even taller from cushion level. Who would've guessed he could? "Having a good time?" he said.

"You'd have to be dead not to have a good time here, and I don't mean undead." I squeezed Dora's hand.

"Glad you think so," the Deacon said. "Costs me enough to keep the police off my back so people can have themselves that good time." A lot of folks in my part of town say that word *po*-lice, bearing down hard on the front end. Not Deacon Washington. He had the perfect voice for radio: deep, mellow, never an accent mark out of place. And nobody who couldn't see him would ever have guessed he was as black as the ace of after-hours clubs, not in a million years.

But he had more fun running Deacon's than he would have selling cigarettes and cars and cleanser and laundry soap to Mr. and Mrs. America, even if it might've tickled his funny bone to have white women in Little Rock or Birmingham or Atlanta sigh whenever his dulcet tones wafted out of the speakers in their sets.

He went on, "I wish I didn't have to worry so much about laying out cash to keep that stinking vampire—forgive me, Miss Dora—off Desmond's back."

"*Oberführer* Kreuzbach is indeed a stinking vampire," Dora said.

"I'm doing the best I can with that." If I sounded as if I felt guilty because I hadn't managed more, that's only because I did.

"He sounds like a fellow who's sneaky enough to tie three or four private eyes up in knots," the Deacon said, letting me down easy. He was a gentleman, Deacon Washington was. Plenty of guys I've run into who call themselves gentlemen wouldn't think so, but to hell with them, too.

The house combo finished their set and walked off the stage. They got the hand they deserved: enough for politeness, not enough to make any of them think he was bound for fame and glory real soon. Oscar Ricks' sound was about as different from theirs as asparagus is from shrimp.

"Where'd you find your new keyboard tickler—Munich?" I asked Washington.

He laughed, which made people nearby look his way. "You aren't so far wrong. Cat's name is Spindelegger, Rolf Spindelegger. He can play some. He can play more than some, to tell you the truth. But he's not exactly on the same page as the guys he's playing with, is he?"

"He's not a jazzman. He doesn't feel it," I said. "The notes are there, but not what went into making 'em. Central Europe and Central Avenue aren't the same thing."

"Some of the guys over there get it," the Deacon said. "Take Django, for instance."

"Django is a Romani," Dora said. "His folk have the same long history of a boot in the face that yours do."

"I heard he was a Gypsy myself," Washington said.

"Roma are called Gypsies in English, but they do not care for the name, any more than I care to be called a lugosi," she answered. "I can also tell you the followers of the fylfot treated them the same way they treated the Jews, though fewer folk in the wider world have bothered to notice."

Me, I'd heard mutters about that in Italy. A lot of Italians didn't miss the Gypsies who'd disappeared. Of course, a lot of the Jews' neighbors didn't miss them, either. And a lot of Americans wouldn't miss colored people … or vampires, come to that. It makes you wonder sometimes. It scares the piss out of you if you let it.

Behind the veil of curtains, Oscar and his buddies were setting up their amplifiers and drum kit. Strange noises came out of the amps as they got the electric guitar and electric bass ready to go. The piano Spindelegger—quite a handle, huh?—had been pounding just sat there. The trio didn't want anything to do with it. It might have been a dinosaur carcass with mammals prowling around it: the past from the viewpoint of the future.

I thought so, anyhow. As far as I could tell, to most people the music the Oscar Ricks Trio made was much sound and fury, signifying nothing. They didn't know what they were missing. Or all my taste was in my mouth. Take your pick.

"You folks will excuse me," the Deacon said. "I've got to go up there and make like a master of ceremonies."

He lumbered away and penetrated the veils layer by layer. He loomed over the guys in the trio. He loomed over me, and I'm not small. I couldn't hear what they were talking about, but I could guess—when would they be ready for him to introduce them? When he sketched a salute, I figured he got his answer.

A few minutes later, at his extravagant wave—Deacon Washington never did anything by halves—the house lights came up. Not to bright, you understand, but to brighter. Curtains slid back. All of a sudden, Deacon's looked to be a much bigger place than anybody in it would have dreamt before. I'd already seen that effect a good many times, of course. It still got to me. It was magic, but magic without sorcery.

"Let's hear it for our own, our very own, our homegrown band tonight!" the Deacon boomed. He didn't have a mike, or need one. "Let's hear it for the Oscar Ricks Trio!"

They got lukewarm applause, about the same as people had given the house combo. Dora was no more than polite herself, but I did my best to raise the temperature of the hand by heating up my own palms. So did a few others here and there: people crazy the same way I am, I expect.

But most of the folks at Deacon's were warier than that. The joint drew Names, the biggest the jazz world had. I'd heard Bird there, and Lady Day. Names. Nobody except his own mama knew who Oscar Ricks was. I wouldn't have myself if he hadn't paid me to do some work for him.

"Thank you very much, everybody," he said gamely. "Here's our latest and greatest, 'Supersonic,' just out on Grampus Records. You like what you hear, grab it wherever you buy your music. Maybe we'll even get paid if you do." He grinned to show people he was kidding—or he wanted them to think he was.

Then the trio started playing. I'd already heard how the amps could make three guys sound louder than your usual big band, let alone a combo. And Oscar could make that electric guitar do tricks like you wouldn't believe. His fingers really did seem to be moving faster than the speed of sound.

I read *The Time Spell* in high school. Who didn't? Either it's assigned in English Lit or you find it on your own before they can assign it and take all the fun out of it. Not for the first time, and not just because of the title of the tune the trio was playing, I felt as though their music were a time spell shoving me into the future.

What would the world look like when everybody listened to music like that? I imagined girls in plastic dresses and guys in bell-bottom pants and velvet shirts, every piece of every outfit blazing with loud colors and patterns, all the people out on the floor jitterbugging as if there were no tomorrow. And maybe, for them, there wasn't. After all, they were already *in* tomorrow, weren't they? Unless they were in the day after, I mean.

I know what you're thinking. *How* much reefer smoke was in the air that night? Afterwards, I had the same thought myself. But that was afterwards.

You might be able to buy "Supersonic" at a record store or a Sears or even a Rexall that had a few platters near the cash registers so you could grab one on the way out like a chocolate bar. But what you buy wouldn't be what the boys played at Deacon's. On a record, a tune runs two minutes, three, four at most. They turned it into a fifteen-minute jam, throwing it back and forth from guitar to bass to drums like boys tossing some other kid's hat around so he can't get it back. I will be damned if they weren't jazzmen after all, and hot jazzmen at that, never mind the odd instruments they chose to show it with. And Jimmy Newcombe tore off a drum solo that had the joint howling.

The next thing they played had the cheerful title of "Salamander Blues." Oscar said it was the flip side of "Supersonic." Again, though, what you bought at the store wasn't the extended version we got.

I knew about the salamander blues. I've had 'em myself, when those people who didn't care for me sicced that salamander on my apartment. It burned down the whole building, of course, and a couple of the ones close by. Luckily, I wasn't there at the time, or I wouldn't be spinning this yarn for you now.

Well, the whole world knows about the salamander blues these days, if not quite so personally as I do. Hiroshima and Nagasaki finally convinced the Knights of Bushido to say uncle. One day, a giant salamander could say hello to your home town, too. Or to good old Los Angeles. Or to Molotovgrad—and the Reds understand as much.

So did Oscar. You listen to that one, especially the way the trio stretched it out, and you want to go and hide somewhere, not that it'll do you any good. Oh. Along with his drum kit, Newcombe had a big bell on a stand. You know, like a church bell. Only it didn't sound like a church bell, unless there's such a thing as the First Congregational Church of Beelzebub. Every note it struck standk of brimstone, as if it were calling down the end of the world. You hope *as if.* You pray *as if.*

They didn't get much of a hand when they finished. Not because people didn't admire the music. I think everybody in the house was stunned.

"Well, they are remarkable," Dora said. "I am still not sure I like them, but remarkable they are. You were right about that." I could barely hear her, not because the room was loud but because my ears were ringing. I expect everybody's were. Those amplifiers *cooked.*

They played some more. They were definitely better than they had been at the Basket Room or on the Santa Monica Pier. They were working out what they could do with what they had. The playerless piano seemed more dinosaurian than ever.

And when they finished their set and took their bows, they didn't get a quarter of what I thought they deserved. Most of the audience didn't know what to make of them. Sometimes you can run too far in front of the crowd for your own good. I'd never imagined that till the Oscar Ricks Trio showed me how true it was.

They unplugged their instruments and the amplifiers and took everything off the stage themselves. I don't suppose they trusted anybody else to do it right, and who could blame them for that?

"I do not know if they will ever make a living playing the way they do," Dora said. "They are unusual, so unusual that most people do not care to follow where they lead."

I leaned over and kissed her. "I was thinking almost the same thing myself!" I said. The look on her face told me she was waiting for *Must be love, huh?* That did cross my mind; I'd be lying if I said anything else. But I was going in a different direction: "I'm one of the weirdos, I guess."

"Well, I could have told you that," she said.

After the trio left the stage, the house combo started setting up again. Deacon Washington didn't have the curtains closed again; that would have insulted them. Their drum guy brought out his rig, which was less elaborate than Newcombe's. The bass man had his big fiddle—he sure wasn't electrified—and a chair. The fellow on alto sax was as skinny as Wardell. Either he was too broke to eat, too strung out to care whether he ate or not, or just one of those guys who don't gain an ounce no matter how big a pig they are.

The piano player came out last. He looked about the way you'd expect Rolf Spindelegger to look: blond and pink and beefy, almost porky. A nice suit camouflaged some of that. As he sat down in front of the black-and-whites, he glared out at the crowd, as if to tell them what he thought of them for sitting through the trash they'd have to endure before he came back.

I hadn't recognized him till then. But I knew that scornful look. I'd seen it twice before—on Gus Friedrichs ... and on Lothar Kreuzbach.

"What is it?" Dora whispered to me. I don't know whether I stiffened or she could smell my surprise and alarm.

"I think we'd better go." I didn't want to name names. We weren't that close to the stage, but vampires' ears are better than yours or mine. Better than yours and mine put together, in fact.

For a wonder, she didn't argue with me. Or maybe she didn't care about the house combo any which way. She got to her feet in one smooth motion—so smooth that both the friendly guys eyed her with something like awe. They didn't care at all when I stood up. Well, I already knew I wasn't their type.

We went out through the blackout curtains. Deacon's has other ways, but that one was closest. Acolyte Adams was manning the cash box. "Let me have a piece of paper, will you?" I said. When he did, I wrote *Kreuzbach is playing piano for you* and handed it back to him.

Dora read it even before Adams did. She showed her fangs. The Acolyte's eyebrows jumped. "What do we do about—?" he began.

"Don't say the name," I warned.

He didn't. He was one sharp bird, Adams. "Are you sure of him?" he asked.

"Much too."

"She we try to—?" He drew his thumb across his throat.

"Good luck with that." Dora said it.

I would have if she hadn't. I did say, "Give him his walking papers. That should do it."

"He hasn't given up," Acolyte Adams said.

"He hasn't given up about anything," I said. "The fylfot boys may have, but he sure hasn't."

"We are stubborn," Dora said proudly.

"I expect you are," Adams said. He tapped what I'd written with his fingernail. "I'll show this to the Deacon. I won't name names, and I'll make sure he doesn't. And we'll see what we can do."

"He's real bad news. I don't think you understand just what bad news he is," I said. He hadn't gone overseas. If they realized you were queer, they wouldn't let you fight for the country. I don't know how much sense that makes, but then again, who expects the government to make sense?

"Be very careful," Dora agreed.

Acolyte Adams took her more seriously than he took me. I was only a neighborhood kid, after all. But I couldn't get too upset with him. Hell, I took Dora more seriously than I took myself, too. She deserved it.

We headed back to Vampire Village. Dawn hadn't touched the sky yet. For Saturday night—well, Sunday morning—we were home early.

I woke up late Sunday. I woke up so late, Sunday morning was already Sunday afternoon. I wished I knew where the hell in or around Gardena Lothar Kreuzbach was staying. For that matter, I also wished I knew how the Deacon and the Acolyte had told Kreuzbach to take a hike.

Nothing I could do about the first wish. City offices on Sunday are as quiet as Vampire Village at high noon. The other one, though .... Acolyte Adams had given me his number. Dora's apartment didn't have a phone, but there was one in the lobby by the manager's apartment. Outgoing calls were a quarter. If you didn't drop one (or five nickels—vampires don't like handling silver, even if it hurts them less than it does with werewolves) in the jar by the phone, Grover Stansfield popped out of the apartment like a jack-in-the-box and read you the riot act.

I waited a while before I went downstairs. Deacon Washington and Acolyte Adams would've been up even later than I was. I didn't want to bother 'em in bed no matter what they happened to be doing in there.

Coffee with sugar and evaporated milk that wished it were cream but wasn't. I scorched some hash for breakfast, then had a devil of a time getting the remains off the bottom of the frying pan. Even steel wool didn't help much.

Once it got to be four o'clock or so, I figured I could use that number without making anybody on the other end hate me. Down the stairs I went. I hadn't expected I would. Only two or three live people besides me lived in the building.

Clink! I crossed the jar next to the phone's palm with silver. I made sure I did it good and loud, so the manager wouldn't give me a hard time. Then I picked up the handset and dialed. Two rings later, Deacon Washington said, "Hello?"

"Hi. This is Jack Mitchell."

"What's up, Mitchell?"

"I was going to ask you the same thing. What happened when you gave a fond farewell to Rolf—what last name was he using?—Rolf Spindelegger, that's it?"

"Oh. That's right. I might've known you'd want to hear about that. He got a trifle testy. Just a trifle, you understand."

"Sure. A trifle, like snow is black." I do like that. It sounds better in Yiddish, but I didn't think the Deacon knew any.

English was enough to make him chuckle. "Something like that. He tried to come for me."

Deacon Washington may be the biggest man I've ever seen. All the same, he was no match for an angry vampire. He managed to live through the encounter any which way, though. "What did you do?"

"I goofered him, that's what," he answered matter-of-factly.

Goofer dust is good for all kinds of trouble. I carry it myself a lot of the time. What goes into it depends on who made it for you, but one common ingredient is … "You think the graveyard earth?"

"It might have been that," he said. "Or there may have been powdered garlic in this batch. It's been a while since I got it, but I think I asked the woman who made it to put some in. As close as we are to Vampire Village, that's only sensible, you know?"

"You'd best believe I do." I told him about my encounter with Bedford Tyler.

He laughed. "I like that!" Then he paused, thinking. "Didn't Despond say he moved away from your building in a hurry?"

"I was the reason for the hurry," I said. "He's down in Gardena now. I haven't been able to run down his address yet."

"Gardena." I wouldn't have wanted my name in the Deacon's mouth, not if he said it the way he said the name of the little South Bay town. "That's where the vampire was playing his blackmail games from, isn't it?"

"Afraid so," I said. "Tyler thinks Kreuzbach is the most wonderful fellow in the world."

"He would," Washington said darkly.

"I know. If you ask me, the ones who still love the Stars and Bars will follow the fylfot, too—follow it come hell or high water."

He kept quiet for close to half a minute. Then he said, "I've had the same thought myself. I didn't figure it mattered much, because most of those ofays are dead." He hardly ever used slang; when he did, it hit twice as hard as it would have from me. He went on, "Of course, their grandsons aren't much better. And Bedford Tyler's an original. Eighty-odd years don't mean much to a vampire."

I thought about Dora, and about how she pined for aristocratic ways long since gone to the ash-heap of history. But she wasn't trying to bring them back, where Bedford would have loved to buy and sell people like me. He wanted to give himself a present of the past.

"You aren't so dumb, are you, Mitchell?" the Deacon added.

"Nice to know somebody doesn't think I am."

He laughed, for all the world as if I were kidding. "Take care of yourself, friend. Desmond and I will try to do the same."

He was going to hang up. Before he could, I said, "Ask you something?"

"Go ahead." By the way he said it, he didn't aim to answer unless he felt like it.

"What's your first name, Deacon?"

He laughed again, this time in surprise. "You don't know that? I thought everybody did."

"Not me. I guess I'm not everybody."

"I guess you're not. But my first name is George. That's right, you're on the phone with George Washington. You'd have to ask my father why, and he's twenty years dead."

"You had fun in school, didn't you?"

"Oh, just a little. Yeah, just a little. I was in high school before I figured out I could tell people who were giving me grief they got my birthday off from school, so why didn't they leave me alone?"

"And you said I was smart! That's genius!"

"Well, yes and no. They mostly stopped picking on me for being George Washington. They didn't stop picking on me for being queer. The people who pick on you for that never let up." The Deacon was usually a cheerful man, but years of bitterness came out of his mouth then.

"You might as well be a Negro or something," I said.

"I don't know what you could mean, sweetheart. This way, I have the best of both worlds." Now he was kidding, kidding on the square. I couldn't say my goodbyes fast enough.

As soon as I hung up, out popped the manager. Stansfield was a gray-haired fellow: old enough to remember when colored folks knew their place and knew they'd better stay there. Yes, he understood what I was. He snapped, "You was bangin' your gums long enough. Oughta chuck another quarter in the kitty."

Now I'd talked with two Presidents' namesakes back to back. If that wasn't some kind of record, damned if I knew what would be. I also knew something else: whenever you argue with your apartment manager, you lose. I bet that's true even if you're white. So I gave him the same big grin I would've used on a sergeant to try to get out of spud-bashing when I was in basic training. "I was just going to, Mister Stansfield," I said, and in it went. Another twenty-five cents, down the drain.

"Awright." He went back inside. I went down the hall. Did I have in mind sneaking back and maybe lifting the whole jar? Who, me? Would I do a wicked thing like that?

Stansfield might've been a prick, but he wasn't a dumb prick. He was wise in the ways of tenants, Grover was. I hadn't quite got to the stairway when his door opened again. He grabbed the jar and took it into his unit.

Exit villain, up the stairs. If I'd had a twirlable mustache, I would've twirled it. Curses! Foiled again! Revenge would have to wait.

In due course, the sun went down. Dora came out of her coffin. By then, I'd fixed myself some more food, eaten it, and policed up after myself. You can take a man out of the Army. Taking the Army out of the man is harder.

"What went on while the White Fire was in the sky?" she asked.

So I told her how I'd talked with George Washington, and how he'd goofered the *Blitzrunen Oberf*. "He wasn't even wearing a powdered wig when he did it, either," I wound up.

Something in her face changed, ever so slightly. Without her saying a word, I was sure as sure could be that she'd worn a powdered wig or two, once upon a time. I was sure she'd looked gorgeous in it, too: she looked gorgeous in anything or in nothing, as I had reason to know.

"Those were elegant times," she replied at last.

"If your wig didn't have lice or fleas in it, sure. Or maybe even if it did, as long as you were George Washington. If you were one of the slaves who had to keep him elegant all the time? I don't know about that."

The look in her eye changed again, this time to mischievous amusement. "You are not a black. You are a Red. We have spoken of this before."

"We've had reason to. I do feel that way sometimes, mostly when I watch the LAPD in action. I had it again when I wanted to liberate Stansfield's phone money according to my needs."

"*Ezüst*," she muttered, and then translated it for me: "Silver."

"A lot of nickels in the jar," I said.

"Here, there would be, yes." She nodded. "And what shall we do with the night ahead of us?"

XV

Kittens. Four of them, in a box that had held cases of Pet Milk. I'd given the grocer I bought Pet Milk from a dime for it. Covering up the bottom was a folded-up bath towel that must have been new once, but not recently. The kittens were, or could be, pets, and they got milk from Mehitabel. Their connection with the evaporated stuff ended there.

However much milk their mama gave them, they always wanted more. They squeaked like starving squeeze toys. That was less annoying than a hungry baby's screeches, but it went on all the time. They never got full together.

Mehitabel came out of the Pet Milk box to eat, to drink, and to use the box with litter in it. Oh, and to drive Old Man Mose away whenever his pink nose got too close. "Nobody's gonna kill my kittens!" she'd yowl, and then she'd try to shred his ears.

"I only want to look at them," he'd say. He would have been more convincing if he'd drooled less.

Not many people came into the office around then. That was bound to be just as well. It did take on a certain aroma. My Old Golds laid down an imperfect smoke screen; you could still tell what was behind them. I'd gone forward through too many smoke screens like that in Italy.

Having four kittens in that cardboard box turned me into a foster father, of course. Even before their eyes opened, even before their little squeaks and mews started turning into words, I was looking for people to foist them on—uh, people who might enjoy having a cat.

Izzy Berkowitz was an easy mark. "Sign me up!" he said over one of our lunches at El Burro Loco. "The kids'll love a cat. My wife and I like cats. I like Missus Katz, too, but Mister Katz keeps an eye on her." He leered and winked.

"Thank you, Groucho. Thank you so much," I said. He bowed over his plate of carne asada. Then we went back to important things, like how to settle Lothar Kreuzbach's hash. Talking about it was turning out to be easier than doing it.

Only we got interrupted. The lady who always stood in back of the counter came over to our table. "Excuse, please. You have *gatitos*—ah, kittens?" Her English left a lot to be desired, which still put it way ahead of my scraps of Spanish. "Can I please to have one?"

I glanced over at Izzy. He knew her better than I did. He nodded right away. "Luisa'll treat it right. And a cat in a restaurant'll never starve."

"Okay. Better than okay, in fact," I said. "I'll bring 'em both up together when they're big enough to do without their mother. You can fight over who gets which."

Instead of going straight back to the office, I hopped off the trolley downtown and ambled over to Al Harris' filth emporium. For once, I went right up to him instead of waiting for the joint to empty out. He noticed. He doesn't miss much, Al. "What's goin' on?" he asked.

"You in the market for a kitten? Will Margie let you get away with having one? Will Skeeter? How's he doing?" I thought of the jackals that had jumped him. I had to remind myself he was related to them.

"Skeeter's doin' okay, thank God. And thank God I could pay the vet's bills. That mutt cost me dough like you wouldn't believe." Al looked up at the ceiling. "A kitten? A kitten could be fun, if Marge wants one. I ain't worried about Skeeter. We get us a kitten, two days later he'll be sure he's its mommy. Tell ya what. Lemme talk to the high command before I give you a yes or no. I'll call you and pass you the word. I bet she says yes."

"Sounds like a plan." As I turned to leave, I added, "Always like talking pussy with you."

"Get outa here! Everybody thinks he's a goddamn comedian!" He sounded as disgusted as I'd hoped he would. Good thing I didn't tell him Izzy's little gem. He might've thrown the register at me.

And then there was one. Mehitabel knew I was looking for homes for her offspring. "I'll miss them," she said. "For a little while, I'll miss them. But they wear me out."

"I'll still take care of'em for you." Mose always sounded so helpful.

Mehitabel bared her teeth. She knew he didn't mean *take care of* the way she would have. They were starting to scramble out of the box now, which meant she had to keep an eye on them while they skittered across the floor and tried to climb my legs. They were still little, but they had sharp claws.

And Margie came through the way Al thought she would. So, yes, down to one.

A day or two later, I saw Rivke when I came out of my building. We waved to each other. I liked her; I think she liked me, too. And I admired her. She'd been through a hell of a lot—and a lot of hell—and here she was. No matter what Dora said when she was feeling snide, it didn't go any further than that.

I worried about Rivke, too, because she'd been through so much. "You okay? You look down."

"Is *gurnisht*." She shoved whatever was ailing her down and to one side. She had a way of doing that. I supposed it helped her not think about too many of the things that had landed on her. Evidently it didn't help enough, not that morning.

That was so obvious, I said, "Like heck it's nothing. C'mon, don't kid me."

She looked surprised I savvied *gurnisht*: one more thing I could blame on Al Harris. "Is nothing can be helped. Just—" She spread her hands, as if to say the same thing without words.

And how was Dr. Jack Mitchell, Boy Shrink, going to deal with that? Hell, Dr. Jack didn't even know where she lived. Somewhere in Boyle Heights, I thought, east of downtown, not far from County General. Did she live with anybody? I had no idea. But I took what wasn't quite a wild guess, not with her looking as miserable as she did: "I bet you're lonesome, is what I bet."

For a second, I thought she'd run away from me as fast as she could. She might've been even less inclined to open up to strangers than I was, which is really saying something. Little by little, she seemed to remember that we got along pretty well and that maybe, just maybe, I wouldn't take advantage of her on account of what I'd figured out.

"How you know?" she asked. What she meant was, *How did I give myself away?* When she got upset, her English fell apart.

"Not hard to see," I said. And if I was able to see it, it couldn't have been.

"But you has—" She stopped short.

"Dora?" I said. She nodded. I went on, "I do now. But I've been … some of the bad places you have, anyway." I made that fingers-on-wrist gesture, reminding her what I was.

She nodded again, jerkily. "Maybe."

Then I exclaimed, "I know what you need!" Understanding smacked me like a sledgehammer. Good thing we were talking about loneliness then, not religion. If religion had hit me that way, I'd've been Buddhist or Hindu from then on.

Rivke looked ready to run again. She must've thought religion *had* hit me. "What?" She sounded wary—no, scared.

"A kitten!" I told her all about Mehitabel's brood. If she had something small and warm and soft and fuzzy to take care of and to care about, she wouldn't feel so lonely herself.

(When I mentioned this to Dora after the sun went down, she gave me a most peculiar look. It was so peculiar, in fact, that I needed a couple of days to realize what it meant. Everything I wanted the kitten to be for Rivke, I was for Dora. I'd thought of myself as her pet before, but never so literally. But that was later. Meanwhile …)

Meanwhile, Rivke stared at me. "A kitten?" she said, as if I'd offered her the sun, the moon, and all the little stars rolled into one.

"Yeah, a kitten. Not quite yet—they aren't big enough to leave their mama. But in a month or so. Can you get away with having one where you live?"

"I do," she said, in tones warning that any landlord or manager who tried to stop her would be making his last stupid mistake. "Thank you, Jack!"

"It's okay. It's better than okay. I know you'll take good care of it." I'd found homes for all of Mehitabel's progeny. I didn't want them wandering the streets the way she had. Cats can do it, sure, but they aren't better for it.

And I'd made Rivke happy. That counted for something, too. Happiness didn't find her every day. Happiness doesn't find any of us often enough, dammit.

You aren't supposed to carry kittens in a shoebox on a Red Line trolley, or even on the Yellow Line that goes from downtown to County General. I did it anyway. Of course the kittens made noise. They didn't know where they were going, or why Mehitabel wasn't with them. They didn't talk or understand well enough to explain anything to them.

The motorman didn't approve. "You got cats in there?" he demanded.

"Who, me?" I couldn't have sounded more innocent if I tried. "Nope. Just some squeaky shoes."

He didn't believe me. Well, why should he have? I was lying. I wasn't even pretending not to lie. But I also wasn't throwing the kitties at other passengers or lighting their tails and blowing things up with them or anything like that. I was riding along with a shoebox on my lap, that's all. So the motorman muttered to himself, but he didn't give me any more trouble. There are advantages to looking as if I could give some back.

When I got to the blood bank, Izzy was waiting outside. I moved the lid an inch or so to let him look in but not let the kittens hop out. "All right!" he said, and then, "Three kittens in there. One for me, one for Luisa, and …?"

"One for a guy on the way back down to the office. I've known Al a while now." I didn't tell Izzy what Al did for a living. You didn't think a private eye can get embarrassed? Shows what you know.

"I've got dibs on the mostly red fuzzball. Is that smartmouthed red tabby of yours the daddy?" Izzy'd met Old Man Mose.

"Right the first time," I said.

We went over to the Mexican place. Of the two calicoes in the shoebox, Luisa chose the one with the red ears. She also gave us lunch on the house. Izzy tried to pay her anyway. She got huffy. "I do this on account of I want to," she said, her back very stiff. She might've been an offended cat herself.

He didn't push it. He knew poor people's pride, all right. He'd probably grown up with it, even if he didn't feel it any more. I sure did. Of course, I still knew it firsthand as often as not.

When Izzy and I went back to the blood bank, he scooped out the kitty he'd chosen. "What you doin'?" it asked in a small, squeaky voice. It stuck out its claws to show how fierce it was.

"Everything's gonna be just fine, kiddo," he said, and rubbed its tummy. It started to purr. To me, he added, "Thanks, Jack. I've got a shoebox of my own in my office. It can explore the new place till I take it home. Chances are it won't like riding in a car a whole lot. It'll cry all night at my place, too, I bet."

"It'll be fine in the morning, though. They get used to things faster than people do."

"I know." He nodded.

I didn't stick around, much as I liked his company. "I've still got my last delivery to make," I said. "I feel like the stork, know what I mean?" I headed for the trolley stop. The last kitty seemed to rattle around in the shoebox. It meowed and squeaked, but didn't say anything. I wondered where it thought its brother and sister had gone.

A couple of blocks after I transferred from the Yellow Line back to the Red, I got off and walked west. When I went into Al Harris' shop, a couple of guys who wore suits were talking with him. I recognized them: a sergeant and a lieutenant from the Vice Squad. I admired the girls in a magazine till he said, "See ya next month," and they left.

Then I went up to the counter. "Shakedown?" I asked.

"Nothin' special. Just what I give the *gonifs* every month. Cost o' doin' business, y'know?" he said resignedly.

"Uh-huh," I said. They've hauled him off to the hoosegow a couple-three times, but he's always beaten the rap. These days, they collect from him instead. Don't get me started about Vice Squad cops. Crookedest bastards in the whole LAPD, and that's saying something.

If they really wanted to hurt his operation, they'd start slapping handcuffs on his customers, not on him. But they don't do that. They mostly don't arrest johns, either, just prostitutes. The only times they go after buyers and not sellers are when they think they can get payoffs for forgetting about everything. Gotta protect the citizens … from having their names show up in the papers.

"Watcha got in the box?" Al pointed.

I set it down on the counter and lifted the lid. Out popped the kitten. "What's this place?" it said.

"Ain't that cute?" Al scratched the little cat under the chin. The kitty made motorboat noises and flopped over on its back. I watched Al turn into a fat tub of goo. Well, he already was a fat tub of goo, but you know what I mean. When he tried to scratch the kitten's stomach, though, it did its best to rip the guts out of his hand.

"Better watch out!" I said.

"Yeah, yeah," he said. A second later, he stopped joking. "Ow!" One of those little claws had scored.

"What'll Skeeter do when Junior there gets him in the nose?" I asked.

"Run away—what else? As fast as he can run." Al rolled his eyes. As I've said, Skeeter isn't a Russian Wolfhound or a Great Dane. He's a salami with a wagging tail. The friendly model, not the ferocious. Al went on, "Margie'll go nuts for this little monster, though. I may close up early and take him home—business is slow anyway."

"That's why I brought him over," I said.

"I know. I owe you one." He had a thought. "You want anything from here? It's yours if you do."

"Thanks. I'll pass, though." Don't get me wrong. I like looking at pretty women doing nasty things. I wouldn't leave the light on in the bedroom sometimes if I didn't. But there's a time and a place and a situation for everything. A magazine doesn't fill the bill.

Or it doesn't for me, anyhow. Al wouldn't stay in business if a lot of guys didn't have different ideas about that.

He just chuckled. Maybe he thought that, even if I did want something he sold, I didn't want to admit it to him. Hell, maybe he was right.

A couple of days later, I left the office before sunset with the last kitten from the litter in another box. "She'd better be going to somebody who'll treat her the right way," Mehitabel said.

"I promise," I said solemnly. I meant it, too. If Rivke wouldn't take good care of a kitten, nobody ever would.

Old Man Mose let out a happy sigh as I headed for the door. "Peace and quiet at last," he said. He didn't bother remembering those kittens wouldn't have been there to start with if he hadn't jumped on Mehitabel. Well, plenty of human daddies don't bother remembering things like that, either.

Going back toward Dora's apartment in broad daylight felt funny. I was taking a half day off, and I don't usually do that. But I had to catch Rivke while she was still in Vampire Village. She went home at sunset. The vampires could take care of themselves after that.

She waited at the corner where I'd told her to meet me. "Let me to see," she said as I came up to her.

I opened the box a little. She peered in. The kitten stuck its nose up toward her. "Who you?" it asked from a distance of, oh, four inches.

She answered in Yiddish first. Then she tried English: "I your new person."

"You feed me?" Mehitabel didn't raise any dummies. That kitty knew what was important, all right.

"I feed you." And Rivke dropped a couple of kibbles into the box. She could've been a Boy Scout—she was prepared. The kitten scrabbled after them and ate them up.

"I think the two of you are gonna get along just fine," I said, and handed her the box.

Never mind that she was Jewish—she smiled like Christmas. "I think so, too," she said.

I was dozing in my desk chair. Old Man Mose was dozing on the sofa. Mehitabel was dozing in the box with a towel on the bottom. She hadn't come back into season yet, so Mose was suspicious of her for eating food he might have got. He wasn't wasting away, you understand, but try and convince him of that.

When the telephone rang, I jumped. So did Mehitabel. Her tail puffed out, too. Mose disappeared under the sofa. He's no braver than he has to be.

After I realized it was only the phone, not a bomb going off or anything, I answered it: "Mitchell Investigating."

"That you, Mitchell?" Not a voice I knew.

"It's me. Who's this?"

"Mickey wants to see you. Three o'clock at his club. You know where it's at?"

I still didn't know who he was, but I knew who he worked for. "I've got it. I know where—I've been there before." I looked at my watch. "I can get there by three."

"Good deal." The line went dead.

Going up the part of the Red Car line that ran along the middle of the Hollywood Freeway always made me feel weird. Not so long before, I'd rescued a guy who'd been shanghaied and zombified and put to work stretching that freeway farther north and west. I still didn't know how many other unsouled pick-and-shovel guys doing all that hard work were out there because they'd sold themselves into zombiedom and how many hadn't had any choice. I don't think anyone else knew, either, or was real interested in finding out.

Then I rolled west along Hollywood Boulevard. A lot of jazz clubs around there; I saw some of 'em. As many as there are along Central, I think. But only Billy Berg's, near Hollywood and Vine, lets colored folks in. I mean, if they're not performing.

I got off the trolley at Hollywood and Highland and took a bus down Highland to Melrose, across the street from Mickey's Rhum Boogie. I walked into the joint at two forty-five. A couple of tough guys were sitting at a table drinking Cokes—probably Cokes improved with something. "What you want?" one of them said.

"I'm Jack Mitchell. Mickey said for me to be here by three. I'm here."

He stood up. "Okay. I know about that. C'mon with me."

We went upstairs and down the hall to Mickey's fancy office. Just as we were getting there, a gorgeous girl came out. She looked mad at the world. Don't ask me why. I know when stuff is none of my business.

Mickey's hired muscle motioned for me to stay back, then went in by himself. He said something to the boss man. The boss man said something back. The tough guy came back out and nodded to me. "He's ready." He stood aside to let me by and took a few steps away from the door so nobody could dream he was snooping.

In I went. "Have a seat, Mitchell," Mickey said, and waved me to the chair in front of his desk. I had a seat. He lit a cigarette, so I did, too. After we had a couple of puffs apiece, he went on, "So what do you know about your Lightning Rune vampire that's new?"

I told him what I knew that I knew, which was mostly about my meeting with Kreuzbach at Danny Becker's Quonset hut and about his playing the piano at Deacon's. "The Deacon canned him after that," I finished.

"The Deacon's queer as a three-dollar bill, but he's got big brass ones." Mickey spoke with grudging but real respect. "You need 'em to tell a vampire to do anything he doesn't feel like doin'."

"Big brass ones and some strong goofer dust," I said.

Mickey grunted. "That shit," he muttered under his breath. Then he shrugged. "If it works, it works, and I guess it worked." He stared across the big desk at me. "What else you got?"

"Nothing I know for sure, but something I think is pretty likely."

"Give."

So I gave. I filled him in on my adventures with Bedford Tyler, and on how Bedford admired followers of the fylfot. I also filled him in on my little venture into breaking and entering. What was he gonna do, arrest me? What he did do was chuckle and then cough so he could pretend I hadn't heard the other. I went on, "I hoped I'd find Kreuzbach's coffin in there with Bedford's, but no such luck. There was only the one of them."

"What if they were both inside it together?" Mickey said.

That clunk you just heard was my jaw hitting his desk. "I didn't even think of that," I said. Did I feel stupid? Oh, a little bit.

"You don't think there can be queer vampires? Better believe there can." Mickey spoke with the air of somebody who knew what he was talking about. "Some of the Lightning Rune fellas went in for that kind of thing, too."

"We used to make dirty jokes about 'em," I said. "I don't know how much I believed that stuff. We mostly did it because we hated bumping up against the bastards. They were bad news. When we laughed at 'em, it let us make like they weren't."

"I don't know about Kreuzbach, but some of 'em sure were like that." Mickey stubbed out his smoke. Mine was already dead. He took out the pack again, then stuck it back in his pocket. "Or maybe they both crammed in there on account of Kreuzbach lost his own coffin, or just to fake you out. You oughta go back and check."

"No can do, dammit." I wished like hell it would've occurred to me or to Rivke while we were in there. Wishing did every bit as much good as it usually does. I explained how Bedford Tyler had lit out for the tall timber of the South Bay.

"You don't have an address for him down there?"

"I know he's in Gardena. That's all I know. The Gardena city hall didn't have anything on him when I went to check."

He said something rude in English, then something ruder in Yiddish. After that, he gave his attention back to me. "Spell this Southern-fried vampire's name for me," he said, so I did. He wrote it down. "Okay. If I have any luck, I'll get back to you. You're doin' better'n I was, I give you that. Kreuzbach's a slippery son of a bitch, no two ways about it."

"No kidding," I said. Why weren't things easy and simple for a change? Because life isn't easy and simple, I figure. Which blames things on God, not on Lothar Kreuzbach or, heaven forbid, on me.

Mickey gave me a gesture that meant *We're done now.* As I walked out of the office, I heard him dialing the phone on his desk. I didn't stick around to listen. I couldn't have if I'd wanted to; his goon was waiting for me. He took me down to where there'd be people when the Rhum Boogie opened up, pointed me toward the door, and said, "See ya."

So I stood on the corner to wait for the bus that'd take me back to Hollywood Boulevard, then rode the Red Car east and south till I could walk back to my office. Old Man Mose and Mehitabel hadn't murdered each other while I was gone. As a matter of fact, they were both sleeping on the sofa, even if they weren't close to each other.

That was progress, and meant visitors—if I ever had any—could get cat hair of many colors on their clothes, not just orange.

The telephone scared Mose off the sofa. While he was disappearing under it, I picked up the call. "Got somethin' for ya," Mickey said.

"Oh, yeah?" *Beware of Greeks bearing gifts* went through my head. Mickey was Greek like—just like, as it turns inside out—snow is black, but the line from high school Latin came back and bit me all the same. And, all the same, I had to ask, "What is it?"

"An address. It's 1612 West 166th Street." He said it again. "You got that?"

"I've got it." I'd written it down the first time he came out with it, because I didn't know he'd repeat himself. I knew whose address it had to be, too. "How'd you get it so fast? How'd you get it at all?"

"I called George, the guy in charge of the Normandie Club." Mickey sounded amused. "What, you think somebody can run a gambling place here without cutting me in?"

"Till right now, I never thought about it at all."

"Well, you should've. He's got the connections down there to find out what he needs to know, and pronto, too. So I told him what he needed to know, and he took care of it for me."

"Thanks," I said.

"It's okay. I'll let you take care of it if you can. That way, my hands stay clean. If you have trouble, or even if you just screw around, like, I'll use some of my own people. That guy, he's gotta go." He hung up. I didn't like agreeing with a mob boss, but I thought something needed to happen to Lothar Kreuzbach, too.

I intended to try to take care of it as soon as I could, but life got in the way. I came down with the worst case of the flu I ever had. I was sick for a solid week, out of my head part of the time. The week after that, once the fever finally broke, I still felt like what the dog left on your lawn.

Dora fed me canned soup and aspirins whenever she could spend her time outside the coffin. She did more than that: she gave the cats their glop and even cleaned their boxes. When I came back to myself, she said, "I cannot imagine what you see in such ungrateful beasts."

"They aren't any worse than people. They're more honest about it, that's all," I said.

"This is not a recommendation." She didn't like cats. I mean, she really didn't like cats.

I had the sense to change the subject. Or, if you'd rather, I wasn't strong enough yet to hold up my end of an argument. I said, "While I was out there in left field, babe, do I really remember hot soup in the afternoon?"

She didn't answer right away. When she did, all she said was, "How am I to know what you remember? I have many talents, but reading minds is not one of them." Her voice sounded uncharacteristically sharp.

"I'm pretty sure I do," I said. "How'd you finagle that, anyway?"

Again, she took her own sweet time about saying anything. At last, she replied, "I saw the Shabbas-goy Jew one morning before the White Fire came into the sky and asked if she would look in on you while I was unable to."

"You asked … Rivke?" I wanted to dig a finger into my ear to make sure I'd heard what I thought I'd heard.

She nodded, her chin up in what looked like aristocratic defiance. "Yes, I did that." She didn't say *What are you gonna do about it?*, but I heard it even so.

"You left the apartment unlocked so she could get in?"

"No. I would never be so foolish. I gave her my key. It is not as if I need it when I am active, being what I am."

"Uh—right. You have it back now that I'm with it again?"

"Yes, of course." Nothing but impatience there.

"That was … awfully trusting of you, wasn't it?"

"She comes to this neighborhood to keep live humans from harming us while the White Fire burns. I did not think her likely to take advantage of me while I had to stay quiescent. Also, as you have said, and as she did, too, she is your friend." Dora stopped, as if reminding herself of something. "She asked me to tell me how much she likes the kitten you gave her." Another pause. "There is no accounting for taste, is there?"

"I guess not. I'll have to thank her when I'm back on my feet again. And I do thank you for everything, babe—including that."

"You are welcome. It was not difficult. Even tending to the cats was not difficult, not once they realized I could use a tin opener and run the water tap." Dora gave me a *Wanna make something of it?* look.

"It seemed like a, well, like a loving thing to do, that's all," I said.

"I have told you before, many a time and oft, that we are not capable of love," she said stiffly.

I nodded. "Yeah, you told me."

"Do you presume to call me a liar?" She might have been a noblewoman grilling a peasant who'd cared to talk back to her. Come to think of it, she must've had a lot of practice doing exactly that.

"Me? I was just agreeing with you, sweetheart." Like any peasant who wanted to keep his head on his shoulders, I sounded as innocent as I could.

"So you say." Dora might have had a fellow with muscular arms standing behind her holding a long-handled, broad-bladed axe. All she had to do was gesture, and … *ka-thunk!*

"So I do. I'm not the only one here who says silly things, though. Am I?" She didn't really have a headsman at her beck and call. And I wasn't really an uppity peasant—even if she was liable to think of me as more on the order of an uppity house pet.

"I have spoken nothing but the truth." She might have thought of me as a pet; all the same, she was the one who could've been an affronted cat.

"Okay. I love you whether you love me or not. You know that's true."

"I know you say it. I know you act as if it is. I know you are quite mad if it is."

"In that case, I'd sooner be crazy than sane. I have more fun this way. And, just between you, me, and the wall, it seems like I'm not the only one who does."

"You amuse me. I shall not deny that. I do deny it has anything to do with love." Sure as hell, Dora talked about me the way I'd talk about Old Man Mose.

"Are you sure? You've fed from me, remember. For all you know, I may be rubbing off on you from the inside out." I winked at her to remind her I didn't expect her to take me seriously.

As if she would have. She was even less amused than the late Queen of Albion. "After you eat a lamb chop, do you want to go out on the lawn and start cropping the grass? Does wool sprout on your back?"

"So much for me being part of you forever," I said.

"You will be part of me forever. You will not be the part of me that thinks, though. And a good thing, too." *So there* danced in her green eyes.

We gave it up after that. Sometimes you have to, or else it gets ugly. This wasn't worth it. If she wouldn't admit to loving me, what could I do about it? Not a thing. If the way she acted toward me made me think she loved me whether she did or not, what could she do about it? She could treat me worse, that's what. I didn't want her doing anything of the kind.

A couple of nights later, one of the other vampires in the building knocked on Dora's door. When she opened it, he spoke to her in Magyar. All the same, I thought I heard him take my name in vain.

And I was right. She translated for me: "There is a call for you on the phone by the manager's office."

I hustled down the stairs. I was getting better; that didn't feel as if I were running five miles in full combat kit. "Jack Mitchell here," I said.

"Hello, Mitchell." It was Mickey. "How come you've been sitting on your *tukhus* with that Kreuzbach *mamzer*?"

"I've been sitting on my can about everything lately. I've been too sick to do anything else," I said.

He grunted. "No wonder you haven't been in your office. I'm sick o' leaving messages with your Hilda gal."

"No wonder at all," I agreed. "How did you find out about this number? Hilda doesn't have it."

"I managed. Took me a while, but I did," he said: an answer that amounted to *None of your business, bud*. Okay, fair enough. He went on, "Since you weren't doing anything about him, I took a swing like I told you I would."

"And?" I said. If he wanted to brag that he'd disposed of Kreuzbach without breaking a sweat, I'd let him. Let him? Hell, I'd congratulate him.

But he grunted again. "I got two of my better people hurt bad, dammit. Your *Oberführer* knows more about booby traps than I figured he did. I couldn't even call the cops—it's not L.A." He sounded revolted.

"That's tough," I said. He didn't even bother pretending his outfit and the LAPD weren't all buddy-buddy. I didn't sound revolted, but I sure felt that way.

"Yeah," he said. "Oh, and the other thing that happened is, George had a fire at his club. Nobody's saying it was arson, but the timing's pretty damn neat. I've got me a wizard watchin' the Rhum Boogie here. He better not fall asleep at the switch, either."

"Luck," I said, and found myself meaning it. He said his good-byes. I hung up the phone. He hadn't told me I was on my own now, but I could read between the lines.

As soon as I felt well enough, I went down to Gardena to scout out the house where Bedford Tyler was staying—and, with luck, the *Blitzrunen Oberführer* he admired so much, too. If Kreuzbach wasn't with Bedford … I'd have to drop back ten and punt.

I got off the Red Car at Vermont and Gardena Boulevard. By what a map told me, the house was just the other side of Normandie and one street south of Gardena Boulevard. I walked past the Bank of America, the post office, and the magic shop that Coptic gentleman ran. Through the front window, I saw him bustling around in there, but I kept going. I had other things on my mind.

Left at Normandie. Down a block. Cross the street. Gardena Boulevard was the business area. Only houses on 166th: mostly clapboard, a few stuccoed instead. Those were the newer ones; the clapboard houses had plainly been there for years. I'd grown up in a house like that, a white one. A lot of these were also white, plus pink and yellow and pale blue and green.

There was 1612, on the south side of 166th just past Denker. I knew it would be on the south side: in L.A. and the surrounding towns, even numbers are always on the south and east sides of the street, odd numbers on the north and west. It was a white clapboard, bigger than the one I'd lived in with my folks. Not big—none of the places there was big or fancy—but bigger.

And that was as much of a look as I could get. All the houses had fenced-off back yards. That's how they do things in these parts. But this one also had an eight-foot-high chain-link fence around the front yard. It looked new, brand new. The dirt the galvanized poles were rammed down into was still raw, not a weed sprouting from it.

The fence did have a gate in front of the cement walkway that led to the house. The gate was closed and locked. The lock looked as if it might have kept out one of the fylfot boys' Tigers, let alone a miserable, down-at-the-heels private eye like me. In case the message wasn't plain enough, somebody'd helpfully put up NO TRESPASSING and NO SOLICITORS signs.

A little old lady came up the street walking a miniature schnauzer on a leash. The mutt wanted to go for my ankle—schnauzers can be mean—but she jerked it up short. I nodded to the fence and the signs. "Nice friendly people," I said.

"They only ever come out at night," she answered. "For all I can prove, they're a couple of lugosis. C'mon, Humphrey. Leave the man alone." She yanked on the leash again. Humphrey reluctantly stopped sizing up the nice, tasty muscle on the back of my calf.

Then he had other things to worry about, because half a dozen lean, mean dogs came up to the other side of the fence and growled at him as if they thought schnauzer was the most delicious thing they'd ever seen. No, not lean, mean dogs. Lean, mean jackals.

Humphrey discovered he had urgent business elsewhere. He wasn't big, but he dragged the old lady in his wake. Three of the jackals loped to the corner of the fence to see if they could find a way to get at him, but they couldn't. Al Harris' Skeeter hadn't been so lucky, even if Al didn't live around here.

The other three jackals seemed convinced I'd do as a substitute snack. They eyed me and showed off what big teeth they had, Grandma. I eyed them, too. The lady'd told me *they* lived here, not *he*. That argued for Lothar along with Bedford. So did the jackals.

They weren't the critters who'd followed Kreuzbach the werewolf. Those had been werebeasts themselves—my dimes burned their feet—and the moon wasn't full now. They were just ordinary jackals, whatever the hell ordinary jackals were doing in a Gardena front yard. Besides sizing me up as a menu item, I mean.

Ordinary jackals or not, they probably gave me another clue that Loathsome Lothar lay inside that ordinary white clapboard house—the one I couldn't get at because of them and the fence and the locked gate.

"More than one way to skin a cat, or even a scavenger," I muttered. I walked back to Denker, then south along it. With any luck at all, there'd be an alley that would let me get at 1612's back yard.

No luck. That yard backed up against the one belonging to the house on the north side of 167th. If I'd been wearing my repairman outfit, I might've gone into the back yard at 1613 to see what I could find. Not in my ordinary duds, though. If somebody shot me in his back yard, he'd get a pat on the back—one burglar fewer for honest people to worry about.

So I'd scouted. And I'd found some interesting things, and I still needed to work out how I'd get in there. Heavy-duty wire cutters? Could I pick that lock? What about the jackals? What about the vampires?

More questions than answers. Welcome to life, in other words. I needed to do some thinking. So I stood there and thought for a while. I didn't take long to come up with an answer, either. It wasn't the answer I wanted, which only made it more likely to be true.

Some jobs are just too big for one guy. Sometimes you need help. I positively hated that. I was a private eye not least so I could be one man against the world. A lone wolf. Not a werewolf, but a lone wolf. The trouble with that is, when it's one man against the world, bet on the world. Most wolves are lone, or at least lonely, these days, because people have damn near wiped them out.

I kicked at the sidewalk. I said a few words everybody knows but nobody ever sees in print. Then I turned around, went back to Gardena Boulevard, and headed east to Vermont to catch the trolley up to my part of town.

When I got to Ancient Egypt, I stopped and walked in. Shenouda Youhanna looked up from a magazine and smiled at me. "Hello!" he said. "Did your friend enjoy the scarab you gave him?"

"He sure did." I smiled back. Either he had a terrific memory or so few people bought anything from him that he could easily recall each and every one. I would've guessed that way myself, but it didn't matter. I said, "Got a question for you."

"Go ahead." His smile grew bigger. Somebody was paying attention to him!

"Okay. What do you do about jackals?"

"Jackals?" He raised an eyebrow. His were black and bushy. They made great signal flags. "I would worry about that in Cairo. I'd worry about it more in a village farther down the Nile. Here in Gardena? No."

"You'd be missing a trick, then. There are half a dozen of 'em not a ten-minute walk from here." I told him about the house with the new chain-link fence over on 166th Street.

"Anubis' minions here? At a house? A nearby house?"

"Afraid so. I've got other good news, too: a werewolf I've met has werejackal friends." I filled him in on my encounter with Kreuzbach, and on the unexpected use I'd found for a handful of flung dimes.

"This is connected with the other?" he asked, though he didn't seem in much doubt. When I nodded, he crossed himself. He did it left-to-right like a Catholic, not right-to-left like a Russian named Vasiliev who'd been in my squad when the war ended. Then he gathered himself. "This is not the smallest of evils. It must be fought."

"You know what, Mister Youhanna? The same thing occurred to me," I said.

When I called Izzy Berkowitz, at first he thought I wanted to know how his kitten was doing. "The little guy's convinced he runs my house," he told me. "We're only there to do what he wants. If you don't believe me, ask him. Luisa says the same thing about hers."

"They sound like Old Man Mose's kids," I said, "but that isn't what I wanted to talk to you about."

"Oh? What is, then?"

"Maybe we can have lunch and hash it out there." I was nervous about saying more than I had to over the phone. I've been snooped on before.

Berkowitz didn't think I was nuts, or didn't act as if he did. "We can do that. You know where to meet me." He didn't name El Burro Loco.

I rode the trolley up to Country General, then managed to find the little eatery without going to the blood bank first. I even got there ahead of Izzy, which surprised me. Luisa spent my waiting time exclaiming about her kitty in English and Spanish. I didn't follow much of the *español*, but she sounded pleased in both languages.

She exclaimed to Izzy when he came in, too. He knew more Spanish than I did. "She thinks I'm a good guy because I hang around with you," he explained as we sat down.

"Why else?" I said. He laughed. Then I talked about the vampire werewolf, about the jackals, were- and otherwise, who followed him, and about what Shenouda Youhanna had to say about all that.

By the time I got done, Izzy wasn't laughing any more. "What is it with you and powers from days gone by?"

"I dunno. I'm just lucky, I guess."

"Some luck."

"Tell me about it." I disposed of my first *taco de lengua* and started on the second one. "Feel like helping me turn 'em back into ancient history?"

"I'd do that if it were only Kreuzbach and he'd never heard of Anubis or any of that stuff. As far as he's concerned, the fylfot's still a going concern. If he feels that way, if he thinks the war's still on, I'll help show him nothing's changed—he's on the losing side."

"We're on the same page."

He grinned at me. "*Nu*, tell me something I didn't know." Then he turned thoughtful. He had a way of doing that. I don't suppose he would have made such a sharp doctor if he didn't. "I wonder if Kreuzbach was in Tripolitania and Egypt before he put on the Lightning Runes. That might explain how he got to know jackals so well."

"And Anubis," I added.

"Yeah, and Anubis," Berkowitz agreed. "Or at least it might explain how Anubis came to notice him."

"If Anubis noticed anybody who followed the fylfot, he would've noticed a vampire who was a werewolf, too."

"Seems that way, doesn't it?" Izzy whistled tunelessly between his teeth.

While he was whistling, one of Luisa's kids left the bill and took our plates away. I grabbed the check before Izzy could. He sent me a wounded stare, as if to ask me how I could do such a thing to him. I bore up under it. He'd bought me more lunches than I'd bought him. Not this time, though.

When I got back to the office, I let Mehitabel know I'd heard two of her kittens were doing well. "That's nice," she said, and went back to licking between the claws on her right front foot. She was ready to fight to the death to keep Old Man Mose from doing anything to her babies while they were small enough to need her. Now that they could take care of themselves—or at least get along with no more help than they got from bumbling humans—she'd stopped worrying about them. They were part of the past, and she cared no more for the past than she did for an empty can of tuna and whitefish. The past was gone; she couldn't do anything about it any more. All that mattered was the present.

Sometimes I think that's why people run things and cats don't, even more than our having those handy thumbs. Others, especially with some Wild Turkey in me, I wonder if they aren't a hell of a lot smarter than we are. And I can easily imagine, oh, some wily Siamese somewhere as the real ruler of the world who lets us think we're the bosses ... as long as we feed him and scratch him under the chin and, when he's feeling generous, on his tummy, too.

I didn't say anything abut that to Mehitabel—or to Mose, either. One of them was liable to know that Siamese, or to know a cat who did. And if he found out I suspected him, good luck to me. I'd need it.

After I went back to the apartment, I said, "Ask you something?"

"You may always ask." As Dora often did, she sounded like a nobleman granting a peasant a boon she knew damn well he didn't deserve. I don't think she meant to do that. It was how she'd talked while she was alive, that's all. And she couldn't help adding, "How I answer or if I answer may be a different story."

"Uh-huh." I nodded. "Okay—what *do* you think of the fylfot boys?"

Her pupils widened the way Old Man Mose's do when he sees a mouse. Whatever she'd expected, that wasn't it. After a moment, she said, "This will have to do with Lothar Kreuzbach, will it not?"

"Right the first time, babe."

"Very well. Of those who followed the fylfot in general, and of their Leader, I think very little. They were barbarians. Savages.

Savages with a veneer of civilization—a cheap veneer, like all of them. They killed more than they could eat, and killed for the joy of killing, not for the sake of food or even revenge."

Some of the fylfot boys' officers, even some who wore the Lightning Runes, talked about the Leader the same way—after they got caught, anyhow. Up till then, though, they sure fought like they meant it.

Dora lifted an elegant hand to show she hadn't finished. "As for Kreuzbach …. You will know I enjoy a certain position here."

"Oh, yeah." I nodded again. If Dora hadn't enjoyed a certain position in VV, I would've been drained dry more times than I can count. To other vampires, I *was* her pet.

"Very well," she said. "Kreuzbach appeared from nowhere and refused to respect who I am. This being so, he deserves whatever anyone can give him." Don't let the noblewomen catch you. You'll be sorry if they do.

Another trip down to the South Bay. By now, people—white people, of course—were starting to move into that proudly restricted tract southwest of the Slauson Tower. Going by there, I wished I'd seen how good I was at arson after all.

This time, when I got off the Red Car at Vermont and Gardena Boulevard, I didn't walk by Bedford Tyler's new abode. I took the bus east to Main and then the other bus north to 154th. From there, I walked the block and a half to Danny Becker's twin Quonset huts.

When I walked into the one that held his office, the secretary waved me to a chair. "He'll be with you soon. He's talking to somebody now."

I sat down. I waited. Half an hour went by. The secretary gave me an apologetic smile. Much good it did me. At last, the door opened. A stocky fellow about my age came out. He combed his hair up in a pompadour and wore a gray suit straight off the Montgomery Ward rack.

He left the Quonset hut without even glancing at me. I know, I know—I'm not what you'd call distinctive. I recognized him, though. I'd talked with him at the Gardena police station when I was just starting to poke my nose into this whole mess.

"You can go in now," the secretary said helpfully.

"Thanks." I could have been more sarcastic. Of course, I also could've been less. When I walked into Becker's office, I closed the door behind me. If that made the secretary unhappy, gee, what a shame.

"Hello, Mitchell," the wizard said. "That took longer than I thought it would. Sorry." I shrugged. We shook hands. I sat down across the desk from him. We both got cigarettes going. All very polite.

Then I asked, "Why was Clyde Shaughnessy here? This isn't Gardena, except for your post-office box."

"You recognized him?"

"Nah. Just a lucky guess."

Becker opened his mouth, closed it again, and then clicked his tongue between his teeth. "That's right. You're a wise guy, aren't you?" he said, as if reminding himself.

"People say so. Sometimes I wish they were right." I leaned forward to tap the ash from my Old Gold into the tray on the desk. "What *was* Shaughnessy after, anyway?"

"He wanted to know everything I knew about the fellow I called Gus Friedrichs." Becker eyed me. "Somehow I don't think that surprises you much."

"It doesn't, and then again it does," I said slowly. "I came down to talk with you about him myself. Which may not surprise you a whole lot, either."

"No, not a whole lot. Some of what I told Shaughnessy, I got from you."

"But wait! There's more!" I exclaimed, as if I were a fast-talking radio pitchman trying to unload knife sets or scrying crystals that wouldn't scry for hell on an unsuspecting public. "As a matter of fact, right this minute dear, sweet Lothar is sleeping the sleep of the undead closer to Gardena police headquarters than we are here. Or I'm pretty damn sure he is, anyway." I told Becker abut my adventures with Bedford Tyler, about jackals were- and otherwise, and about the house on 166th Street with the brand new fence around the front yard.

He listened. He listened hard, which I took for a compliment. When I got done, he said, "Well, if you'd got here an hour and a half ago, I would've had more to tell Shaughnessy."

"Yeah, well .... With the hours I keep these days, getting here an hour and a half ago would've taken something like an exhumation, if you know what I mean."

"I've heard you have a lady friend who helps you keep hours like those."

"That's right." I didn't remember telling him about Dora, which didn't mean he couldn't have found out for himself. He was a wizard. That gave him a head start when it came to finding things out. And I'd given him reasons to be curious about me. "What d'you think?"

He made a small production of lighting another cigarette. After he blew a stream of smoke up at the Quonset hut's curved ceiling, he said, "Friedrichs or Kreuzbach or whatever his true name is needs to have something happen to him. The war's over. The Leader's dead. Whatever his name is, your *Oberführer*'s got no business bringing it here. And that goes for the guy who used to live in your apartment building, too. His war's over. Uh, used to inhabit, I should say."

"Yeah. Used to inhabit." I stood up and stuck out my hand again. "I was hoping you'd say something like that. Will you help?"

He grabbed that outthrust hand. "Man, I thought you'd never ask!" We both laughed. Then he got serious again. "You mentioned Shenouda Youhanna. He should be in on this, too. I've dealt with him before. He knows all kinds of things I'd have to research, knows them so he's got them at his fingertips."

"Good thought. Thanks. I'll talk with him." I stubbed out my latest smoke and turned to go. "I'll let you know when we're gonna try it."

"Should be interesting." Becker made a face. "One of the lieutenants who ran my transport section used to say that before we took stuff straight up to the front. One day, a 105 came down right on his truck, and then we had another lieutenant."

I winced, too. I hadn't heard that exact phrase, but I'd heard others that meant the same thing. *There they are, the bastards. We're stuck with getting there anyway.* Interesting? That was one way to put it.

"Both white men, of course," Becker added. "Not like the Blue Square Express would have colored officers, either."

"God forbid!" I said.

When I walked out of the Quonset hut, there stood Clyde Shaughnessy. Three butts lay by his feet, and he had a fresh smoke in his mouth. "Hello, Mitchell. Fancy meeting you here."

"Hello, Officer. You've got a good memory." I reminded myself never to play cards with Shaughnessy. He had a devil of a poker face. I've never been able to mask myself like that, so I hardly play cards at all these days.

"What brings you here again? Still messing with the mob?"

I could have told him to mind his own beeswax. If he'd been an LAPD cop, I would have. But he seemed to be a guy who deserved to be taken seriously, so I said, "Not exactly," and told him about my adventures with Lothar Kreuzbach.

"Jesus Christ!" he said when I got done. "I was in the Navy. Hate like hell to think a son of a bitch like that made it across the Atlantic. What do you aim to do about it?"

"Whatever I can—unofficially, of course."

He stepped on his latest smoke to put it out of its misery. "I'm outside city limits. Anything that happens here is unofficial. And so, unofficially—luck."

"Thanks." I meant that. I had the feeling I'd need it.

I got off the westbound bus a stop farther west than I would have if I'd been going back up to the apartment or the office. Then I walked a little farther west still, till I came to Ancient Egypt.

The place wasn't busy. I'd never seen it busy. I wondered how he paid the rent. Was somebody running numbers out of his back room, the way Loverboy Lester had been downtown? That was none of *my* beeswax. But once you start dealing with the mob you see it everywhere, whether it's really there or not. And you start wondering if there's any pie it doesn't have a finger in.

If there is, it's not a big one—I'll tell you that.

Youhanna smiled when he recognized me. "Good morning, sir! What can I do for you today?"

"Today? Today Danny Becker sent me over here."

That got his attention. "You are acquainted with each other?"

"No, not really. He tripped over my foot, and when I picked him up off the sidewalk he told me I ought to come see you." I hate questions like that.

Youhanna's eyes were large, dark, liquid … and, at the moment, reproachful. "I wonder how he would tell the story if I telephoned him."

"Hey, go ahead. Be my guest."

He might've thrown me out on my ear. Chance I took. If he did something like that, though, I'd know I didn't want him along when the going got rugged. But I turned out not to need to worry. "Never mind," he said, his voice as mild as tea with milk. "Why did he sent you here after you so generously picked him up?"

I bared my teeth at him in an almost-grin. Nobody this side of Dora'd ever given me the glove so politely. But he deserved a straight answer: "He said you know Egyptian things better and deeper than he does. Better and deeper than he can."

"He is a learned man. He may give me too much credit, and himself not enough."

"Either way's okay by me. Are you interested in hunting jackals?" I nodded toward the house on 166th, just the other side of Denker.

"It is … possible. Would he be along if I went on this hunt?"

"Odds are pretty good. And some other people. And I've heard—unofficially—that the police here might not get too upset."

"Have you?"

"Unofficially," I said again.

"I understand. Anything may be said. This is less true of things said officially." However he scratched out a living, he knew which way the world turned. He wrote a couple of phone numbers on a sheet of scratch paper. "The top one connects here. The other will reach me at home. Call whenever you care to. I will use the time before you come down to ready myself."

"Thanks." I stuck the paper in an inside jacket pocket.

"May I do anything else for you?"

I pointed to a statuette with a jackal head and a human body. "Let me have that one, will you? It will remind me of what I'm getting into."

"Are you sure you would not be putting a spy inside your fortress?"

"I'm not sure of anything." The older I am, the truer that gets. "But do you think the real Anubis would want anything to do with a follower of the fylfot?"

"A point." Youhanna took the little statue off the shelf. He put it in a box and swaddled it in tissue paper. "Two dollars plus sales tax."

"Plus sales tax." I set $2.10 on the counter.

He gave me three cents in change. " 'Render unto Caesar the things that are Caesar's.' " Yes, indeed, he was a Christian, even if one of an odd flavor.

I walked east to the Red Car stop. I would've jumped on a bus if one had come by, but none did. The trolley rolled up from the south. I gratefully hopped aboard and headed north, toward Los Angeles and civilization—if you left the LAPD and Jim Crow out of the mix, anyhow.

Gardena's police seemed a better bargain than L.A.'s. Past that? Past that, it was a small town. What lay south of it, I didn't particularly want to know. More small towns that eventually faded out into farms and orchards. Nothing that would ever amount to anything, in other words.

When I walked into the office, Mehitabel and Old Man Mose were curled up together on the sofa. By now, Mose had got used to her—as long as she wasn't in heat, I mean. He half-opened his eyes. "Oh. It's you," he said, and started to close them again.

"Who were you expecting, the Abominable Snowman of the Himalayas?" I asked.

"What's that?"

"Something big and ugly that probably isn't real."

"All humans are big and ugly. If it isn't real, it can't feed me. And if it can't feed me, I don't care about it." Old Man Mose knew how to cut to the chase. Having set things to rights, he did go back to sleep.

Of course, he didn't need to worry about money. I did, worse luck. I called Hilda and asked if I had any messages. Most of the time, she just said no, which kept conversations short and sweet. This morning (no, it had got to be afternoon), though, she said, "A Mister Lipshits from Van Nuys called. He's interested in engaging your services, he says." She gave me his number.

Automatically, I wrote it down. I didn't make the obvious joke. If I knew Hilda, she would have laughed. I didn't make it even so. Sometimes I'm such a good boy, I scare myself. All I said was, "What does he want me to do?"

"He didn't say."

I sighed: "Van Nuys." Van Nuys is somewhere up in the San Fernando Valley. That much I knew off the top of my head. It isn't any place where I'm in the habit of going. The San Fernando Valley is part of Los Angeles … after a fashion.

"Maybe it's work." Hilda was a born optimist.

"Maybe." I wasn't. But what the hell? If you don't bet, you can't win. I dialed Lipshits' number.

Somebody answered: "Hello?"

"This is Jack Mitchell. I'm looking for Mister Lipshits."

"I'm Irving Lipshits."

"You talked with my secretary earlier today." No, I don't tell people I have an answering service.

"Oh, yeah, I did. I thought it would be exciting, talking to a real-life detective."

I told him what he could do with exciting. All corners and sideways. Then I hung up. From the office, Van Nuys is a toll call, too, and not a cheap one. Naturally.

After that, it was trying to find out when everybody who wanted to show Lothar Kreuzbach—and maybe even Bedford Tyler—why following the fylfot wasn't such a good idea could get over to the house on 166th Street at the same time. People with families, people with jobs that didn't let them get away when other people could …. I wasn't a sergeant who could give orders. While I was in the Army, I never wanted stripes. Now I figured out why they mattered.

"Lothar will die of old age before we can work out how to deal with him," I said to Dora.

"That seems unlikely," she answered. She wasn't wrong, either. She didn't make me feel any better.

"How much trouble can he make before we finally have a go at him?"

"How much trouble can he make if we botch what we want to do because we try without someone we prove to need?"

I gave her a dirty look. "Do you have to be so damn sensible?"

"Vampires often are. Blame experience."

She'd shown me that was true for her. For vampires generally? I wasn't convinced. "Then why does Kreuzbach follow the fylfot?" I asked. "Why does Tyler wish the Stars and Bars were still flying?"

"Blame experience," Dora repeated. "They do what they do now and in the recent past because of what happened to them in their earlier time, their live time. If things went wrong there, then the experience they have is corrupt, and also how they reason about it now."

I grunted. What was I going to do, tell her she ought to act like an idiot, the way Irving Lipshits did? That didn't strike me as a winning argument. I did say, "Are you sure you want to be part of this? I know it adds your power, but it also means Lothar and Bedford can use theirs against you."

"I understand this." She sounded uncommonly patient. She must have realized she needed to sound that way with me. "Live people have advantages over us, as we have some over them. Going out under the White Fire is not the smallest of these. But those who use that advantage do not always enjoy what comes of using it."

"You mean it's not sporting?" In Italy, the fylfot boys and we mostly didn't try to kill each other's medics. Mostly. Neither side was perfect about that, and accidents did for some, too. Both sides also mostly didn't shoot guys who were squatting with their pants around their ankles, either. Again, mostly. Some snipers made a point of potting soldiers they caught like that. A couple of them met nasty ends when they tried to surrender afterwards. Things like that don't get written down. They happen anyway.

"It is not sporting, no, but I did not mean that," Dora said. "Yes, vampires who learn about such dealings may seek to avenge themselves, but—"

"Uh-huh." I nodded uneasily, once more thinking of those snipers.

"*But*"—Dora overrode me—"that is not what I meant, either. There are times when giving one of us to the White Fire is justified. This may well be one of them. But there are also occasions, many of them, when those who finish us that way find they have no luck from that time forward. Their lives prove shorter than they might have otherwise, and filled with misfortune and pain. You should think on this."

"Should I?" She might have been a grownup telling a little kid, *The boogeyman'll get you if you don't watch out*, trying to scare him out of whatever mischief he's dreamt up.

She might have been. Or she might not.

"Talk with your comrades," she said. "If this Becker is any kind of wizard, he will know whether I speak the truth. I daresay Doctor Berkowitz also will. He is no sorcerer, but for a mortal he knows a great deal about my kind. If one is a doctor at a blood bank, that is a necessity."

"It would be, yeah." I changed the subject. I wanted to think she was bluffing, but she sure didn't make it easy.

And so, when I got to my office the next day, I did call Izzy and put the question to him. I'd known him longer than Danny Becker, and trusted him more. He didn't say anything at all for close to half a minute. When he did, it was, "You come up with the good ones, don't you?"

"I try," I said modestly.

"Yeah, I've seen that. You're pretty good at it, too. Trouble is, it's not a question with a simple, obvious answer."

"The older I get, the more it looks like most questions are like that."

"Doesn't it just, buddy? Oh, doesn't it just? The way it looks to me is, your lady has it pretty much right. You *can* throw away your luck forever if you give a vampire a sunburn for the fun of it. You can throw away your health, too. That doesn't always happen, but it happens often enough to make me leery of trying it unless there's no choice."

"Any idea why?"

"There's no scientific explanation I know of. If the theoretical thaumaturges have found one, I haven't heard about that, either. But I don't know everything there is to know about that end of things. A proper wizard may be able to tell you more."

"Okay. I'll see what I can find out there. Thanks." I said my goodbyes, then called Danny Becker.

"I don't have answers. I have some recent speculations, though," he said after we went through our small talk and I got to ask my question. "You know how there are little granite hills in Scandia they call *jätehöge kullar*?"

"I'll take it for granite," I assured him.

"Okay." He gave me a sour chuckle. "It means 'giant hills.' Giants that don't take cover before sunup turn to stone, the way vampires go up in smoke. When they do, there's a lot of radioactivity involved, and that can make you sick or kill you if you get a big dose. Some mages think the same kind of thing is involved in vampire combustion. No proof—the experiments aren't exactly easy to arrange."

"If that's so, how come sometimes nothing happens when you give a vampire to the sun?"

"You find out, Mitchell, you win the Kewpie doll. Maybe the wind is blowing the ashes away from you, not into your lungs. Maybe you're in a state of grace and God's protecting you."

"As much as God ever protects anybody," I said. "Some of the things the fylfot boys and the Knights of Bushido did ..."

"I know. Everybody knows. A lot of us still manage to believe anyway. I can't begin to tell you whether that's good or bad."

"If God doesn't feel like taking care of us, we've just got to take care of ourselves," I said. Danny didn't try to tell me I was wrong.

XVII

Dora and I stood outside the apartment building, waiting for Izzy Berkowitz's Ford. A chilly breeze off the ocean blew dead leaves down the street. No streetlights on the block, but I had no trouble seeing them anyway. Twilight still paled the western sky; by Dora's standards, we were out early.

In the east, the moon had risen not long before. Yes, it was full. Of course it was full. I turned to Dora and said, "Is Kreuzbach liable to be more dangerous as a vampire or a werewolf?"

"By himself, I would say as a vampire," she answered. "As a werewolf, he will not be thinking and scheming as well as he might. But, as a werewolf, he also has a connection with those werejackals, which is not to be despised. As a werewolf, he may also have a connection with Anubis. I cannot give a precise value to that. If the connection is there at all, that value will not be small."

"Yeah." I lit an Old Gold. They help me think, and I can use all the help I can get there. "Looks about the same to me. Just wondered if you had a different slant on things."

"It seems the most certain of all the uncertainties we face." Dora was about as clear as the time a sundial shows on a cloudy day.

Before I could find a comeback, a car turned on to our street and slowly came up it towards us. Sure enough, a Ford. It stopped in front of us. "Hello, folks. Hop on in, why don't you?" Izzy called out the open passenger-side window. "Now we get to see just how far out of our depth we really are."

"You know how to cheer people up, don't you?" I said as I held the back door open for Dora. She slid in, graceful as a cat—not that she would have appreciated the comparison.

"I'm famous for my bedside manner. Famous, I tell you," Berkowitz said as I got in after Dora and slammed the door behind me. Before he put the car in gear, he half-turned in the driver's seat and nodded to Dora. "Good to see you again, Miss Urban."

"And you, Doctor," she replied. When she didn't feed off me—which was most of the time, because I couldn't make blood as fast as she needed it—she fueled up at County General.

As if plucking that thought from my brain, Izzy said, "We haven't done anything that looked like this much fun since we visited the US Rubber factory, have we? Blood-bank chitchat just ain't the same." He said *ain't* with the air of a man who knows he's doing it wrong on purpose.

"Indeed, it is not." Dora hardly used contractions at all, let alone wrong ones.

"I hope we don't have as much fun as we did down at the tire plant," I said.

"Fun. Uh-huh, fun." Izzy chuckled harshly. "Anybody'd guess you'd been through the mill a time or two."

I laughed the same way. "Can't imagine why." While I'd slogged up the Italian boot, Izzy'd been a medic in Gaul. He got to see all the delights of war, but wasn't supposed to shoot back when bullets came his way either accidentally or on purpose. The best of both worlds … it wasn't.

Dora glanced from me to him and back again with the air of someone watching a couple of children at play. Which is what we had been during the war, only most kids' games don't kill you when you play them. Then again, to vampires mortals can't help seeming like children—dangerous children sometimes, but children all the same.

Izzy turned left on to Vermont and headed south. Vermont had streetlights. The poles changed style when we left the city of L.A. for the county, then again when we came into Gardena. That stretch of Vermont was familiar to me; it looked the same from a car as it did from the trolley.

It wasn't familiar to Izzy. He grunted in surprise when we passed the gaudy Rainbow Club, then again when we went by the more sedate Monterey Club. "I forgot they have those poker joints here," he said. "It's a game of skill, right?"

"My wallet always told me it was," I said sadly. "That's how come I don't play poker any more."

"A sensible attitude," Dora said. "If everyone had it, the clubs would not be able to stay in business."

"You expect people to be sensible?" Izzy Berkowitz snorted at the absurdity of the notion.

"I said 'if.'" Dora's voice was prim and precise.

"Yes, ma'am," he said.

"Light after this one is Gardena Boulevard," I told Izzy. "Turn right there and go down a couple of blocks. The magic shop's on the other side of the street."

"Gotcha."

They seemed to have rolled up the sidewalks on Gardena. It wasn't late, but all the businesses had shut down for the night. We were the only car on the street. Izzy made a U-turn—no danger in that, not when he could see all the nothing in front of and behind him—and slid into a parking space in front of Ancient Egypt. Another car—a new-looking Pontiac—sat two spaces over. After a second, I realized I'd seen it before, over by the Quonset huts on 154th. It belonged to Danny Becker.

We all got out of Izzy's Ford and went into the shop. Sure enough, Becker and Shenouda Youhanna were talking animatedly about jackals and crocodiles when we came inside. Since I was the only one who knew everybody, I introduced people around.

"Pay attention," I said. "There'll be a test later on tonight."

"What do we get if we ace it?" Izzy asked.

"If we're real lucky, we get to stay in one piece." I wasn't kidding. I wished I were. I'd been that scared at the US Rubber factory, in the zombie dealerships that led up to what happened there, and a handful of times in Italy. Some people enjoy the feeling: it reminds them they're alive. Me, I don't, not for hell. It reminds me I'm liable not to stay that way.

By the look on Izzy's face, he'd known that feeling, too, and liked it no better than I did. Danny Becker'd seen the elephant, too. Shenouda Youhanna seemed cool enough. Maybe he'd been in combat, too, or maybe he just knew how to keep up a bold front. That also counts for something.

Dora I didn't worry about. Being undead leaves you preternaturally if not supernaturally calm. Whatever needed doing, she'd do. And if that meant flying away from trouble and leaving the rest of us, including me, in the lurch, then it did. She was what she was, same as the rest of us.

Danny Becker grabbed his carpetbag. After we went outside, Izzy pulled a doctor's medical bag out of the Ford's trunk. "Are we ready?" I asked brightly. Nobody said no. I wished someone would have. We started walking toward the house with the jackals in the yard.

Gardena Boulevard had streetlights. So did Normandie. Those were big streets. People made money on them. Once we started west on 166th, we left the light behind. People just lived on 166th Street. Nobody at the Gardena city hall figured streets like that needed lights. Those guys and the Los Angeles city fathers thought the same way.

Oh, we did have the full moon. If having it would've cost Gardena one red cent, though, I guarantee you they would have come up with some kind of scheme to take it away from us.

We hadn't got very far along 166th when we heard a howl that stopped us in our tracks. Even Dora didn't go on right away, and Dora, being what she is, is the poster girl for sangfroid.

"Well, well," Izzy said, at the same time as Danny Becker was going, "How about that?" Both meaningless phrases carried the same message: *That scared the bejesus out of me, and I'm doing my best not to let on.*

When I stepped off the curb to cross Denker, my legs felt light and loose, as if they wanted to run if only I'd let them. I remembered that from Italy, too. Speaking of *if only*s, if only I'd been able to forget it after the war ended.

I hopped up onto the sidewalk on the far side of Denker and pointed west. "It's the one with the chain-link fence around the front yard," I said, and reached into a pants pocket to jingle some dimes. I was as ready as I could be to cope with werebeasts. Whether that was ready enough ... I'd find out.

Shapes in the moonlight on the other side of the fence, smooth, sharp-nosed, sinuous. More like coyotes than anything else I can think of, but with a sophistication coyotes don't have. Jackals.

"Are those ordinary critters or brought out by the full moon?" Izzy asked.

"Could be either," I said.

Shenouda Youhanna said something in a language that seemed to have more consonants than it knew what to do with: Coptic, I suppose. The jackals separated into two groups. By the way they snarled, they didn't like separating, but they did it anyhow. Youhanna came back to English, saying, "Those are the werejackals," as he pointed to one bunch.

I flung dimes at them. They barked and whined and made unearthly noises to show they didn't care for that one bit. Even more to the point, they ran away from us—the silver hurt them. Now we only—only!—had the regular jackals to worry about.

Becker walked up to the locked gate and touched the lock with his forefinger. Then he jerked it away with his own yip of pain. "That's ... a stronger ward than I looked for," he said.

"You okay?" I asked.

"I hope so. I don't *think* it was venomous," he said.

"That might not endear you to the neighbors," I agreed. Then I fumbled in my pockets till I found the little leather case where my lockpicks lived. If magic wouldn't get us in, burglary might.

Even with the full moon, the light wasn't what I wished it were. But that mattered only so much. You pick locks more by feel—almost by smell, I sometimes think—than by sight. When you pick them. This was a good one, and it gave me trouble. I always knew I should have practiced more often.

The regular jackals on the other side of the chain-link fence didn't help, either. They were growling and yipping while I worked, which sure didn't do my concentration any good. Neither did thinking about what would happen after I got the gate open, if I did. They had big, sharp teeth. *The better to eat you with, Grandma.*

Then Shenouda Youhanna said something else in—I guess—Coptic. The jackals' yips and barks turned to frightened whines. Their tails went down between their legs.

"What did you tell them?" I asked as one of my picks pushed up a tumbler.

" 'Pride goeth before destruction, and an haughty spirit before a fall,' and also 'As a dog returneth to his folly, so a fool returneth to his vomit.' From Proverbs, you understand."

"Yeah." I didn't bother telling him he'd got the last verse backwards. If he hadn't done it on purpose, nobody ever did anything like that. Then I noticed Dora'd taken a step away from the rest of us. She was hanging on to the fence to hold herself up. Ice rivered through me. "Are you all right, babe?"

"I cannot hear words from … from that book without feeling them like a scorpion's sting," she said, her voice weaker than it should have been. "But they were not aimed at me, so I should recover soon." She took her hand away from the chain link. When she didn't fall down, she seemed satisfied.

Youhanna fell over himself apologizing. "I did not think, I did not think! Forgive me, I beg!" He made a point of not saying *I pray*.

"It is already better," she answered gamely. I hoped she wasn't lying. For all kinds of reasons, I hoped she wasn't.

Since I couldn't help her if she was, I went back to lockpicking. I hated doing it with an audience—everybody standing there watching me, wanting me to hurry up and get it right. I couldn't hurry up. You only fubar things if you do. But, at last, I got it right. The lock clicked open.

"Way to go, Jack!" Izzy said.

I knew I should have been happier, prouder, whatever you want to call it. That was one *nasty* chunk of ironmongery. I took it off the hasp and let it fall to the sidewalk with a dull clunk. Then I opened the gate.

"This is where the fun stuff starts," I said. That was why I wasn't happier. I felt like a dull clunk myself. Going into the yard—probably going into the little clapboard house, too—would be easy. Getting out again? That'd be a different story.

"Let's do it," Danny Becker said. The way the words came out of his mouth, in a tight, self-contained burst like the one an experienced machine gunner would use, told me he'd made himself advance on other places where most of him didn't want to go. War will do that to you.

We moved toward the house. Kreuzbach and Bedford Tyler didn't have to wait for us in there. They could fly off and likely get away. I didn't think they would, though. For one thing, they had to know we'd fix it so they couldn't safely use the place again. They'd need to start over from zilch. And, for another, the fylfot boys always were a pack of arrogant bastards. They had their goddamn nerve, thinking they were entitled to own other people just like them.

We walked up on to the porch. I tried the front door. It wasn't locked. It creaked when it swung open. Had Kreuzbach watched too many horror movies? Or had he and Bedford just forgotten to oil the hinges? You worry at, worry about, the small things so you don't have to sweat the big ones. That was me, all right.

I wished for a Tommy gun with a drum full of silver bullets. That beat the hell out of a handful of dimes, which was what I had. I might as well have wished for the big full moon while I was at it. The moon stayed up there in the sky, where I couldn't reach it. It didn't even throw any light into the front room—that faced north.

"Watch out for booby traps and trip wires," Izzy said softly. He knew what was what. I nodded. So did I. It was as if the few years since the war ended hadn't happened. Does the war against the things the fylfot boys and the ones who fought for slavery want ever really end?

Confident I knew what was what, I ran my hand over the wall to the left of the doorway. There'd be a light switch there, maybe two on one plate. If there was just one, it would turn on the porch light and let me see the front room, at least a little. If there were two, one would be for the porch light and the other, with luck, for a lamp in the front room, which would be even better.

There were two. The one closer to the door would work the porch light. Confident I knew what was what, I cautiously felt out the other. No gossamer wires leading away, no sign anybody'd messed with it at all. My strength was as the strength of ten because my heart was pure. Or something like that. I flipped the second switch.

You know how you always realize you've made a mistake right after it's just too late to do anything about it? That was me at one particular moment with my last lady friend before Dora. Not her fault, not mine—or, if you'd rather, the dishonors were about even. It was a mistake all the same.

So was flipping that goddamn switch. No, it wasn't rigged to shoot a zillion volts through me as if I'd sat down in an electric chair. Whoever'd set it up—probably Lothar Kreuzbach but maybe Bedford Tyler—didn't think anywhere near so small.

All of a sudden, I wasn't—or I didn't perceive that I was—standing in the doorway of a small prewar clapboard house on 166th Street in a dinky L.A. suburb nobody who lived more than fifteen miles away had ever heard of. I was on a battlefield, lit only by the full moon.

It might have been Italy. Then again, it might not have. I could see buildings with pieces bitten out of them. Somewhere off in the distance, heavy artillery boomed. Shells, big shells, made freight-train noises overhead. The air stank of wood smoke, smokeless powder, shit, swampy mud, and, faint but unmistakable underneath the rest, the sick-sweet spoiled-meat smell of death.

"I don't think we're in Gardena any more, Toto," Izzy Berkowitz said with what I thought was commendable calm.

He'd made the trip to wherever the hell this was, then. A quick look around told me the rest of them had, too. I felt better—not good, but better. You don't want to be out there all by your lonesome when everything goes sideways.

"This is crazy, man." Danny Becker might've been a hopped-up hipster digging the Bird—hopped up himself, chances are—launching into a solo.

"We're playing on the other guy's field," I said. "Can you do anything about that?" I didn't say, *What kind of wizard are you if you can't?*, but I thought it pretty loudly. Unfortunately, I knew the answer to that. He was the kind of wizard who cranked out copies of records or batches of shot glasses with a picture of a bare-naked lady on them or whatever else needed duplicating.

He didn't say anything to me. I couldn't blame him. Things started getting livelier, there under that double eagle of a moon. Werejackals loped towards us. I suppose they were werejackals, but they hadn't got all the way into beast form, not quite. They still kept some human. It didn't improve them.

Behind them stalked their commander—Anubis, the jackal who walked like a man. Except it wasn't exactly the Egyptian god. It looked more wolfish than jackaly, if you know what I mean. One more time, not an improvement.

And a jackal walking on its hind legs should've been wearing a linen kilt if it really was Anubis, not a *Blitzrunen* officer's *Feldgrau* tunic and a high-crowned officer's cap with a patent-leather visor.

"This is blasphemy," Shenouda Youhanna said. "Understand me—I do not follow the old faith of the Nile valley. It is blasphemy nonetheless." He sounded more offended than furious.

Skulking along behind the fylfotish almost-god came Bedford Tyler, jackalishly following the jackal. He was decked out in a gray that wasn't *Feldgrau* but might as well have been. He looked stupid in a Civil War kepi, but then to me he looked stupid most of the time. Here he was, carrying a Confederate flag, the way he wished he were and maybe the way he had been a mortal's lifetime earlier.

I wished for grenades full of holy water. I didn't get them, any more than I'd got the Tommy gun with silver bullets. I had dimes. I threw some of those out in front of us, the way soldiers will plant mines in front of their foxholes to discourage unfriendly people from sneaking up on them.

A werejackal stepped on one of the small silver discs I'd flung out there. The werebeasts hadn't liked that a bit even back in what I fondly thought of as the ordinary, mundane world. Here, fire spurted up under the jackal's foot. It let out a horrible howl—not piteous, but horrible. The fire didn't want to go out as the jackal limped away.

Kreuzbach growled fiercely. But he didn't come forward very far or very fast. He'd seen silver hurt one of his henchbeings, even here in this metaphysical realm where he was bound to be more at home than my friends and me. He'd set it up, after all, he and Bedford. But even here, the two of them didn't have everything their own way. I had the feeling they'd thought they would.

Bedford Tyler didn't seem to have worked that out as fast as the *Blitzrunen Oberführer* had. Well, I'd always reckoned Lothar the brains of their vile little outfit. Of course, I'd also reckoned Bedford a coward. If he wasn't, why had he fled down to Gardena when I threatened to let the sun shine in on him? Why hadn't he tried to take me out before I could?

Whatever his reasons in the real world, he didn't have them here. Forward he came, waving his goddamn Stars and Bars and let out a series of high, shrill yips and yowls that might almost have burst from a jackal's throat rather than a man's—or even a vampire's.

I realized with something like awe and something like disgust that I had to be hearing the genuine, the authentic, the fabled and legendary Rebel yell. No one alive in our time remembers quite what it sounded like. Ancient veterans who'd been young soldiers under that flag had tried to re-create it at the seventy-fifth anniversary of the Battle of Gettysburg a few years before the Knights of Bushido threw dragons at the Sandwich Islands and our ships anchored there. But not a man jack of 'em had been a day less than ninety, and geezers' croaks don't match up to youngsters' yells.

Bedford, though, Bedford had hardly changed a lick from those days till these. If he wanted to rip out a real Rebel yell, he could. And he did.

And he shifted the Stars and Bars he carried from his right hand to his left and drew his officer's sword from the scabbard. It flashed fire even in the moonlight and smoke. No, those weren't flashes. Real flames—real metaphysical flames, anyhow—licked along the length of the blade. What those flames would do if that blade bit into flesh … was something I didn't care to think about. Or to learn from experience, come to that.

Bedford charged past Kreuzbach and past the werejackals who played the role of cannon—or rather, dime—fodder for him. He didn't fear my makeshift minefield. Silver pains vampires, yes, but it doesn't hurt them the way it hurts werecreatures. And, unlike the werejackals and the wolfish almost-Anubis Kreuzbach, Bedford wore shoes.

So on he came, yelling like a vampire possessed (although how would you go about possessing a thing that had no soul?) and waving that flaming sword like … well, like a damn fool, if you really want to know. I wasn't the only one who thought so, either. Dora said, "Bedford, stop waving that sword like a damned fool," which proved the point.

It also made Bedford Tyler mad. "Shut your stinkin' trap, you rotten furrin slut!" he shouted. He never would've dared talk to Dora like that in the real world. She scared the whey out of him. But he was a big man, or could imagine himself one, here in Kreuzbach's metaphysical realm. Imagining yourself a big man was what following the fylfot was all about—and what owning slaves was all about, too, I suspect.

"You will regret speaking to me so," Dora said in a voice that made Sibir or Greenland seem downright tropical.

He shouted at her some more, and cussed her up one side and down the other while he was at it. Now, I wouldn't've talked to a lady that way on general principles, but I don't think Bedford'd had any of those even in his mortal days. But Dora proved to have it right. She usually did.

Because Bedford was so busy slanging her, he didn't pay any attention to me sneaking up on him. You live through a year in Italy, you will have learned how to do a proper sneak, I promise you that. So he almost jumped out of his undead hide when I popped up just out of reach of that sword of his and chucked goofer dust at him.

It worked even better than the garlic powder I'd given him in the real world, back what seemed a million years ago now. You never know for sure what all goes into a batch of goofer dust, not unless you know the wizard who put it together and maybe not then. But this one must've been a lulu, because he started coughing and choking as if he'd breathed in mustard gas.

He rubbed at his eyes at the same time as he was rubbing at his nose, and he doubled over and puked up blood. I didn't think that was as big a deal as it would've been with a live person, because what else would a vampire puke up? But it wasn't a *good* sign, for sure.

When he doubled over, he dropped the flaming sword. Dry grass caught fire by his feet. Sick or damaged as he was, he got out of there as fast as he could. That wasn't cowardice. Vampires can exist through almost anything, but fire is part of the *almost*. If they get burned, they don't heal. Ever.

Next question you're going to ask me is, do metaphysical flames burn a vampire the same way real ones do? Damned if I know, but Bedford Tyler sure as hell thought so. Of course, in that realm he was pretty metaphysical himself, if you care to contemplate the notion of a metaphysical vampire.

The fylfotted Anubis-jackal that was a metaphysical Lothar Kreuzbach snarled at me. But he wasn't about to give up. He was made of sterner stuff than Bedford; I'd known that all along. He made some quick passes, so quick I couldn't tell whether he had hands or paws at the ends of his arms, front legs, whatever you want to call them. Call them what you will. They did what he wanted them to do.

How do I know? Because a glowing fylfot appeared above his head: as grotesque a parody of a halo as you can imagine. It didn't just appear, either—it started to spin. That was when I started to worry. The fylfot boys called their emblem the *Hakenkreuz*, the hooked cross. When a hooked cross spins … well, you don't want to get in its way.

Sometimes you don't have a choice. Kreuzbach's *Hakenkreuz* zoomed toward me. Have you ever got buzzed by an angry mama bird when you stray too close to her nest? I've almost had my head taken off a couple of times that way. Or I thought so at the time, anyway. Man is the animal that makes metaphors.

Except the buzzing *Hakenkreuz*—and I could hear it, as if it were a circular-saw blade at high revs—wasn't a metaphor. It wanted to take my head off. For real. But I managed to duck and jerk away just enough. All it managed to chew off was part of the brim of my fedora.

Damn. I always liked that hat.

The *Hakenkreuz* zoomed up for another pass at me or at one of my friends. I didn't think I could duck twice. I thought I'd been lucky to duck once.

Izzy Berkowitz fumbled at himself. *What has he got in his pockets?* I wondered. He didn't seem to know himself. Then he found whatever he was looking for. It was small, and glowed blue. When you're looking at things by moonlight—even metaphysical moonlight, it turns out—their proper colors leach out of them as if they've been drained by hungry vampires. Unless they shine by themselves, that is.

Shenouda Youhanna touched the scarab I'd bought Izzy with a trembling forefinger and said something that wasn't English. I understood it anyway, don't ask me how. I think we all did. It was a prayer. *Mother Isis, help us!*

Hearing a prayer to Isis didn't hurt Dora. She bared her fangs in what looked like exultation. I knew just how she felt. Isis *was* a mother goddess. She had no patience with the bloodthirsty nonsense the followers of the fylfot practiced. What halfway decent person or deity would?

A beam of blue light, the same color as the faience scarab, shot out at the *Hakenkreuz*. It dodged and jinked, for all the world as if it were in a dragonfight during the war. Plainly, it didn't have the power to fight back; all it wanted was to get away. It couldn't. That blue beam touched it, and it went to destruction in a shower of sparks.

Lothar Kreuzbach roared in fury or fear or anguish or all of them at once. I looked back at the scarab. It was gray under the moonlight. Whatever power it had held was gone out of it now.

And, while it hadn't hurt Kreuzbach, it hadn't finished him off. He kept fighting, the way the fylfot boys had till they couldn't fight any more. He waved the werejackals out into wings on either side of him, then waved them forward to encircle us. Silver or no silver, forward they came.

"What do we do now?" Dora asked: a reasonable question, under the circumstances.

"You can get away," I said.

"Not yet," she answered, which was as much as I could've hoped for. She *was* a vampire. She always thought of herself first. She was made that way. That she thought of the rest of us at all would do for a miracle till a bigger one came along.

We turned so we faced every which way. All of us who had silver—all of us but Dora, I mean—got it out and got ready to do our best or our worst with it. Farther away than any of us could hit him with the silver we had, Lothar laughed a dreadful jackal laugh. He thought he had us. I only wished I thought he was wrong.

Then? Then a bigger miracle came along. I didn't think so at first. I thought I was losing my mind, is what I thought. The noise filled the whole world—excuse me, the whole metaphysical realm. Of all the things I never expected to hear there, a dog's happy bark might've topped the list. A big happy dog's bark, I should say. A happy dog as big as an … as an I don't know what.

I had to look over my shoulder to see the big dog. The big happy dog. The big fat happy dog. The big fat happy yellow dog.

The way I put that together, one piece at a time, may suggest to you that I was none too swift, there in that metaphysical realm Kreuzbach and Bedford Tyler had cobbled together. Now that you mention it, I wasn't. Then again, you have to understand that I'd never met Skeeter in person. I'd heard Al Harris talk—and talk—about him, and I'd seen a couple of photos. Black-and-white photos, naturally. That was it.

Almost it, I should say. The idea that Skeeter the Big Fat Happy Yellow Dog would charge to my rescue, or anybody's rescue, also needed a little while to start percolating. Well, not *charge*, exactly. Would waddle to my rescue.

But here he came through that metaphysical realm, big as a city block of skyscrapers and friendly as a swimming pool full of chocolate custard pie. Love conquers all, they say. I think they're talking about Skeeter.

The werejackals took one look at him and decided they didn't want to be anywhere near him. They ran like hell. He trotted after them, barking as if they were his best friends in the whole world. His legs didn't move very fast, but he covered one hell of a lot of ground at every stride. The werejackals were streaking away flat out, and Skeeter … Skeeter was gaining on them.

When the werejackals realized that, one of them—Tail-Gunner Joe, he was, Tail-End Charlie—turned and fought. At first, I thought he'd be too small for Skeeter to notice, and Skeeter would just stomp him into the ground. But notice him Skeeter did. *Oh, good!* he must have thought. *He wants to play!*

Out came his tongue, long as a couple of buses. It curled around the werejackal and wrapped him up in a big, wet, warm blanket. I don't know whether Skeeter let him drop, half drowned or all drowned, or swallowed him whole without even noticing him going down. The other werejackals ran even faster. Skeeter came after them, inevitable as a tax collector. He had to lick them all to show them how friendly he was. Not much remained of them after he did.

Which left Lothar Kreuzbach in the role of almost-Anubis. There he was, the *Blitzrunen Oberführer*, face to face with Skeeter the Big Yellow Dog. I would've paid good money to know what Lothar was thinking. He'd gone to all that trouble to set this up—and then Skeeter'd crashed his party. Life is full of surprises, but I don't imagine he fancied this one a whole hell of a lot.

Still, he had no quit in him. The Lightning Rune troops hardly ever did. And so he tried to attack. LR troops did that all the time, right up to the point where they had nothing to attack with any more. Kreuzbach was no different from the rest of the bastards.

He threw one of those spinning fylfots at Skeeter. Skeeter thought it was a stick or a ball. He knocked it out of the air with a paw and stepped on it. It wasn't the same after that, somehow.

Lothar shouted something guttural and foul. He started to swell. He got about as big as the angel of Angel's Flight—say, twenty feet tall. Next to Skeeter, he was still a doll. He ran toward him anyway.

Skeeter was delighted. He licked Kreuzbach the way he had with the werejackals. The *Oberf* screamed … wetly. He was big enough for Skeeter to pick him up and know he was doing it. Then Lothar tried something. I saw lightning bolts that looked like the *Blitzrunen* bite into Skeeter's tongue. Skeeter didn't like it. He let out a startled yip, and his jaws closed.

And that was the end of that. Next thing I knew, I was standing in the doorway of the house on 166th Street. My friends were right behind me. We all stared at one another. Each of us was looking at somebody else when we all said the same thing at the same time: "How did you *do* that?"

Everyone denied everything. If it was anybody's fault, it may have been mine. I at least knew Skeeter existed, which put me ahead of the rest of them. But I'm not a wizard, and I never would have dreamt up an overgrown Big Yellow Dog coming to the rescue like the cavalry in the last reel of a bad oater.

It didn't really matter anyway, did it? The thing had happened, and who cared about how any more? We did what we'd meant to do with that house before things got strange—we made it as unfriendly to vampires as we could. Dora had to go outside while we used garlic powder and goofer dust on the doors and windows and in the coffins. Bedford Tyler might come back to the real world, but he wouldn't have a welcoming home when he did. I didn't think we needed to worry about Kreuzbach, but how could I know for sure? He was one tough cookie. Well, we'd turned out to be pretty tough ourselves.

We looked on what we had done, and we saw that it was good. And I said, "Let's get out of here." And we saw that was good, too, and we did it.

XVIII

There I was, up on Hill Street near Al Harris' smut palace with a package under my arm. But I was walking toward the dirty-book store, not away from it, and the package wasn't one of those flat paper bags you could stick a filthy magazine in. It was fatter, and wrapped in butcher paper.

When I walked into the place, the doorbell gave forth with its usual quiet, half-embarrassed ring. For once, I went straight over to the counter instead of hanging around till Al and I were the only ones in there. I plopped the package down on the painted plywood.

Al looked at it. "What the hell ya got there?"

"A present."

Now he looked at me. "What the devil you bringin' me a present for?" Yeah, instant suspicion. "I ain't done nothin' for you lately."

Before I could answer, a guy came up and set a magazine on the counter without looking at me at all. I didn't look at him, either. That's etiquette in those places. Anyway, the brunette on the cover would've drawn my eyeballs even if it weren't. Al rang him up and put the magazine in one of those bags. He nodded his thanks, then scooted away.

Al's gaze swung back to me. "*Nu?*"

"Don't worry. It's not for you."

"Whaaat?" He stretched out the word. "Who is it for, then?"

"Skeeter. Fanciest steak I could find."

As soon as I named the dog, Al's face softened. He was nuts about that mutt. Margie was, too—the kid they didn't have, I guess. But the suspicion didn't go away. That's how he stayed in business, by suspecting everything and everybody. "So how come you're buying presents for my dog?" he asked, reasonably enough.

"I can give you the whole *megillah* if you've got an hour and a half," I said. Al wheezed laughter at somebody like me coming out with a word like that. I'd hoped he would. I went on, "The short answer is, you wouldn't believe me if I told you."

"Since when do I ever believe the *dreck* you come out with?" Al laughed some more. But then his gaze sharpened. No flies on Al Harris, no sirree Bob. No flies at all. "Wait a minute. Wait just a damn minute. Somethin' funny happened this morning when Margie gave him his Dr. Ross. He was a little off his feed, like."

"Really?" I could see how Skeeter being off his feed would seem funny to Al. That dog lived to eat.

"Uh-huh." He was dead serious. "Margie, she made him open his mouth so she could look inside, make sure his teeth were all right an' everything. An' they were, but he had what looked like a burn on his tongue. She made me take a gander, and I seen it myself. So tell me, Mister Hotshot Private Eye, how's a dog get a burn on his tongue, huh?"

"Maybe he smokes too much," I answered, deadpan. So I hadn't imagined everything after all. When something that weird happens, you do wonder. Or I do.

" 'Maybe he smokes too much.' Har-de-har-har. You're a card, you are. You oughta be dealt with, card. But tell me straight, okay? That burn got anything to do with you?"

"It had a lot more to do with jackals than it did with me," I said, and that was true enough. What was Lothar Kreuzbach thinking when those ginormous Skeeter jaws crunched down on him? Besides *Oops!*, I mean.

"Jackals, huh? You know jackals with Zippos?" Al had one. He lit a cigarette with it.

"Not any more."

"Jackals," Al repeated. "Miserable things. Did Skeeter get even?"

"In spades, doubled and redoubled." And wasn't that the truth, the whole truth, and nothing but the truth, so help me Perry Mason?

"Okay. For that, I'll take this." Al set his hand on the butcher-paper package.

"You have someplace where you can keep it cold till you go home tonight?"

"Oh, sure. You know the chop-suey joint a few doors toward Third?"

"Vaguely." I'd walked by it, but I hadn't eaten there.

"I have lunch there every so often." Al chuckled. "Old man Ming, he comes in here every so often, too, but you didn't hear that from me. Anyway, he'll let me stick it in his icebox for a few hours."

"Good deal. I hope Skeeter starts making a pig of himself soon."

"This ain't bad, not like when the goddamn jackals jumped him. Just a little burn. If it wasn't on his tongue, you'd kiss it and make it better, y'know?"

"I'm glad." I didn't think the *Blitzrunen Oberführer* was glad, though. To tell you the truth, I don't think he had any opinions about that or anything else at the moment.

We said our goodbyes. A couple of fellows were looking over Al's stock in trade. I figured he'd wait till he had the store to himself, then lock up for long enough to take the steak over to old man Ming. And Skeeter would eat like a champ tonight.

When I got back to the office, Mehitabel's nostrils flared. All of a sudden, she seemed like an animal that hunted for a living. "You smell like meat," she said. "How come you smell like meat?"

"You do!" Old Man Mose hadn't been paying attention before. Now he was. "Where is the meat?" he asked. "If you smell like meat, how come we aren't getting any of it?" He knew what counted: his stomach.

"You don't get any meat right now, besides your cat food, I mean—"

"Cat food isn't meat! It's not exactly meat, anyway. It's meat people have done things to. It doesn't smell like fresh blood. You do," Mehitabel said. Cats don't understand cooking and canning. Among other things, I mean.

"Give us the meat, already," Mose said. He didn't add *and nobody gets hurt*, but that's what he meant.

So I had to break the bad news: "I can't give you the meat. I got it for a dog."

They were not happy with me. "A *dog*?" By the way Old Man Mose said it, the word was filthier than anything in Al Harris' bookstore. Mose has had run-ins with dogs before. If you hear him tell the stories, he won all the scraps. Maybe he did. But he doesn't go out of his way looking for them. You can take that to the bank.

"Why did you want to waste a piece of yummy-smelling meat on a no-good, stinking dog?" Mehitabel sounded sure I had no possible alibi for such an awful crime.

I thought I did. "Because he saved my life, that's why. And he saved my friends, too. He deserves it."

"No, he doesn't. He's a dog." To Mehitabel, it was obvious.

Old Man Mose did some of what passed for deep thinking with him. "If you can't feed me that piece of meat, the least you can do is go out and get me another one."

"And one for me, too!" Mehitabel said.

"Have the two of you saved my life?" I asked.

"No, but we will," Mose said.

"How?"

He pinned me with a copper-green glare. "Next time you fall asleep with your feet up on the desk, we won't tear your throat out, the way Fluffy did with that lady."

I winced. I can't tell you how he'd heard Fluffy's sordid story, but he had. And I wouldn't have put it past him or Mehitabel. They'd be getting even with me, and they wouldn't worry about who'd feed them once I wasn't around any more. Not that that would do me any good.

So I went back to the butcher shop and got some steak for each of them. It wasn't as much as I'd bought for Skeeter, and it wasn't a fancy filet like his, but they didn't have to know that. The way they purred while they gobbled it up made the dough I spent seem almost worthwhile. Almost.

And, with any luck, they wouldn't decide to find out what *I* tasted like if I did go to sleep in the office. I ever run into that Sturgeon character, I'll give him a piece of my mind for putting ideas in my cats' heads.

I didn't plan to admit to Dora what I'd done. She would have laughed at me. She would've asked who ran things, me or the cats. She would've known the answer, too. And she wouldn't have liked it, feeling the way she did about our four-legged overlords.

The phone rang. I picked it up. "Mitchell Investigations."

"Hello, Mitchell." That raspy voice had to belong to Mickey. "Got any news for me?"

"It's taken care of," I said.

"Is it?" I think I impressed him, which wasn't easy. "Well, good." He hung up on me.

A few days later, I went down to Gardena. I wanted to find out what had happened to Bedford Tyler. I knew I'd hurt him, but I didn't think I'd finished him, worse luck. If I got the chance to do it now …

But the house on 166th Street seemed vacant. The gate in the chainlink fence stood open; I wondered whether anybody'd bothered to close it since I picked the lock. No jackals in the yard, which argued no one had.

That old gal and her dog came up the street. She remembered me from the last time I'd been casing 1612. "Nobody's living there now," she told me. "Guy moved out night before last in a heck of a hurry."

"Did he?" I said, and she nodded. "Have any idea where he went?"

"I sure don't. Don't want to, neither." She eyed me. "You the law?"

"No, ma'am." I never lie about that. You get yourself into a whole peck of trouble if you tell somebody you're a cop when you're not.

"Bet you're one o' those Sam Spade, Philip Marlowe kind of guys, then."

"Ma'am, if I were I'd be better looking and the pretty girls'd fall all over me," I answered.

She cackled laughter, as if I were joking. "I've seen plenty worse, pal," she said.

Damned if my ears didn't get hot. You'd think I'd be embarrassment-proof by now, but I guess you'd be wrong. And some of the blood that rushed to my head must've gone to my nose, too. I'm no bloodhound. I'm not even a cat—ask the two who hang around with me. But I knew what I was smelling. "You have a problem with the plumbing around here?"

"You mean the piss?" she asked matter-of-factly. No, she wasn't shy. Or prissy.

"Well, yeah."

She jerked a thumb at 1612. No, at the yard behind it, since she said, "The back yard there was swimming in the stuff a few days ago. It's mostly soaked in by now. Clarence—he lives a few doors down—he said it smelled like dog piss to him. You can tell it's not cat piss, I give him that much. But past that ..." She shook her head. The way her gray curls bounced around her head reminded me of a dandelion flower gone to seed.

"Clarence has a good nose." All I could think of was Skeeter lifting an enormous leg against a tree. That might have been all my imagination. How did he turn small again? How did he get back to Al and Margie without their even noticing he'd been gone? I've got no answers. But if it wasn't Skeeter, how did all that piss get there? I've got no answers for that, either.

"He's got a big nose, I'll tell ya that. Not quite Durante big, but big." The old lady decided she'd wasted as much time on me as she was going to. She flicked her dog's leash. "Come on, Humphrey! Get moving." He did, slowly. She rolled her eyes and found a few more words for me after all: "He's a lazy beast." Her voice was fond.

"Good for him," I said, and she laughed again. She went up to Denker and turned right, heading south.

I went up to Denker myself, only I turned left. I walked the block back to Gardena Boulevard, then turned left again and went down to the toy city hall and the Gardena PD headquarters next door. The sergeant sitting at the front desk wasn't quite as disreputable as the ones the LAPD sticks there, but he was working on it. He had a cigarette in his mouth, a full ashtray on top of the desk, and a half-empty coffee mug and a half-eaten donut next to the ashtray.

"What can I do for you?" He did pause to swallow before he asked the question. Any LAPD desk sergeant would've talked with his mouth full. See what I mean?

"Is Clyde Shaughnessy around?"

"Yeah, I just seen him a coupla minutes ago. You know where to find him?"

"If he's in his office, I do."

"Go on back, then." He jerked a thumb toward the corridor that would take me to Shaughnessy's office. Then he picked up the donut again. A second later, it was quite a bit more than half eaten.

Somebody was in Shaughnessy's office, or else the typewriter'd decided to go in for automatic writing. No, it was the cop. He was banging away with two fingers, faster than I can with all ten. My mama made me take typing in high school. She said it would be good for me. And it was, only not the way she meant. Almost all the people in the class were girls who wanted to be clerk-typists or secretaries or something like that. I made a lot of friends there. Yes, I did. And I got lucky with one of them. I wonder what ever happened to dear, sweet Martha.

Oh. Yeah, I did learn to type.

Shaughnessy looked up from the form or the report or whatever it was. "Hello, Mitchell," he said. "Fancy meeting you here!"

"Small world, huh?"

He had a cigarette smoldering in a glass ashtray by the typewriter, so I lit an Old Gold. He picked up his smoke, took a drag, and put it down again. "It is, yeah," he said. "I was gonna call you."

"Were you?" I sucked in smoke of my own.

"Uh-huh. You've been asking around after a vampire named Bedford Tyler. Some pretty funny stuff going on not long ago at the house he rented." He didn't say lugosi. Did he think it, along with other names like that? Would he have said it if he were talking with his buddies in the cop shop, not to a near-stranger like me? It's possible. It's not a sure thing. He was tough to read.

"You gonna blame me for the lake of dog piss in the yard?"

"You've been over there." His voice went hard and flat.

"You already knew I was looking for Tyler. Okay, I found him. His buddy, too. Friedrichs, Kreuzbach, whatever you want to call him. Now what?"

He drummed his fingers on the typewriter keys, hard enough so the typebars moved and made some noise, not so hard that they went all the way up and hit the paper in the machine. "I can't prove you had anything to do with whatever went on in there the night of the full moon. Whatever happened there, nobody here's broken-hearted about it."

"I'm glad. I'm sure the big dog is, too."

Shaughnessy started to say something, then stopped and sent me a long, cool stare. "You're a wise guy, aren't you?"

"I do my best. You aren't the first one who's thought so."

"No, huh? Why am I not surprised?"

"If you were surprised, you'd be a lot dumber than I think you are."

"Thank you … I guess." The cop's cigarette had burned down to a tiny butt. He stubbed it out of its misery, then lit a fresh one. Another man who ran on smokes and coffee. After his first drag, he looked at me again, in a different way this time. "One more question before you take off?"

"Sure, go ahead."

"Where the hell did you or your wizard get a dog *that* big?"

I started to laugh. I shouldn't have, but I couldn't help myself. Once I started, I had trouble stopping. Finally, my inner top sergeant gave the loon in me a direct order—*shut up!* For a wonder, I followed it. "Oh, my," I said. "Oh, my."

"I didn't know I was such a comedian." Shaughnessy sounded as dry as a piece of scorched toast. In his own low-key way, he was a wise guy himself. Quite a few cops, the ones who're smart enough to see how much of what they do is crap, have that style.

"Sorry," I managed. "The funny thing is, I don't know how to answer you, because none of us knows how he got there, either. We were glad he did, though. You bet we were. We were in a tough spot right then."

" 'There are more things in heaven and earth, Horatio, than are dreamt of in your philosophy,' " Shaughnessy said.

"A cop who quotes the Bard? Now I've seen everything!"

"A wise-guy private eye who knows what I'm quoting? Now *I've* seen everything!"

We left it there, honors even. I walked to the door. The sergeant at the front desk had started on a new donut, a raspberry jelly one. He looked as if he had blood running down his chin. "Get what you needed?"

"I did, yeah. Thanks."

He said, "Good," but he looked disappointed. Civilians weren't supposed to get what they wanted in cop shops. I went outside. It was a nice day. Sunny. Not too hot. Not too cold. So nice, instead of waiting for the bus, I walked up to the Red Car stop at Vermont. Then I headed back to the office.

The Central Avenue promenade. There's nothing like it anywhere. It makes you come alive—though Dora, whose hand I held, wouldn't have put it just like that. Not even the LAPD cars crawling along the crowded street and the boys in blue swaggering up the sidewalk and expecting everybody else to get out of their way could ruin it, no matter how hard they tried. They were part of the scene, too.

"Here we go," I said. Dora and I turned off Central and on to one of the dark little side streets that weren't part of the scene. Because they weren't, nobody bothered with them. Nobody'd bothered with this one for a long time.

Every step took us farther from the bright lights behind us. Quiet slammed down like a blackjack. It was the kind of dark little side street where a real blackjack could slam down, too—not that anybody who tried coshing Dora would have much luck.

If you know, you know. If you don't, all the explaining in the world won't do you any good. We turned into an alley even darker than the street. I couldn't see a damn thing. Dora didn't have any trouble. Right at the end of the war, the fylfot boys' sorcerers came up with a spell to let people see in the dark by heat. Like so much of what they tried then, it was too late to do them much good. But I bet they stole the idea from vampires.

"Here we are," Dora murmured, so low I could barely hear her.

"Okay." I put my hand out. Yes, there was the shabby bannister to help keep you from falling off the shabby stairway in the dark. I got a splinter. Giving people splinters was the other thing the bannister was for.

We went up the stairs, along the rickety walkway, and through the first set of blackout curtains. The light inside wasn't bright, but it seemed so by comparison to where we'd been before. Acolyte

Adams was presiding over the cash box. He started to stick out his hand for the cover charge, then stopped when he recognized us.

"Ah," he said. "Go on in. But before you do, any news for me?"

"It's over," I answered. "Kreuzbach is finished."

"He is, yes," Dora agreed.

Adams is all about keeping everything inside himself. All the same, he grinned like a crazy fool for a second before he could pull his face straight. "That's ... very good," he said, his voice under full control. "May I hear more?"

Another couple came through the curtains. "Long story," I said. "I'll tell you inside."

"All right." Voice tart, the Acolyte added, "The two of you are regulars these days."

I winked at him. "Why not? The price is right."

Dora and I went inside through the second set of curtains. Acolyte Adams couldn't even answer back. He had to deal with the people behind us—actual paying customers.

We made ourselves a nest of pillows and cushions and what have you. We'd just got ourselves comfortable when a serving girl asked what we wanted. Dora ordered scotch over ice; I stuck with Wild Turkey.

The girl was very pretty. She wore enough to stay technically decent, but not much more than that. She might've been eighteen. I hoped she was. I asked her, "Does your mama know you work here?"

"Oh, yes, sir, she sure does." The way she said it told me she'd heard the question before, probably a good many times.

"What does she think of it?"

"My pay is good. She likes that. And she says the Deacon and the Acolyte, they ain't gonna give me no trouble." She rocked her hips forward and back—not quite a grind, but almost—to show what kind of trouble she meant. "They're gentlemen, is what they are."

They're queer, is what they are, I thought. But the girl wasn't wrong. In their own way, they *were* gentlemen. Being queer had to be part of what made Adams as tightly wound as he was. Being queer and colored sure didn't help him relax. In case the bar girl was too young and naïve to know about stuff like that, I kept my big mouth shut. Dora noticed me not talking. It amused her.

Sooner or later, the kid was bound to find out about those things, but she wouldn't find out from me.

She swayed away. When she came back with our drinks, she said, "Shorty says these are on the house." Shorty was tending bar tonight.

"Thank him for us," I said, and tipped her as if we'd paid Deacon's fierce prices for the booze. That made her smile. I turned to Dora. "A toast!"

"To what?" she asked. Maybe she thought I wouldn't have anything ready. I'm scatterbrained enough to make that a fair bet.

But not this time. "To Skeeter!"

Dora almost laughed. To get a vampire to almost laugh, you've got to be doing something right. "To Skeeter!" she said, and we both drank.

Deacon's house combo played on the little stage. They weren't bad enough—or good enough—to make you notice them if you didn't feel like it. The elevators in some fancy department stores use spells that have you listening to that same kind of music. They're way cheaper than putting a combo in every elevator car, I'm sure. They take up less space, too.

A man walked past our nest, a drink in his hand. I noticed him out of the corner of my eye—till my head snapped around as I recognized him. He'd played a big, beefy he-man and brawler in more movies than I could shake a stick at. Deacon's was the last place I would've expected to find somebody like that. Or, if you look at it the other way, maybe the first.

Dora also saw him. She started by looking at things backwards, which I hadn't. "You never can tell, can you?" she murmured.

"Not even a little bit. You can't even tell if there's anything to tell about," I said. She gave me an odd look. I couldn't tell if it was a queer look, which, I suppose, was the point.

Acolyte Adams found us then. "Enjoying yourselves?"

"Nah. I hate it. I'm a masochist—that's why I come back so much," I said.

I didn't faze him. "So glad to hear it," he said, and then sat down cross-legged on the thick carpet next to our cushions. "You have a story for me?"

"Have we got a story for you!" I said. Izzy Berkowitz would've killed me, but he would've been laughing while he did it. Dora and I told the story together, all the way up to where things looked worst. I took over then. After all, I knew more about Skeeter than she did.

"A big yellow dog?" Adams sounded as if he didn't believe it, or as if he didn't want to believe it.

"A great big huge tremendous enormous gigantic yellow dog," I said helpfully, wondering if there were any job openings for a thesaurus.

"How did a big yellow dog"—the Acolyte ignored my synonymosis—"happen to ride in—"

"To waddle in."

"—to ride in just at the right time?"

"The only thing I can think of is, he'd had trouble with jackals. The real him had."

"Huh," Acolyte Adams said.

"That is a better explanation than any I found for myself," Dora said, which made me proud. She had brains and more experience than any live person could get. If I came up with something she'd missed … it had to mean I was lucky. And that I knew Al Harris and knew about Skeeter. I could imagine Dora doing all kinds of things. Traipsing into a shop that sold dirty books wasn't one of them.

"As long as the blackmail is over, as long as that Kreuzbach won't be giving the Deacon and me any more trouble, I'm happy." Adams didn't sound happy, but then, he hardly ever did.

"Without reincarnation, the *Oberführer* isn't coming back," I said.

"Reincarnation requires a soul. Giving that up is part of what becoming a vampire means," Dora said.

"Part of what following the fylfot means, too," I said. "You can't do that and stay a human being, not if you mean it the way the Lightning Rune soldiers did."

"Hating for no reason …. Do you do it because you've already lost your soul, or does doing it make you lose yours?" Acolyte Adams asked. We batted that back and forth till it started getting light outside and Dora had to head home to her coffin. Not what I expected at Deacon's, but a long way from the least interesting night I ever spent there.

Sometimes L.A. is too damn hot. Sometimes it's too damn smoggy. Sometimes the fog blots out the sky—and anything else more than ten feet away from you. Sometimes the wind blows in hard. Hell and breakfast, sometimes it even rains. It snowed once, when I was a kid.

But sometimes it's perfect. The kind of weather the Chamber of Commerce only dreams about. The kind of weather than makes people from Wichita and Duluth and Sandusky and Little Rock pack their bags. *The devil with what we got here, Mary Lou! Let's head west!* they say. And they do it, too. Swarms of them.

I came out of the apartment building on an afternoon like that. It was so gorgeous, I wished Dora could see it and enjoy it without bursting into flames. The sky was blue. The sun was bright. It wasn't 105, or even 90. Orange blossoms were in the air. Like Baby Bear's porridge, everything was just right.

But I had no one to share it with. That made me sad. Not many people out and about in Vampire Village in the middle of the afternoon. Ah, well. I headed for the Red Car stop.

And there was Rivke, walking along to make sure no live people were troubling vampires who couldn't do anything about it till night fell. We waved to each other. I started to cross the street to say hello, but a smoke-belching Hupmobile from before the war made me jump back on the sidewalk. Till a breeze swept things away again, the air smelled of exhaust fumes, not citrus.

"How are you?" I said once I could make it to her side of the road without getting car-squashed.

"Very okay." That wasn't anything someone who'd grown up speaking English would've said, which didn't mean I couldn't follow it.

"Good. Me, too," I said, and then, "How's the kitten?"

Rivke's face lit up. "She grow so fast! She talk so much!"

"They do that, yeah. Listen, I know her mom and pop. Don't let her talk you into signing anything. She'll wind up with everything you've got."

She frowned as she chewed on that, then brightened again. "Oh! You make joke."

"Think so, do ya?" I grinned at her. "Yeah, I made a joke. A dumb one, the way I mostly do."

"You not dumb, Jack! You far from it," she said seriously. I don't know why she thought so, but she did. She spread both arms wide and waved her hands up to the sky. "Is so beautiful! Till I come here, I never think is weather like this."

"It's nice," I agreed, as proud as if I'd had something to do with it.

"They say Holy Land has such weather."

"I don't know anything about that." I knew something about Italy. Weather there was pretty good in spring and fall. But in Italy, at least when I was there, you always smelled death, sometimes far away, sometimes right up close. That takes the edge off your joy. Of course, what Rivke went through was bound to throw my year slogging up the boot into the shade.

"You never think about it?" she asked.

"I don't know. I have a hard time thinking anything's holy these days."

"Ah." Her smile faded, as mine had. "Yes, is that."

The war is over. It's been over for a few years now. Everybody says so. For people who never went overseas, I imagine that's true. But if you were in it, you take it with you forever.

Rivke might've been thinking along with me, because she said, "This America is good place. You can be safe here, even if Jew. Almost safe, anyhow. As safe as Jew can be. Is easy here. But sometimes I remember where I been before."

"Yeah. You aren't the only one." I hesitated, then went on, "I still dream about the war sometimes. Not good dreams. Nightmares. And sometimes—mostly when they thought I wasn't listening—my folks would talk about things they saw, things that happened to them, in the Deep South, before they came out here."

Don't get me wrong. It's not easy being a Negro out here. I don't think it's easy being a Negro anywhere in the land of the free and the home of the brave. But it's a hell of a lot easier in L.A. than it is where my mom and dad came from.

I'm not sure how much of that Rivke followed. She got what counted, though. "I not the only one?" she breathed, as if that hadn't crossed her mind till I said what I said. And I bet it hadn't. Feeling you're by yourself, that's always rough. Crawling across the overgrown field toward the machine-gun nest is easier if half a dozen other dogfaces are crawling along with you no matter how shit-scared they are. They'll keep you alive if they can, and they know you'll do the same for them.

And then I stopped remembering bad times an ocean and a half away, on account of Rivke flung her arms around me and kissed me like she meant it. I might've been a life preserver for somebody who'd been in deep water a long time, but I'll tell you, I was one mighty goddamn happy life preserver.

"Thank you!" she said, right in my ear. "Thank you, thank you, thank you!"

"It's okay." It was way better than okay, but I didn't tell her that. I started detaching myself from her. "This is the best thing that ever happened to me on the way to the streetcar, y'know?"

She jumped away from me as if I'd turned salamander. And she blushed all the way to the roots of her hair. Staring down at the sidewalk, she mumbled, "You must think I is terrible person."

"I think you're great," I said, and spent a while convincing her I meant it. She thought I thought she was a scarlet woman or something. Sure as hell, she'd brought where she came from with her to Vampire Village. I managed to convince her we were still friends. And we were, even if I didn't think I'd tell Dora all about it. She managed to wave goodbye to me as I walked on toward the trolley stop.

When the Red Car clanged up, I put my money in the fare box and found a seat. Easy enough at that time of day. I hopped off about three blocks from my office. Have to say, I was grinning while I walked. It was a beautiful day, and out of the blue a pretty girl'd kissed me. You could do worse.

There's a Richfield station halfway between where I get off and the office. The big old neon Richfield eagle shines at night. During the day, it's just a filling station. The guys who work there wear dark blue uniforms and caps that look like officers' hats, so they make you think of cops.

Except I recognized one. He was busy pumping gas into a De Soto while I crossed the street. As the car pulled away, I said, "Fancy meeting you here, Oscar."

"Oh. Hey, Mitchell." Oscar Ricks spread his hands. They had grease stains. "It's a steady job. What the hell am I gonna do? I got sick of starving, sick of hustling, sick of scuffling."

I've heard that song from more musicians than I care to remember. A few grab the world by the tail. Most of the time, the world grabs them instead. "I'm sorry, man. I liked what you were doing. It felt like a spell that let me hear the future, know what I'm saying?"

"That's what I was aiming at. Electric instruments are the coming thing for sure. But most folks turned out to be too square to dig it."

"Think you'll go back to it?"

"I'd like to, if I can make it pay. It's more fun than pumping gas and changing wiper blades and doing brake jobs. But I gotta eat. My family's gotta eat."

"What are the other guys from the trio doing?"

"Otis, he's selling clothes at a Jim Clinton. And Jimmy … ask me no questions and I'll tell you no lies."

Which meant that whatever he was doing, the LAPD didn't like it. Burglary, reefers, running numbers? Oscar was right—I didn't need to know. I stuck out my hand. He shook it. "Luck, man," I said. "You start gigging again, let me know. I'll be there."

"Okay. Don't hold your breath, though. I kinda like regular money."

Regular money? What was that? I went on to my office, hoping somebody'd call or stop in. I'd done my own stretch of starving and scuffling. I was liable to do more. And when I opened the door and walked in, Old Man Mose greeted me with, "Took you long enough. We're starving. Feed us!"

"Yeah, yeah," I said, and I did.